Praise for JM Al

'**There is a new star in the classical firmament.** Philocles is engaging, inspiring and feels absolutely real. This is **historical writing at its best and crime writing worthy of prizes**. Riveting'

Manda Scott, author of the Boudica series

'**If you like C J Sansom's Tudor sleuth Matthew Shardlake, you'll love this** – a gripping murder mystery set in a fantastically fully-realised ancient Athens, which **will keep you guessing to the very end**'

James Wilde, author of *Pendragon*

'**Intriguing . . .** a **refreshingly different** setting portrayed with a convincing air of authenticity. **I hope it's the first of many**'

Andrew Taylor, author of *Ashes of London*

'**It's about time** someone did for ancient Athens what Lindsey Davis' Falco novels do for Ancient Rome. **Alvey sets the scene perfectly**, with easy brushstrokes and lightly worn learning. In Philocles we have an aspiring playwright, man of the people and reluctant detective. **I look forward to his next case . . .**'

Jack Grimwood, author of *Moskva*

'**Historical sleuthing finally gets its grown-up trousers.** The book's got wit and knowledge and the winning knack of immersing the reader in ancient Greece and the whole theatrical scene there. It shows a thorough understanding of time and place, and has **a dark** heart of thuggery and murder. Finally, someone has taken on Saylor and Davis and brought us out of Rome at last!'

Robert Low, author of the Oathsworn series

'Alvey has combined the best features of a crime novel and a work of historical fiction. The result is **a pacy, exciting and intelligent story set in a rich world**. The plot is clever and solidly rooted in history, the characters vivid, sympathetic and lifelike and **the world of Athens is gloriously recreated**. Best of all, **while** *Shadows of Athens* **is taut and historically detailed, it also displays a quirky sense of humour** – [I] loved it'

Simon Turney, author of *Caligula*

'**Historical crime writing that virtually reinvents the genre**. Ancient Athens is recreated with a **masterly** touch, while the beleaguered Philocles is the perfect protagonist to lead us through this **vividly evoked** menacing world'

Barry Forshaw, *Financial Times* crime critic

'The historical detail is excellent, and the story and characters expertly spun out – a **very entertaining** and satisfying read'

Glyn Iliffe, author of The Adventures of Odysseus series

SCORPIONS IN CORINTH

JM ALVEY

ORION

First published in Great Britain in 2019 by Orion Fiction,
an imprint of The Orion Publishing Group Ltd.,
Carmelite House, 50 Victoria Embankment
London EC4Y 0DZ

An Hachette UK Company

1 3 5 7 9 10 8 6 4 2

Copyright © JM Alvey 2019
Map artwork by Hemesh Alles

A CIP catalogue record for this book is
available from the British Library.

ISBN (Paperback) 9781409180654
ISBN (eBook) 9781409180661

Typeset by Input Data Services Ltd, Somerset

Printed and bound by Clays Ltd, Elcograf S.p.A.

MIX
Paper from
responsible sources
FSC® C104740

www.orionbooks.co.uk

For the organisers, authors, academics and audiences of the St Hilda's Mystery and Crime Fiction Weekend; an annual delight in Oxford since 1994, and a catalyst for my transformation from reader to writer.

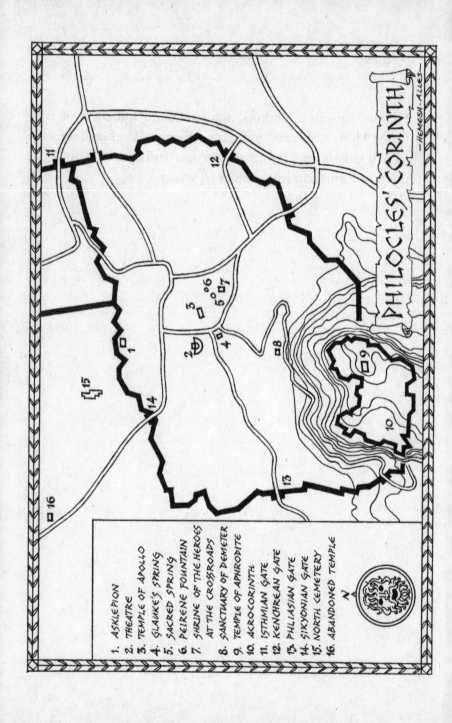

PHILOCLES' CORINTH

—HEMESH·ALLES—

1. ASKLEPION
2. THEATRE
3. TEMPLE OF APOLLO
4. GLAUKE'S SPRING
5. SACRED SPRING
6. PEIRENE FOUNTAIN
7. SHRINE OF THE HEROES
   AT THE CROSSROADS
8. SANCTUARY OF DEMETER
9. TEMPLE OF APHRODITE
10. ACROCORINTH
11. ISTHMIAN GATE
12. KENCHREAN GATE
13. PHLIASIAN GATE
14. SIKYONIAN GATE
15. NORTH CEMETERY
16. ABANDONED TEMPLE

N

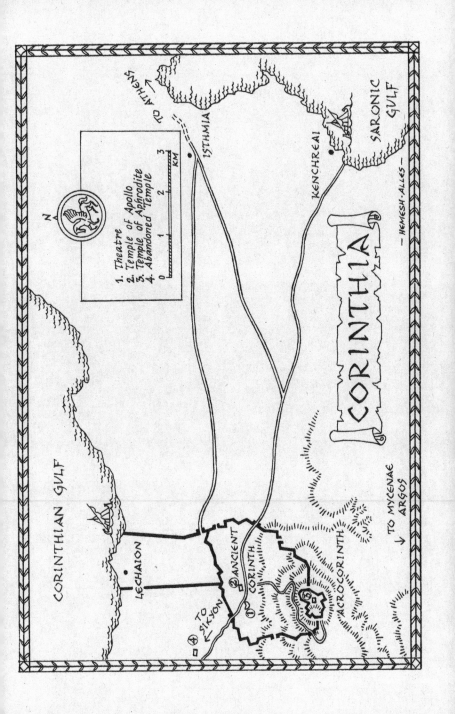

CORINTHIA

— NEMESH·ALLES —

N

1. Theatre of Apollo
2. Temple of Aphrodite
3. Temple of Aphrodite
4. Abandoned Temple

0 1 2 3
KM

CORINTHIAN GULF

SARONIC GULF

TO ATHENS →

ISTHMIA

KENCHREAI

LECHAION

② ANCIENT
CORINTH

① TO
SIKYON

ACROCORINTH

↓ TO MYCENAE
ARGOS

Chapter One

'Oligarchs have no sense of humour. They're famous for it.' Hyanthidas slid the dish of olives across the tavern table.

'Then we have a problem.' I edged my papyrus sheets away from the bowl's oily rim.

'Cutting a dozen jokes is hardly going to wreck the whole play.' The musician still didn't understand, but then, he was a Corinthian.

'The trouble is where I have to cut them.' I shuffled through the pages to find the turning point in the drama. 'If we can't get some decent laughs in the political debate, it's going to kill the pace stone dead, but we won't get a chuckle in this town with jokes about Athenians who no one has even heard of. Or worse, by mentioning ones the audience will know for all the wrong reasons.'

I handed a sheaf of papyrus to my beloved Zosime, who was sitting patiently beside me on the bench by the tavern's whitewashed wall. 'Here we are.'

I read aloud from the scene where our play's hero and his second in command were allocating tasks to their men, now that this boatful of warriors returning from

I

Troy had decided to build a city on the wild shore where they found themselves stranded.

'Send Myronides and a few men out to stake our claim to this land, but don't expect him to be any good at masonry. I hear he's far better at pulling down walls than building them.'

That had been hilarious in Athens. Myronides was the name of the general who had led our armies to successive victories in Boeotia, before underscoring his domination by having the city of Tanagra's fortifications demolished.

Here in Corinth, though, he was remembered as the general who'd defeated a Corinthian army not once, not twice, but three times in rapid succession, to assert Athenian dominance over the Megarans whose lands lay between our two great cities. That might have been fifteen years ago, but memories of such humiliations linger. There would be men around us in this tavern this evening who'd marched and fought in those battles. They wouldn't laugh at being reminded of that when they were in our audience at the theatre.

'I see what you mean, but you won't get any laughs making jokes about the city's influential men.' Hyanthidas raised his voice to make himself heard. 'Everyone knows it's foolish to cross the Council. No one will risk a grin at their expense.' He helped himself to sausage and cheese.

As he did so, I saw he was busily scanning the tavern for anyone he knew, taking advantage of being taller than most, even sitting down. I knew how much he had been looking forward to coming back home. He'd spent most of the past year in Athens after I'd hired him to compose and play the music for our comedy in the Dionysia drama competition.

'Those jokes still have to go.' Zosime took the remaining pages out of my hands and tapped the whole manuscript into a tidy stack with her elegant, artist's fingers. 'You're here to convince everyone that such conflicts between your cities are over.' Born in Crete, she was as impartial as she was beautiful.

'I know.' I reached for a piece of bread.

Strictly speaking, we were here to convince the locals that Athenians, Corinthians and anyone from any other Greek city would all be equals as new citizens of Thurii, the colony currently being built across the sea in Sicily. Perantas Bacchiad, the wealthy Corinthian and Council member who was paying our bills on this trip, was a vocal supporter of the Thurii project, just like Aristarchos, who'd introduced me to him in Athens. Aristarchos had been my play's original patron, footing the costs of our Dionysia performance as a rich man's tribute to our city and our gods. He's a firm supporter of Hellenic expansion westward into the untamed lands of Sicily and the mainland beyond, rather than looking east and risk butting heads with the Persians again. My play reflected that.

I yawned. I was starting to feel like Sisyphus, endlessly rolling his boulder uphill only to have the bastard thing slip and hurtle all the way down to the bottom of his cursed mountain again. I'd already rewritten the songs that the play's chorus would perform so that all references to unity, equality and common purpose now clearly and only referred to the colony that the actors were preparing to found in those days long ago, after the fall of Troy.

Back in Athens, the chorus had celebrated our democracy where all men are equal before the law and every citizen plays his part in our city's good government, justice and legislation. But now we were in Corinth, where their Council of wealthy merchants rule by decree to suit themselves and their friends. Oligarchy. Rule by the few. Barely distinguishable from tyranny as far as Athenians are concerned, though I'd be keeping such thoughts to myself. A good guest doesn't insult his hosts and we were being paid handsomely to restage my play, after *The Builders*' first performance had been so well received back home.

I yawned again. I was longing for a comfortable bed. Our journey had taken two days on the leisurely coastal trading ship that had brought us from Athens. First, we'd sailed to Aegina, where a business associate of our patron had put us up for the night. Unfortunately, I'd barely slept, restless in an unfamiliar house and tense about bringing my play to this new audience. When we'd sailed for Kenchreai the next morning, choppy seas had me hanging queasily over the ship's rail until we were tied up at the dockside of Corinth's eastward port on the Saronic Gulf.

I poured myself a little more of the excellent local wine, well watered down. I had to get these rewrites right to satisfy our new paymaster, and time was short. I needed an insider with local knowledge to suggest some notables whom I could make the butt of a few jokes without risking the Council's wrath.

'Where's Eumelos?' I looked around the tavern for the man who'd met us on the docks at Kenchreai, identifying himself with an agate signet ring that was the twin of the one Perantas Bacchiad had worn in Athens.

I'd recognised his type at once; open-handed with a broad smile and a hearty welcome, while his shrewd eyes darted this way and that, never missing a detail. The rich and powerful of every city always have fixers like him to call on. I was thinking that such a character would make a great comic lead for my play in next year's Dionysia.

Eumelos had had wagons waiting for our personal luggage as well as the hefty wicker baskets holding the play's costumes and masks. He had also persuaded the crew to unload our baggage before the rest of the ship's varied cargo, so I guessed the right amount of obols had discreetly changed hands.

The journey from the port on the eastern side of Corinth's famous Isthmus was a short one and an easy walk. Eumelos saw us settled in the comfortable house that Perantas Bacchiad had put at our disposal. As the sun was sinking, he'd recommended this local tavern for dinner, and we'd left my personal slave, Kadous, to supervise the house slaves that Perantas had loaned us as they unpacked our bags and baskets.

'He's over there.' Hyanthidas twisted around on his stool and pointed.

Eumelos was sitting with his back to us, his shoulders

as broad as any wrestler's. It was hardly his fault that we couldn't find two tables together. The quality of the food and the wine proved why this place was so popular. He gestured as he explained something to Menekles, sitting beside him. The two men were much of a height, though Menekles wasn't as heavily muscled. Sitting opposite, shorter and stocky, with his curly hair and beard both needing a trim, Apollonides was chuckling into his wine.

Seeing that the actors liked our new friend reassured me. I trusted both men's judgement, since anyone who makes a successful living on the stage soon learns to spot charlatans and chancers.

Our play's third actor, and the fourth man at the table, was unremarkable in height and heft. I saw he wasn't smiling, though thankfully Lysicrates looked a little less dour than he'd done on the voyage here. He'd been the most reluctant to accept Perantas Bacchiad's offer, arguing that we should stay home and start rehearsals for next year's Dionysia. I still didn't know why, and I could only be thankful that Apollonides and Menekles had persuaded him to earn this generous bonus. The show simply couldn't go on without all three of them.

Someone on the far side of the room struck a chord on a lyre. Several voices united in a drinking song, as well known in Athens as it was here.

'All praise to Praxilla of Sikyon!' Hyanthidas raised his wine in a toast to the famous composer.

Zosime raised her own cup. 'Praxilla!'

She glanced at me as she drank, her dark eyes bright

6

with amusement above the rim of her cup. Visiting a city where women poets and musicians performed their work in public was merely one of her reasons for insisting on coming on this trip.

Sitting in this Corinthian tavern, I was forced to agree it was a little hypocritical of Athenian men to sing Praxilla's songs as they caroused while insisting their own wives' and daughters' musical talents were kept for strictly private, family entertainment.

Eumelos stood up to lead another rousing song, waving his cup of wine. His voice rose above the rest, powerful and tuneful. He was tall as well as broad-shouldered, a commanding presence.

I wondered if he had ever performed in a theatre chorus. Our first task here was recruiting twenty-four Corinthians to take the place of the Athenian citizens who'd performed as the chorus of builders that the play was named for. Once we'd got those new singers rounded up, I would be their chorus master, with ten days to get them fit to perform.

It was a role I felt wholly unsuited for. I wished Chrysion, who'd led our chorus in Athens, could have come with us. He was back in Athens, recruited by my friend and rival Pittalos, whose new play would grace the upcoming winter's Lenaia festival. Besides, while actors were expected to travel when plays went abroad, chorus masters never did. It's long-established custom for the playwright to take on that duty.

I watched Eumelos singing with exuberant enjoyment. Teaching two dozen complete strangers how to perform

The Builders' songs and dances would be a good deal easier if I had someone local at my right hand. Someone with a knack for getting things done.

Hyanthidas stood up, beckoning. I followed his gaze and saw a strikingly handsome woman in a long, pleated green dress entering the tavern. A watchful escort followed a few paces behind her. Friend, slave or brother? In Corinth, as in Athens, it was impossible to tell.

Zosime sat up straight. 'Is that Telesilla?'

I was as interested as she was. As we'd sailed along the Saronic Gulf coast, Hyanthidas had told us about his long-time lover. They'd never expected to be apart for so long when he'd come to Athens looking for a few months' lucrative work playing his flutes at rich men's drinking parties. Then Aristarchos had heard the talented musician and we had hired him to stay for nearly a year.

Hyanthidas had written to Telesilla and she'd agreed he couldn't pass up the opportunity, for the sake of his art as well as the money. She was a poet and composer herself, so she understood that. On the other side of those scales, she wasn't prepared to join him in Athens and sit twiddling a distaff and spindle all day, unable to perform.

She saw Hyanthidas and greeted him with a loving smile. Her escort turned to go and she made her way over. As she cut between the tables towards us, she passed our three actors.

Eumelos was still on his feet, singing loudly with ever more expansive gestures. Noticing Telesilla, he set down his cup with a thud that spilled wine across the table. He stepped into her path with his arms spread wide.

I could see Lysicrates' surprise and concern. I was taken aback myself. Eumelos must have been drinking hard to get so drunk so quickly. Maybe recruiting him for our chorus wasn't a good idea if he habitually soaked up wine like a sponge.

Eumelos embraced Telesilla. She tried to hold him off, her hands pushing back against his chest. I saw her consternation as she realised that, taller and stronger, he wouldn't be denied. He folded his long arms around her and buried his face in her lustrous black hair.

Hyanthidas was scowling like Zeus polishing up a thunderbolt. I couldn't blame him, but a tavern brawl on our first night in Corinth wouldn't be an ideal start to our visit.

Thankfully Apollonides and Menekles were already there, taking hold of Eumelos' arms to force him to release the woman. Lysicrates stepped between the Corinthian and Telesilla. I saw the actor lay a solicitous hand on her shoulder, doubtless asking if she was all right, as well as introducing himself.

Apollonides and Menekles got Eumelos turned around and ushered him back to their table. Menekles raised a hand, summoning a fresh jug. I hoped some cold spring water could dilute whatever the big man had been drinking.

Lysicrates brought Telesilla to our table. She was as baffled as she was indignant. Seeing no trace of embarrassment or, worse, guilt on her face, I breathed a little easier. Hyanthidas didn't deserve to come home and discover the woman he loved had been letting someone else pluck her heartstrings.

'What was all that about?' he asked, all concern.

'I have absolutely no idea.' With her shock receding, Telesilla was annoyed. 'Who is that oaf?'

'Eumelos. He works for Perantas Bacchiad.' I would have said more but Zosime elbowed me gently in the ribs.

'Here, have my seat.' She smiled at Telesilla as she stood up. 'Philocles, let Hyanthidas sit there.'

I saw the Corinthian woman's tension ease as Hyanthidas sat beside her on the bench. He put his arm around her shoulders, drawing her close. She shook her head, clearly puzzled. 'He was calling me Kleoboulina.'

'Who's that?' Zosime looked at me as she claimed Hyanthidas' vacated stool.

'I have no idea.' Mystified, I looked at Lysicrates.

The actor could only shrug. 'He never mentioned her to us.'

'Whoever she is, she has my sympathies,' Telesilla said tartly. 'He was begging for my – for her – forgiveness.'

'Why?' Zosime handed me the wine jug. I saw it was nearly empty.

'Who knows?' Telesilla's voice shook.

'Who cares?' Hyanthidas said coldly.

My beloved reached across the table to offer Telesilla a comforting hand. 'I'm Zosime, and this is Philocles Hestaiou.'

'I'm very pleased to meet you both.' As Telesilla did her best to shake off her bizarre encounter with Eumelos, she looked more closely at Zosime. 'But you're not Athenian, are you?'

Zosime smiled. 'My mother was from Crete and we lived there for some years. My father's Egyptian. He's a potter and I'm a vase painter.'

Telesilla was only too pleased to pursue this new conversation. 'What do you paint?'

I raised the wine jug. 'Let me get a refill.'

'I'll help.' Lysicrates followed as I headed for the nearest waiter.

'More of the amber, well watered, if you please, and another cup.' I handed the slave the jug and pointed to our table. 'We're sitting over there.'

As the man hurried off, I turned to Lysicrates. 'What are you lot drinking? Something mixed by satyrs?'

'We ordered the same jugful as you,' he protested, 'and we shared it between us.'

'Has Eumelos had anything to eat?' Wine on an empty stomach makes a lot of mischief.

Lysicrates nodded. 'I don't know why—'

'No!' Eumelos' bellow silenced the entire tavern.

Everyone stared as the big man lurched to his feet, scarlet-faced. He set the table rocking so violently that the cups and wine jug crashed to the floor.

'Where is she?' Eumelos roared. He spun around, his eyes staring and his jaw slack.

Menekles and Apollonides got warily to their feet, staying beyond the big man's reach. I snatched a glance at Zosime. She had darted around behind our table to sit on the bench with Telesilla. Hyanthidas stood in front of them both, his fists clenched. Lysicrates had moved quickly and was standing braced at his shoulder. If Eumelos tried to get to the women, there'd be no avoiding a fight.

The big Corinthian's vacant gaze swept straight past them. Then he looked back at me as I stood there in the middle of the tavern. I saw that his eyes were eerie hollows of darkness. Dionysos save me; the man looked possessed.

'You! How did you get in here?'

Drinkers scattered as Eumelos forced his way towards me. Stools toppled and crockery smashed as he wrenched tables out of his path. Men and women were surging out of the tavern door, spilling into the street with cries of alarm.

I took a few swift strides towards the door, before I turned and stood my ground. Now Eumelos had his back to Zosime and Telesilla as he came towards me. I only hoped Lysicrates and Hyanthidas could find a rear door and get the women out of the tavern.

Looking past the big man's shoulder I could see Apollonides and Menekles coming to help. The three of us should be able to subdue the Corinthian, though I had no idea what we'd do next. We didn't even know where Eumelos lived to carry him home to sleep off whatever he'd drunk.

Eumelos staggered towards me. 'Where are they? Please, I beg you, for the love of Athena, tell me!'

I was ready to dodge a punch. Instead, he seized my hands. This close to, I realised he was older than I'd first assumed. I'd guessed there were only a few years between us, but I saw he was at least a decade my senior.

His grasp was hot and dry, and his face wasn't flushed with wine. His cheekbones and brow burned scarlet like a man stricken with a fever. If this was some sudden sickness, could we escape the malady? My blood ran cold at the thought of falling ill so far from home.

His grip on my fingers tightened. 'Where are they?'

'I—' I didn't know what to say, but as long as he was clinging to me, he couldn't attack anyone else.

His gaze shifted, looking past me. He gasped. 'Alkias!'

I twisted to see who he was talking to, but there was nobody there. The only people left in the tavern besides us were the huddle of staff by the door to the back room where wine and water were stored.

I felt violent tremors running through Eumelos as he squinted at me again. 'What did Alkias say? Where have they gone?' He was blinking like a man in bright sunlight even though most of the tavern's oil lamps had been toppled and snuffed in the rush of people leaving.

I did my best to assess the situation. I could see Menekles standing ready, looking for my signal. Unfortunately, I had no idea what to do. Apollonides was by the rear door now, talking urgently to a man who I guessed was the tavern owner. I wondered if he'd sent a slave to fetch some help. If this was Athens, someone would be running to alert the Scythians, the public slaves who keep order, paid for by everyone's taxes. I had no idea if Corinth's wealthy Council spared any coin to protect their citizens.

'But – no, wait – she is blameless!' Eumelos cried out, anguished.

My fingers were numb. I snatched a glance at Hyanthidas. He and Lysicrates stood shoulder to shoulder, hiding Zosime and Telesilla. Lysicrates' attention was shifting from me to the street door and back again. I guessed he was calculating their chances of getting the women safely out of the tavern without attracting Eumelos' attention. I tried to catch his eye with a warning frown. I didn't like those odds.

Eumelos let go of my hands. His eyes rolled back in his head, and he collapsed, as boneless as an octopus. He lay as still as death on the floor, with spilled wine pooled around him like blood.

Stunned silence followed the thunderous crash. I looked around to see everyone gaping with astonishment that equalled my own.

Chapter Two

Eumelos stiffened, rigid as a spear shaft from head to toe. Then a convulsion racked him, arching his back like a bow. In the next breath he was twisting and thrashing, his arms flailing wildly. I backed away, my heart racing. But before I took a second step, the frenzy was over.

'What's—'

Another spasm seized Eumelos. Breath rasped through his nose as his jaw clenched, his teeth bared. He rolled from side to side, with his arms drawn up and his knees pumping. He looked as if he were fighting some eerie, invisible presence. Fighting and losing. I backed away, sick with dread, and begged Apollo, whose great temple guards Corinth, to watch over us all.

Hyanthidas arrived at my side. 'The Asklepion—'

Eumelos started whining like a man bereft. We could only watch as convulsion after convulsion tortured him. Every time he lay still, I held my breath, praying this was his release. Time and again, his torment resumed.

I've seen men die in battle. I've seen friends fade and fail from slow sickness as relentlessly mortal as a spear through the eye. I sat beside my father's deathbed with my family. I'd never seen anything like this.

The end caught me unawares. Belatedly, I realised I'd counted a dozen breaths while Eumelos lay limp as a slaughtered lamb.

Zosime's voice shook as she peered around Lysicrates. 'Is he dead?'

I summoned up my courage and knelt. Reaching for his throat, I felt for the beat of his heart, but I couldn't be sure if I was mistaking the trembling in my fingers for his pulsing blood. 'I can't tell.'

'Try this.' Apollonides offered me a silver platter. Athena only knows where he'd got it.

I held the gleaming metal over Eumelos' mouth and nose. Snatching it away, I studied it closely. Not trusting myself, I repeated the process. This time I was sure. Faint and swift to fade, shallow breath nevertheless misted the metal.

I got to my feet, brushing away a potsherd I hadn't even realised I'd knelt on. 'He's still alive.'

Hyanthidas stepped forward. 'Asklepios' shrine is to the north and west of here, by the city walls.'

Menekles approached. 'We'll need a litter to carry him.'

'Stay back!' I warded them off with upraised hands. 'We don't know what ails him.'

'Philocles,' Apollonides protested, 'we were drinking with the man.'

'Sharing a cup?' I challenged. 'No, so we can hope you've escaped any contagion.'

'So who's going to carry him to the doctor?' Menekles

demanded. 'You're hardly going to sling him over your shoulder.'

That was fair comment. Eumelos was half a head taller than me, and I'm built for running not wrestling.

'We need a couple of strong slaves and a litter,' Apollonides insisted.

'We'll fetch Kadous.' Zosime answered. She was still by the table, her face taut with concern.

'No.' I could tell I was going to be saying that a lot. If this mysterious ailment struck me down, I needed my faithful slave to stay fit and well, to look after Zosime in this unfamiliar city. He would see her safely back to Athens, and to her father, Menkaure.

'Go back to our lodgings with Menekles.' I turned to the actor. 'Send word to what's his name, Eumelos' man, the one who was waiting there to welcome us.'

'Dardanis.' Menekles snapped his fingers as he recalled the name of the slave who managed Eumelos' household.

'That's him.' I nodded gratefully. 'Tell him to get here as quick as he can with a couple of strong lads.'

If the big Corinthian had some insidious disease, the chances were good that those closest to him had already been put at risk. As for my friends, and the woman I loved, I made a silent vow to Athena and to Dionysos. I would keep them as far from this peril as I possibly could.

I looked at Apollonides and then at Lysicrates. 'Go on, all of you. Get out of here.'

'I'll come with you to the temple,' Lysicrates said curtly. 'Any doctor will have a thousand and one questions. You know what they're like.'

'You'll need someone to show you the way. Telesil-la—' Torn, Hyanthidas looked at his beloved.

I saw the fear in his eyes. Whoever Eumelos had mistaken her for, the stricken man had embraced Telesilla as close as any lover.

'She can come with us,' said Zosime.

'No.' Telesilla spoke just as quickly.

We all waited for her to continue, before realising she was as much at sea as the rest of us.

'I can escort you home,' Apollonides offered.

'Thank you,' Telesilla replied, relieved.

She looked at Hyanthidas who nodded his agreement, as well he might. After spending plenty of this past year drinking with him in Athens, Hyanthidas knew the actor could handle any challenge he might meet on Corinth's streets.

'Excuse me!' The tavern keeper bustled up, red-faced with indignation. He snatched the silver platter up off the floor. 'Who's going to pay for all this damage?'

At least that was a question I could answer, though I felt I was taking the coward's way out. 'Send word to Perantas Bacchiad. This is his trusted man, Eumelos. Give him a fair account of your losses and let him know we've taken his man to the doctors at the shrine of Asklepios.'

'Who might you be, to claim acquaintance with the Bacchiads?' The tavern keeper wasn't remotely convinced. He also had burly slaves to back him, currently lurking in the doorway to the back room.

'I am Philocles Hestaiou Alopekethen of Athens.' I did my best to mimic Menekles in the role of the hero

Meriones, the central character in our play. Menekles plays the part with utmost dignity and seriousness, which makes the comedy unfolding around him all the funnier. Though there was nothing to laugh at here tonight.

'We have come to stage a play in your theatre, as Perantas Bacchiad's gift to the people of Corinth.' I indicated everyone else with a suitably sweeping gesture.

I saw the tavern keeper was torn between his desire to have us empty our purses, and wariness over offending one of this city's richest and most powerful men.

He settled on a scowl. 'Get him out of here. My people need to clean up this mess!'

'Of course.' Hyanthidas stepped forward to thrust his hands under Eumelos' armpits.

I understood what he was thinking. If the woman he loved had been so close to the stricken man, there was no point in him keeping his distance. I picked up Eumelos' ankles, and we carried the unconscious man outside.

The seating outside the tavern had been shoved aside by fleeing customers but nothing was knocked over or broken. We laid Eumelos carefully on a long table and pulled up a couple of stools.

'You'll need this.' Zosime handed me my cloak. I'd forgotten it completely, left behind on our bench inside. She was right though. These nights on the cusp of summer and autumn soon grow chilly.

She wrapped her shawl around her shoulders, drawing up a fold of finely woven wool to cover her hair. She looked as modest and respectable as any Athenian citizen's wife, the legitimate mother of his heirs, and no one here in Corinth would care that she was none of those things. I also noticed that she had my rolled sheets of papyrus safely tucked through the woven belt securing her pleated rose gown. Yet another reason for me to love her.

'I'll be back with Dardanis as quick as I can,' Menekles assured me as they set off.

'Let's get you home.' Apollonides bowed to Telesilla and offered her his arm.

As everyone else headed in different directions, Lysicrates took a seat on the far side of the table. Eumelos lay still as death between us. I held my palm over his face just long enough for the faint warmth of his breath to reassure me that he still lived.

The street was deserted, with just a few lamps burning here and there to help latecomers find their own doors. A feral dog paused to stare at us, brindled ears pricked. It loped off before anyone could throw something, doubtless in pursuit of a fat rat for its supper.

We heard the irate tavern keeper berating his slaves. His insults were punctuated by thuds as furniture was set back upright, and the slithering clatter of broken crockery being swept up and dumped in buckets. Despite the noise, my eyelids drooped.

'Here we are.' Menekles' voice roused me with a start.

Yawning, I scrubbed the sleep from my eyes and saw the actor was being followed by two thick-set slaves. One carried a bundle of sailcloth and the other had two rough-hewn poles sloped over one shoulder.

Lysicrates stood up. 'Where's Dardanis?'

'He's—' Menekles turned and did a double take that would make any audience roar with laughter. 'He was right behind us. Where's he gone?'

He looked at the two slaves who exchanged a vacant glance. Whatever duties they'd been bought for, quick wits clearly wasn't a requirement.

'He was right behind us,' Menekles protested again. 'I went back to the house, and Tromes, you know, Perantas' slave, he said he'd take me to Eumelos' house. It's not far, and when we got there, Dardanis got these two out of bed. He told me to lead the way, to show this pair of plough oxen where to go.'

He spread his hands, beard jutting as he demanded a response from them. The two slaves just stared back, as dumb as doorposts.

'He must have gone to tell Perantas,' I guessed.

So when I faced our Corinthian patron, he'd already have heard at least two versions of what had happened here tonight. So much for hoping that someone would let me off that particular hook. I remembered what the oracles always say. Be careful what you wish for. You may just get it.

Regardless, it would be my responsibility to tell the Bacchiad if Eumelos lived or died. 'Let's get him to the Asklepion. Menekles, please go back to the house and stay with Zosime.'

'All right,' he said, still irritated. 'You'd think Dardanis would've had the courtesy to tell me what he was doing.'

As the actor departed, muttering under his breath,

Hyanthidas and I manhandled Eumelos onto the litter. The slaves picked up the poles and started walking. Neither said a word. I was starting to wonder if they were even Hellenes.

Hyanthidas led the way. Lysicrates and I followed the litter. We weren't far from the Lechaion Road, which cuts straight as an arrow northwards from Corinth's main marketplace toward the long gulf that separates the Peloponnese from Boeotia, Phocis and Aetolia. Passers-by looked at us, incurious, and most courteously stepped out of our path. The two slaves navigated around the ones who insisted they had right of way.

When Hyanthidas turned down a side street, we cut between quiet houses, their gates safely barred for the night. The sky was clear and there was enough moonlight to show us our way without difficulty. Sooner than I expected, the city walls loomed up ahead of us and I saw the sanctuary that surrounded the temple dedicated to Asklepios.

A long, shallow ramp ran along one side of the tall wall that faced us. We followed it up to the entrance. As we went in, we saw the temple enclosure on our right-hand side, and the doctors' hall to our left. During the day, the colonnades surrounding the pillared temple in the right-hand courtyard would be thronged with people praying for a cure or giving thanks for divine healing. At the moment, all we heard were the faint snores of travellers who'd sought overnight shelter here.

Hyanthidas knocked on the door to the doctors' hall. A man opened it and, seeing the litter, he wasted no time.

'Come in. Quietly.' His air of calm competence was wonderfully reassuring, just in those three words.

Inside the broad hall, oil lamps in high niches cast soft, golden light. The floor was packed with pallets and the air was stuffy. The patients slept on, some stirring restlessly beneath their blankets, while others sprawled, oblivious in slumber. I wondered which ones would wake recovered, or be granted a sacred vision by Apollo's healer son.

'Our friend . . .' I looked at him helplessly. 'He began raving, and then fell into convulsions.' I kept my voice low, but my words couldn't help disturbing the closest sleepers.

'Follow me.'

The doctor turned right and led us towards the northern wall. His head barely topped my shoulder and he was almost as broad as he was tall. He picked up a lamp from a table by a door and led us through it to a stairwell.

The steps turned left as we descended, slowly and carefully. Fortunately the stairs were wide enough for Hyanthidas and I to flank the litter and make sure Eumelos didn't slide off. As we went out through another door into the clean, cool night, I heard the soft trickle of a spring or a fountain somewhere in the darkness.

As my night vision returned, I saw we were in another courtyard. The temple's architects had dealt with the sloping ground hereabouts by building this second sanctuary on a lower level. To our left, three dining suites for private celebrations at the temple had been built directly underneath the doctors' hall. The rest of the courtyard

23

was surrounded by colonnades where wooden partitions separated long tables.

'Put him in there.' The doctor was a Cycladean by his accent, maybe from Naxos. He nodded at the closest cubicle.

The slaves did as they were told, still without a word, before retreating to sit, apparently unperturbed on the steps leading down to the open courtyard. I waited beside the table with Lysicrates and Hyanthidas.

Several of the sanctuary's sacred snakes slithered away into the shadows as the doctor lit two lamps waiting ready among the jars and vials on some shelves. A smaller table held an array of medical instruments and plain-glazed pots. 'Who is he?'

'Eumelos—' I broke off, appalled.

That was as much as I knew about the man. If this was Athens, even if we'd barely passed the time of day, I'd know his father's name and his voting tribe. It would be easy to find the district brotherhood where his father had proclaimed his son's citizen rights, and those brotherhood officials would tell us where to find his family. Here in Corinth, I had no idea how to learn anything useful about the stranger.

'He works for Perantas Bacchiad,' Hyanthidas offered. 'His signet ring is token of that.'

The doctor looked at the agate carved with a splendid portrayal of Perseus riding Bellerophon and sniffed, unimpressed. Then he looked closely at Eumelos' face. 'Tell me exactly what happened.'

'We were in a tavern, sharing a jug of wine.' Lysicrates

rubbed the back of his neck. 'It went to his head awfully fast. Then he started seeing things. He mistook a woman he didn't know for someone else entirely. He was talking to people who weren't even there.'

'Go on.' The doctor examined Eumelos' hands and arms, testing every joint from his fingers to his shoulders, as the three of us described the Corinthian's terrifying convulsions.

'I take it he has no history of the falling sickness?' The doctor looked up from studying Eumelos' well-muscled legs and sandalled feet.

'I've no idea,' I said helplessly. 'But he has a fever.' I didn't think the gods added such torment to that brutal punishment for hidden sins.

The doctor stepped back from the table. His broad face was thoughtful. 'His skin is hot to the touch, but this is no fever born of sickness.'

'So this is no disease that we might succumb to?' Hyanthidas' face betrayed his anxiety.

'I don't believe so.' The doctor pursed his lips. 'I don't think it's the falling sickness either. Those so afflicted so often piss themselves, though not always, of course.'

I looked at the other two. We all wanted to ask what the doctor thought was wrong. Or rather, we all wanted somebody else to ask.

The doctor eased the big Corinthian's mouth open and cautiously sniffed his frail breath. Sliding back an un-resisting lid, he ran a fingertip around Eumelos' eyeball and rubbed it against his own thumb. As I winced, I saw Lysicrates grimace.

'Help me undress him,' the doctor ordered.

That wasn't easy with the big man now limp in his stupor. Lysicrates and I lifted Eumelos' shoulders. Hyanthidas unbuckled his belt and the doctor began easing his tunic up under his buttocks. As the Cycladean freed the fabric, lifting it as far as Eumelos' waist, something slipped free. Not the purse tucked inside his tunic and held secure by his belt, but something smaller. It rolled across the table and fell to the floor with a sharp clatter.

'What was that?' the doctor demanded.

We all stepped back carefully, looking this way and that among the dark bars of shadow cutting across the tiles.

'There!' Hyanthidas crouched to retrieve a vial of thick blue glass as long as a man's thumb. It was stoppered with a wax-crusted cork.

'What's this?' the Cycladean demanded.

'A pick-me-up, that's what he said.' Lysicrates nodded at me and we laid Eumelos down. It looked as if undressing him could wait.

'He drank this?' The doctor looked at the actor, exasperated. 'You didn't think to mention this earlier?'

'He emptied it into his first cup of wine, but he was perfectly fine after that,' Lysicrates protested.

'Until he wasn't,' the doctor said caustically. He freed the cork and sniffed it warily. 'You say he was distressed, but he wasn't actually weeping? You were drinking for some time, but he never left the table to piss?'

'No,' said Lysicrates, defensive.

The doctor set the little vial down and tugged

Eumelos' tunic up, exposing his groin and belly. His deft fingers probed the area between the unconscious man's hips, just above his cock. He nodded, speaking quietly to himself more than to us. 'Bladder full to bursting.'

Then he seized a fold of skin deep in Eumelos' groin, pinching it viciously hard between finger and thumb and twisting his hand for good measure. We all exclaimed in pointless outrage, but Eumelos had no need for our sympathy. Not a flicker of response crossed his slack face.

The doctor drew the fabric down to cover the stricken man's nakedness. 'Your friend has been poisoned, or rather, he was persuaded to poison himself, with the contents of that vial.'

'What's in it?' Now Lysicrates looked at the blue glass bottle with loathing.

'Thornapple, mostly, judging by the scent.' The doctor folded his arms.

'That's a medicine,' Hyanthidas objected.

'In the right hands, in a carefully measured dose.' The Cycladean shrugged. 'Not like this.'

'Will he recover?' I asked, hoping against hope. 'If he's endured this far?'

'I have no reason to hope so,' the doctor said, dispassionate. 'I believe he'll be dead by morning.'

He looked at the three of us, brisk and businesslike. 'You can stay or you can go, as you see fit. He may as well rest here for the night. He's feeling no discomfort so I see no need to move him.'

He left us in the cubicle without waiting for an answer. Hyanthidas and Lysicrates stared at me, appalled.

I looked at them, horrified and equally at a loss.

Lysicrates was the first to break the silence. 'What's that they say about Corinth? Look for a scorpion under every stone.'

'How dare you?' Hyanthidas was outraged.

'Please,' I interrupted. 'There's no need to quarrel among ourselves.'

'You said he took the dose himself,' Hyanthidas insisted. 'Whoever mixed it must have made some mistake. This is just a dreadful accident.'

Lysicrates shook his head. 'This man's been poisoned by some enemy. The gods only know what he was mixed up in. We all know that Corinth—'

'Enough!' I clapped my hands. They both subsided, though I saw them slide sullen glances at each other. I made a series of swift decisions.

'I'll stay here, until we know if the Fates have truly cut Eumelos' thread. You, go and reassure Telesilla.' I jerked my head to send Hyanthidas on his way. 'Tell her there's no need to fear any sickness.'

I turned to Lysicrates. 'Can you find your way back to our house?' I was relieved to see him nod. 'Tell everyone what's happened. And tell Zosime I'll be back as soon as I can tomorrow.'

I glanced at the slaves sitting stolidly on the steps. 'Send that pair home, and tell them to tell Dardanis to call on us first thing in the morning. I should be back by then, but if not, you find out exactly what he's told Perantas. And tell Zosime I love her.'

'Always.' He managed a crooked smile.

28

I watched them all leave, wondering how long the musician would be annoyed about Lysicrates insulting his home. I still didn't understand what the actor had against Corinth. I also wondered uneasily if he was right about Eumelos' fate. Had some enemy found the means to poison Perantas' man? I didn't like the thought of being caught up in someone's murderous quarrel in a strange city.

The doctor had left the little blue vial on the shelf with the lamps. I went to look at it but there was nothing to tell me where it might have come from. If Zosime's father had been with us, I could have asked what he thought. Menkaure is widely travelled and as a potter, the Egyptian has a keen eye for ceramics and glass. But he was back in Athens, staying in our little house to make sure no thieves took advantage of our absence and ransacked the place.

Still, somebody might recognise the vial, if they were familiar with whatever novelties traders brought to this seafarers' crossroads. I made sure the little cork was rammed down and dropped the vial inside my tunic. The cold glass slid down my ribs to be caught by my belt.

Footsteps echoed in the courtyard. The Cycladean reappeared with a thin mattress rolled up under one arm and carrying a folded blanket. 'Your friends said you were staying the night.'

'Yes, thank you.' I took the bedding.

The doctor looked at me with measured sympathy as he snuffed all but one of the lamps. 'You realise that all

29

you can do here is give him an obol for Charon.'

I nodded. 'But no one should die alone.'

The doctor smiled briefly. 'Asklepios bless you both.'

He left and I unrolled the pallet across the open end of the cubicle. After all the day's upheavals, I welcomed the colonnade's stillness. With the blanket as well as my cloak, I wrapped myself up, warm and comfortable. Sleep soon claimed me.

When I woke up the next morning, Eumelos was stiff, cold, and dead.

Chapter Three

I slid the Pegasus seal ring off Eumelos' rigid finger with some difficulty. The gold band left a noticeable dent in his skin. His jaw was clamped so solidly shut that I couldn't put an obol in his mouth, so I settled for wedging the tiny coin between his waxen lips. It had been minted in Athens, but our money is accepted by Hellenes everywhere so I didn't imagine Charon would quibble.

I felt sorrow for an untimely death rather than grief. I barely knew Eumelos, so this was hardly a personal loss. At least he was at peace after last evening's violent seizures. Though the torment was only beginning for his family and I was sorry for that. They would want to know why he had drunk the dose that killed him. Had he been tricked into doing that, or had he sought his own death? Hades help him if he had. There are so many easier ways out of this life than such a brutal poison.

Once I'd delivered the ring to his family, I needed to call on Perantas Bacchiad. I'd inform our Corinthian patron of this tragedy and see what he wanted to do next. He must know who to contact among Corinth's ruling Council to get this murky death investigated.

Uneasily, I supposed it was always possible that he'd decide to cancel our play's performance. Still, there was nothing to be gained by delay. Quite the contrary. If we were going to be packing up and heading straight back to Athens, the sooner we knew it, the better.

I slid the ring onto my middle finger. I'd better take care not to lose it. The gold band was noticeably loose, and the expertly carved agate was heavy.

'Farewell.' I laid my hand briefly on Eumelos' chest. 'I wish you peace in the asphodel fields of the Underworld.'

I rolled up the thin mattress and left the blanket folded on top of it. The morning light showed me the wide basin filled by a spring over in the south-west corner of the courtyard, and I washed the night's staleness from my mouth and sluiced my head and face. A few hearty shakes got the worst creases out of my cloak and I repinned it around my shoulders. The sky was a clear, pale blue and the morning was still cool enough to raise gooseflesh on my forearms.

Going in search of the Cycladean doctor, I found a hatchet-faced Arcadian in charge of the hall full of patients sitting at the table by the door to the stairs. He was concocting assorted doses, mixing herbs and powders from an array of plain glazed jars. He looked up, his expression enquiring. 'Good morning?'

'I came here last night with a man who had been poisoned. He died, so I must tell his family.' I slipped the Pegasus ring off my finger and held it out, so no one thought the corpse had been robbed. 'I'll be returning this to them.'

'Chresimos told me to expect you. My condolences.' His sympathy was sincerely meant. 'We will care for your friend until his family come to take him home.'

'Thank you.' I nodded gratefully and made my way out of the hall. Outside the entrance, at the bottom of the long ramp, a welcome sight greeted me. Kadous was leaning against the temple wall. He stood up as I drew close.

'How long have you been waiting?'

The Phrygian shrugged. 'I left the house at first light. We weren't sure if you could find your way back.'

'It would have been a challenge,' I admitted. 'Did you get everything unpacked?'

'We did.' He cocked his head. 'Will we be staying?'

My father prized quick wits in his slaves, and Kadous was one of the most astute he'd ever bought.

I sighed. 'That remains to be seen.'

We reached the Lechaion Road and walked south towards the heart of the city. Ahead, I could see the great, grey bulk of the Acrocorinth, barely gilded by the morning sun. Its rugged crags rose up beyond the houses and temples, with the lofty citadel within the embrace of Corinth's long walls that stretched all the way behind us back to the sea.

Our Athenian acropolis is the heart of our city, the sanctuary where we honour our gods, and our refuge where they defend us in time of gravest danger. By contrast the Acrocorinth looms over its city. Its brooding cliffs are four times the height of our acropolis and the twin-headed summit offers ten times the space for

33

temples and fortifications. Now I'd seen the famous mountain for myself, I could see why no army would advance into the Peloponnese if Corinth was set against it. By the same token, no Peloponnesian foe could threaten Athens as long as Corinth was our ally. Aristarchos had reminded me of that more than once.

'This way.' Kadous headed down a side street. I committed the route's turns to memory, so much easier in the daylight. I'd simply been following Hyanthidas last night, too distracted to pay much attention. We soon arrived at the sizeable residence Perantas had put at our disposal. Kadous knocked and Tromes opened the gate. He was the most senior of the Bacchiad slaves sent to serve our temporary household's needs.

We walked into the spacious courtyard, ringed on three sides by pillared porches and two-storey buildings. The family house, when a family lived here, was straight ahead. Stairs led up to guest apartments above the storerooms and slave accommodation on either side.

Zosime was sitting at the table in the courtyard, eating bread and figs for breakfast. Apollonides sat beside her, sipping at a cup. He studied my face. 'He died?'

'He did.' There was nothing else to say about that.

'He emptied some poison into his own wine?' Zosime had evidently heard the full story from the others.

'He did.' I unbuckled my belt and the blue vial dropped to the beaten earth. Until she reminded me, I'd forgotten about it, with the glass warmed by my body overnight. I scooped it up and tossed it over. 'If we can find out where that came from, we might learn more.'

Apollonides studied the vial. 'I can ask around the markets, to see who might make or sell such work.'

'Just keep your eyes open,' I cautioned. 'We don't want to add to his family's grief by starting rumours, or to slander some innocent by accident.' I had no idea how Corinth's laws dealt with unfounded accusations but Athenian courts exact harsh punishment.

The door to the storerooms on my right opened and Menekles appeared, holding a handful of masks by their linen ties. Lysicrates followed, with his arms full of the tightly woven stage skins that our new chorus would wear beneath their costumes.

Behind them, I glimpsed two more of the slaves we'd been loaned. Their faces were shifting between curiosity and apprehension. Tromes clapped his hands briskly and shooed them backwards, before disappearing through the main door into the house, intent on his own duties.

Menekles' full lips thinned as he saw my expression. 'He's dead then.'

Lysicrates shaded his eyes from the bright sun with a hand. 'Have you any idea where we're supposed to go for rehearsal space? Eumelos said he'd arranged that for us.'

'He'd already spread the word about our chorus auditions,' added Apollonides. 'Singers will be turning up tomorrow and we need to know where to meet them.'

Clearly the actors were assuming the play was going ahead and expected me to fulfil all the chorus master's duties.

I held up the Pegasus ring. 'This must go to his family,

35

along with the grievous news. Once I've done that, I'll go and see Perantas Bacchiad. Someone in his household should know something about the arrangements for the play.' I hoped so, anyway. I looked at Menekles. 'Do you know the way to Eumelos' house?'

The actor nodded. 'Tromes showed me last night. It's close by.'

Apollonides got to his feet. 'I'll help finish checking through the baskets.'

'I need something to eat first.' I sat beside Zosime and helped myself to sweet, ripe figs and bread.

'Did you get any sleep?' She squeezed my hand.

'I did, by Asklepios' grace,' I assured her.

The actors stood motionless, watching me eat, as though they were poised for some cue on a stage. In the silence, I heard those slaves in the storeroom whispering.

I snapped my fingers to attract Kadous' attention. 'Tell Tromes to tell his people to keep their mouths shut around the markets. There's going to be enough gossip without them adding to it.'

'I'll see to it.' The Phrygian spoke loudly enough to be heard by those two in the shadows who instantly fell silent.

'Come on.' I swallowed my mouthful and nodded at Menekles. As I stood up, Kadous opened the gate for us.

Eumelos' home was only a couple of streets away. I was surprised to find it was a modest residence, though. I thought he was supposed to be a prosperous merchant.

An unknown youth opened the gate to our knock, his sharp-cheekboned face drawn with anxiety and

36

exhaustion. 'Is there word from the Asklepion?'

I could see he was desperately clinging to hope, at the same time as dreading the worst.

Menekles looked past him. 'Where's Dardanis?'

The lad's eyes widened. 'Isn't he with you?'

Menekles was puzzled. 'No.'

I held up a hand to quell the lad's next question. 'Good morning, I'm Philocles Hestaiou. Please excuse me, who are you?'

I couldn't see a family resemblance to Eumelos, but that's not necessarily any guide. I needed to know to whom I was speaking, before I shared the dreadful tidings.

'I'm Nados.' He stepped back to let us into the narrow courtyard. 'Eumelos' business partner. Junior partner,' he added hastily. 'One of three. There's Aithon in Kenchreai and Simias in Lechaion.'

'Where does your master's family live?' I hoped he'd say Lechaion. That would be an easy walk, there and back before noon. Going all the way to Kenchreai and dealing with a shocked widow's concerns and questions would take up the rest of my day.

Nados frowned. 'His family?'

'His wife and children? I'm afraid I have grievous news. Eumelos died last night.'

But Nados was shaking his head. 'It's just us. Eumelos never wed. It's—'

He tried to go on, but grief choked him, as tears spilled down his cheeks.

'Oh.' I realised that I'd simply assumed that a man of

37

the merchant's age and good standing would be married.

The lad grimaced, distraught. 'He – he – he always said a man would be a fool to tie himself to one woman, in Corinth of all places.'

That seemed an odd thing to say, but people say the strangest things in the first shock of bereavement.

It also made a sort of sense. There are supposedly a thousand sacred prostitutes dedicated to serving the Temple of Aphrodite, up on the Acrocorinth. Never having a chance to visit them is a byword for bad luck in life, among men at Athenian drinking parties anyway.

It was one of Zosime's reasons for coming with me on this trip. She said she didn't want me getting lonely while I was here, and bringing back some unwanted souvenir.

Menekles and I waited as the boy fought to hold back his emotions. After a few moments, Nados took a deep, shuddering breath, and scrubbed the tears from his cheeks with the heel of one hand.

'He was planning to visit his favourite brothel last night, after he'd seen you settled. That's why we weren't expecting him back here before dawn.'

Menekles looked thoughtful. 'That might explain why he needed a pick-me-up.'

'Perhaps.' It still didn't explain where he'd got the dose from, or why it had killed him. Someone needed to be asking those questions. 'Can you take me to Perantas Bacchiad's house? We need to tell him what's happened, and someone must take charge of the funeral arrangements.'

'Let me get my cloak.' Nados drew another shaky

breath and squared bony shoulders. He was a few fingers taller than me, and old enough to have done his hoplite training, but it would be a few years before he filled out.

He went into the house and I looked around the courtyard while we waited. The paving was smooth and a terracotta-tiled porch was furnished with elegant tables and stools. The wall was painted with skilfully executed acanthus fronds and I knew from Zosime that such tasteful artistry didn't come cheap. Eumelos' house might be small but he didn't stint on home comforts.

Nados reappeared, and paused on the threshold, talking to a grey-haired woman who was trying to stifle her sobs. A girl in a plain dress stood close, ineffectually patting her shoulder. If they were both household slaves, along with Dardanis and those mute litter bearers, that was more evidence of Eumelos' prosperity, and this was only one of his three properties.

The more I thought about the puzzle of his death as we waited, the more uneasy I was becoming. The obvious answers to the riddle made no sense. Granted, there could well be explanations I was unaware of. Even wealthy men have heartbreaking sorrows. A man can look enviably rich while he is drowning in debt. Still, I was going to need hard proof before I'd believe that Eumelos had killed himself.

Nados crossed the paving to join us, his eyes red-rimmed with grief. 'Let's go,' he said hoarsely.

We had a longer walk to Perantas Bacchiad's house, and our path took us through the heart of the city. We passed through the bustling agora where the Council's decrees were displayed on all sides, engraved on gleaming bronze tablets. The market stalls selling fresh vegetables, fruit and fish were as well-stocked as any in Athens and equally busy with household slaves buying the day's provisions.

We passed the sacred fountain house at the Peirene Spring, where Bellerophon had first bridled Pegasus, with divine Athena's help, and water had sprung from the ground where the irritated beast stamped his hoof. I admired the grandeur of Apollo's temple elevated on a shallow rise in the land. The god, and the Corinthian Council who met there, watched over colonnades on all sides where countless deals were being done. I heard voices with every Hellenic accent as well as dialects from much further afield. I recalled Eumelos telling me, as we walked side by side from Kenchreai, how Corinth's merchants trade as far as the Phoenician settlements out on the wild coasts beyond the Pillars of Heracles.

There were monuments and statues on all sides, dedicated to any number of heroes. I hadn't realised just how many shrines this city boasted. I would have liked to stop to learn more, but this was hardly the time.

At the far end of the agora, Nados took the lesser road heading northwards beyond the temple's hill, and we passed another of Corinth's famous shrines; the spring sacred to Glauke, though she had been a mortal woman rather than a goddess.

Her ghastly fate was another famous poisoning in Corinth, I recalled uneasily. The poor girl had been rivals with Medea for Jason's love. The vengeful sorceress sent her a dress saturated with burning venom. Maddened with pain, Glauke threw herself into the waters in the vain hope of quenching her agonies.

Personally, I wouldn't have wanted to drink from such a spring, but the Corinthians filling water jars from the basins didn't seem bothered.

As we approached the city's theatre, Menekles had other things on his mind.

'Nados, do you know where Eumelos intended to hold our chorus auditions? Where we are supposed to rehearse?'

The lad was startled out of his melancholy thoughts. 'Yes, of course. He made all the necessary arrangements at the Shrine to Demeter and Persephone, and spread word for singers to attend at the third hour of the day tomorrow. I can take you up there and make introductions.'

'Thank you.' Relieved, Menekles slid me a grin.

My answering smile was fleeting. I'd wait and see what Perantas Bacchiad had to say, before assuming our play would go ahead.

'Here we are.' Nados wiped sweating hands on his tunic, blinking hard to ward off fresh tears.

Perantas enjoyed a spacious terracotta-tiled house not far beyond the theatre. Look one way from the upper windows and he would have a fine view of the Temple of Apollo and the Acrocorinth beyond. Look the other way and this wealthy man would see all the way to Lechaion and the sparkling waters of the Gulf of Corinth.

We wouldn't be admiring such vistas unless we could

get through the closed gate. A handful of burly men leaned against the wall in the shade. Three were holding sturdy vine staves and they all stared at us, unsmiling.

'Good day to you. I'm Nados—' The lad's voice cracked under the twin burdens of nervousness and grief.

I looked for the gang's leader. My guess was the sleepy-eyed man with muscular arms folded across his broad chest and a collar of gold plaques around his bull neck. I raised my hand to show him the Pegasus ring.

'I'm Philocles Hestaiou of Athens. We're in Corinth at Perantas Bacchiad's invitation, come to stage a comedy in your theatre. Perantas sent his man Eumelos to see to our needs but he has been struck down—'

'I know who you are.' The bull-necked man jabbed a thick finger at me, scowling. 'And you don't wear that ring unless you're ready to swear allegiance to the Brotherhood of Bellerophon.'

I had no idea what he meant by that, but I could see the gold rectangles of his collar were stamped with the image of the fabled hero's winged horse. 'I'm here to return this to Perantas.'

The bull-necked man gestured and one of the others knocked on the gate. 'Make sure that you do.'

As the gate opened, a bright-eyed Nubian in a finely woven linen tunic welcomed us in. Slave or servant, it was impossible to tell, but I recognised the type. Rich men prize their personal scribes, if they're wise.

'This way, if you please.' He bowed and didn't bother looking back as he led us into the inner courtyard. Not a slave, I decided, not with that much self-confidence, and the gold rings that shone against skin even darker than Zosime's father's.

We followed him, for lack of any other option.

Perantas was an unremarkable man in an expensive, deep-dyed red tunic. He was neither handsome nor ugly, of average height and build, but I knew from our single meeting in Athens that he could command attention in a gathering with a few well-chosen words. He sat in a pillared porch's shade amid painted olive trees, dealing with the correspondence that mounts up like autumn leaves around the great and the good of every city.

He laid a crisp sheet of papyrus aside. 'Good day.'

I slipped the Pegasus ring off my finger and laid it on the table. 'I sincerely regret to inform you that Eumelos is dead.'

'So I have heard. Please, sit.' Perantas paused as the Nubian brought stools for the three of us. 'Tell me everything,' he ordered.

Menekles related the evening's events in the tavern without theatrics. The story was dramatic enough. I took up the tale when we departed for the Asklepion.

When I fell silent, Perantas looked at Nados. 'Where is Dardanis?'

The lad stared at him, bemused. 'Isn't he here?'

If he wasn't, I wondered who had told the Bacchiad the news. Perhaps someone at the Asklepion wore one of those Pegasus rings. I guessed a man like Perantas had informants across this city. Either that, or Tromes had sent word while I was eating breakfast. He was Perantas' slave after all, so that's where his loyalties would lie.

Perantas turned his attention to Menekles. 'When did you last see Dardanis?'

'He was following on behind me and the slaves with the litter when we left Eumelos' house last night. He must have headed off somewhere else before we reached the tavern.'

The man could hardly have got lost in that short distance. I could see the actor shared my concern for the absent slave.

'You say poison killed Eumelos.' Perantas looked at me. 'Presumably given to him by someone he trusted.'

'Not by Dardanis.' Nados was shocked into a vehement protest. 'They've been together since Eumelos was trading from a shack by the Kenchreai docks ten years and more ago.'

'Then where has the slave gone?' Perantas demanded.

None of us had an answer for him.

Perantas drummed contemplative fingers on a stack of documents. 'There are factions in Corinth who wouldn't be sorry to see this play abandoned. Some of my rivals have made no secret of that. They believe we should be strengthening our alliances across the Peloponnese instead of making common cause with Athens over some new colony in Sicily.'

'You think one of them is responsible for Eumelos' death.' That was an alarming idea.

Perantas paused for an instant too long before replying. 'Not now that Dardanis is missing. Surely the slave must have poisoned his master and run away. It's the obvious explanation.'

'I cannot believe he would do that,' Nados stuttered.

'It's surely as likely as Eumelos killing himself.' Perantas looked at Nados, dark eyes intent.

'I don't . . .' The boy subsided into an incoherent mumble.

Perantas turned to me. 'If we don't seize the initiative, this calamity will hand my opponents a stick to beat me with. They won't accuse me outright, but there will be whispers around the agora before sunset today that accuse Eumelos of shady dealings on my behalf, to lay that guilt for his death at my door.'

I didn't like where this conversation was heading. I hadn't expected Perantas' priorities would be so far from my own. Aristarchos, my Athenian patron, would have set justice for the dead man far above his own concerns.

I tried again. 'That's all the more reason to drag the truth into the daylight, to kill such rumours.'

'How long will it take to establish what happened? How would we set about such a task? I don't wish to sound callous, but who would uncertainty in the meantime serve?' Perantas and I could have been the only two people in the courtyard. 'It's not as if he had a family who are clamouring for answers.'

'We have a duty to the gods, above and below, to establish the truth.' I wasn't going to face the Furies' displeasure on Perantas' say-so.

'And that duty is best served by doing nothing,' Perantas said quickly, 'at least for the moment. If Eumelos has been murdered, let's keep whoever might be responsible waiting and wondering. If word spreads that I believe

45

this missing slave is guilty, that might lure the real poisoner into some misstep. If such a poisoner even exists. Meantime, you need not get entangled in Corinth's politics. You can continue with your auditions and rehearsals. Let Wetka know if there's anything you need.' He nodded at the Nubian who was waiting patiently a few paces away.

Menekles shifted on his stool. 'So we are going to stage the play?'

'Of course.' Perantas was adamant. 'If someone truly killed Eumelos to put a stop to your performance, I'll see them cursed by all the heroes before I let them succeed. As for Eumelos' funeral, you can make the arrangements, Nados, and see to his business affairs. There's no need for me to be involved.'

He shuffled some papyrus into a neat stack and reached for his pen. It was clear we were dismissed. Menekles and I stood up. Nados was slower on the uptake, shocked by his new responsibilities.

'Come on.' I tapped his shoulder.

The lad was silent as we walked back to the gate, clearly overwhelmed. I knew how he felt. I contemplated the Acrocorinth looming ahead of us. Without Perantas backing us, without his contacts and influence in this city, solving the mystery of Eumelos' death would be a challenge equal to pushing a boulder up that faint path winding up to the summit. I remembered that Sisyphus had been a Corinthian king in the age of heroes, and I wondered if he rolled his burden for all eternity up a ghostly echo of that great mountain in the Underworld.

I'd be a fool to take it on. I had all my duties as chorus master as we prepared to perform the play, and we'd already lost valuable rehearsal time.

On the other hand, I wanted to know the truth, and not just out of duty to the gods. If Perantas Bacchiad had enemies so determined to stop our performance that they were prepared to murder Eumelos, I hated to imagine what else they might contemplate. We needed to know if our own lives were in danger. It's not as if we had friends in Corinth to watch our backs.

Outside in the street. I picked up the pace. 'Come on. We've got things to do.'

Chapter Four

Hyanthidas and Telesilla were sitting on the bench in the courtyard talking to Zosime when we got back. Good. I had questions I hoped the musicians could answer.

So did Menekles. 'Where is the Sanctuary of Demeter and Persephone? That's our rehearsal space,' he explained as Apollonides and Lysicrates appeared in the doorway to the storeroom.

Lysicrates looked at me. 'We're going ahead with the play?'

'We are,' I said grimly, 'and we're keeping our eyes open for anyone out to make trouble. Perantas Bacchiad says rival factions in Corinth would like to see us fail.'

'What did he say about Eumelos' death?' Apollonides demanded.

'Perantas prefers to believe that this missing slave is somehow responsible.' I raised a hand as everyone protested. 'I know, I don't believe it either. There must be some other explanation. What was Eumelos saying to you in the tavern? Was there any hint of trouble in his personal life? In his business dealings?'

Lysicrates shook his head. 'We were talking about Athens and Pericles' building plans.'

'He hadn't visited our city for years,' added Menekles, 'so he was interested to know what had changed.'

There was nothing remarkable in that. I sighed. 'Let's hope Dardanis turns up soon, and that he knows something of use. Meantime, we may as well get on. Everyone, pull up a stool.'

Zosime made room for me on the bench. I took a breath; first things first. 'Nados, where is the Sanctuary?'

He was more than ready to let me take charge. 'On the road up to the Acrocorinth.'

'And the priestess is expecting us? Good,' I continued as he nodded. 'When did Eumelos say we would hold our chorus auditions?'

'Tomorrow morning.' The lad looked distressed. 'But I have to be at home. That's where he will be laid out—'

As soon as word got around that Eumelos had been carried there from the Asklepion, the lad would have his hands full with visitors.

'We can go to the Sanctuary and introduce ourselves,' I assured him. 'We'll hold auditions as planned tomorrow. You need only concern yourself with the funeral. Go and reclaim your master's body.'

'We'll come with you.' Telesilla stood up and so did Zosime. The women exchanged a glance that told me they'd agreed on that earlier.

'Thank you.' Nados was pitiably grateful.

'One more thing,' I said quickly. 'Do you know which brothel Eumelos intended to visit last night?'

'The House of Pearls.' Nados glanced towards the Acrocorinth. 'Close to the Temple of Aphrodite.'

Hyanthidas nodded. 'I know it.'

'Let's see what the women there can tell us. They may know something that might shed light on all this.' I stood up to kiss Zosime farewell.

She murmured as her lips brushed my cheek. 'I'll see what Eumelos' people can tell me about Dardanis.'

As the trio departed and Kadous closed the gate behind them, the actors closed up our circle. I turned to Hyanthidas. 'Tell me about the Brotherhood of Bellerophon.'

'It's one of the city's hero cults. We have a lot more of them here than you do, though most of them are much the same as religious associations in Athens. Devotees commemorate their chosen hero with rites at his shrine, followed by feasting and drinking. Members often have trades or commercial interests in common. They support each other's businesses, help out those who fall on hard times, and defend the interests of widows and orphans.'

So far, so familiar, but the musician clearly had more to say. 'And?' I prompted.

Hyanthidas ran a hand through his curls. 'Some become politically active.' There was a distinct edge to his voice. 'They ally themselves with powerful men on the Council, and those men use their support to pursue their political aims, repaying the favour with preferential contracts and loans. The Brotherhood of Bellerophon are all in favour of strengthening Corinth's ties to Athens. After all, Athena advised Bellerophon to lay in wait for Pegasus by the Peirene Spring. She gave him the golden bridle that tamed the winged steed. They say that binds our cities together.'

'And anyone who says different gets a smack in the mouth?' guessed Menekles.

'At the very least,' Hyanthidas confirmed.

Lysicrates and Apollonides started to protest that hero cults were peace-loving associations, but Menekles told them about our encounter outside Perantas Bacchiad's gate.

'He's a prominent member of the Brotherhood,' Hyanthidas explained. 'They'll be in favour of Perantas sponsoring our play.'

'Who *won't* like the idea?' Menekles asked.

Hyanthidas hesitated. 'Hard to say. I've been away too long to know all the agora gossip. There have always been factions opposed to Corinth making any alliance with Athens. They think that weakens Corinth's claim to pre-eminence within the Peloponnesian League—'

Lysicrates let slip a derisive murmur.

'What?' Hyanthidas demanded, annoyed.

'Well, the Peloponnesian League—' Lysicrates colour-ed slightly. I could see he hadn't meant to provoke the musician, but equally, he wasn't about to back down. 'It's just an excuse for the Spartans to bully their neigh-bours whenever something puts their nose out of joint. It's not like the Delian League—'

'You mean it doesn't demand money, year on year, even in peace time?' Hyanthidas retorted.

Lysicrates wasn't having that. 'The Delian League defends all Hellenes with ships and hoplites in time of war, and by supporting the rule of law and democracy.'

'And who do you have to thank for that?' Hyanthidas

challenged him. 'The Peloponnesian League, who drove the tyrants out of Athens—'

'Enough!' I said loudly. 'We're getting off the point.'

The last thing I needed, or expected, was to see my two friends falling out. To my relief, Lysicrates subsided. I got to my feet. 'Let's go and see this rehearsal space.'

Menekles and Apollonides instantly agreed, equally dismayed by this quarrel.

While everyone found their sandals, I seized the chance to have a quick word with Kadous, telling him to go to Eumelos' house to give Zosime any help she might need.

'Ask his slaves where they think Dardanis might be. When you get back, see what Tromes and these Bacchiad slaves think of these hero-worship associations.'

We set out for the Acrocorinth. Well before we reached the Sanctuary of Demeter and Persephone, I was glad I'd left my cloak behind. Even with the heat of summer behind us, the day was warming up, and that first stretch of the road below the great grey cliffs was one of those long, gradual slopes that you don't realise is rising quite so high until your legs and lungs protest. When you're forced to take a breather, you're surprised to see how far you've come.

When we drew to a halt by mutual, unspoken consent, I could see the city spread out below us. Red-tiled roofs were sparsely scattered on the dry, rocky slope we had climbed, while down where water was plentiful, houses were tight-packed around the agora, overlooked by the Temple of Apollo. Beyond that cluster of fountains and shrines, the city spread northwards into a sprawl of workshops and smallholdings. Here and there, plumes of smoke indicated kilns baking the pottery and tiles that Corinth was famous for.

Further still, I could see olive groves, fields of grain, vineyards, fruit orchards and patches of scrubby pasture, all defended by the city's long walls running down to the sea.

I could see clear across the fertile plain to the coast, with the high ground of Megara a dark shadow along the horizon. Once we reached the summit I'd bet we would see the Isthmus, separating Corinthia from Attica, as clearly as any bird flying over it.

'I never thought I'd be seeing those hills from this side. Not without a spear in my hand.' Lysicrates scowled as he stared northwards.

I saw that he was looking back across the years as well as the distance. 'You were in those battles?'

It wasn't quite twenty years since Athenians and Corinthians had first gone to war over Megara. The Corinthians had objected to the Megarans growing ever closer to Athens. That friendship enabled us and our allies to hold the Isthmus against any Peloponnesian threat. I suddenly realised that Lysicrates would have just done his hoplite training and been in the front rank of those sent to fight.

Like the tumbling pebble that starts a landslide, that quarrel had precipitated over a decade of bloodshed as allied cities on both sides fought to settle old scores. I'd marched and shared in Athens' victories under General

Tolmides before barely escaping death when he led us to defeat at Coronea. Fighting for Megara hadn't even been worth it. A few years ago, an uprising had massacred the Athenian soldiers garrisoned there.

'Good friends of mine died on those fucking hills. Corinthian spears spilled their life blood on the black earth, and it was all for nothing.' Lysicrates had tears in his eyes.

'I'm so sorry.' I prayed silently to Apollo and to Athena, asking their forgiveness for not asking my friend why he didn't want to come here. 'Let make a sacrifice together at the Sanctuary, for the sake of every mother's son lost in battle. Let's pray that our performance fosters goodwill and preserves the peace, for the sake of our young soldiers at home and lads like Nados here.'

Before Lysicrates could answer, Hyanthidas decided we'd had enough rest and set off, striding up the hill. 'Come on.'

Menekles and Lysicrates followed. I laid a hand on Apollonides' arm, holding him back a few paces. 'Did Hyanthidas hear what Lysicrates just said?'

'I don't know, but apparently Lysicrates said something last night at the Asklepion, about there being scorpions under every stone here? Hyanthidas really didn't like that.' Apollonides sighed. 'This morning, before you got back, they had another falling out. Lysicrates was talking about Iktinos. You remember him?'

'Of course.' I was hardly about to forget the murderous brute. He'd used his knife to deadly effect, serving rich men in Athens conspiring to provoke unrest for their own profit.

'Lysicrates mentioned that you thought he was Peloponnesian, and Hyanthidas took that to mean Corinthian. Things went downhill from there.' Apollonides wiped sweat from his forehead. 'It'll blow over. They're just wound as taut as lyre strings after seeing Eumelos struck down.'

'They'll have plenty of other things to think about as soon as we start rehearsals.' Meantime, I hoped for swift answers to the mystery of Eumelos' death.

Especially now that Apollonides had given me something else to worry about: we never had discovered where Iktinos had come from. Aristarchos and I were convinced he'd been in the pay of someone outside Attica keen to stir up strife in Athens. Some enemy of our democracy. Someone who had reason to hate me and Aristarchos for foiling their plot to discredit us both. Could that unknown foe have followed us and killed Eumelos to stop our play? But then, why kill the fixer, when attacking me or one of the other Athenians would make far more certain of that?

I was still fretting when we reached the Sanctuary, high on the Acrocorinth's slopes. Broad steps on one side of the road led up to a spacious courtyard with a little temple at one end and a sacrificial altar raised up on a terrace at the other. Dining suites had been built all around the sacred precinct, on both sides of the road.

Some were simple dining rooms for private family celebrations. Others were larger halls for feasting, flanked by rooms where guests could wash, slaves could cook, and people could find space for sitting and enjoying quieter conversation when the music and dancing started.

Temples in Athens offer such facilities and I'd attended lively gatherings when the Alopeke district's men honour the gods with rites and sacrifices to celebrate their sons' citizenship rites. I'd never seen anything on this scale though. The midden pit was heaped high with the ashes from sacrifices, when Demeter's share was dedicated on the flames of her altar, as well as with other debris from feasting.

A priestess was coming down the steps from the temple precinct, wearing the long yellow gown of her office and with a finely embroidered veil draped over her high-piled hair. She paused halfway, her hands folded at her waist. We hurried up to meet her.

'Good day.' As serene in her authority as the goddess she served, she might have been ten years my elder, or twenty, it was impossible to tell.

Hyanthidas and the actors all looked at me. Naturally, we have priestesses in Athens, but their duties are purely ceremonial. We're used to dealing with men managing a temple's day-to-day affairs.

'Good day. I'm Philocles Hestaiou of Athens.' I really would have to get used to these self-confident Corinthian women. 'We're here at Perantas Bacchiad's invitation, to perform in your city's theatre. His man Eumelos made arrangements for us to hold our chorus auditions here, and to rehearse.'

She smiled briefly. 'Indeed. Follow me.'

She led us along a narrow alley cutting between two

long buildings. Turning a corner, we found a sort of courtyard bounded by blank walls and with two dining rooms opening off one side. The far end was open to the hillside and a soft breeze brought us the scent of wild herbs.

The priestess gestured at the two dining room doors. 'Both of those are at your disposal.'

'Many thanks.' I hesitated, wondering if I should tell her that Eumelos was dead, but she left before I could decide.

The others were pacing out the courtyard. Over by the wall opposite the doors to the dining rooms, Apollonides scored a line in the well-trodden earth with the toe of his sandal. 'If we call this the edge of the stage, that leaves enough room for a dancing floor.'

Menekles was peering into the closest dining room 'Swept clean, and quite empty,' he pronounced. 'Plenty of storage space.'

'Let's get everything up here as soon as possible.' Apollonides rubbed his hands together briskly. 'Along with some wine. If Corinth's finest singers make that climb to audition, we owe them a drink for their trouble.'

'A decent vintage.' Lysicrates looked at me. 'There'll be more singers than we can use and if the ones we disappoint leave pissed off, they'll just come to the theatre to boo.'

Menekles glanced up the slope towards the temple precinct. 'I take it we can use the springs here for fresh water?'

'I imagine so.' Eumelos would have known. I was

realising how much we would have relied on the Corinthian.

'I'll ask the priestess while you three head back down to the house. Get Tromes to round up some slaves to carry all the baskets up here.' I turned to Hyanthidas. 'Meantime, why don't you and I go and see what we can learn in that brothel?'

I was hoping he'd make a joke out of that, but the piper just shrugged. 'We're already halfway there.'

'Sort out some wine for tomorrow when you've done that.' Apollonides was already on his way out of the courtyard.

Menekles let Lysicrates go on ahead. 'The sooner we have our new lines to learn, the better, Philocles.'

'Of course.' I did my best to keep my face expressionless. I hadn't had a moment to think about the rewrites, and I couldn't see young Nados advising me on jokes that would raise a laugh in Corinth without insulting the rich and powerful.

Hyanthidas and I followed the actors out to the broad steps leading to the road. Encountering a temple slave, we were able to confirm we had permission to get water from the Sanctuary's springs. Then we resumed the climb to the Acrocorinth. The road grew considerably steeper, leaving neither of us with breath to spare for conversation.

I stopped looking back, because that meant looking down and words like 'precipitous' were taking on a whole new meaning. When I realised I wasn't looking at bushes at the base of those cliffs, but was gazing down the length of fully-grown pine trees, I felt so dizzy that I stumbled. Moving on, I kept my eyes firmly forwards.

Fortifications ringed the vast summit. The walls were truly imposing, built on foundations of massive stones that surely only the titans could have wrestled into place, back in the days when gods and heroes walked these lands. The guards on the gates were much less impressive, waving us through with barely a glance. Still, I reckoned few enemies would arrive in any fit state to fight after this climb.

Plenty of visitors were making their way up here, regardless. The Temple of Aphrodite was a fitting vision of beauty on the summit's highest point, with its pillars and pediments of gleaming white marble. As well as all the brothels, which housed the goddess' handmaidens, these heights boasted other shrines and sacred springs. We made our way through enough taverns and peddlers to satisfy any pilgrim's every need.

'This way.' Hyanthidas clearly knew where he was going. I wondered what Telesilla thought about that.

Courtyard gates stood hospitably open and I caught glimpses of girls with inviting smiles lounging in pillared porches. They were sipping from pottery goblets and dressed in seductively short dresses. I tried not to think how thirsty I was.

I wasn't tempted by anything else. Even if I didn't love Zosime to the exclusion of all others, I knew the hazards of visiting whores. I wasn't going to risk having a doctor searing an outbreak of blisters on my cock with a hot blade.

'Here we are.' Hyanthidas knocked on a gatepost as we entered a clean-swept courtyard.

'Good day. My name is Eirene, and you are most welcome to my house.' A woman in a long, pleated gown appeared from a doorway, looking much the same age as my mother. 'How do you wish to worship Aphrodite?'

As she spoke, I caught a glimpse of a heavy-set man, sitting in the shadows of the porch inside the gate. He looked considerably more alert than the guards who had let us enter the Acrocorinth's citadel.

'Good day.' I thought quickly. 'My friend Eumelos speaks very highly of your house.'

The whore mistress smiled. 'And we are always glad to welcome his friends.'

Clearly she didn't know he was dead.

'Does he have a favourite girl? Could she spare me a few moments?' This didn't look like the sort of place where a man wipes himself off and leaves once he's spent his seed. Eumelos might have confided something in the drowsy languor that follows such pleasure, something the girl didn't even realise was important.

The brothel-keeper gave me a measuring look. 'If you're willing to pay for her time.'

'Of course.' I should have expected that.

'Eight obols.' Mistress Eirene held out her palm. 'And your friend?'

'I'll wait out here,' Hyanthidas said hastily.

That was a relief at these prices.

'Sekis, wine for our guests.' Eirene glanced at her henchman before turning to me. 'This way.'

I followed her into the house and along a corridor of curtain-hung doorways. I couldn't hear any sounds of commerce but then, we had reached the heat of the day. Business around Athenian brothels usually only picks up as the sun starts to sink.

'Arete.' The whore-mistress tugged a curtain aside, startling a round-faced girl sitting on a bed sorting ribbons. 'Make our guest welcome while I fetch some wine.'

'Of course.' The girl crossed the room to a water clock, filling the upper pot from a waiting jug. Drops from the spout at the bottom began measuring my time here into the lower vessel.

She untied the woven belt that held her draped dress demurely closed. Once she unpinned the silver brooches at her shoulders, the flimsy linen would fall away to leave her alluring curves naked as the day she was born.

'I'm in no hurry,' I said quickly. 'We can wait for the wine.'

I was glad to think I'd be getting a drink. Though, on my oath to Dionysos, I should at this price. Still, Mistress Eirene seemed generous with her girls. The room was clean and furnished with an expensive bedstead, an elegant ebony table and bronze lamps for the evening trade.

'What's your pleasure?' Arete twirled a seductive finger in a dangling ribbon woven through her intricately plaited hair. As she stepped close enough for her generous breasts to brush my arm, I smelled floral perfume. I could see her dark nipples through the sheer cloth.

I took a step away. 'Some wine, and conversation.'

To my relief, the slave Sekis arrived with a jug and cups decorated with naked couples enjoying athletic amusements. He set them on the table and departed without a word. I offered a sip of wine to Dionysos and downed the rest in one parched breath. That was my thirst dealt with. Now for the real business at hand.

'Tell me,' I asked as casually as I could. 'Did Eumelos have any particular cares when you last saw him?'

'No.' The girl looked at me blankly.

'Do you know anyone he was at odds with?' I persisted. 'Anyone who wished him ill?'

'No.' She shrugged, unconcerned.

I couldn't decide if she was truly witless or playing the pretty fool, used to men who only value what's between a woman's legs. I decided to break the bad news and see how she reacted.

'I have to tell you that Eumelos is dead.'

The girl couldn't have been more shocked if I'd slapped her. Scarlet-faced, she burst into noisy tears.

'Hush, hush.' I hastily ushered her to the bed and sat her down.

'We were going to be married,' she sobbed.

Whatever she said next was strangled by cataclysmic weeping. I went and poured more wine, coming back to sit beside her, putting one arm around her shaking shoulders.

'Just a sip,' I coaxed her. 'Who knew what you planned?'

This was the last thing I expected to hear. As soon as

I got back to Eumelos' house, I would ask Nados what he knew about it.

'He loved me,' Arete wailed, her perfumed ribbons bobbing. 'He did! He—'

She dissolved into incoherent misery as the curtain swept back to reveal the mistress of the house. I don't suppose she'd been more than a pace away outside in the hall.

I stood up. 'I brought bad news—'

'I heard.' Mistress Eirene stood to one side, holding the curtain. My invitation to leave was unmistakeable.

I drank the wine I'd poured for Arete since I'd paid for it. Then I went dutifully out into the corridor before Eirene called on her burly slave to throw me out.

More whores peered around their own curtains, agog with curiosity and concern. Some were half-dressed, some wholly naked. Several had small children close by, girls and boys, none older than five or six years. Olive-oil-soaked sponges and wine-vinegar rinses can't always save a woman from the hazards of pregnancy. Certainly not ones who roll those dice four or five times a night.

At their mistress's nod, two girls hurried to console Arete. I followed Eirene out into the courtyard.

'Forgive me,' I began. That seemed safest.

'Why?' she asked tartly. 'Did you kill him?'

If she favoured straight talking, I was happy to oblige. 'Who would want to stop Eumelos marrying that girl?'

She startled me with a bark of laughter. 'He had no thought of wedding her, no more than any of the others who've mistaken his kindness for affection. She lost her heart to him, little fool, and he knew it, but if she'd breathed a word of such hopes, he'd have dropped her like a hot coal.'

'You're certain?'

'Absolutely.' She was adamant. 'He does it without a second thought. So, how did he die?'

'Poison.' I matched her piercing stare, look for look. 'Supposedly he took a potion to stiffen – his resolve. Did he get that here?'

'No.' She shook her head. 'When a man brings a limp leek to our table, and I grant you, Eumelos did from time to time, we have plenty of tricks to perk up a client without resorting to herbalists' concoctions. Who knows what they might be peddling? I won't have such things in my house.'

'No?' I took a step closer, to press her harder.

Hyanthidas set his cup of wine on a table and moved to stand between the two of us and the bruiser by the gate.

Eirene wasn't remotely intimidated. 'No, and I think you had better leave.'

'As you wish.' I thought about asking for some of my money back but seeing her henchman's scowl, I decided against it. At least the wine had been excellent. Hyanthidas and I walked out into the lane and headed back towards the citadel gates.

I heaved a sigh. 'I'm sorry I dragged you up here.'

'You think it was a waste of time?' He sounded surprised.

Now I was puzzled. 'You think she was mistaken? The brothel keeper?'

'Oh, I'm sure Eumelos had no plans to marry,' Hyanthidas assured me, 'but who might have believed the girl, if she told them that he did? Whose inheritance would that threaten?'

I wondered about that all the way back down the mountain. Then we went to find a wine merchant. We still had auditions to hold and a play to rehearse.

Chapter Five

I was wondering about Eumelos marrying when Zosime stirred beside me the next morning. We'd slept long and soundly after making love the night before. I couldn't imagine a day when the merest touch of her hand wouldn't send my blood pulsing with desire. Could Eumelos have felt like that about his little whore?

Seeing me staring up at the ceiling, Zosime raised herself up on one elbow. 'What's the matter?'

'This time yesterday, I had no idea who might have killed Eumelos. The notion made no more sense than him killing himself. Now I have three possible motives for murder.' I eased my arm around her shoulders and cuddled her close. 'Someone who wants to stop our play. Someone out to make trouble for me and Aristarchos. Someone who wanted to stop him marrying.'

I had no idea where to look for answers. If we were in Athens, I'd have no such problems. Once I knew Eumelos' voting district, I could approach the local officials, vouched for by the elders of Alopeke who'd known me since I was a child, since my father had presented me to them as an Athenian citizen. Then I could find the dead man's family.

Once I knew his trade, my brothers and I would ask around until we found someone who knew someone who'd had dealings with him. That would surely offer some scents to follow. Meantime, Aristarchos would be making enquiries in the very different circles where he moved, learning all he could about Eumelos' patrons and their enemies.

But we were in Corinth. I didn't know how this city worked, and knew precious few locals I could trust.

Zosime drummed thoughtful fingers on my bare chest. 'No one in Eumelos' household expected that he'd ever wed. Old Abrosyne was breaking her heart over it yesterday. He should have had a wife and daughters to wash his body and lay him out, not just her, me and Telesilla.'

I kissed her hair. 'Thank you for doing that.'

'We all have a duty to the unjustly dead,' she said sombrely. 'I don't want the Furies hounding us.'

I pictured the weeping slave woman I'd seen talking to Nados. 'Abrosyne is his housekeeper? Do you think you could ask her if Eumelos ever mentioned a woman called Kleoboulina? That's what he called Telesilla in the tavern.'

'I can ask.' Zosime was still thinking about this supposed wedding. 'But who could the whore have told that she expected to be married? She'd hardly tell her other customers.'

'I can't see it,' I agreed. Even in a brothel, men like to kid themselves they're the one a woman is wishing for while they're thrusting between her thighs. A whore pining for someone else risked a slap or worse.

'Who would this Eirene tell?' Zosime went on. 'Especially since she didn't believe a word of it.'

'Maybe one of the other whores heard Arete boasting?' I hazarded. 'Then told a customer?'

Zosime shifted in bed so she could look me in the eye. 'How much time did you spend gossiping with whores, in your brothel-going days?'

'None.' I kissed her.

She kissed me back. 'So how could someone who'd kill to stop Eumelos marrying hear any rumour of a wedding?'

'And if everyone says he wasn't the marrying kind, surely they would wait for proof before risking a step as drastic as murder?' But I still wanted to know whom such a marriage might have disinherited.

We heard a door slam and voices down in the courtyard. The household was rousing.

Zosime got out of bed. 'I'm meeting Telesilla at Eumelos' house, to help Nados with the visitors coming to pay their respects.'

'See if any of them has any idea where Dardanis might be hiding.' I watched her see to the morning's necessities.

Back in Athens, she'd wear a simple draped dress, swiftly created from folded cloth wrapped around her body, pinned with shoulder brooches and secured with a belt. Here she was wearing a long, pleated gown, reaching down to her sandalled ankles. Elegant and decorous, that's what my mother and sisters wore back home, and Zosime never did. While there are no actual laws forbidding such garb for non-citizen women, there

68

are certainly harsh penalties for resident foreigners like Zosime masquerading as Athenian-born. After all, access to an Athenian citizen's enviable rights and privileges depends on having two citizen-born parents.

But this was Corinth and, as in most Hellenic cities, a citizen's rights went to a citizen's sons and no one cared about their mother's status. Women didn't have to watch what they said, where they went, and who with in case their Athenian birth was ever called into question. Women like Telesilla could be musicians, free to perform and to compete in public competitions.

I wondered uneasily what opportunities Zosime might notice here, for a vase painter as talented as she was. Could she be tempted to stay in a city where she was every other woman's equal and her children wouldn't be dismissed as bastards? I was selfishly glad that her father had stayed in Athens, to guarantee she would go home with me. Though a skilled potter like Menkaure could easily find work here. He was a much-travelled man, and making another fresh start in a new city would hardly daunt him.

Zosime put on her earrings and looked quizzically at me. 'How long are you staying there?'

'I'm up.' I dressed quickly, used the chamber pot, and washed, before following her out. These guest accommodations consisted of an inner room and one that opened onto the staircase leading down to the courtyard. That was where Kadous was sleeping.

Everyone else was already eating barley bread and fruit. I served myself some breakfast.

'Did you get everything taken up to the Sanctuary?' I asked Apollonides.

He nodded, chewing, grape juice glistening on his beard.

'Did you find a wine merchant?' Lysicrates asked.

'I did, thanks to Hyanthidas, and he's a man who does plenty of business with Perantas so he'll send the bills straight there.'

I broke off as an urgent knock rattled the gate.

Tromes opened up to reveal Nados, plainly dressed as befitted a mourner, and clutching a sheet of papyrus. He came over to us, fighting tears. 'I was trying to find Eumelos' will and came across this. I'm not sure what he meant by it, but—'

'Let's see.' I took the crackling sheet. The single word at the top was plain enough. Auditions. Then I read a list of names, each one with a cryptic symbol drawn beside it.

Menekles peered over my shoulder. 'What does that signify?'

'I have no idea,' I said, mystified. 'Let's hope Hyanthidas can shed some light on it.' I rolled up the papyrus and tucked it through my belt.

'I had better get back.' His duty discharged, Nados turned for the gate.

'Wait a moment.' Zosime brushed crumbs from her dress. 'I'll come with you.'

Her departure spurred the rest of us on. We left Tromes and the other slaves clearing away the breakfast dishes and headed for the city's great temple and shrines, and the road to the Acrocorinth beyond.

The walk up the lower slopes of the mountain to the Sanctuary of Demeter was much easier in the morning cool. Hyanthidas was already waiting at the side of the road, by the steps leading up to the temple precinct.

He wasn't alone. A dozen or so men were loitering close by. Half were wearing boxers' leathers to protect their knuckles in a fight. The rest carried olive wood staffs that they could use on the climb to the summit, or wield as weapons just as easily.

'Good morning.' The bull-necked man with the golden Pegasus collar offered me his hand and an ominous smile. 'We weren't introduced. I'm Thettalos.'

'Are you here to audition for our chorus?'

His grin widened to show his teeth, as friendly as a hunting dog. 'Let's say that I am.'

'And your friends?' From what I could see, his closest companions all had rings or brooches or belt buckles that bore the Pegasus symbol.

Thettalos shrugged. 'If you like.'

I didn't like this, not at all, but I couldn't see how to get rid of him and his associates. I could see several men coming along the road, looking uncertainly in our direction. I didn't think would-be singers would be keen to run the Brotherhood's gauntlet. I didn't imagine the priestess would be too thrilled either, to have this mob cluttering up her steps.

'Stop hanging around out here. You make the place look untidy.' I went past Thettalos and headed for the courtyard we had been granted for our rehearsal. The Brotherhood of Bellerophon followed.

Hyanthidas had already fetched the keys and Apollon-ides unlocked the two dining rooms. 'We've put all the costumes and masks in there.' He gestured towards the further door, before showing me jugs and cups in the room close at hand. The crockery was stacked on the ledge where cushioned dining couches would usually be set. 'I suggest we use this for the wine, and when we need a breather or a quiet conversation.'

'Good idea, and let's keep the costumes and masks in their baskets for the moment.' I had no idea who might have travelled from Corinth to Athens for the Dionysia and seen our play back in the spring, but we might as well keep its surprises secret for as long as we could.

I turned to Thettalos, pointing to the tall water jugs. 'You lot can make yourselves useful and fill those. Leave those walking sticks in here. You won't need them until you head home.'

He wasn't smiling now. 'I don't—'

'I assume Perantas Bacchiad sent you to help us?' I enquired mildly.

He looked at me for a long moment. 'He did.'

I watched him pick up a jug and hand it to one of his contingent. They exchanged a few curt words. I guessed the noble Brotherhood weren't keen on doing women's work. If some of them went off in a huff, I'd be more than happy to see them go.

Lysicrates appeared in the alleyway. 'Philocles, the wine has arrived.'

By the time we had the amphorae safely stowed, Thet-talos' men had finished fetching the water. Lysicrates and

Menekles began mixing jugs of the fragrant wine with a judicious measure of spring water.

The tantalising flourishes of Hyanthidas' pipes brought us our first handful of would-be chorus singers, and more soon followed. One thing I'd noticed about Corinth was the city's abundance of sundials, and the citizens were proving punctual.

We had a small table and a handful of stools, and Apollonides helped me carry them outside. I armed myself with papyrus, pen and ink from the writing supplies I found stowed with the costume baskets. I guessed we had Nados to thank for all that. If Eumelos *had* been killed to stop our play's rehearsals, the murderer should have remembered that few men are truly irreplaceable.

'Who's first?' I smiled at the waiting Corinthians.

One stepped forward, bolder than the rest. 'Timoleon, son of Timophanes of Lechaion.'

I made a note of his name as he looked at Hyanthidas sitting in the shade.

'Do you know Arion's Hymn to Helios?'

'I do.' The piper obliged with the first line of the tune.

At his nod, Timoleon began singing. His voice was clear, strong and true. Sitting beside me, Apollonides leaned close to speak quietly behind a raised hand.

'If they're all as good as this, we'll be done by noon.'

'As long as he hasn't got two left feet.' I marked Timoleon down as a definite prospect, and beckoned the next hopeful forward.

Apollonides should have known better than to tempt the gods. Divine Apollo had a good laugh at our expense.

This eager singer had brought his own lyre, and sang one of his own compositions. It was hard to decide what was more excruciating; the banal lyrics twisted to fit the rhythm, the lyre that was out of tune, or the singer's thin and nasal voice. I didn't even bother noting his name.

'Thank you. Please, have a drink while we continue.' I smiled blandly as the man stood there, obviously expecting a leading role in our chorus.

Thanks to all the gods, the next singer was a marked improvement. Not as good as Timoleon but most choruses are made up of those who perform better alongside others than they do as soloists. We listened to twenty or so more men who similarly ranged from definites through possibles to no-hopers. I allowed myself to hope we'd have a choice of strong performers rather than having to take a few weaker ones to make up our number.

Then, as the next contender stepped forward, I saw Thettalos heading towards me.

The singer scowled at the bull-necked man before addressing me and Apollonides. 'Ameinocles of Vayia. I play as well as sing.' He wasn't carrying a lyre, but there was a bone flute thrust through his belt.

Thettalos arrived, planting his hands on our table and leaning forwards to loom over me. 'You don't want him.'

I leaned backwards against the wall, lacing my fingers over my midriff. 'As chorus master, that's for me to decide.'

I stretched my feet under the table, ready to kick Thettalos' ankles out from under him if he tried anything stupid, but the bull-necked man retreated to join his allies in a corner.

I had already noted that none of the Brotherhood had auditioned and three still carried their olive wood staffs. Now I saw several glowering at some new arrivals who were standing together.

A trill from Hyanthidas launched Ameinocles on a familiar hymn of praise to Dionysos. The man had a serviceable voice. I also saw his eyes were fixed on Thettalos.

When Ameinocles finished singing, I thanked him and turned to Apollonides. 'Get the first dozen possibles together and try them with a few dance steps. Get Lysicrates to clap out a beat. I need to talk to Hyanthidas.'

As the actor took our list and began calling out names, I beckoned to the piper. With everyone's attention on Apollonides as he paced out steps for the chorus hopefuls to follow, I drew Hyanthidas into the doorway of our costume store and showed him the list Nados had brought to us. I had remembered right. Ameinocles of Vayia was on it.

'What does this mean?' I tapped the looping squiggle of ink beside the man's name.

Hyanthidas frowned as Lysicrates' clapping hands struck echoes from the enclosing walls. 'I have no idea.'

A sudden shout interrupted us.

'Watch where you're going!' A wiry man who'd shown no interest in auditioning threw his hands up as the dancers circled close. He shoved the nearest hopeful, sending him staggering into the man beside him. 'Mind my fucking feet!'

'I was nowhere near—'

More men than I expected coalesced around Ameinocles as quickly as the rest of Thettalos' Brotherhood emerged from the alleyway. Everyone else stepped back, to press against the walls.

'Want to make something of it?' As lean and vicious as a shark, a lanky youth at Ameinocles' shoulder grinned at the bull-necked man.

'I made your sister beg for more, the last time I fucked her.' Thettalos smacked his lips. 'Maybe I'll try your mother next time I don't have the coin for a whore. I hear she'll spread her knees for free.'

'Cocksucker!' spat the youth.

'Your sister could suck the resin out of a pine knot,' Thettalos assured him. 'But I'm guessing you already know.'

The youth had no answer, woefully outmatched in this battle of insults.

Everyone's attention except mine was fixed on the pair, agog to see who'd attack first. I was scanning the crowd, trying to work out who was here to fight and who'd be leaving as quickly as possible.

That's why I saw the wiry man who'd been so quick to accuse the dancer of treading on his feet punch the singer standing in front of him. It was an expert, single blow, hitting the hapless man's kidney. As the singer yelped, his knees buckling, the wiry man staggered backwards, hands clasped to his face and protesting. 'What the fuck did I do?'

As if that was some signal, the witless youth sprang forward, intent on Thettalos. The bull-necked man swiftly sidestepped to let one of his lackeys jab the youth in the guts with his staff. As the youth doubled over, retching, the lackey used the stick on the backs of his knees. The youth sprawled forward, landing hard. The lackey kicked him in the face.

Thettalos had no time to gloat. Ameinocles was coming for him, that flute in his fist. He lunged and the bone pipe swept across Thettalos' face, before coming back, fast as thought, to stab at the bull-necked man's eyes.

Thettalos threw up his hands, instinctively protecting his face. That was exactly what Ameinocles wanted. Dropping into a low crouch, he stabbed his weapon into Thettalos' side. Something cracked; the bone flute or Thettalos' ribs, I couldn't tell.

Ameinocles followed up his advantage as the bull-necked man reeled away. He walked straight into the bronze buckle of another man's belt. Thettalos' Brother had launched it at Ameinocles' face with a vicious snap of leather. The metal cut so deep into his forehead that the edge of the buckle must have been sharpened.

Blood gushed down Ameinocles' face to soak into his beard. He surged forward with a roar and wrestled the Brother to the ground. Getting one strangling arm around his foe's neck, his other fist pummelled the man's face unmercifully. Soon both were unrecognisable beneath masks of blood.

What had started as a couple of fights was becoming a pitched battle. These men looked intent on killing each other. One spun around to smash his opponent's face into a wall. Another had a knife and slashed an enemy's forearm open to the bone. One animal was using his teeth, jaws clamped onto the side of a screaming foe's hand. Someone else was locked in a wrestler's clinch with Thettalos now. Hobnails in the soles of both men's sandals were ripping bloody gouges in their shins and calf muscles.

Hyanthidas had one hand on the dining room door, ready to slam it in the face of anyone attacking the pair of us. The only weapon I had to hand was a pen but I was ready to use that if I had to.

My fellow Athenians had all withdrawn to the second doorway. Lysicrates had used the table to make a rampart in front of them. Apollonides was armed with a stool and Menekles held a broken wine jug, ready to ram the sharp pottery into any assailant's face. Most of the singers who'd come to audition had fled. I only hoped no one had been badly hurt.

'What the fuck happens now?' I asked Hyanthidas. I wondered if Eumelos would have warned us to expect this sort of trouble.

'Temple slaves.' Hyanthidas was hoarse with relief.

A handful of well-muscled men in plain tunics appeared. My heart sank. There weren't nearly enough of them to break up this mayhem. But as soon as the first Brother shouted a warning, allies and enemies alike scattered like quail hearing an eagle's cry.

Most ran for the open hillside, some pausing to gather up their blood-spattered comrades. The rest fled down the alley, towards the temple steps and the road.

The slaves made no effort to stop them. Inside a few moments, the courtyard was empty, littered with lost sandals, several belts and bloody clumps of hair. The oldest temple slave stepped forward to address me. His hair and beard were grizzled and his calm, hooded eyes told me he'd seen worse than this more than once.

'The priestess would like a word.'

'I'm sure she would,' I said heavily.

Chapter Six

By the time the priestess finished with me, I had taken a different sort of beating. It might not have left any marks but I felt as thoroughly bruised as that witless lad must be.

I found Hyanthidas and the actors waiting down by the road. Lysicrates and Apollonides both carried small bundles but before I could ask what those might be, the actors had urgent questions.

'I take it she wasn't pleased?' Menekles said with misgiving.

'Has she thrown us out?' Lysicrates clearly expected bad news.

'No.' I didn't hide my surprise. 'She says we're not to blame for the fighting. It happens quite often in Corinth, when rival hero cultists clash.'

'Really?' Apollonides was astonished.

'So maybe the fight today had nothing to do with our play?' Menekles was relieved.

I nodded. 'Though the priestess doesn't want to see the Brotherhood back. She says her temple slaves can keep order for us.'

As we set off downhill, Menekles was still puzzled by

the priestess of Demeter's response. 'That's all she said?'

'Pretty much.'

Actually, she'd had considerably more to say but I didn't particularly want to relive the experience. It had been a blend of a scolding from my mother and a tongue-lashing from an exasperated teacher, back when I'd been learning my letters and mathematics in the Lyceum's colonnades. I'd half expected her to whip out a fennel stalk to smack my legs, and I'd probably have let her, out of sheer confusion. I've never faced such stinging reproach from a woman who's not a blood relation.

We walked silently back to our lodging, all of us preoccupied with our own thoughts. When Tromes opened the gate, Apollonides strode forward to unfold the bundle he carried on the table in the courtyard. Wrapped up in the torn cloak, I saw several shoulder brooches, a bronze arm ring, two mismatched sandals and a belt.

'The spoils of battle,' he said sarcastically.

Lysicrates had a similar haul of lost and abandoned possessions. 'Nothing that any of us want to tread on when we're rehearsing.'

Hyanthidas reached for a tarnished bronze brooch, scowling. 'This is the Kin of Agamemnon's insignia.'

Twin lions, lean and muscular, faced each other, standing proud on either side of a pillar with their forepaws up on its pedestal.

'What about this?' Lysicrates had found a belt with a ram's head stamped into the leather.

'Hermes' Herdsmen,' the piper said curtly.

Menekles held up a dolphin brooch. 'And this?'

'Melikertes' Men.'

'How many of these hero cults are there?' Apollonides sorted through the debris.

'How often do they beat the shit out of each other?' Lysicrates asked acidly.

'Does it matter?' Hyanthidas demanded.

His mood was easy to read. I knew how proud he was of his city. He'd said often enough how Corinth was thrice blessed by the gods, with its fine harbours to east and west of the Isthmus. Goods from furthest west and the most distant cities eastward are bought and sold here, carried across that short stretch of land to save sailors from all the hazards of the lengthy voyage around the whole Peloponnese.

He'd regaled us with tales of the elegant shrines and fountains, of great temples dedicated to Apollo and Aphrodite, and the mighty Acrocorinth that defended his home's peace and prosperity. He'd assured us of a warm welcome and the applause we would win with our play.

Now he was embarrassed. The brawl made his home look as inviting as a midden thronged with snarling vermin. He was furious with the men who'd disgraced Corinth so thoroughly. That didn't mean he wouldn't bite someone's head off, if any of us thought we could criticize our hosts.

Apollonides was still sorting through the rubbish. 'Does this mean anything?' He held up a belt buckle ripped loose from its strap with a thick club of knotted wood embossed on the bronze. That was instantly recognisable from countless vases and statues.

'The Sons of Heracles.' Hyanthidas glowered.

I noted more than a few of the trinkets bore that insignia. 'What do they want for Corinth?'

The piper sighed. 'They insist that Heracles is the ancestor of all our cities' ancient kings. They think that all the states of the Peloponnese should be united in the League, following Sparta's lead. But they were always more interested in talking bullshit and drinking wine,' he protested. 'They never used to get involved in street brawls.'

'Things have obviously changed while you were away,' I said lightly. 'There's no way you could have known.'

From Hyanthidas' expression, that wasn't much consolation.

'I take it the Brotherhood of Bellerophon don't agree?' Menekles set down a brooch engraved with the familiar winged horse.

'Not at all,' Hyanthidas said, emphatic.

'And the Sons of Heracles will dislike Corinth's new friendship with Athens.' Menekles sighed.

'Wait a moment.' I pulled Eumelos' list out of my belt. Don't ask me why, but I had managed to keep hold of it, though the papyrus was badly crumpled. I laid it on the table, careful as the layers of thin-sliced stems flaked apart.

'Does that look like a knotted club to any of you?' I tapped the looping notification scrawled beside the first name. Then I reached for the brooch with the two lions, and pointed to another recurrent drawing. That one was two rough triangles side by side. 'What about that? Could it be this Kin of Agamemnon's insignia?'

It wasn't immediately obvious. Whatever his other talents, Eumelos was no artist.

'What are they all about?' Apollonides wanted to know about this cult.

'They want to strengthen Corinth's ties with Argos,' Hyanthidas said reluctantly.

'That means they're no friends to Athens either,' Lysicrates pointed out.

I tapped the crumpled list. 'So Eumelos knew of at least two hero cults who would like to see our play fail. He knew they could do a lot of damage by sneaking into our chorus, so he made a note of the ones he knew were good singers, like Ameinocles of Vayia.'

'So let's see who we don't want.' Apollonides startled me by producing our list of chorus hopefuls. I'd thought that had been lost in the chaos.

'Tromes.' I looked across the courtyard. 'Pen and ink.'

The slave quickly obliged. He was always close by and ready to serve. In unguarded moments, I'd seen him looking apprehensive, even anxious, as he watched us and waited for some instruction. I could well imagine that Perantas Bacchiad was a demanding and unforgiving owner.

I drew a black line through the names that appeared on both lists before writing out a clean copy and handing it to Hyanthidas. 'Can you let these men know we'd like to enlist them in our chorus?'

He looked dubious. 'Some of them might not be so keen now.'

'Do what you can to reassure them.' There was nothing else I could say.

'When can we hold more auditions?' Apollonides looked around the table. 'Tomorrow?'

'The day after.' I raised a hand to quell Menekles' protest. 'We have Eumelos' funeral to go to.'

Lysicrates had other concerns. He tapped a third distinct squiggle on the list of hero cult affiliations. 'What does this mean?'

'Does it matter?' Apollonides looked at him. 'We're not taking anyone Eumelos was going to warn us about.'

'If there's another hero cult out to make trouble for us, they don't need to be in the chorus to do that,' I pointed out.

'I'll ask around.' Hyanthidas studied the mysterious scrawl as he rolled up the papyrus I'd given him. 'I'll see you at the funeral.' He looked around the table, and then headed for the gate.

'Let's take a trip to Corinth.' Menekles sucked his teeth. 'It seemed like such a good idea.'

'Do you want to head home?' Apollonides began sweeping the detritus off the table and into a rubbish bucket. 'With our tails between our legs like whipped dogs? We'd never hear the last of it.'

'I never wanted to come in the first place.' Lysicrates headed for his room.

Apollonides and Menekles watched him go up the stairs and slam the door behind him.

Menekles tossed the bronze arm ring into the bucket. 'So what shall we do with the rest of our day, if we're not rehearsing?'

'Take a walk and see the sights?' Apollonides suggested.

Menekles looked at me. 'You can finish those rewrites.'

'I can indeed.' I stood up quickly before they could ask awkward questions about how I was getting on.

The knock that rattled the gate was as well timed as any distraction in a play. Tromes opened up and Kadous entered as Menekles and Apollonides went out.

I beckoned the Phrygian over and pushed the bucket of rubbish towards him. 'See if Nados recognises any of these hero cult insignia and what he knows about them. Then ask him where to get rid of it all.' I had no idea if Corinth had regulations like Athens to prevent randomly tossed garbage.

A new thought occurred to me. 'If you can sell any of it, use that silver to buy some goodwill with Perantas' slaves. See what they have to say about Eumelos. I take it there's still no word of Dardanis?'

Kadous shook his head. 'None.'

I supposed that was too much to hope for. I gestured up at our room. 'Tell Zosime I'll be working here for the rest of the day.'

Ordinarily I'd have enjoyed the fresh air in the courtyard as I wrote but I didn't want anyone looking over my shoulder to see how little progress I'd made. So I went up the stairs and opened the shutters, dragging a table and stool to the window to get the best of the light.

I spent the rest of the day scribbling fruitless notes and

crossing most of them out. When Kadous brought me some food he cleared away the crumpled papyrus that littered the floorboards without a word.

Daylight was fading when I heard Zosime's voice. I set down my pen and capped the inkwell. At least I had the first stirrings of an idea now for rewriting that wretched scene.

Going down to the courtyard, I looked at my beloved and realised this wasn't the time to ask her about jokes to suit Corinthians. I opened my arms wide and she stepped into my embrace. Not weeping but not far from it. I gestured to Kadous, miming drinking from a cup with my free hand. Nodding, he went to fetch wine.

'It's so sad.' Her voice was muffled, her face buried in my shoulder. 'Eumelos had so many friends. They've been coming to pay their respects all day.'

'Not the Brotherhood of Bellerophon?' I asked uneasily.

'What do you mean?' Zosime took a step back to look at me.

'I'll tell you later.' I waved that away as Kadous brought us ochre-glazed cups and a jug of black wine watered down to ruby red.

Zosime sat on the bench by the table. 'We lost count of how many people came to make their farewells. From Corinth, Lechaion, Kenchreai and any number of villages out in the Corinthia.'

'Word's spread fast.' I wondered if winged Rumour

might bring back some answers to solve the puzzle of his death.

'No one had a bad word to say about him.' Zosime sipped her wine. 'Oh, he was known to drive a hard bargain, but everyone agreed he was always fair.'

'What was his business, exactly?'

'Mostly, he traded in salted and pickled fish from Gades. He bought it from the Phoenicians who sail into Lechaion in the spring and sold some locally, as well as sending the rest to Kenchreai. He'd sell that to merchants trading as far as the Euxine Sea.'

'Did he have many rivals?' Though I found it hard to believe anyone would commit murder over salted fish.

Zosime shook her head. 'Everyone wanted to be his friend. He was always hearing useful things about what could be profitably traded where, and he would broker deals for other merchants, when those Phoenicians were filling their holds with luxuries before heading home before the autumn storms.'

'Maybe one of those merchants had debts he couldn't settle?' I speculated.

Maybe Eumelos had learned something perilous that convinced someone to shut his mouth. Every new thing I learned seemed to take me further from any hope of an answer. If Eumelos' business affairs had prompted his death, his killer could have come from anywhere. The murderer could already be sailing to some distant port, or beyond to barbarian lands.

Zosime thought otherwise. 'How would a business rival persuade Eumelos to put an aphrodisiac in his wine?

Would you take an unknown potion from someone who owed you money?'

'It makes no sense, does it?' I admitted.

'Nor does suicide.' Zosime reached for my hand. 'He's been encouraging young Nados to start buying and selling on his own account, lending him the silver he needs. Abrosyne says he's done the same for Aithon in Kenchreai and Simias in Lechaion. He did the same for two young men who worked for him before, teaching them a merchant's tricks and tips, and backing them when they set up in business for themselves.'

'Yet he had no sons of his own. No children at all, nor a wife.' That still puzzled me.

'No relatives have come to the house,' Zosime said sadly.

'He could have lost his family to some cruel misfortune.' I gave her hand a comforting squeeze. The Fates visit every family with untimely deaths. Zosime was still a child when Menkaure lost her mother in childbed. I had seen one sister buried with her infant, and Kadous had come back all the way from Egypt with the grievous news of my brother's death in battle. Such loyalty is merely one reason why I value my Phrygian slave so highly.

'No one believes that he killed himself,' Zosime said, emphatic. 'He had no business troubles, and even if he had, Eumelos wouldn't take a coward's way out. People don't believe the potion he drank is what poisoned him, or they say he must have been tricked into swallowing it.'

'But how would someone persuade such a shrewd man to do that?' We were making no more progress than a dog chasing its tail.

Before we could continue, Tromes opened the gate to Menekles' knock. I saw Apollonides instantly register the sorrow clouding Zosime's face.

'Sweetheart!' He hurried over to embrace her. 'We must visit the markets together. The crimson and scarlet woollens here are as glorious as everyone says, and much cheaper than at home.'

'Their perfumes are well worth a look, too, or should I say a sniff.' Menekles offered Zosime his wrist.

It wasn't much of a joke but it made her smile and I was grateful to him for that.

'We went to the North Market first.' As Kadous brought more cups, Apollonides poured us all some wine.

I could see Menekles wanted to ask how I was getting on rewriting those key scenes. For the moment though, he was content to tell Zosime about their afternoon sauntering around Corinth to take her mind off a day spent in a house of mourning.

When Apollonides finished extolling the exquisite local almond pastries, she raised a hand. 'Why haven't you been rehearsing? How did the auditions go? Where's Lysicrates?'

'I'm here.' He appeared at the top of the stairs leading to the rooms he was sharing with the others. 'Have you heard about all the excitement?' He joined us and poured some wine. I tried to catch his eye, but he was avoiding everyone's gaze.

By the time Menekles had told the tale of our eventful day, Zosime was looking pensive. 'I hope there won't be any trouble at the funeral.'

'They wouldn't dare risk divine disfavour for such impiety,' I said with rather more confidence than I felt.

Lysicrates looked up at the lavender sky. 'We should get an early night if we're going to be up before dawn.'

There was no argument there. Soon after Kadous had served us fresh-griddled fish, wheaten bread and a local dish of spiced chickpeas, we all retired to our rooms. In bed, I held Zosime close until her breathing softened into sleep. I was still wracking my brains over Eumelos' death but I came up with nothing before I followed her into welcome oblivion.

Kadous woke us with softly persistent knocking and I opened my eyes to the darkness that shrouds all funerals. We dressed quickly in our plainest clothes and joined the others in the courtyard. Kadous was yawning from staying awake through the night to wait for the slave that Nados sent to summon us, so I told him to head for his own bed as soon as he closed the gate behind us.

We found a sizeable gathering at Eumelos' house, silently waiting in the pitiless grey light before dawn. There must have been a hundred men and women, young and old. Looking discreetly around, I couldn't see anyone wearing any sign of the Brotherhood. That was a relief.

The gate opened and the funeral procession emerged. The slaves who'd taken Eumelos to the Asklepion now carried the litter bearing his body. The corpse was richly dressed and crowned with a laurel wreath. Nados and two other young men walked ahead of the bier in the place of a dead man's sons, dressed in black as befitted the chief mourners. They carried torches and the tears on their cheeks gleamed in the flickering light.

It took me a moment to realise the woman following the bier with her hair covered was Telesilla. As the man behind her played a dirge on his flute I recognised Hyanthidas. The sorrowful little procession moved on and Telesilla sang a soaring lament that brought tears to my eyes. Everyone here to mourn Eumelos shuffled their feet and sniffed as her glorious singing gave voice to their heartbreak.

We've all been to funerals where you feel that people are only there to make sure that some unloved or despised deceased is really dead. This was completely different. As we walked through the sleeping city, through this last fading hour of the night, I heard whispers all around us struggling to accept that a man so full of life and vigour was indeed lying dead on that bier.

The procession threaded through the agora, past the theatre and northwards out of the city to the west of the Asklepion, where the land slopes sharply down to the plain. The grave in an extensive burial ground had already been prepared and Eumelos was laid to rest. I looked for any gravestones to tell us he was being buried in the same plot as his family but there was nothing to be seen.

Zosime slipped her hand into mine as we stood

witness to the funeral rites. Nados, Aithon and Simias cut off handfuls of hair to cast into the grave. This was no perfunctory nod to offering a lock for the dead. Their voices shook with grief as they poured their libations to their lost friend and mentor. As the young men offered fervent prayers to the gods above and below, others all around us added their own intercessions. Killers usually fear being pursued by an angry ghost. Whoever had murdered Eumelos should be more afraid of his vengeful friends.

As the first true sunlight flooded the Corinthian plain with the soft golden promise of warmth, the two mute slaves began filling in the grave. Nados turned to address the gathering waiting in respectful silence.

'Thank you for honouring our beloved Eumelos. Please, come back to his home, to eat and drink and celebrate his life.'

As he managed a shaky smile, I realised he was searching for someone in the crowd. As soon as he saw me, he raised a hand, and I saw Simias and Aithon focus on me as well. They clearly wanted to talk, so as everyone else moved off, I waited with Zosime.

The three young men came over to us. They were all much of an age, with Simias perhaps the oldest. He was shorter than Nados, heavily browed and muscled like a rower.

'Philocles, it's good to meet you.' Aithon had a faint Thessalian accent but I guessed he had lived here long enough to qualify for Corinthian citizenship, since he was participating so fully in the funeral.

'I wish it had been under better circumstances. What can I do for you?'

Nados ran a hand over his ragged hair. 'We still can't find Dardanis, and we can't find Eumelos' will.'

'We can't find his savings either,' Simias added, anxious. 'We've searched everywhere.'

'Didn't he keep a strongbox in a temple?' I guessed the priests of Apollo acted as the city's bankers, and most sensible merchants only keep money for their day-to-day needs at home.

'He did, but that's not the problem.' Aithon explained. 'He told me that he kept his silver reserve here in Corinth, where Nados could make up all the accounts.'

The tall Corinthian took up the tale. 'But he told me that Simias kept the accounts, as well as his private strongbox, in the Lechaion house.'

I looked at the stocky man. 'While he told you that Aithon kept everything safe in Kenchreai?'

'He said no one would think of looking there to rob us,' Simias confirmed.

Zeus help me, what had Eumelos been thinking? I looked past the three young men to the dark scar of his grave. There was no way we could ask the dead man now, not unless someone fancied following in Odysseus' footsteps and making their way down to the Underworld.

Chapter Seven

We arrived at Eumelos' house to find the courtyard paving dull with water. Abrosyne and the household slaves had barely finished the cleansing rites after the dead man's departure. They hurried to serve wine and food to the gathering throng. I wondered how many of these men and women had truly been the merchant's friends, and how many were just here to fill their bellies.

Thettalos was eating heartily and grief wasn't dulling the appetites of his handful of companions. They all wore Pegasus insignia, though only Thettalos showed any sign of the fight at the Sanctuary. There was the dark shadow of a bruise under his beard and his legs looked like he'd been mauled by a wolf. As he made his way towards me, his warning scowl made sure no one jostled him.

I toyed with the idea of slipping away through the crowd but that would be pointless as well as childish. So I waited to hear what the brute had to say.

'We will have our vengeance for our brother. Never doubt that, Athenian.'

I was a little surprised to see unshed tears of genuine grief in his eyes. 'May the Furies bless your endeavours.'

He drew a deep breath. 'You need a chorus. Perantas said—'

'—the play will be staged.' I nodded. 'We'll hold our auditions and rehearsals without your help, thanks all the same.'

I tried, and failed, to avoid sounding acid. Thettalos' lip curled.

'If you think you can defend yourselves, three actors, one scribbler and a piper—'

'If you want to defy Demeter's priestess, that's between you and her and the goddess.' I let him see my anger, though I kept my voice low out of deference to the mourners around us. 'She said you are no longer welcome in the Sanctuary.'

'Then don't come crawling to me,' he sneered, 'with a knife in your guts.'

'The further I stay from you,' I retorted, 'the safer I reckon I'll be.'

As I turned my back, I saw Abrosyne looking uneasy as she passed by with a jug in her hand. More slaves I didn't recognise carried laden platters to and fro, their eyes hollow with anxiety. I could hardly blame them, but I had no reassurance to offer. I had no idea what would happen to them if Eumelos' will had gone missing.

Nados, Aithon and Simias kept looking at me, between shaking hands with mourners sharing some fond memory of Eumelos and expressing their shock at his death. The crowd was spilling out of the gate into the street now. Hushed condolences were giving way to louder reminiscences and even an occasional laugh as someone was caught unawares by some amusing recollection.

I remembered my father's funeral. I hadn't been much older than these three, but I'd had my brothers to share the burden. We'd had so much more besides. There were our mother's brothers, as well as cousins on our father's side. Our married sister Kleio's husband, Kalliphon, was a true friend, and we could turn to the district brotherhood that we'd belonged to since we were children. Those guarantee every Athenian citizen's rights and see to it that a dead man's dependants are dealt with fairly, even if no will can be found.

Aithon excused himself with a shake of a weather-beaten man's hand. Simias and Nados extricated themselves from their respective conversations, and I could see they all had something to say to me.

Taking Zosime's hand, I edged my way to the elegantly painted portico at the side of the courtyard. The handful of people there politely yielded the space to us, so we were unlikely to be overheard. That was good, because I had some hard questions to ask, after thinking through what they'd said at the graveside.

'Did Dardanis know where Eumelos kept his silver reserves? Did he tell you this same tale about the strong box and the accounts being kept in different places?'

The trio exchanged apprehensive glances and nodded.

'Was he involved in keeping the day-to-day records of your trades? Did he handle correspondence, cargo lists and such?'

'He's an excellent secretary,' Aithon confirmed.

'He carries letters back and forth for us all,' Simias added.

'So he knew more about Eumelos' business than any of you. Don't we have to consider the possibility that he is Eumelos' killer? That he's fled with the fortune?'

Perantas Bacchiad was ready to blame the slave because that was most convenient for him. Now I was forced to wonder if he was right.

'I know you're afraid that Dardanis fell foul of who-ever murdered your master, but surely he'd have turned up dead or injured by now? How could someone seize him between here and our lodging without Menekles and those two noticing some scuffle?'

I nodded at the doleful slaves who'd carried their master to his final resting place, now lugging heavy water jars from the nearest fountain. 'If Dardanis can't be found, surely he doesn't want to be found? If you can't find Eumelos' will, did Dardanis know where it was kept?'

'He wrote it,' Aithon said, sullen. 'Eumelos revised his bequests every year.'

'Sensible, since he was a man with many trading inter-ests.' I looked at the three of them. 'So I'm guessing his will was a lengthy document. Have you any idea what it said? Who might have a claim on his property?'

'He said we'd be treated fairly.' Nados sounded utterly bereft. 'But none of us expected him to die. No one did.'

He gestured vaguely at the crowd in the courtyard, and I smiled blandly at the closest men and women trying unsuccessfully to conceal their curiosity about our conversation. I turned back to the trio.

'Dardanis knew where the silver was hidden. Dardanis knew that without a will, you'd be too busy sorting out the confusion to pursue him.'

'Eumelos trusted him,' Simias protested. 'More than anyone else.'

'Enough to drink whatever medicine Dardanis gave him? A pick-me-up before he visited a brothel?' I steeled myself for their response.

'He wouldn't do that!' Nados' shout echoed around the courtyard, silencing the chattering crowd.

I turned to challenge the motionless figures with wide-eyed stares and gaping mouths. This tragedy didn't need a chorus. As I glowered, stealthy movement caught my eye. A wiry man slipped behind a portly mourner, heading for the gate. As well he might. That was the bastard who'd started the fight to wreck our auditions.

I took a stride to follow him. Men and women shuffled like startled hens, only inconveniencing each other and thoroughly blocking my path.

'Let me through.' Simias pushed his way through the crowd.

He wanted to be anywhere but here. I remembered that feeling all too well from my father's funeral.

'I have to . . .' Nados disappeared into the house. Aithon followed him without a word.

Conversation resumed, awkward and abashed. A few people decided it was time to leave. I saw Hyanthidas leaning against the opposite wall of the courtyard. He looked as weary as Eumelos' slaves. At his side, Telesilla couldn't stop yawning.

I wondered if he'd seen the wiry man. I took a step, only to find Zosime holding me back.

'Why are you blaming the slave?'

'Who else is there? Who else is missing? No one likes to imagine such betrayal, but slaves have been known to kill.'

'When they're driven to it by brutality,' she retorted. 'Everyone says Eumelos treated his household fairly.'

'No one knows what goes on behind closed doors.' That was a feeble answer and I knew it.

Zosime gave me a withering look. 'Abused slaves run away. They reach a new city, they change their name and no one is ever the wiser. Why would Dardanis risk murder with Corinth's two ports within such easy reach? When a killer will be pursued by gods and men alike?'

I couldn't deny her logic but she hadn't answered my first question. 'Then where is Dardanis?'

'Killed by whoever killed Eumelos, who knows how quickly a missing slave will be blamed.' Zosime had no doubt about that. 'Do you think Kadous could do such a thing?'

'What?' This abrupt swerve in the conversation wrong-footed me.

'Would he ever kill you, to rob you and run away, after serving you faithfully for so many years?'

'Of course not, but that's different.'

'How?' Zosime demanded. 'Everyone says that Dardanis was as loyal to Eumelos as Kadous is to you. I spent the whole day here, when his body was brought back from the Asklepion. These people knew both of them. None of us did. They all swear Dardanis couldn't do this.'

'Then where is he?' Though she was right about one thing. I wouldn't know the missing slave from a stranger on the highway. We'd barely exchanged twenty words and I struggled to remember the man's face. But I'd definitely recognised that wiry man and he was getting away. 'I'm sorry. We'll discuss this later.'

I shook off Zosime's hand and headed for Hyanthidas. Before I could reach him, the crowd at the gate parted, and a handful of stern-faced men entered. They wore plain tunics of undyed wool, and I guessed that the same barber kept their hair and beards clipped close. Temple slaves.

The leader pointed at me. 'Are you Philocles Hestaiou of Athens?'

'I am.' There wasn't much point in denying it.

'You're summoned before the Council of Corinth, to answer for the disruption you've brought to our city.' His tone was matter-of-fact.

'When do the honoured Council wish to see me?' I asked warily.

'Now.' He didn't need to explain how much trouble I'd be in if I baulked. None of these men carried chains, but I guessed such things wouldn't be hard to come by.

'By all means.' I agreed.

'Follow me.'

As the slaves' leader turned around, I looked at

Hyanthidas with desperate appeal. He gave Telesilla a swift kiss of farewell and fell into step beside me. As we reached the gate, the temple slaves flanked us. If we weren't under arrest, we certainly couldn't run.

Glancing over my shoulder, I saw Telesilla join Zosime, both women unable to hide their concern.

'Just answer the questions you're asked,' Hyanthidas advised in an undertone. 'Don't elaborate. Don't speculate.'

I nodded, my mouth dry, as we walked through the streets. Corinth's citizens and visitors were going about their daily business in the agora. It felt as if every one of them stopped to stare as we went past.

We climbed the shallow slope to the mighty temple's broad precinct. A great statue of Apollo seated with his lyre watched us approach, impassive. The temple slaves led us across the sacred paving and into the temple's porch. Gleaming bronze plaques on all sides were engraved with the Council's decrees.

In Athens, we chisel our laws and annual records into stone to ensure that the will of the people endures, unaltered. Oligarchies prefer metal that can be melted down and recast whenever some new faction emerges to overrule their predecessors.

We entered the larger of the temple's two inner chambers. The god rose above us, beardless and beautiful in gleaming bronze, his hair a cascade of loose curls. His quiver was slung across his back, and the arm holding his bow was outstretched. Lithe and muscular, he stood as tautly poised as any archer who has just loosed an arrow. His divine gaze swept over our heads, looking out through the temple entrance as if to see where his shot might have landed.

I didn't need reminding that Apollo is as ready to strike down the impious and dishonest with his arrows of misfortune and disease as he is to reward good men for their virtues and grant them his gifts of healing, alongside his divine son, Asklepios.

A half-circle of folding stools were set in front of the magnificent statue, with carved and polished legs and glossy leather deep-dyed with the scarlet that Corinth is justly famed for. The men who would plant their back-sides on such luxury were talking in low voices, gathered in small groups. They were well nourished, expertly barbered and expensively dressed. Every one wore gold and silver rings and brooches as well as a finely woven wool cloak. All had obsequious attendants hanging on their every word.

'This isn't the full Council,' Hyanthidas murmured as the temple slaves withdrew. 'That's good.'

I wanted to ask why, but the gathering had noticed our arrival. The hangers-on withdrew to stand silently against the temple walls while the great and the good of Corinth settled themselves on their stools. I noticed Perantas Bacchiad, but he looked at me with bland disinterest, as if we'd never met before.

A stocky individual sat in the centre of the half circle. His ample belly and broad arse spoke of a youthful wrestler's muscles now softened for lack of exercise and too much rich food. His vanity was apparent in his carefully curled beard and the way his long grey locks were combed to compensate for his relentlessly receding hairline.

He looked at me as though I was filth to scrape off the bottom of his sandal. 'Philocles Hestaiou of Athens.'

I'd faced a more hostile audience when my first play had failed so miserably at the Lenaia. This lot didn't have cheese rinds to throw either.

I smiled cheerfully. 'Good day to you, honoured sirs.'

The merest hint of a smile from Perantas answered me as the greybeard scowled.

'You have caused considerable disturbance since your arrival.'

This time I decided to wait for a question.

'Well?' the greybeard barked, irritated. 'Tell me why we shouldn't forbid you the use of our theatre, in the interests of civic order?'

Old soldiers will tell you the best way to win a battle is not to fight in the first place.

I addressed the whole gathering rather than the greybeard alone. 'Granting such a favour is in your gift. We would never presume otherwise.'

I wasn't about to argue over whether or not we were responsible for the near-riot at Demeter's shrine. Any debate would concede the possibility that we might be somehow at fault. Whatever I said could be twisted to leave some of these men suspecting there could be no smoke on the breeze without some smouldering fire.

Hyanthidas clasped humble hands, head ducked and

shoulders rounded. 'We can remove ourselves to Sikyon without delay.'

That was news to me since Sikyon's no great friend to Athens, but I made sure my smile stayed respectful and hopeful.

The Council men stirred like billy goats catching the scent of a wolf.

'I see no reason why that should be necessary.' A leather-faced bald-pate glowered at the greybeard.

Our opponent wasn't about to yield. 'Can you give us your assurance that you will cause no further trouble?'

I shrugged my cloak back to show that my arms were as unmarked as my face. 'As you can see, I have not raised a hand to any Corinthian, nor to any visitor to your glorious city. I have given no man any cause to strike me. Nor have any of my companions and nor will we do so, as I have sworn before Demeter's priestess on her sacred altar. We only wish to offer your city our entertainment, and to honour the gods as we do so.'

I raised my hands in supplication to the magnificent statue. Granted, Apollo's the god of music rather than drama, but I imagine he appreciates any good perfor-mance. Menekles would be proud of me.

I saw Perantas shift on his seat, though he wasn't the next to speak. An old man with dewlaps like a scenting hound studied me thoughtfully.

'I see no reason to deprive our people of this trivial amusement.'

'I see no reason to even consider a vote,' a square-jawed man said firmly.

More than half the Council members present at this sudden meeting voiced their agreement. I still didn't understand why, but the mood in the lofty chamber had turned against the greybeard, as surely as a change in the wind drives off the threat of a storm.

Now Perantas spoke. 'I believe this concludes our business.'

'Quite so.' The square-jawed man was already rising, gesturing to his attentive minion.

I looked sideways at Hyanthidas. 'Are we dismissed?' I murmured.

'Give it a moment,' he said quietly.

So I stood still, smiling so cheerfully that my face ached, as the Council members and their underlings went past. Most barely spared us a glance.

Once the temple slaves started folding the fancy stools, I turned to the musician. 'What was that all about?'

Hyanthidas began walking towards the door. 'The man who wanted to provoke you is called Philolaos Kypselid. Most of the councilmen he'd summoned here just want a quiet life, so they can concentrate on making money. If Philolaos could convince them you were a troublemaker, they'd have followed his lead and forbidden the play for the sake of civic peace.'

'Until they thought we'd take the play to Sikyon?'

Hyanthidas grinned. 'Sikyonians claim their city's the equal of Corinth. The Council will always agree such ridiculous and offensive pretensions must be squashed at every opportunity. That and no one wants Sikyon looking to Athens for an alliance that doesn't go through Corinth.'

I would be glad to get home to straightforward Athenian politics. 'What's this Philolaos Kypselid got against us? Do you think he'll try to turn the Council against us again?'

'I don't know why you're such a thorn in his foot, but I wouldn't bet against him trying something else,' the piper said frankly.

'Should we—' I broke off, seeing Perantas' Nubian secretary, Wetka, walking towards us.

'My master's compliments,' he said, composed. 'Do you need any assistance with your preparations for your performance?'

'Keep Thettalos and his fools away from us,' I said, uncompromising.

'My master's apologies.' Wetka didn't miss a beat. 'What else—?'

'Nothing. Never mind. Off you go.' I waved him away as we reached the threshold.

I'd just seen two men in urgent conversation beside one of the great temple's outer pillars. The wiry man was talking to a fresh-faced youth who had been hanging around on the edges of Philolaos' entourage. He probably thought his long hair made him look like Apollo. I reckoned he looked like a yearling sheep in need of the shears.

I drew Hyanthidas into the shadows and pointed as discreetly as I could. 'Do you know who that rat-faced bastard is?'

'No.' The musician looked at me, curious. 'What's he ever done to you?'

'He helped to wreck our auditions.' I swiftly explained how the man had thrown the first punch. 'I saw him at Eumelos' house, too, at the funeral.'

'I wonder if Wetka knows who he is.' Hyanthidas looked to see where the Nubian had gone.

'No.' That had been my first impulse but I'd thought better of it. 'We don't want word getting back to Thettalos. He could well decide to take matters into his own hands, and we've already seen he's free with his fists. Any more brawls will only strengthen Philolaos Kypselid's case against us.'

'Shall we follow him, and see where he goes?' Hyanthidas studied our quarry.

I shook my head. 'Too risky. He saw me notice him earlier at the funeral. Let's get back to the house. There's something I want to check.'

As soon as Tromes opened the gate to us, I hurried up the stairs to fetch Eumelos' crumpled list. As the slave brought wine for me and Hyanthidas, I studied the third mysterious symbol; a small rectangle with a horizontal line near the top.

'Does that look like a box or a chest to you?' I asked the musician.

'Possibly,' he said slowly.

Hyanthidas looked at me, and I could see he knew what I was thinking. He swallowed his wine and stood up. 'I'll ask around and see what I can find out – discreetly,' he added, before I could warn him to be careful.

Chapter Eight

Hyanthidas appeared the next morning as we were eating breakfast. 'Pull up a stool,' I invited him.

'You were right.' He reached for the jug and poured himself a cup of fresh spring water. 'Those men on Eumelos' list all have ties to the Heirs of Hephaistos. The ones with that chest symbol next to their names. These days Philolaos Kypselid is their most generous supporter, according to the agora gossips.'

Athena help us, yet more foes. 'What do they want?'

'Corinth for the Corinthians. They hate Athens even more than the Sons of Heracles do.'

'Would one of you care to explain? Why do they worship Hephaistos?' Zosime dipped a spoonful of honey from the jar and drizzled it over soft cheese. 'And what's the significance of a chest as a symbol?'

'The tyrant Kypselos' mother, Labda, was lame.' Apollonides reached for more bread. 'Lame ancestress, so the family honour the lame god and his cult.'

Zosime nodded. 'That makes sense.'

'That's why she was allowed to marry a commoner like Kypselos,' added Menekles, 'even though her father, Amphion, was a Bacchiad.'

'Bacchiad? Like Perantas?' Zosime looked at me.

'Same family, but generation upon generation ago. The Bacchiads were the kings of Corinth back in the age of heroes, but the rest of the family wanted their share of the power and riches. The last king, Telestes, wasn't inclined to generosity, and he ended up dead, most likely at the hands of some cousins. After that, the Bacchiads ruled through a Council and Chief Magistrate, who were always men chosen from among their own bloodline.'

'Then came the prophecy,' Apollonides said with relish.

'Prophecy?' Zosime leaned forward. Clearly she hadn't heard this tale in Crete when she was growing up.

'The oracle said that Labda's son would overthrow the Bacchiads. They sent men to kill the infant, so Labda hid him in a chest and they went away empty-handed.' Apollonides laughed. 'When Kypselos did eventually seize power, they say he had a magnificent cedarwood chest inlaid with gold and ivory, and sent to Delphi.'

'Corinth flourished under his rule for a generation,' Menekles remarked, 'and the city grew richer still under the tyranny of his son, Periander, despite how cruel and capricious they could both be. That was—' he looked at the other actors '—around the time Draco was drawing up Athens' first law code?'

Apollonides nodded. 'Then Periander quarrelled with his sons and they left Corinth. They were convinced he'd killed their mother. When the old tyrant's strength was failing, the younger son, Lycophron, was persuaded to come back from exile in Corcyra to take over, but only on condition that Periander left the city. But the son was killed before he could return.'

Hereditary rule never lasts. We learned that long ago in Athens and far sooner than most. Now we strive to show all other Hellenes the benefits of democracy.

'With no one fit to inherit Periander's power, the Corinthians opted for oligarchy again,' I told Zosime. 'Though this time the Bacchiads had the sense to share the Council's seats with the other powerful families.'

Lysicrates scowled. 'Now they keep firm hold of that power and wealth by trading on the people's fear of some new enemy every ten years or so. The Spartans. The Megarans. Whatever strife they think will make them a profit.'

'So much for today's history lesson.' I clapped my hands quickly before Hyanthidas could object to that harsh assessment. 'Now that we know who else Eumelos would have warned us about, let's go and recruit our chorus.'

I indicated to Tromes that he and Kadous could clear the remains of our breakfast away. Though, as everyone agreed and got up from the table, I wished I could turn my full attention to the play. There were far too many distractions. I couldn't help wondering how Nados, Aithon and Simias were getting on with sorting out the mess of Eumelos' affairs, with no will to settle the dead man's property, and all his accounts and silver missing. I kept thinking how effectively Zosime had argued that Dardanis couldn't be the killer.

Presumably Perantas and the Brotherhood of Bellero-phon could help Eumelos' lads, I told myself sternly. Assuming there were some Brothers who didn't think all problems could be solved by breaking heads.

Menekles was the first to rejoin me in the courtyard with his cloak. 'How are the rewrites coming?'

'Very well.' As Athena is my witness, that wasn't a lie, not exactly, anyway.

When I had got back yesterday, I'd sat down with Zosime to discuss a new idea. She thought it had poten-tial, though she wanted to talk to Telesilla about exactly how to make it work.

As well timed as any cue on stage, Tromes opened the gate to a knock and we saw Telesilla standing there, carrying a lyre.

I gave Zosime a quick kiss. 'What have you got planned for today?'

She looked at me, determined. 'We're coming to the rehearsal with you.'

Telesilla nodded with equal resolve. 'There's much less likely to be trouble if two women are there.'

Zosime smiled sunnily. 'We can pay our respects to Demeter and Persephone.'

Evidently this wasn't up for debate. I looked at everyone else but nobody seemed inclined to argue. I capitulated.

'Say a prayer for us all.' Hopefully the divine mother and her daughter would look favourably on our endeavours.

We walked through the bustling city and took the

winding road up to the Sanctuary. There were no loitering brutes braced for battle today, and our courtyard had been swept clear of any detritus left from the brawl. Apollonides set about pacing out the areas that would serve as our stage and the dancing floor. Menekles fetched stones from the hillside to mark their boundaries.

An encouraging number of the singers whom we'd already seen were waiting for us, thanks to Hyanthidas' powers of persuasion. More turned up as Lysicrates fetched the keys from the priestess.

I addressed the hopeful newcomers first. 'Who's here to audition today?'

A tall Megaran stepped forward, looking at Telesilla. 'Praxilla's "Folly of Adonis"?'

She strummed a resounding chord. The Megaran launched into the song, and several others joined in with the chorus. I exchanged a grin with Apollonides.

It proved an honest omen. We soon had a full complement of twenty-four singers, and those who weren't chosen took their dismissal without rancour. None of those named on Eumelos' list even turned up, and we didn't see any hero cult insignia.

We began teaching our new singers their songs, with me taking the lead and Apollonides, Menekles and Lysicrates bolstering the rest. It had been a few years since I'd last been in a chorus, but with every word and note of my own play so familiar, I soon found my pace and my rhythm.

By the time we felt the full heat of the day approaching, we were making impressive progress. I should visit the next Isthmian Games, if these singers were any indication of the standard of Corinth's performers.

I judged it was time for a break. 'We've made an excellent start. Thank you all. Let's start again at the eighth hour and try pacing out our first steps.'

A handful of the chorus cheered, their enthusiasm heartening.

Menekles raised a hand. 'Who's coming with me to fetch some water?' Three singers dutifully obliged.

I saw Kadous appear in the alleyway leading from the road, carrying a basket of provisions. Some of the chorus members had come prepared while the others were discussing the merits of the lengthy climb to the Acrocorinth's taverns, compared to heading down to the agora. As those seeking lunch elsewhere wandered off, Zosime began unpacking Kadous' basket. The singers who were staying found seats in the shade.

Hyanthidas appeared at my shoulder. 'Come with me.'

His grim face unnerved me. 'What is it?'

He didn't answer, taking hold of my elbow. I let him steer me to the dining room where our costumes were stored. Apollonides was sprawled on the ledge where dining couches would rest. Telesilla was frantically mopping his face with a dripping rag.

'What's happened?'

Telesilla stepped back. I gasped. Apollonides was flushed like a man with a fever and blisters covered his face. Some were as big as my thumbnail.

My first thought was sheer terror. I'd never seen a pox

like this, and it must be lethally virulent to have struck him down so swiftly. Then I realised Apollonides was gesturing at a mask on the floor. I hurried to pick it up before someone stood on it and crushed the shaped and painted layers of linen and gypsum.

'No!' Telesilla smacked my hand. 'That's what did the damage!'

'How?' I was as confused as I was concerned.

Apollonides struggled up to sit up. 'I was checking the masks,' he rasped. 'the ties on that one looked loose, so I put it on—'

He broke off, struggling for breath. His lips were a purplish hue, ghastly against his scarlet face. Now his eyelids were swelling, tears blinding him.

I thought of the dress that Medea gave to Glauke, which burned the poor girl alive. Heracles had burned himself alive to escape the agonies of a robe soaked in Hydra's blood, after Deianeira was duped into giving that to him by the vengeful centaur Nessus. Corinth had so many tales of poisoned garments.

'Stay down!' I pushed Apollonides backwards, then scooped up his legs, forcing him to lie flat on the ledge. 'Telesilla, keep washing his face. Hyanthidas, fetch more water.'

Frantic, I wracked my brains. I wanted to get Apollonides to a doctor but we were so far from the Asklepion. There might well be doctors up on the Acrocorinth, serving the shrines and the brothels, but I had no idea where to start looking for one who could be trusted. Besides, Apollonides wouldn't manage the climb to the summit, any more than he could to walk across the city to the Asklepion. His breath was growing laboured and I could see his limbs trembling.

I begged Apollo to save this man named to honour him. I asked the god to curse the villain who'd done this with the worst torments he could devise.

A shadow dimmed the daylight coming through the doorway. Lysicrates swore. 'This fucking city!'

Hyanthidas was right behind him. 'Don't you—'

'Enough!' I snapped. 'What else can we do?'

'Nothing.' Telesilla leaned over to study Apollonides' forehead as best she could in the dimness. 'I think he's had the worst of it.'

She didn't sound nearly certain enough to reassure me. I watched her cross to the closest basket and realised that rag in her hand was the torn sleeve of one of our stage skins; the lightweight, closely woven cloth that covers every actor and chorus member from the neck down.

I swallowed my instinctive protest as she tore off another piece, soaked it in water and laid it on Apollonides' face. We'd brought a few spares in case of rips and accidents, and her prompt action could well have saved his life.

Menekles appeared in the doorway. 'Why are we all in here?'

'The masks have been dosed with something that blisters the skin.' Mindful of Telesilla's warning, I ripped the other sleeve from the ruined stage skin and drew it over my hand before picking up the fallen mask. 'Let me get some light.'

As the others stepped back from the doorway, I turned the mask over to look inside, but could see no sign of anything amiss.

'All of them?' Menekles looked over at the basket holding the masks and wigs.

'Feel free to try them on.' Apollonides pressed the back of a hand to his mouth to stifle a cough, his chest heaving.

I told myself he must be feeling better, to crack a joke like that. I wished I could believe it. Lying there with wet linen draped over his face, he reminded me horribly of my last sight of Eumelos, shrouded for burial. My blood ran cold. Was this the same poisoner's work?

From my vantage point in the doorway, I surveyed the chorus men around the courtyard. None of them had noticed anything amiss. Kadous was pouring watered wine for those who wanted a drink, chatting amiably.

'We don't want them knowing about this.' I spoke the thought aloud.

'No indeed.' Menekles stood beside me.

Eumelos' death could be dismissed as an unfortunate coincidence, with Perantas blaming a faithless slave for his murder. Rival hero cults fighting seemed to be a fact of life in Corinth, so the uproar the day before yesterday could be waved away.

Poisoned masks gave those events a different complexion. This was a direct attack. No one could blame our chorus singers for walking away if they learned what had happened.

'What's wrong?' Zosime joined us. 'Aren't any of you having some lunch?'

'See if you can help Telesilla.' I stood aside to let her enter and find out what was amiss.

'How can we stage a play with no masks?' Lysicrates demanded in a savage undertone. 'We can hardly hand them over to a laundress.'

'Let me think.' I silently begged Dionysos to inspire me with some solution. 'We had better get the costumes all thoroughly washed though, in case they've been given the same treatment. Everything, the stage skins and the tunics.'

At least that was in our favour. The chorus of builders that our play was named for wore everyday clothing: ragged tunics smudged with mortar and stone dust. Though the actors' solo speaking parts were a different matter. My heart sank.

Lysicrates got there ahead of me, literally and metaphorically. He was heading for the furthest basket that held all their props and costumes. He knelt to study the buckled straps and knotted ropes.

'Well?' Menekles demanded, tense.

Apollonides forced himself up on one elbow, dragging the wet cloth from his face.

'No fucker's tampered with this.' Lysicrates slapped the woven wicker.

'You're sure?'

I wished those words unsaid as he glared at me.

'I tied these knots myself. I didn't want anyone nosing through our stuff on board ship.'

'So the damage is limited,' Menekles said, bracing.

'The chorus masks are still fucked,' Lysicrates spat.

Standing just outside the door, Hyanthidas raised a hand. 'People are starting to look this way.'

'Get back to your rehearsal,' Apollonides said hoarsely. 'I'll be buggered if I'm going through this for nothing.'

Menekles looked at me. 'He can't leave here in daylight. If anyone sees him, the rumours will fly faster than whatever pox he's supposed to have.'

I nodded. 'Saying Apollo's arrows have struck him down as a sign of the god's displeasure with our play, no doubt.'

'As soon as the priestess sees him, she'll throw us out of here regardless.'

I looked sharply at Lysicrates, unable to tell if he'd welcome Demeter's handmaid putting an end to our trip here. He wasn't wrong though.

'Go on.' Zosime shared a glance with Telesilla. 'We can look after him.'

I realised everyone was looking at me. I drew a steadying breath. 'Very well.'

'Eat something first,' Zosime called out as we left the room.

Belatedly investigating the provisions Kadous had brought did at least give me the opportunity to quietly alert him to unwelcome developments. The Phrygian's eyes widened, but one of the first things a wise slave learns is never to let his face betray him.

The rest of the chorus returned and we resumed our rehearsal. We had no choice. It was either that or abandon the play. The singers were keen and proved as deft at picking up the dances as they were with the songs. By the time dusk closed around our courtyard, I could call a halt to a good day's work without arousing suspicion.

I even allowed myself a moment of quiet satisfaction. A couple of songs had collapsed in spectacular fashion, as several of the Corinthians couldn't help laughing at the situations they found themselves in, but that had been heartening in its own way. I prayed to Demeter that it was an augury their fellow citizens would find our play just as hilarious. Hopefully our chorus would start spreading the word among their friends and acquaintances, saying they'd be fools to miss the performance.

That brief moment of respite passed. I headed for the windowless dining room. The doorway was ominously gloomy and any lamps within remained unlit. I couldn't hear anyone talking. Menekles and Lysicrates joined me, visibly apprehensive. Hyanthidas stayed sitting on his stool, tossing his pipe from hand to hand.

Telesilla appeared on the threshold. 'Has everyone gone?'

I nodded. 'It's just us here.'

She stepped out into the evening, and Apollonides followed her, wearing a broad-brimmed floppy straw hat and a cloak. I recognised it as one of his costumes from the play's marketplace scene. With a fold of the cloak drawn up over the hat, his face would barely be visible to any passer-by.

I felt weak with relief. 'How are you?'

'Better.' His voice was still hoarse though he seemed to be breathing normally. 'Somewhat.'

As he lifted the hat's brim a little, I saw that hectic redness had faded but the blisters on his forehead and cheeks were still shocking. A few had already burst to leave raw sores.

'Do you think you can walk back down to the city, or should we send for a litter?'

'I can walk,' Apollonides assured me, 'and I'm going to the Asklepion. We need to know what did this. Perhaps that can tell us who deserves a kicking.'

'Let's hope so,' I agreed. When we did, perhaps we would have a use for Thettalos and the Brotherhood of Bellerophon after all.

Chapter Nine

Before we left, Menekles secured both dining rooms with a sharp tug on the leather thongs threaded through holes in the wood. Those drew the substantial bolts home across each door's inner face. He rattled the keys in his hand. 'I'd better give these back to the priestess.'

'So she can give them to whoever sneaked in here last night?' demanded Lysicrates. 'What will we find tomorrow? Shit all over the costumes? Piss in our wine?'

Hyanthidas scowled. 'We don't know that the priestess gave the keys to anyone.'

'Then how did someone get in?' Lysicrates challenged him.

'I wonder how many people have used these dining suites over the years.' Menekles was studying the keys.

They were the usual Spartan design; a bronze rod as crooked as a dog's hind leg, and precisely measured to be the right length when it was threaded through the keyhole. The end would engage with the ridges in the top of the hidden bolt, to push it back as the key was twisted. We watched him fit the two keys together. They were identical.

Menekles looked up. 'What's the betting every lock

in this place is made to the same pattern?'

'Why shouldn't they be?' countered Hyanthidas. 'When they're not in use, these doors only need to be locked to keep out animals and vagrants.'

Telesilla nodded, threading her arm through his. 'Who would imagine someone risking the goddess' wrath by dishonouring her sanctuary?'

They were both right, but so was Lysicrates, and I couldn't see how I could agree with both of them without annoying everyone.

'Shouldn't we ask the priestess if anyone came asking for access?' Zosime wondered.

Yet again, everyone was looking at me. I wished Chrysion had warned me that a chorus master is expected to solve every problem. I quailed at the thought of confronting the formidable priestess with what could only sound like an accusation.

'What would that achieve? Even if she did hand over the keys, whoever persuaded her must have lied. I can't imagine it was anyone she'd recognise. Whoever did this would hardly send someone she'd know, to lead us straight to their door.'

'She needs to know these doors need guarding,' Menekles observed.

'Until someone bribes a temple slave,' Lysicrates said sourly.

'There's no need for that,' I said quickly, seeing Hyanthidas was ready to rebuke him. 'We don't need Demeter smiting us all because you showed her servants such disrespect.'

Lysicrates had the grace to look abashed and I moved quickly on.

'But we might well learn something useful if we keep watch on this courtyard ourselves.' I turned to Kadous. 'Do you think you could make yourself comfortable out on the hillside? Find a place where you can see without being seen?'

'Comfortable enough.' He grinned. 'Not so comfortable I'll fall asleep.'

I smiled momentarily despite myself. He and I had shared a wretched scrape in the ground through one long night on campaign in Boeotia. We'd been part of a small detachment sent to reconnoitre the enemy's position. Snoring from the next hollow on the hillside had kept both of us wide awake.

'If you see someone making mischief, go and rouse the temple slaves,' I told him, serious once again. I didn't want the Phrygian taking on some unknown assailant with Hades only knew what allies hidden in the darkness. 'I'll let the priestess know you'll be on watch, so she can tell her men to stay alert.' I held out my hand and Menekles gave me the keys. 'You can all start walking. I'll catch up as soon as I'm done.'

As Kadous headed out to find some lair on the hillside, we left the courtyard through the alley between the buildings. Out on the broad steps, everyone else headed for the road downhill while I went up to the temple precinct. One of the goddess' handmaidens directed me up to the altar, where Demeter's priestess was sacrificing a brace of pigeons.

I'm used to seeing Athenian priests with gore up

to their elbows after cutting a sacred bull's throat, but seeing a holy woman holding a bloody knife was a novel and disconcerting experience. I coughed nervously to let her know I was there.

She turned, carefully holding the dripping blade away from her gown. 'How can I help you?'

'Someone has been interfering with our props and costumes.' As I explained, I did my best to be clear that we weren't levelling any accusations at her temple or its slaves. 'Of course, we don't want to burden your people with additional duties,' I added quickly, explaining Kadous would be keeping watch tonight.

The priestess wasn't amused, though I couldn't tell if she was more irritated with me, or with the unknown bastard who had poisoned our masks. 'Any intruder will soon regret their folly,' she assured me tartly.

'Thank you.' I only hoped we got a chance to learn who had sent anyone her irate slaves caught, before they beat him senseless.

I bowed, low and respectful, and beat a hasty retreat. The others hadn't got too far ahead, cautious on the downhill path as the dusk thickened, so I soon caught up.

As we reached the agora, Hyanthidas and Telesilla turned for their own home with barely a word of farewell. As we took the Lechaion Road towards the Asklepion, I wondered how to reassure the musicians that none of us blamed them for some unknown Corinthians' misdeeds.

We walked on in silence. I guessed Lysicrates and Menekles were preoccupied with their own thoughts and I could hear the breath rasping in Apollonides' throat, even though our pace was far from strenuous. Now that I was reasonably sure he wasn't going to die on us, I began to worry that he might not recover fast enough to manage his taxing role in the play.

As the lead, Menekles only had the one part to play, though Meriones' presence was substantial, on stage from the first scene to the last. Lysicrates had the third principle speaking role, as well as a bevy of characters coming on for two lines and a laugh.

In between, Apollonides bore the burden of playing Thersites, the second largest part. His banter with Meriones relied on immaculate timing for my jokes to work. He also had his own roster of minor characters, demanding swift entrances and exits, with quick changes of mask and costume behind the scenes. Back in Athens, the effort had left him sweating and breathless, and no one had poisoned him there.

More than that, back in Athens, if some misfortune had struck down any of our actors, Chrysion could have stepped into any of their parts. In case of a second disaster, I could have taken to the stage. Any one of our Dionysia chorus could have taken on the leader's role, and we knew enough experienced singers who could learn the steps to make up our numbers inside a day or so. We had no such resources in Corinth.

We reached the Asklepion eventually. With the first stroke of divine favour that we'd had since reaching Corinth, the doctor supervising the sleeping patients was Chresimos, the Cycladean who'd examined Eumelos.

'Good evening.' He looked at us with mild curiosity,

recognising me and Lysicrates. 'How can I help you tonight?'

Apollonides stepped forward, pulling back the fold of his cloak and taking off the floppy straw hat.

'He was trying on a mask.' Menekles explained what had happened.

Chresimos pursed his full lips. 'Let's take a closer look.'

Once again, he led us through the hall of pallets, down the staircase, and out through the door to the lower courtyard. This time we could see the glow of lamps here and there, and hear low voices and a hiss of pain from other cubicles along the colonnade.

As Chresimos led us to the closest examination table, I couldn't help a shiver of apprehension. This was where Eumelos had died. Zosime slid her arm around my waist, and I hugged her close, grateful for the comfort.

'Up on the table,' Chresimos said briskly as he lit the lamps.

Apollonides obliged, doing his best not to flinch as the doctor brought the flame frighteningly close in order to study his blisters.

'Breathe for me.' Chresimos set down the lamp and stood with his ear close to Apollonides' mouth. He listened intently for a few long moments.

'Well?' Menekles asked, tense, as the doctor stepped away.

'By my guess?' Though the Cycladean sounded wholly confident. 'Someone smeared the inside of the mask with hellebore sap.'

He smiled at Apollonides. 'Thankfully, you took it

off at once and washed your face quickly. I can give you an ointment to soothe those blisters and there's every reason to think you won't be badly marked. As for your throat . . .' He walked to the shelves at the end of the cubicle and found a yellow-glazed pot with a lid pierced by a hole.

'I'll give you some herbs. Put a palmful in this pot and fill it halfway with boiling water. Put the lid on tight, at once, and suck on the steam like this.' As he spoke, he took a hollow reed from a bundle on the shelf. He slid it through the hole in the lid, miming taking the end in his mouth. 'Make sure you keep your lips tight around it. Do that morning and evening and you'll feel your breathing ease inside a few days.'

'I will, thank you.' Apollonides' voice shook with relief.

Lysicrates and Menekles echoed his gratitude.

'Honour Asklepios with an offering. That's all I seek in return.' Chresimos glanced at me. 'Of course, in the right hands, hellebore's a medicine, like thornapple. Whoever's making this mischief for you certainly knows his herbs.'

'So it seems.' It was stretching credulity to snapping point to think that Dardanis had poisoned Eumelos to rob him and abscond, mere days before someone else entirely used toxic sap on our masks to ruin our play.

'How long will the hellebore persist?' asked Lysicrates. 'When do you think the masks will be safe to wear?'

'I have no idea,' the doctor said bluntly. 'As soon as anyone wearing one starts to sweat, whatever has soaked into the linen will most likely be reawakened to burn their skin.'

'Then we're fucked.' Lysicrates threw up his hands. 'We may as well go home.'

'No,' I said, adamant. 'Whoever did this is not going to win.'

If I was the chorus master, I was going to have the final say.

'Let me get you that ointment and those herbs.' Chresimos took a lamp and left us looking at each other across the table.

Apollonides was swinging his feet. For a man who looked as if he'd blundered into a beehive, he was remarkably cheerful. 'Do you think he can recommend a tavern? I don't know about anyone else but I want something to eat and a decent jug of wine.'

'Me too,' Menekles agreed.

Lysicrates stayed silent, scowling. He didn't say a word as the doctor returned with a small pot of ointment and a larger jar of dried herbs.

Once we'd expressed our thanks again, we made our way out through the doctors' hall. Closing the door behind us, Menekles looked across to the temple. 'We'll come back first thing tomorrow and make an offering.'

'Absolutely.' Apollonides nodded.

Lysicrates still didn't say anything as we made our way down the ramp. He didn't offer an opinion when Menekles pointed to a bustling tavern and suggested we see what it had to offer.

We found a table and learned the evening's dish from

the kitchen was lamb stew and barley bread. That suited us all well enough and we asked for a jug of black wine to go with it. Once we were served, Apollonides filled our cups and offered his first sip to Asklepios. We all did the same, and the dark ruby drops vanished into the well-trodden earth floor.

Zosime dipped her bread in her bowl. 'What are we going to do about the masks? Do you think Hyanthidas will know someone who could help?'

'Someone discreet,' warned Menekles. 'We don't want gossip doing our enemy's work for them, telling the chorus their masks have been poisoned.'

'Though if someone *did* start saying that, knowing who they were might tell us something useful,' Zosime pointed out.

'We don't want whoever did this thinking we've found a way to frustrate them,' Apollonides said thoughtfully. 'They'll just try something else.'

'True enough.' Menekles nodded. 'Carrying our masks across the city to someone's workshop will set tongues wagging from Lechaion to Kenchreai.'

'And offer anyone who wants to wreak more havoc an easy target,' Apollonides agreed.

I sipped my wine and pictured hero cultists ripping open our baskets and hurling our masks into the gutters, stamping on them to shatter the painted gypsum.

'There's plenty of room where we're lodging.' Zosime began spooning up stew.

I pictured some mob forcing their way through that gate, when she was there all alone. I imagined Perantas' slaves scattering to let our enemies run riot. Why should they put themselves in harm's way for the sake of an Athenian play?

I tore a hunk of bread in half and tried not to despair. 'We've got to work out how to salvage the masks before we decide who's doing what and where.'

'What do we tell the chorus?' Lysicrates demanded.

I sought for a plausible answer. Thankfully we had brought a collection of old masks with us for rehearsals.

'We can say the masks for the actual performance need some repair and a little reinforcement after being bounced around on the voyage here.'

I silently asked Dionysos to make sure that word never got back to Sosimenes in Athens. He was arguably the city's finest mask maker and would see this as a grave slur on his workmanship.

But it was true that a play's festival masks are usually only worn once. If we'd been taking the play to one of Attica's country theatres for the rural Dionysia, the actors would have used all-purpose wooden masks, proof against the rigours of travel, and the local chorus would have provided their own. But Aristarchos wanted our comedy to have the greatest possible impact, so he'd covered the costs of shipping everything here.

'That's a problem for tomorrow,' Menekles said, bracing. 'Let's eat up, and get a decent night's sleep.'

We finished our meal and made our way back to our temporary home. I don't think Lysicrates said another word.

Chapter Ten

I lay awake at first light, trying not to disturb Zosime. Trying not to wonder if we'd be better off taking a ship back to Athens and leaving Corinth to its cultists' quarrels.

She stirred and rolled over to face me. She smiled. 'Slip.'

'What?' For all the sense that made, she could have been speaking Phoenician.

'Slip,' she repeated. 'Liquid clay. The stuff that Disculos and the others use to paint their designs on the vases and bowls.'

It took some effort to picture the pottery where she and her father worked, back in Athens. I recalled marvelling at the way artists used liquid clay as paint to outline and detail their designs. That drab grey background was burnished to glossy black by the final, fierce heat of the kiln, leaving the rest bright red. Such mysteries are another divine gift to our city from our grey-eyed goddess.

'I still have no idea what you mean.'

'We can paint the insides of the masks with slip,' she said confidently, 'as long as we're careful not to make them too wet and risk it soaking through to the outer layers of plaster. Once the clay dries, that'll put a solid barrier between whatever the masks have been dosed with and anyone who's wearing them.'

'A layer that will scour their skin.' I hated to think what gritty, clay-soaked cloth would feel like on Apollonides' blisters.

'Not if we add another inner layer of linen, and maybe some wool for padding.'

'Perhaps.' I wasn't convinced, but I'm not a mask maker. On the other hand, I certainly didn't have any better ideas.

She raised herself up on one elbow. 'We need to find a pottery workshop to supply us with clay and some brushes. I'll go and ask Nados for advice. He must know where Eumelos got the pots for selling his pickled fish locally.'

I reached up to cup my hand around the back of her head, and drew her down to kiss her. 'I'll go. I want to talk to him about something else. You go up to the Sanctuary with the others and I'll see you there.'

I got up, dressed, and made my way quietly through the outer room where Kadous' bed stood empty. Down in the courtyard, one of Tromes' underlings was drowsing on a stool by the gate. At my nod, he got up, drew back the bolts and I left.

The streets were silent beneath the pale sky, and I didn't see anyone on the short walk to Eumelos' house. One of the silent litter bearers opened to my knock.

'I wish to see your master, Nados. Please offer my excuses for disturbing him so early.' Though I wasn't sure how the slave would do that, if he was truly mute.

He gestured to the painted porch. I took a seat and contemplated several battered chests stacked beside two rows of dusty baskets crammed with scrolls.

Nados appeared so swiftly that I guessed he was already up and dressed. A jaw-cracking yawn interrupted his attempt to greet me politely. 'Excuse me.'

'Not sleeping well?' I offered a wryly sympathetic smile.

'Barely at all,' he admitted, rubbing one cheekbone with the heel of his hand.

I waved a hand at the battered scroll baskets. 'I take it you've been turning the place inside out looking for Eumelos' will?'

He nodded, dejected. 'We're about ready to strip the plaster off the walls.'

'That seems a little extreme.' I wasn't entirely sure that was a joke. 'I assume you have checked for loose flagstones?'

He nodded, yawning again. 'There's nothing hidden under these floors. So we're going to Lechaion today, to search the house there from the rafters down. After that, we'll head for Kenchreai. After that . . .'

He shook his head, teetering between exhaustion and despair. 'We'll have to start making the rounds of all the temples, to see if there's a strongbox somewhere that none of us knew about. Assuming we can convince the priests and priestesses that we have a right to open it without Eumelos' will to name us as his heirs.'

I thought of the dizzying number of shrines and

temples in and around Corinth and its ports. 'Good luck.'

Nados managed a weary smile. 'Let's just hope we find something before we have to hike all the way out to Isthmia and ask the priests at Poseidon's temple there.'

I hadn't even thought of that. I hesitated. Simias and Aithon must be as exhausted as Nados and it hardly seemed fair to add to their burdens. On the other hand, I needed their help.

Nados might be preoccupied, but he noticed my indecision. 'What brings you here so early?'

I explained what had happened to Apollonides, and shared the doctor's verdict on our poisoned masks, as well as Zosime's idea for a solution. 'We need supplies from a pottery brought discreetly up to the Sanctuary. Supplied by someone who won't ask questions or gossip at his workshop gate.'

'Let me think.' Nados raked his fingers through his curls. 'There's a man who should be able to help,' he said a few moments later. 'He owes – he owed – Eumelos several favours. You can find him—'

'Forgive me.' I hoped he could see I was sincerely sorry. 'Whoever's behind this undoubtedly has people watching us. As long as they think they've succeeded and we don't realise our masks are tainted, with any luck this is all they'll do. We need someone else to make these arrangements. Can you do this for us? And please don't tell anyone about this except Aithon and Simias. The fewer people who know, the better our chances are that somebody guilty will let something slip.'

Nados didn't look thrilled but he nodded, nevertheless. 'I suppose so.'

'There's one more thing.' I steeled myself against his disbelieving look. 'It could help us both.'

'Go on,' he said reluctantly.

'If we find out who supplied this poison, we might discover who supplied the dose that killed Eumelos. If we were in Athens, there are people I could ask if I needed to find a herbalist or a doctor who'd trade his scruples for silver, but here in Corinth, or in Lechaion, or Kenchreai?' Belatedly I realised that we needed to cast our net wider than the city. 'How can I possibly learn who might do such favours for one of these hero cults set on wrecking our play? We need your help, yours, Aithon's and Simias'.'

A sardonic gleam brightened the lad's tired eyes. 'You've changed your mind about blaming Dardanis for killing Eumelos?'

I held up my hands in surrender. 'I was never certain that he had done it. I just couldn't see any other answers.'

'Where do you think he is?' Nados' chin quivered. He looked far too young to be bearing all these burdens.

'We can hope he's hiding somewhere,' I said, bracing, 'until he hears that the guilty man has been brought to justice.'

We could hope, though I reckoned that was as likely as that sour-voiced singer with the badly tuned lyre taking a winner's wreath at the Isthmian Games. If Dardanis knew who'd killed his master, the slave would still be running, if he had any sense. Or he was already lying dead, hidden where no one would ever find him. But I didn't want to say that, and Nados didn't want to hear it.

The lad drew a resolute breath. 'We'll see what we can find out.'

'Many thanks.' I rose to my feet. 'Please excuse me. I have other errands to run before today's rehearsal.'

My route took me to the agora, where the market gardeners of the Corinthia were starting to set up their stalls and unload their handcarts and baskets. Friends and acquaintances greeted each other with cheery shouts that echoed back from the deserted shrines and empty colonnades. No one paid me any attention, busy with their own concerns.

The tantalising scent of warm bread drew me to a bakery on a nearby corner and I bought a small barley loaf. There were no wine sellers out this early but the Peirene Spring flowed clear and cold and I was able to quench my thirst. As I did so, I prayed to Athena, asking for her favour, for the sake of Athens' ancient ties with Corinth.

As I went on my way, I saw mighty Apollo was looking down on me from the silent temple precinct, sitting aloft with his lyre. I paused to salute the god and to ask for his assistance in seeing this poisoner punished, not least for so foully misusing the medicines that his son's devotees at the Asklepion used for good.

Even so, it was still indecently early when I arrived at Perantas Bacchiad's house. The double gate was firmly closed and the high walls looked blankly down on me.

The Brotherhood of Bellerophon were presumably still snoring in bed.

I knocked briskly on the iron-studded wood. When there was no answer, I knocked again, harder. After another pause, I tried a third time.

A small shutter behind criss-crossed metal bars slid open. 'Yes?'

'I am Philocles Hestaiou of Athens and I need to see Perantas Bacchiad.'

Whoever was behind the gate was unimpressed. 'Wait there.'

I heard retreating steps instead of sliding bolts. I waited. Two sets of footsteps returned.

'Good morning. How may I help you?'

That was a Nubian accent. Perantas' secretary, Wetka.

'You can open this gate and tell your master I need to speak to him.' I was in no mood to compromise.

'If you could come back—'

'No. I need to see him now, before today's rehearsals. Unless he wants us to abandon the play.'

Silence on the other side of the gate lasted so long that I feared the shrewd Nubian was calling my bluff. Then the bolts rasped and the latch rattled as the gate opened, just an arm's length. The nightwatchman peered suspiciously past me, to be certain I was alone before he stepped back to let me enter.

'This way, if you please.' Summoned from his bed so early, Wetka didn't look nearly as crisp and neat as he had done on our previous meetings.

He led me to a porch running alongside this outer

courtyard. As he went into the house, a girl brought me bread and fruit. I could have saved my obols at that bakery. I had time to eat every last grape and crumb before Wetka reappeared to take me to Perantas.

The Bacchiad was eating almond cakes and sipping sweet spring water, sitting beneath his painted olive trees. He looked at me with something between amusement and irritation. 'What can I do for you so early in the day?'

I noted he didn't invite me to sit.

'Good morning,' I said politely. It was time to be diplomatic. 'Please excuse me, but this couldn't wait. There's been an attempt to destroy our costumes and masks.' I'd already decided that was as much as I was going to tell him. As I'd said to Nados, the fewer people who knew the details, the better.

Perantas tossed his half-eaten cake aside. 'What happened?'

'It's of no consequence.' I fervently asked Dionysos to make that true. 'But we don't want a second foray to enjoy more success. No one will risk a run-in with Demeter's slaves during the day, but we need the Brotherhood of Bellerophon to stand guard over our gear at night.'

Hard as I'd tried to find an alternative, this was the only solution I could come up with. I couldn't spare Kadous every night, if I wanted him awake and guarding Zosime by day.

Perantas' expression was distinctly unfriendly. 'I'm to make your apologies to Thettalos, am I? He told me what you said to him at Eumelos' funeral.'

'I will make my own apologies,' I said steadily, 'for any offence I have caused. But the central issue is seeing the play successfully staged. You said yourself that we owe it to Eumelos' memory. As I will explain to the Priestess of Demeter. She is the one who banned the Brotherhood from the Sanctuary, not me,' I reminded him.

'Do you have her permission for their return?' His surprise suggested he'd had his own encounters with the goddess' formidable servant.

'I will have, by the end of the day,' I assured him.

Though that really wasn't a conversation I was looking forward to. I silently begged Athena to intercede on my behalf with Demeter.

Perantas gave me a long, measuring look and then turned his attention to the almond cakes again. 'I will send word to Thettalos.'

'Good day.' I didn't wait to be dismissed, bowing politely and turning to Wetka with a cheery smile. Stony-faced, he led me back to the gate.

Since I was making such good progress with my list of unpalatable labours, I headed straight up to the Sanctuary and humbly asked the first slave I found for the boon of a private audience with the priestess.

I expected another lengthy wait. I can only assume curiosity got the better of the goddess' handmaiden. The slave quickly returned and led me into the little temple's inner sanctum. The priestess was standing in front of the superb marble statues of Demeter and Persephone. All three looked at me with the penetrating gaze of women who can see right through every foolish stratagem that a man might dream up.

I told the priestess everything, from Eumelos' death, through to the doctor's assessment of Apollonides' blisters, and all the trials and tribulations besetting Nados. I didn't insult her by asking for her discretion. If you can't trust a priestess to keep her mouth shut, who can you rely on?

Even so, she was less than pleased to be asked to approve the Brotherhood's return, even merely to serve as our night-time guards. I drew on every performance I've ever seen in the theatre, falling to my knees as I begged for this favour, in order that our comedy could be dedicated to Eumelos' memory.

I don't know if that made the difference, or if she simply wanted to shut me up, but she cut me short with a gesture.

'You have my permission, but tell Thettalos he'll answer to me for any unnecessary violence.'

I decided against asking what she might consider necessary violence.

'Thank you.' I retreated from the inner sanctum, bowing low to the priestess and the mother and daughter goddesses alike. 'Thank you.'

Outside, as I crossed the paved precinct and looked down the hill, I saw our chorus members were already gathering in our rehearsal courtyard. Hastily checking the sundial on a nearby building, I was relieved to see I wasn't late. It only felt as though I'd already put in a full day's work.

'Any disturbances?' I asked Kadous as my faithful slave came to greet me.

'None.' He looked nearly as tired as Nados.

'Good.' I nodded at the costume store. 'Get some sleep.'

As I joined the others, I heard Apollonides wryly explaining how a branch had flared up with unexpected sparks when he'd been piling firewood on the courtyard brazier last night.

'A sudden gust caught them and I realised I should have remembered what my father told me about checking the wind before taking a piss.' His face was far less red and swollen today. The Cycladean doctor's ointment was doing its job.

I supposed a faceful of hot embers was as good an explanation for his blisters as any. If I hadn't ever seen anyone who'd suffered such a bizarre accident, I don't imagine anyone else here had either.

We spent another intensely productive day rehearsing our songs and dances. Nados' potter arrived with the supplies we had asked for while most of the chorus were away finding lunch. None of the rest showed any curiosity about the jars and baskets being carried into the costume store. Whatever Zosime and Telesilla might be doing in there was presumably women's work and, thus, none of their concern.

Menekles and Apollonides began running quickly through their speeches, to teach the chorus their cues. While they were doing that, I explained to Lysicrates how I was planning to rewrite that debate scene. I saw him smile for the first time since we'd arrived in Corinth, and he quickly thought of a couple of excellent jokes for me to include.

As we resumed rehearsals, he still didn't seem to be talking to Hyanthidas, but I decided I'd take whatever good fortune the Sanctuary's goddesses saw fit to grant me.

Two arrivals brought our rehearsing to a timely end. The first was Thettalos and a handful of the Brotherhood coming to stand guard overnight. He had the chastened expression of a man who'd just had a bracing conversation with Demeter's priestess. That didn't stop him looking at me with barely veiled loathing.

The other newcomer was one of the litter-bearers from Eumelos' household. Diffident for such a large man, he made his way towards me through the departing chorus members. I was surprised to hear him speak in heavily accented Greek from somewhere far to the west.

'My master Nados sends this for you.' He handed me a note, the papyrus sealed and folded.

Nados had scrawled a few words and drawn a rough map. I held directions to lead me to Zopyros, a herbalist trading up on the Acrocorinth.

Chapter Eleven

I beckoned to Menekles. 'Talk to Thettalos, please. Don't tell him what's happened to the masks. Just say we need his men to watch over everything we're storing here. When Zosime's ready to go, see her safely back to the house, you and Kadous.' Hyanthidas would escort Telesilla home.

'Of course.' The actor glanced at the note in my hand. 'Where are you going?'

I explained.

'You're not going alone.'

'Of course not.' I beckoned to Lysicrates and Apollonides and showed them the map, relating my conversation with Nados.

'Right.' Lysicrates cracked his knuckles with a vehemence that made me uneasy.

I turned to Apollonides. 'You should wear your hat and cloak.'

He nodded and headed for the dining suite where Telesilla and Zosime were still diligently hoping to salvage our masks. As Menekles headed over to greet Thettalos, Lysicrates and I were left standing alone.

'This herbalist may know something, he may know

nothing. It's just a place to start looking.' I kept my tone as light as I could. 'If we get into a fight, that will only play into our enemies' hands.'

Lysicrates' expression was unforgiving. 'I don't have to lay a hand on someone to scare the shit out of them.'

Apollonides returned and we began the climb to the Acrocorinth. I couldn't decide if it was better or worse to have those terrifying drops on either side lost in shadow as the light faded.

The road was much busier now with men eager for an evening's entertainment. The citadel gates stood open, though the crowd meant there was some delay before we were waved through. As that gave us all a chance to get our breath back, I could hear Apollonides wheezing and that worried me: the sooner we got back to the house the better so he could suck on his medicinal steam.

While we waited, I looked out over the Corinthian plain, stretching northwards to the gulf. Approaching night drew a veil over the buildings around the agora and the sprawl of smallholdings blurred into invisibility. Lit windows and lamps on gateposts were golden pinpricks of light in constellations that mimicked the stars growing brighter overhead.

Apollonides cleared his throat and spat into the scrubby grass at the side of the road. 'Let's get on.'

Inside the Acrocorinth's walls, the taverns and brothels were busy. Unshuttered windows were bright with oil lamps while loud music and laughter spilled out through open doors. The night was fragrant with herb-scented fat spitting on the charcoal braziers offering grilled sausages and skewered morsels to hungry passers-by.

The atmosphere was taut with anticipation. We passed a vine-covered portico where a group of men sat, each one with a giggling girl on his lap. Each prostitute wore her hair threaded through with trailing ribbons. Wherever they might have come from, a Greek city or some barbarian wilderness, they wore their dresses Spartan-style, with the cloth pinned on one shoulder and falling away to leave their other breast bare. One of the revellers fondled his temporarily beloved's ripe nipple between his finger and thumb, his wet mouth greedy for her pouting lips. I felt my own interest distinctly aroused.

Despite himself, Lysicrates grunted. 'Maybe Corinth does have a few things to offer.'

High on the summit, the altars in front of Aphrodite's temple were blazing as the divine portions of sacrifices sent their savour to the heavens on clouds of smoke and steam. Those who had paid for those slaughtered beasts would be dining on the choicest cuts and enjoying the finest wines in private suites like those at Demeter's Sanctuary. I wondered if the acrobats and dancers from the famous temple were truly as athletic and as inventively erotic as they were so widely reputed to be.

Closer at hand, fire-baskets on street corners did away with any shadows where those with less pious motives might be lurking to prey on the unwarily drunk and the happily drained. They offered me light to check Nados' map to make sure we were on the right route.

Our path took us into a quieter, less well-frequented

district. We passed high walls with high windows, closed shutters and bolted gates. I was glad to have Apollonides and Lysicrates flanking me.

When we reached a small, irregular square with uneven paving there was no sign of life anywhere. With a sinking feeling, I wondered if this expedition had been a waste of time and effort.

'Can I see that map?' Lysicrates paused beneath the single lamp offering assistance to whoever was so thoroughly lost. After studying the papyrus for a moment, he knocked briskly on the door. 'We're here.'

The herbalist opened up with commendable promptness. He was younger than I expected, a slight man in an expensive tunic with his long hair slicked back with oil. 'Good evening. Good evening. It's a pleasure to welcome guests to our beloved city.'

If he could tell visitors from locals at a glance, we were dealing with no fool. 'You're Zopyros?'

'I am.' His smiled widened.

'A friend recommended you.' Lysicrates waved the scrap of papyrus before tucking it through his belt.

'I am honoured.' He stepped back from the threshold, inviting us in. 'How may I serve you?'

He was clearly expecting a brisk night's trade selling nostrums to those who knew where to find him. Small jars, some made of glass, some painted pottery, were tightly packed on the table in the centre of the room. Shelves on all sides held plain glazed jars, similar to those holding medicaments at the Asklepion. Lamps turned glass bottles of coloured oils into glowing jewels. The air was heady with perfume, undercut with the insidious scents of exotic intoxicants.

I looked for any blue glass vials like the one that had poisoned Eumelos, but none were apparent. Lysicrates strolled around the room, apparently studying the jars on the shelves. As he did so, he put himself between the herbalist and the only other doorway. It made sense for a man like Zopyros to meet his customers alone, especially ones with some embarrassment to confess. It also made sense for him to keep an ally close, in case someone was more interested in taking his silver instead of his medicines.

'Gentlemen?' he prompted.

I smiled hopefully. 'What do you sell to sustain a man's ardour?'

He grinned, conspiratorial. 'Any number of effective compounds. Is the issue—' he paused delicately '—an excess of haste in coming to a conclusion, or undue sloth in rising to the occasion?'

I tried to look convincingly sheepish. 'The former.'

'The latter,' said Lysicrates a breath later.

The herbalist looked momentarily puzzled before his expression brightened at the prospect of two sales. He glanced hopefully at Apollonides to see if he had a third customer but the actor kept his back turned, studying the bunches of dried flowers hanging by the front door. With any luck, he seemed embarrassed by our inadequacies. Friendship only goes so far.

Our new friend rubbed his gold-ringed hands together. 'Let me assist you.'

I noted he wore no sign of any hero cult affiliation. Presumably he sold his wares to whoever had the coin to pay him. I couldn't decide if that made him more or less contemptible, if he was indeed the man we sought.

'For you, good sir.' Zopyros' darting hand plucked a bottle from the array on the table, swift as a stork plucking a frog from a puddle. 'This should enable you to satisfy the most demanding of women.'

Unerring, he picked out a second tightly corked vial and offered it to Lysicrates. 'This will lend you the necessary vigour to enjoy a most rewarding visit to Corinth.'

Arms folded, unsmiling, Lysicrates leaned against the back door. He made no move to take the potion. 'Which one will leave us dead in our beds?'

The herbalist's ingratiating grin faded. 'I don't know what you mean.'

'A friend of ours took a dose to invigorate himself and it killed him,' I said bluntly.

'I've had no reports of any such accidents befalling my customers,' Zopyros said warily, half-turning so he could see us both. 'I can only offer my sincerest condolences.'

He seemed genuine but, just as easily, he could be lying through his teeth. I spend my days with men who can convince any audience that they're kings and heroes from the days when gods walked the earth.

'It's hard to make a complaint when you're stuck on the far side of the Styx,' Lysicrates observed coldly.

'Who said it was an accident?' I stared at Zopyros. 'We believe that our friend was murdered.'

'But you have no proof, otherwise you'd have gone

to the Council.' He looked back at me and I saw in his eyes that, at very least, he'd heard about Eumelos' death. Given the numbers at his funeral, that was not such a surprise.

'An innocent man wouldn't say that.' Lysicrates' voice hardened. 'An innocent man would say how dreadful, maybe ask for details about how our friend died, perhaps offer to help identify the poison that killed him.'

'Maybe ask why we suspect foul play,' I agreed. 'Maybe ask how he could help find out who was responsible. The dose that killed our friend came in a blue glass vial. Will we find more of those if we tear this place apart?'

'Not here,' retorted Zopyros, 'but you'll probably find them if you ransack more apothecaries' shops. Let us suppose that a man in my trade was fool enough to sell risky doses to rich fools. He wouldn't want to get them mixed up with honest aphrodisiacs and cures for cock rot. He'd keep them in distinctive bottles, and he'd keep them well out of sight.'

I had no answer to that.

'Besides, what would finding a stock of blue glass prove?' Zopyros was rallying, as the shock of our arrival faded. 'You can't prove that I mixed whatever dose your friend took, or even that it passed through my hands, can you?' he challenged us, before answering his own question. 'Of course not. Nobody could. So fuck off!'

As he raised his voice, we heard movement behind that rear door. The handle rattled, but since the door opened into the shop, Lysicrates simply leaned against it, bracing his feet and smiling unpleasantly at Zopyros.

For an actor who specialises in female roles, he conveyed unspoken menace unsettlingly well.

I snapped my fingers to reclaim the herbalist's attention. 'If you didn't sell the dose that killed Eumelos, who did?'

I took a step forward, only to halt. I didn't see where he had got it, but the herbalist was holding a knife. He jabbed the stained blade towards me, the gesture as forceful as his voice. 'I told you to fuck off!'

There was a thud against the door as someone attempted to charge the obstinate planks with a shoulder. Lysicrates held firm.

'What do you think?' I asked Apollonides.

Right on cue, he turned around, pulling back his cloak and hat. 'I think I want to know who did this.'

Timing is everything, in daily life, as it is in the theatre. Zopyros couldn't hide his reaction to the actor's blistered face. His lips parted on an infinitesimal indrawn breath. The barest hint of satisfaction proved beyond any doubt that he knew he was looking at his own handiwork.

That distracted him just long enough for me to knock that knife out of his hand. It's a trick my dead brother Lysanias taught me and the gods only know who taught him. I smacked the back of Zopyros' knife hand in the same instant that my other hand slapped the inside of his wrist.

The trick only works when you catch someone unawares. When it does work, it works spectacularly well. The blade flew across the room to scatter the bottles on the table. A handful toppled to the floor. One cracked and the aniseed scent of an indigestion cure filled the air.

Zopyros stared at me in utter disbelief. Then whoever was in the back room launched another assault on the planks. Lysicrates stepped aside so quickly that the door flew open to slam back against the shelves.

Zopyros' would-be saviour hurtled into the room, unable to stop himself crashing into the table. Every bottle and jar went flying. As the man tried to recover his balance, Lysicrates was on him. He forced the man to the floor, his knees pinning the back of his victim's thighs. The actor wrapped his arms around the man's neck in a wrestling hold. The hapless man's spine arched with a cracking sound. He slapped the floor in a desperate attempt at submission. Lysicrates loosened the stranglehold, but not enough to offer him any chance of escape.

I snatched up Zopyros' knife and levelled the blade at the herbalist. To my utter astonishment, he burst out laughing.

'All right, all right.' He raised his hands in surrender. 'Please, stop before you cost me any more breakages. I'll guarantee my brother's good behaviour.'

The man gurgled what sounded like agreement. Lysicrates looked at me, brows raised.

'As long as he stays on the floor.' I still had the knife, and any more fighting would be three against two. Unless that careless assumption got us all killed. 'Is there anyone else back there?'

His hands still raised, Zopyros shook his head. 'Just the two of us.'

'You expect me to trust a Corinthian?' Lysicrates released his victim and stood up. He walked to the door, to satisfy himself the room beyond was empty.

I considered shutting the herbalist's brother in there before deciding against it. The last thing we needed was him slipping out through some unsuspected exit to summon reinforcements. He could stay where he was, flat on the floor, forehead resting on his crossed forearms.

I looked at Zopyros, unsmiling. 'Are you proud of your achievement?'

'Forgive me.' The herbalist bowed to Apollonides. 'This was business. It's nothing personal.'

'It's pretty fucking personal for me.' Apollonides outstripped Lysicrates' menace without breaking a sweat.

'Who did you sell the hellebore to?' I demanded. 'Who bought the poison that killed Eumelos?'

'The hellebore lotion—' Zopyros turned his hands palm upwards. 'My customers pay for my discretion.'

Lysicrates smiled nastily. 'If you want them to think that we beat it out of you, I'm happy to oblige.'

'We can smash every bottle and jar in the place,' Apollonides agreed, 'to make your bruises look more convincing.'

Zopyros looked at me. 'I was thinking more in terms of you paying for such information. I am simply a businessman.'

'No,' I said flatly. 'You can tell us, or you can answer to the Council, when we accuse you of murder and attempted murder.'

'No,' Zopyros said instantly. 'I have no idea what

happened to your friend. I'll swear to that on any altar you name. As for the hellebore lotion, that wouldn't kill anyone, not unless they tried eating a mask.'

'So what was the plan?'

Zopyros folded his arms. 'If I tell you what I know, can you promise me that my customer won't hear what you've learned from me?'

'That depends on what you tell us.' I wasn't making any deals.

The herbalist grimaced. 'Then I'll deny everything, if anyone comes asking, when I'm standing before the Council if needs be. Kittos here will go on oath that we've never even met.' He nudged his brother's foot with his toe.

'Here all night, alone.' The man's voice was muffled as he lay there facing the floor. 'No customers at all.'

Mention of customers made me realise we needed to leave before someone came genuinely looking for a rise under their tunic.

'We'll keep your secrets as long as you keep ours. As long as you don't tell whoever's paid you that we know what they've done.'

'Do you think I'm a fool?' he protested. 'If they poisoned your friend, and believe me, I had nothing to do with that, they've proved that they're willing to kill. I was only paid to make sure your play was a shambles, with your chorus ripping their masks off halfway through.' He glanced at Apollonides with mingled satisfaction and regret.

My blood ran cold as I realised how close our enemies had come to success. 'Who paid you?'

'A man called Sosandros.' Zopyros shrugged.

'Who does he work for?' I demanded.

Zopyros shrugged again. 'I've no idea.'

I tried another approach. 'What hero cult does he belong to?'

This time Zopyros hesitated.

'If you can't tell us anything useful,' Lysicrates growled, 'we'll just have to smash everything in here, to make sure you can't make any more mischief.'

'Maybe break both your arms for good measure,' Apollonides agreed darkly.

A blind man could see this was no idle threat.

'Isn't it just easier to tell us?' I invited the herbalist. 'We won't tell anyone.'

'I have heard,' Zopyros said reluctantly, 'though I cannot vouch for the truth of it, that Sosandros is sworn to the Sons of Heracles.'

So it was no coincidence that we'd found so many trinkets decorated with the divine hero's club after the brawl on that first day.

'Who's their paymaster?' Lysicrates looked at me.

I shrugged. I had no idea.

'Wait a moment.' Apollonides was still intent on the herbalist. 'Was it just the chorus masks that were poisoned? What about the rehearsal masks, the stage-skins and the costumes?'

'As far as I know, it's just the masks for the performance,' Zopyros assured him. 'Sosandros talked about using the hellebore on the costumes but I said that risked blistering the hands of whoever sorted them out before the play. Then the whole game would be up.'

It really was just a game to him. I resisted the urge to punch him so hard he'd be shitting teeth for days.

'Let's go,' I said shortly.

Apollonides put his hat back on to shadow his face and opened the door to the street. I thrust Zopyros' knife deep into the table and bent it until the blade snapped. Tossing the hilt on the floor, I followed the actor out. Lysicrates was close behind me, walking backwards to keep the herbalist and his brother in view until he slammed the outer door shut.

We walked swiftly back towards the bustling heart of the citadel by unspoken agreement. When we reached a busy thoroughfare, Lysicrates was the first to speak.

'Do you think we can trust him to keep his mouth shut? He's proved he's a treacherous bastard.'

'I think we can trust him to serve his own interests. Letting this Sosandros know he's betrayed him would hardly be good for his health.' I shook my head. 'That's not what bothers me. Zopyros admitted to poisoning the masks but he swore he had no hand in Eumelos' death.'

'So he's a lying arsehole.' Lysicrates had no doubt about that. 'He knew we had him caught, so there was no point in denying he supplied the hellebore. But he'd hardly admit to supplying the means for a murder in a place like this. The Council would probably hand him over to their executioner without a trial.'

'Maybe so.' I wasn't convinced.

Though I was certain of one thing: the attacks to stop our play would continue.

Chapter Twelve

I was trapped in a labyrinth with no idea how to find the way out. Turning a corner showed me three more routes. They all looked exactly the same. Any one might be a dead end. I might stumble into some pitfall in this ominous gloom, to lie lost and injured until I died of thirst. But I had to go on. In the shadows behind me, I could hear running footsteps, getting faster and closer. Was my pursuer man, or beast, or something monstrous in between?

I woke up with a gasp. After an endless moment, I realised I had been dreaming. I lay there limp with relief. Then I looked for any hint of daylight through the window shutters. No such luck. But I didn't dare sleep again, and risk returning to that dreadful maze.

Zosime rolled over to press her naked body against the length of mine. Her toes stroked the top of my foot. I drew a breath. She laid a finger on my lips before leaning over to kiss me. Her thigh slid over mine. As she kissed me again, longer and deeper, she reached for my hand and cupped it around her breast.

I freed my lips from hers. 'Have you . . . ?'

'All taken care of, before you got home.'

As she spoke she straddled me, shrugging off the blanket. She moved slowly at first, the feel of her against me softer and more inviting with every stroke. I grew harder, my breath coming faster. She took me inside her in one swift movement and her hips bore down on mine. I caressed her nipples until I felt her flesh tighten around my manhood. I took firm hold of her hips, moving more quickly beneath her. She rode me ever faster until ecstasy rippled through her.

I bit my lip. 'I can't—'

With one swift movement, we swapped places. I was already so close to the brink, it wasn't long before I was spent in a glorious spasm. I sank down to lay my head between her breasts, hearing her heartbeat gradually slow. Beads of sweat trickled and tickled between my chest and her belly.

She stroked my hair. 'Better?'

'Oh, yes.' I kissed her soft skin.

Now Hypnos had me in his clutches. I didn't care what city we were in, still less whatever else might be happening. As Zosime shifted beneath me, I rolled onto my back. I was asleep before she came back to bed.

I slept so deeply that sunlight shone bright around the edges of the shutters when I finally woke. Opening the window that overlooked the courtyard, I saw the others sitting around the table as a kitchen girl served breakfast.

I waved to Kadous as he looked upwards. 'Water for washing, please.'

I made myself presentable as fast as I could but the others were ready to leave for the Sanctuary by the time

I got downstairs. I tore open a hunk of barley bread and filled it with mashed chickpeas, fragrant with herbs and garlic. 'Let's go.'

Zosime took my hand as we walked through the city and followed the rising road up to Demeter's Sanctuary.

'What happened last night?'

I told her the tale of our visit to the Acrocorinth. 'So it looks as if it's just the performance masks that were poisoned.'

She pursed her lips, unconvinced. 'We'll look utter fools if we're wrong. I'll check the costumes anyway.'

'How?' I objected. 'You can't cover yourself in blisters.'

'I can moisten cloth and test it against the inside of my arm or my thigh, somewhere that won't be obvious. I'll wash it off if I feel the slightest tingle.' She wasn't going to be dissuaded. 'I'm sure Apollonides will share his ointment if needs be.'

A few steps ahead, the actor halted as he heard his name. 'What's that?'

'Never mind.' Zosime smiled at him.

Apollonides' thoughts had already moved on. 'I've been wondering, in case someone in our chorus can't keep his mouth shut, should we keep the leatherwork to ourselves?'

He looked at me meaningfully, as if there was a real possibility that some Corinthian passer-by might understand and go running to tell our enemies.

Lysicrates stopped walking as well. 'We don't want someone breaking in to cut everything to pieces.'

'I suppose so,' I said reluctantly. One of the very best jokes in the play relied on the special props that my brothers had devised. It wouldn't be nearly as funny without the whole chorus involved. Then again, half a loaf is better than none. Four of us in on the secret should still raise a good laugh. 'I'll need to make a few changes to that scene.'

Menekles took a few long strides to draw level with me. I expected him to ask me about the other rewrites, but he had something else on his mind. He'd been talking to Lysicrates and Apollonides.

'What are we going to do about these Sons of Heracles?'

'I'd say we do nothing. If we make any move against them before the performance, if we give them an excuse for more violence, we've handed a weapon to all of these factions who want to stop our play.' A good night's sleep had clarified my thoughts. 'As long as they think we don't know about their hellebore lotion, there's no reason for them to risk anything else. They'll just bide their time, come to watch the performance, and wait for their poison to strike us down.'

'Do you think this weasel, this Zopyros, will keep his mouth shut?' Menekles didn't sound convinced.

'I think so, to save himself aggravation.' Though there wasn't anything we could do if he went running to tell tales.

Menekles still wasn't satisfied. 'What do you think they'll do, when they realise they've been foiled?'

I heaved a sigh. 'I have no idea.'

Menekles grimaced. 'If we'd known what we were getting into . . .'

Still, the day was fine, and a fresh breeze made the climb to Demeter's Sanctuary that much easier. The chorus was already assembling and the last few singers arrived close behind us. We were soon ready to start rehearsing while Zosime continued working on the masks. All we lacked was musicians.

Apollonides came out of the costume store, concerned. 'There's no sign of Hyanthidas or Telesilla.'

'Has anyone seen our piper on their way up here?' I called out to the chorus.

Their only answers were shrugs and shaken heads. There was no cause for alarm just yet, I told myself sternly. The musicians simply didn't have a houseful of talkative actors to wake them if they overslept.

That didn't loosen the clutch of dread in my guts. Hyanthidas had composed all the music that enhanced the actors' performances, not only the songs for the chorus. He was integral to our play and irreplaceable.

I beckoned to Menekles. 'Where did you last see Hyanthidas and Telesilla?'

He looked at me uncertainly. 'We parted ways in the agora.'

'This is their own city,' Apollonides protested.

Lysicrates came over to join us. 'That's supposed to keep them safe? When we know there are any number of bastards here who would happily do us harm?'

I wished I could dismiss that as his grudge against Corinth but I could imagine too many plausible and violent scenarios. I also saw the chorus singers looking at the four of us, growing curious about this delay.

I looked for any signs of guilty knowledge, for any veiled satisfaction that might suggest a hero cult spy in our ranks. I saw absolutely nothing. I couldn't decide if that was reassuring, or if it merely proved that Corinth's festivals train actors as talented as the city's singers.

'They could have eaten some bad fish and spent the night each hugging a bucket.'

The three actors looked at me dubiously.

'Let's find out.' I saw Kadous returning with a jug of fresh spring water, and beckoned him over. 'Do you know where Hyanthidas lives?'

'I can find out,' the Phrygian said, obliging.

'It's not like him to be so late, without sending word.' I resolutely ignored catastrophic possible explanations. 'Go and make sure there's nothing they need.'

'Of course.' Kadous understood what I wasn't saying.

I clapped my hands. 'Let's make a start. We haven't got time to waste.'

Menekles stepped forward onto the stretch of well-trodden ground serving as our stage. In the guise of the Homeric hero Meriones, he claimed this stretch of as-yet-unknown land for his shipload of Hellenes. His posture was noble, his gestures commanding, and his deep voice echoed around the courtyard.

Apollonides, playing Thersites, hovered like a gad-fly. He challenged every bold proclamation. He seized on every hesitation. Finally, he forced Meriones to admit that, yes, they were hopelessly lost.

His voice wasn't as strong as I was used to. Thersites didn't caper and leap as he tormented Meriones. Several times, Apollonides seemed on the verge of breathlessness.

I couldn't spare any time to worry. The chorus' first cue was approaching. Thankfully, Lysicrates is one of those people who can pluck any note out of thin air. He stepped forward to sing the first line, confident and full-voiced.

The chorus followed his lead with impressive promptness, and I led the singers through our first dance. There were a few mis-steps but nothing caused more than a hasty scurry to catch up.

As we finished singing, Lysicrates stepped forward in his first, and main, speaking role. Incongruous in his tunic and without his beard hidden by a mask, he greeted these ancient Achaeans as Egeria, a voluptuous and voracious Etruscan matron. These wayward mariners had washed up on the wild, wooded shores of Italy, far from any hope of civilisation.

Even lacking costume and wig, Lysicrates was mesmerising. Several of the chorus doubled up laughing as lustful Egeria pursued startled Thersites.

'Let me show you my favourite hidden hollow,' she cooed, before turning to the audience, lascivious. 'I'll soon have this straying lamb entangled deep in my undergrowth.'

I wasn't smiling. Back in Athens, Lysicrates had chased Apollonides all around the stage. Now Thersites edged away, step by wary step. Egeria stalked him with the measured intent of my mother's ferrets pursuing a leather-gnawing mouse.

Distracted, I nearly missed my own cue. As the chorus leader, I had to take the lead in the debate between the Achaean warriors and the noble Meriones over how their new colony would be governed.

I really wished I wasn't in the midst of the singers, as the first proposal to be made was the oppressive Spartan system; condemning the locals to serfdom and training citizens as warriors with merciless rigour. In Athens, the chorus emphatically rejected this. Here in Corinth, I wanted to see the faces around me, in case someone's expression betrayed the Sons of Heracles' sympathies with the Spartans.

The debate moved on to hereditary kingship, with Meriones and Thersites bickering loudly over who was more fit to rule. The chorus briskly dismissed such pretensions from both of these heroes, endorsing all men's duty to help their neighbours, so that when hard times came, they could expect help in return. Not quite what the chorus in Athens had proclaimed, but more palatable to a Corinthian audience.

The singing was loud and enthusiastic and everyone was making encouraging strides with their dance steps. When we finished, I clapped my hands in appreciation.

'Let's go straight to the next choral piece. The song about building this new city in the wilderness.'

I avoided Menekles' eye. I didn't need to see his unspoken question about the play's rewrites. There were other issues we needed to discuss if we were using our special props differently.

Since the singers knew nothing about that, they were content to carry on celebrating the glories of the temples they would build to honour the gods. Hyanthidas' inspired music made this song a highlight of the whole play. Back in Athens, I'd assumed he was inspired by the new buildings that Pericles persuaded the People's Assembly to finance, to raise our city from the rubble left by the invading Persians. Now we'd come to Corinth, I realised this melody showed Hyanthidas' pride in his own city.

I desperately wanted to know where the piper was, to be reassured that all was well with him and Telesilla. But Kadous didn't reappear until we were ready to halt for the noon break. At least we'd managed a nearly complete run through by then.

'Well done, everybody. Get some food and drink, and we'll start again when the heat's passed.' I managed an encouraging smile as I included all the Corinthians in my praise.

As I walked towards Kadous, I couldn't hide my concern. He raised a discreetly placating hand, so I guessed the worst hadn't happened. I'd be happier if he was smiling though.

'Well?' I demanded, low-voiced, as soon as I reached him.

'Come with me.'

I glanced over my shoulder to see Menekles and Lysicrates watching us with expressionless faces. I managed a tight grin and gestured to indicate that I'd be leaving for a while.

I followed Kadous between the buildings. 'Where is he?'

'In the agora.'

Not what I was expecting, but better than in the Asklepion. We reached the broad steps down to the road where we could walk side by side.

'What's the problem?'

'You need to hear that from him,' Kadous said carefully.

So it was something he wanted to steer well clear of. As we walked down to the city, I wondered what hidden rocks might be about to wreck my shipload of Achaeans. If Hyanthidas refused to play, our performance could not go on.

Neither of us spoke till we reached the agora and its cheery, noisy bustle. I surveyed the busy market stalls and the crowded colonnades, as well as the devotees and visitors crowded around the fountains and shrines.

'Up there.' The Phrygian pointed to the paved precinct around the temple of Apollo.

Our missing musician sat on the lowest ledge of the pedestal that supported the god's reclining statue. Leaning back, with his ankles crossed and hands interlaced behind his head, Hyanthidas gazed out across the heads of the crowds. His eyes were so distant I don't think he'd have noticed a centaur strolling past. Kadous fell back, to follow a pace behind me as I walked up the slope.

'Good to see you're safe and well.'

Startled out of his preoccupation, Hyanthidas sat up straight. 'Philocles. I should have sent word—'

'Never mind,' I said mildly, taking a seat beside him. 'Is Telesilla all right?'

He reddened beneath the summer sun's bronze on his cheekbones. 'She's fine. She's at home. She . . .'

I let the silence between us lengthen, keeping my expression amiable, inviting him to continue.

'She says I'm making a fuss about nothing.' The tense undercurrent in his voice told me they'd had a blazing row.

'What's the problem?' I kept my tone light, hiding my concern as best I could.

Another silence opened up amid the tumult on all sides.

'It's Lysicrates,' Hyanthidas burst out. 'I know he didn't want to come here, but he insults my home and my countryfolk at every opportunity. I want to shut his mouth with my fists.'

I was shocked. 'I know he's said a few things out of turn, in the heat of the moment—'

'That's not the half of it,' Hyanthidas said savagely. 'I know what he says when I'm not there to hear him. How women performing in public is shameful. How I stand by while Telesilla degrades herself. How he reckons that Nados, Aithon and Simias most likely conspired to poison Eumelos, so they could steal his silver for themselves. That they probably beat Dardanis to death and buried his body in a ditch. What else can you expect from Corinthians? This is a city of whores and liars, after all.' He glared at me. 'And the rest of you just sit there and let him spew his slanders, never daring to contradict him.'

Now I was struggling for words. 'I never heard—'

'You deny he called us cowards?' Hyanthidas challenged me. 'Poisoners as treacherous as Persians? As hard to catch as bilge rats? That must be Medea's legacy, mustn't it? She always disappeared when she was cornered. So Lysicrates says.'

'I do deny it, absolutely,' I snapped. 'When's he supposed to have said all this nonsense?'

'Last night,' the piper spat. 'When you came back from the Acrocorinth empty-handed.'

My rising anger was instantly quenched. 'Who told you this?'

Hyanthidas shook his breath, stubborn. 'No. He won't get a thrashing on my account.'

That meant a slave had been gossiping. That's why Kadous had insisted I hear this for myself. One slave accusing another won't end well for either of them. Except this wasn't gossip. Gossip has at least some passing acquaintance with the truth, however badly that gets mangled as it passes from person to person. This was different. This was a putrid concoction of lies.

'Last night on the Acrocorinth,' I said carefully, 'we found the man who sold the hellebore lotion that was used to poison our masks. By the time we got back to the house, Apollonides was wheezing like an old donkey in the mountains. No one was sitting about chatting, never mind insulting Corinth. We tucked him up in bed and then we all went straight to sleep.'

Hyanthidas wanted to believe me. At least I hoped that's what I was seeing in his face. But he had no reason to doubt whoever had told him these falsehoods.

'Tromes.' I realised who the liar must be. 'When we got back, when he asked if there was anything we needed, he asked if we'd enjoyed our visit to the Acrocorinth. We said we hadn't.'

To be strictly accurate, Lysicrates had still been in a filthy mood, and had said the whole fucking evening had been a complete waste of fucking time. Then Menekles told Tromes to boil some water for those herbs the doctor had given Apollonides. But telling Hyanthidas all that would hardly help matters.

'This morning?' the piper demanded. 'Who said what over breakfast?'

'I've no idea,' I said reluctantly. 'I slept late. Kadous?' I looked at the slave, and my nod gave him permission to speak.

He answered steadily, looking Hyanthidas in the eye. 'They talked about today's rehearsal and decided that the more rest Apollonides gets, the sooner his lungs will recover from the hellebore's effects. Then they discussed how to play their scenes differently, to save as much of his strength as possible for when he really needs it.'

I was so relieved to hear this explanation for the changes I'd seen this morning, that I nearly missed what Kadous said next.

'Besides, Tromes wasn't even there.'

'Not at all?' I wanted to be certain.

Kadous shook his head. 'He was nowhere in the house, from before first light. He hadn't come back by the time we left.'

I turned to Hyanthidas. 'He was with you?' Telling more lies. But I couldn't understand why he would do this. Tromes was Perantas Bacchiad's man.

Now Hyanthidas was looking suspicious. 'I didn't see him until we were just about to leave for the Sanctuary. He turned up at my door, all hot and bothered. He's been coming by to seek my advice ever since you arrived, asking if I think he should tell his master how much you hate Corinth and the Corinthians.'

'Perantas may own him,' I said slowly, 'but I'll wager the weight of his lying tongue in silver that Tromes is serving a different master.'

A master who'd bought his treachery with a fat purse. Or someone who'd promised him that fat purse, provided our rehearsals collapsed into acrimony. I wondered exactly where Tromes planned to flee as soon as he had the coin he needed to reinvent himself as a free man. Assuming he didn't drop dead first, poisoned by a cup of wine he was given to celebrate this vile scheme's success. All of this explained the anxiety I'd seen in his eyes from time to time. The apprehension that I'd mistaken for fear of Perantas' displeasure.

I looked at Hyanthidas. 'I swear to you, on my honour, here in Apollo's presence, that you've been deceived. None of us have been slandering Corinth. Ask Zosime if you wish. She'll tell the truth without fear or favour.

She's no Athenian who'll stay silent out of loyalty.'

It cost me a pang to say so, but it couldn't be denied.

Hyanthidas' cheeks coloured with embarrassment. 'That's what Telesilla said.'

'We are both blessed in the women who love us,' I said with the friendliest smile I could manage.

The musician gratefully seized that peace-offering. 'We should ask their advice about this.'

'Absolutely.' I agreed whole-heartedly. 'Meantime, we should get back to the Sanctuary, and continue our rehearsals.' I gestured at the agora. The midday crowds in search of food, drink, shade and conversation were beginning to thin.

Hyanthidas got to his feet. 'I'll go and fetch my pipes.'

From his self-conscious look, I guessed he'd also be apologising to Telesilla.

'Take your time.' I stood up and looked around for someone who could sell me and Kadous some late lunch and a cup of wine.

When Hyanthidas returned, we walked slowly back up to the Sanctuary. On the way I wondered wrathfully who had so nearly succeeded in setting us at each other's throats.

I was angry with myself for not seeing this trouble brewing. I was also cross with Hyanthidas for being so ready to believe these lies, after all the time we'd spent together in Athens. That didn't make Lysicrates blameless. He'd been inclined to think the worst here in Corinth and far too ready to say so.

No wonder some enemy had decided to try the trick

that had worked so well for Cadmus of Thebes. When he sowed the dragon's teeth and found armed warriors springing from the ground, one carefully thrown stone had seen them all turn on each other.

By the time we arrived at the courtyard, I was thinking about a different stratagem. I remembered my dream of being lost in the Minotaur's labyrinth. Theseus was Athens' own hero and he had found his way through that lethal place by following Ariadne's thread. Maybe finding out who was paying this treacherous bastard Tromes would give us some answers about who was out to wreck our play. The man who had started by murdering Eumelos.

Chapter Thirteen

I forced myself to concentrate on the afternoon's rehearsals, and thankfully we made good progress. As the sunlight softened and the shadows lengthened, I called everyone together. 'Let's decide where we need to do most work.'

The Corinthian singers were eager to put their hands up, to acknowledge the passages in the play where they were dissatisfied with themselves thus far. I could see their growing determination to make this an exceptional performance.

Once we had a plan for tomorrow's rehearsals, Hyanthidas packed his pipes away.

'Everything all right?' Menekles asked him, pausing as he took a cup of water to Zosime.

'Family matter,' Hyanthidas said briefly. 'Sorted out now.'

Lysicrates was passing behind them. He clapped a hand on Hyanthidas' shoulder. 'If there's anything we can do, say the word.'

That casual gesture probably did as much to convince the musician that he had been lied to as anything I had said.

As the chorus was leaving, Thettalos and his hench-men arrived to stand watch through the night.

'This is a waste of my time,' he announced to no one in particular. 'There are ten or twenty families and local societies dining here tonight. No one will try anything stupid with so many potential witnesses.'

Zosime heard him as she came out of the costume store. 'Or they'll think it's an ideal time to sneak in, with so many people to lose themselves among if they're caught making mischief.' She closed the door and pulled the leather thong to draw the hidden bolt across.

Apollonides emerged from the wine store with an am-phora. He shook it with a hollow slosh and handed it to Thettalos. 'There's enough here to quench your thirsts overnight without sending you to sleep.'

'As long as you remember to add enough water.' As he secured our second storeroom, Lysicrates' smile didn't quite draw the sting from his words.

Seeing Thettalos' belligerent scowl, I winced. Lysi-crates looked surprised. 'What did I say?'

I shook my head. 'It can wait.'

Menekles rattled the keys. 'I'll take these to the priestess.'

'We'll wait for you down by the road.' I slipped my arm around Zosime's shoulders.

When we reached the broad steps, she twisted free of my embrace and searched my face. 'What is going on?'

Apollonides and Lysicrates were equally curious. Hyanthidas wouldn't meet anyone's gaze and Kadous' expression was studiously blank.

'I'll explain when Menekles gets back.'

'Let's stop blocking the path.' Hyanthidas started walking down to the road.

He had a point. A steady stream of people were heading up to the temple precinct, carrying their offerings for the priestess' deft knife. Those who'd arrived earlier were returning with the meat left after the goddesses and their handmaidens had taken their cuts. Demeter and Persephone must have a particular fondness for suckling pig, judging from the savoury scents rising from cooking braziers. More people arrived carrying covered dishes and wine amphorae. Pipe trills and lyres being tuned prompted snatches of song and laughter.

This everyday activity reminded me that Corinth wasn't so very different from home. We are all Hellenes, sharing one language and worshipping the same gods. These good citizens enjoying their celebrations had nothing to do with the hero cults that were so obsessed with their rivalries and ambitions. These ordinary Corinthians were the people we'd come to entertain.

'How did you get on today?' I asked hopefully as we followed the piper. There was still enough daylight to see that Zosime's arms remained smooth and unblemished.

'Everything seems safe to wear.' She smiled briefly. 'Your herbalist must have told the truth.'

'That's good news.' Though I realised that also meant the corrupt bastard was probably telling the truth when he said he had no idea who had poisoned Eumelos.

'This smell of food is making me ravenous,' Menekles

175

said cheerfully as he caught up with us. 'Where are we eating dinner?'

Still several paces ahead of us, Hyanthidas stopped and turned. 'At my house.'

'Are you sure?' Apollonides asked.

I could see why he was uncertain. Someone offering his home's hospitality didn't usually look quite so tense. Hyanthidas looked like a man facing a thrashing.

'Is Telesilla expecting us?' Zosime wanted to know.

Hyanthidas nodded. 'Though I will go on ahead and see what I can do to help.' He looked at me. 'Explain what's been going on, and why we need to talk well away from treacherous ears.'

'What do you mean?' Menekles was alarmed, but Hyanthidas was already hurrying away.

I sympathised with the musician. I'd be embarrassed to hear someone was telling this tale about me. I was also irritated that he'd left me holding this particular boiling pot.

'Philocles?' Zosime slipped her arm through mine.

I started walking. 'We should have been on our guard for treachery closer at hand.'

The others drew closer, trying to hear what I was saying without treading on each other's heels. By the time we reached the agora, I had told them the whole sorry story.

'Kadous can bear witness to today's events,' I concluded. As the others assured him that wasn't nec-essary, I turned to the slave. 'So where is Hyanthidas' house?'

'Follow me.' He led the way.

As we followed, the three actors and Zosime fell silent, preoccupied. I left them to their thoughts. I'd had my say.

Hyanthidas' house was a good distance from the agora, tucked away in a district of narrow streets and modest houses. This made me unexpectedly cheerful. It felt considerably more like home.

A young man standing by an open gate waved when he recognised Kadous. I remembered him from our first evening here, when he'd escorted Telesilla to the tavern. Inside the small courtyard, we found a single-storey building that ran across the far side of the paving and turned a corner to continue towards the gate.

'Good evening,' the slave said politely. 'May I take your cloaks?'

As we were unpinning and handing over our wraps, Hyanthidas appeared from the furthest door of the house carrying a table top long enough to be awkward even for a man of his height.

Lysicrates hurried forward. 'Let me help you with that.' He cleared his throat uncomfortably. 'It seems I owe you an apology.'

'It seems there are plenty of those to go around.' Hyanthidas was equally self-conscious.

'Not until we've eaten.' Telesilla was sitting on a stool beside a cooking brazier, stirring a bubbling pot. Whatever she was cooking smelled delicious.

'What can I do to help?' asked Zosime.

'As soon as they've got the table set up, could you fetch

the other dishes? Arion will show you where everything is.' Telesilla nodded at the slave.

Menekles, Apollonides and I hurried to fetch the furniture while Zosime followed Arion into the house.

With us working together, dinner was soon ready. A broad shallow dish held what I guessed was a layered salad, judging by the bowl of spiced raisin dressing beside it. A fat nut omelette was waiting to be sliced. There were anchovies fried in wine, shredded cabbage in a pepper and thyme sauce, and fine wheat bread. Our musicians were going to entertain us in fine style.

'Mix the wine,' Telesilla told Hyanthidas as she deftly cracked eggs into a bowl. Beating them briskly, she stirred the golden liquid swiftly into her cooking pot.

The piper poured amber wine and fresh water into a tall jug. He looked at us with a strained smile. 'Who shall we offer our libations to this evening?'

'Apollo,' Menekles said promptly. 'Asking his aid to heal any rift between us, and to help us confound those who contrived this misunderstanding.'

Hyanthidas handed the actor a cup. 'Let's invite Athena's blessings as well, and seek the gift of her wisdom.'

We offered the first sips of wine to the divine guardians of both our cities, murmuring contrition for past follies, and resolving to do better. With the air cleared, we sat around the table.

Arion hefted the cooking pot from the brazier. Fish in cheese sauce was spiced with pepper, lovage, and rue berries and finished with a dusting of ground cumin. The shallow bowl held shredded meat and salty cheese on slices of barley bread layered with cucumber, pine nuts and chopped onions. I tasted ginger and coriander in the olive oil and wine dressing, sweetened with honey and raisins.

'You are a wonderful hostess,' I told Telesilla. 'Layered salads are a particular favourite of mine, and Zosime always says how time-consuming they are to prepare.'

'You are most welcome.' She was looking a lot happier than she had done when we arrived. 'Please, eat.'

None of us needed any further urging. Eventually, though, none of us could eat any more. Kadous and Arion began to clear away the meal's remnants and Hyanthidas mixed another serving of wine.

'So.' He resumed his seat. 'What now?'

I took a long swallow of wine. 'Tromes may be Perantas Bacchiad's slave but I take it we're agreed that he's sowing discord on someone else's orders?'

Lysicrates set his cup down on the table. 'It makes no sense for Perantas to pay us to stage the play while he's urging Tromes to wreck it behind our backs.'

Apollonides looked troubled. 'He won't be pleased if he learns we've been keeping this from him. Tromes is his property. He has a right to know.'

'But we only have half a story,' Menekles countered. 'Surely Perantas will want to know everything?'

'If we tell him now, there's every chance he'll hand Tromes over to someone like Thettalos,' I said with distaste. 'To beat some answers out of him.'

'How long will it take to get to the truth,' wondered

Menekles, 'as opposed to whatever Tromes thinks Perantas wants to hear?'

'Or whatever he thinks might save his neck.' Zosime grimaced.

'Assuming Thettalos doesn't beat him to death first.' Telesilla shook her head.

We all fell silent. The only sound was Kadous and Arion over by the storeroom door scraping the leavings off our plates into a refuse pail.

Kadous looked up and our eyes met. We both knew that, whether we told Perantas sooner or later, Tromes' fate was sealed. The Bacchiad wouldn't forgive such betrayal from a slave and the law would endorse whatever brutal vengeance the wealthy man chose to exact.

'So how do we learn the full story?' I looked around the table.

'Set someone to follow Tromes?' Lysicrates suggested. 'To see where he goes and who he meets?'

'Who do we send?' Apollonides gestured around the courtyard. 'We're the only ones who know what he's been doing, and he'll recognise any of us.'

Menekles agreed. 'Besides, there's no chance we could get close enough to hear what he might be saying, so how could we learn anything useful?'

'What about one of Eumelos' lads? The one from Kenchreai, what's his name, Simias? Tromes won't know who he is.' Lysicrates leaned forward, elbows on the table. 'They have a cockerel in this fight, if whoever's behind this shit-stirring killed their mentor.'

Hyanthidas shook his head. 'The more people we tell,

the more risk of word getting back to Perantas, even by accident.'

I saw Menekles' gaze stray towards Arion. 'We can't use our own slaves,' I said firmly.

'Absolutely not.' Telesilla was adamant. 'If an accusation comes down to one slave's word against another, they'll both have their evidence tested under torture. I won't put Arion at such risk.'

I nodded. 'The law's the same in Athens and I value Kadous too much for that.'

'Besides,' Hyanthidas pointed out, 'Tromes knows both of them by sight.'

'You're talking as if we're taking this before a court.' Lysicrates drummed his fingers on the tabletop. 'I take it Hyanthidas would have to come forward as the accuser, because none of us have any standing to bring a case before Corinth's courts. Then there would have to be a preliminary hearing, to test the evidence before a prosecution could be launched. How long would that take to arrange?'

He shook his head. 'It's not just that our argument is as threadbare as a beggar's blanket. I can't see an Athenian magistrate being convinced, if one of us was acting for a bunch of Corinthians accusing a man of our city's most well-born, especially after we'd spent nearly a year away from home. Do you want to face counter-accusations of disloyalty to your fellow citizens or of vexatious litigation? Assuming the case wasn't thrown out for lack of credibility or proof, then we'd still have to wait for a date when your Council will be sitting in judgement. There's no chance that could happen before we stage the play.'

The actor reached for his wine as Telesilla and Hyan-thidas nodded reluctantly. 'We don't have time for all that. Not when whoever's working against us will use all his influence to weight the scales of any legal proceedings in his favour. We need to thrust a spear through the spokes of his chariot wheels and wreck this bastard's plans once and for all.'

'Tromes is just the stick someone's using to knock this olive harvest down from the tree,' Menekles said thoughtfully. 'Why not see if we can use him ourselves?'

'To draw whoever's behind all this into the daylight?' Apollonides clearly liked that idea.

So did I. 'If we can get them to betray themselves in front of Corinthian citizen witnesses, they'll have no defence in court or anywhere else.'

'If we can snare them in front of enough Council members, no case need ever come to court,' Hyanthidas remarked. He liked that idea even more.

'As long as they're the right Council members,' Tele-silla pointed out. 'If we don't know who we're laying this trap for until it's been sprung, we can't know who their allies might be.'

'The Sons of Heracles, or the Heirs of Hephaistos.' Zosime looked around the table. 'It's someone involved with one of these hero cults, surely? No one else wants to wreck our play.'

I turned to Hyanthidas. 'Who's paying for the Sons of Heracles' pleasures?'

'I don't know, but I'll find out,' he assured me.

I wondered what else we could do. 'What about the Council members who Philolaos Kypselid tried to enlist, when he accused us of causing a riot? You said they were more interested in making money than hero cult intrigues. Wouldn't they make good witnesses?'

'They would,' he agreed.

'We still need a plan to lure whoever's suborned Tromes in front of them,' Lysicrates pointed out. 'In some way that betrays him without the possibility of question.'

Hyanthidas got up from his stool. 'Who wants more wine?'

'Just some water for me, thanks.' I had a feeling I'd need my wits about me to devise the plot we needed now.

Chapter Fourteen

I slept surprisingly well that night. When I did stir, I heard the household slaves starting their day. Perantas' slaves, I reminded myself. They must all be convinced by our performance this morning. It was safest to assume that Tromes had told the slaves under his direction whatever lies would enlist their unwitting aid.

Zosime and I rose and dressed, barely exchanging a word. We went down to the courtyard and the others joined us. The kitchen girls served us with bread, cheese and fruit while Tromes brought jugs of fresh water and sweet black wine for mixing a morning cupful.

Apollonides was diligently sucking on the reed stuck into his pot of steaming herbs. He set it aside and looked at me. 'So now we've all had a chance to sleep on it, are we really going to do this?'

'Will we need to cut today's rehearsal short?' Menekles looked concerned.

'If we do, it's hardly going to matter.' Lysicrates reached for the water jug.

'We don't want to prompt too many questions.' Apollonides shared a nod with Menekles. 'Not until the deal is done.'

I can recommend actors as fellow conspirators. Even without a script, they were wholly convincing. Hopefully Tromes would be able to put these pieces together and see the full picture. This wasn't a play where two characters could remind each other about people, places and plans they both already knew, purely to inform the audience.

I hoped I could match the actors' easy sincerity as I kept my eyes fixed on my plate. The temptation to look at Tromes was consuming me but I dared not yield. A single careless glance from Orpheus had undone all his struggles to win Eurydice back from the Underworld.

I cleared my throat. 'We'll know what we're doing once Kadous gets back.'

'What are we going to say to Hyanthidas?' Apollonides seemed genuinely troubled.

'Nothing,' Lysicrates said curtly. 'Not after what he said to me last night.'

If I hadn't known he was acting, that vicious edge to his voice would have sent a shiver down my spine.

'What's done is done,' said Menekles, placating. 'But, now we know where we stand, we're entitled to look after our own interests.'

'We can go where we please,' agreed Apollonides, 'and take our play with us.'

Lysicrates glowered. 'Somewhere we're not going to be fucked about and fucking insulted.'

'You gave as good as you got last night,' retorted Zosime.

I watched Tromes out of the corner of my eye. His

face was as expressionless as any prudent slave's, but his unfocused eyes told me he was listening intently. There was a tension in his lean body as well, as if he were poised to fight or flee. If I'd had any lingering doubts about his duplicity, this would have convinced me.

A heavy-handed knock rattled the gate. Tromes went to open it. As Kadous entered the courtyard, he looked uneasy. I could only hope Tromes took that for nervousness. Anxiety was surely natural when a slave was up to no good, even if he was following his master's orders.

'Well?' Lysicrates demanded.

Zosime muttered something disapproving under her breath and spread soft cheese on bread with forceful knife strokes. We'd agreed last night that anger would explain her silence as the actors played their parts.

I beckoned my loyal slave over and held his gaze with my own. That was as much to stop me looking at Tromes as to help Kadous recite the fiction we'd invented with Hyanthidas and Telesilla's help. 'Tell me.'

The Phrygian knotted his hands behind his back. 'The Sikyonians are definitely interested. They're willing to pay you handsomely.'

'How much?' Lysicrates asked at once.

Apollonides had other concerns. 'Did anyone mention knowing a piper who'd be willing to work with us there? Did you remember to ask?'

'Hush.' I cut them both short with a gesture and a glare. Kadous didn't need these interruptions if he was going to recall everything we needed him to say. 'Did they propose a meeting place, where we can discuss our terms?'

Kadous nodded. 'There's a ruined temple not far from the city, out on the Sikyon road. Their representatives will meet you there in the last hour of the day before sunset.'

'Very good.' I nodded sincere approval. 'Go and get yourself some food.'

'Thank you,' he said with heartfelt relief.

The actors were quick to continue the conversation, determined to keep Tromes' attention on the five of us as Kadous disappeared.

'We'll need to get the baskets of costumes and masks brought down from Demeter's Sanctuary.' Menekles looked thoughtful. 'Before anyone has reason to think we'll be leaving.'

'Especially Perantas Bacchiad. I don't fancy trying to fight my way past Thettalos and his merry band,' Apollonides said fervently.

'We don't want to move anything too early,' countered Lysicrates. 'We could give ourselves away just doing that. The Sanctuary slaves will be bound to ask what's going on.'

'We should ask for carts to be waiting for us by the Sikyonian Gate, as soon as we've come to terms,' Apollonides decided.

'We still have to get the baskets to the gate.' Lysicrates frowned, thoughtful.

Menekles looked at me. 'Do you think young Nados would lend us some of Eumelos' slaves?'

I pretended to think about that. 'I can send Kadous to sound him out.'

In fact, I had already given Kadous very precise instructions for his conversation with Nados. He'd be going to Eumelos' house as soon as we departed for Demeter's Sanctuary. For one thing, that would take my Phrygian into a household where Tromes had no good reason to follow. However seemingly casual the disloyal slave's questions might be, and however unarguable Kadous' defence against them surely was, that he could not betray his master's confidence, there was always the risk that he would say something to arouse Tromes' suspicions.

We wanted the traitor heading into Corinth, looking to confirm as many of our lies as he could, before he took our carefully woven tale to whoever was paying him to betray us.

We finished our breakfast and got ready to set out for our rehearsals, as if this were any ordinary day. Kadous followed us to the corner of the street, then turned off to head for Eumelos' house. Apollonides stumbled convincingly and knelt to retie his sandal's laces.

'Well?' Menekles asked, apparently gazing idly up at a nearby window where a woman was shaking out a blanket. She draped it over the sill and disappeared from view.

'He's gone back inside and closed the gate.' Lysicrates stood up and brushed dust from his knee.

'It would look a bit obvious if he rushed out as soon as we left.' I tried not to worry that we'd somehow given ourselves away.

'What do you suppose he'll do, if he thinks we suspect him?' Apollonides wondered as we started walking.

'Tell Perantas Bacchiad we're supposedly going to Sikyon?' Menekles hazarded. 'Playing the loyal slave warning his master about our deceitfulness?'

'Hoping to cause a breach between us that will still achieve his new patron's aims?' Lysicrates laughed without humour. 'Maybe Perantas will reward him. Then he'll be getting paid twice.'

'What do *we* do then?' Apollonides didn't relish the idea of such complications.

'We explain everything,' Zosime said briskly. 'Perantas can hardly blame us for trying to find out who's been setting out to wreck the play.'

I took her hand. 'It's not as if we've really had any dealings with Sikyonians.'

Though I wouldn't give a clipped obol for our chances of learning who Tromes' hidden paymaster might be if he did go running to Perantas. That would mean the slave was confident he could brazen this out, denying Hyanthidas' accusations, even with the rest of us bearing witness to what Lysicrates had actually said.

Would the Bacchiad really take his slave's word over four Athenian citizens' testimony? When their word was backed by a true-born Corinthian? Tromes would have to trust absolutely in Perantas' goodwill, to risk his life on the Bacchiad's favour.

I couldn't see it, not after talking to Kadous last night. I guessed Tromes would simply disappear. If he took to his heels straight after telling Perantas about our supposed meeting with Sikyon's representatives, he could hope for a day's head start. He would want to get as far away from Corinth as he could before the confusion he'd created was cleared up. He had to know that Perantas would send someone like Thettalos to pursue him.

A slave's betrayal is the foulest treachery and it cannot go unpunished. I guessed Perantas would insist on some bloody, brutal punishment that would ensure the rest of his household wouldn't dream of such disloyalty without suffering the vilest nightmares.

I was in a sombre mood by the time we reached the Sanctuary.

Zosime waved a hand. 'There's Hyanthidas.'

The piper was sitting on the edge of a step. As he got to his feet, he was smiling. 'Arion tells me the neighbours were thoroughly convinced by last night's play-acting.'

'Naturally,' Lysicrates said with a wicked grin. 'We must have rattled their window shutters.'

'Let's hope Tromes goes looking for gossip around your local fountain.' I hadn't found the argument they'd staged as the first act of our plot amusing. The insults they'd hurled at each other had been a little too cutting and rather too pointed.

'I told Thettalos and his brutes to head for their beds.' Hyanthidas handed me the angled brass keys as we walked through to the courtyard.

Lysicrates looked around before nodding with satisfaction. 'Nothing amiss.'

'Make sure you two don't look too friendly when the chorus arrives,' Zosime warned. 'We don't know who any of them might be talking to at lunchtime, even in all innocence.'

Lysicrates immediately looked at Hyanthidas with cold disdain. The piper's lip curled as he looked down his nose at the actor. Turning their backs on each other with lofty contempt, they both stalked away.

I sighed as I walked to the costume store with Zosime. She squeezed my hand. 'Don't fret.'

'You don't think they meant some of what they said last night?'

'I'm sure they did.' She was unconcerned. 'Until they heard themselves saying such ridiculous things aloud. All the while, they were looking each other in the eye and remembering the friendship they'd shared in Athens. Now they've got that poisonous nonsense out of their systems, they'll be fine.'

'Let's hope so.' I threaded the key through the door and jiggled it to force the bolt back.

We didn't have any further opportunity to discuss my misgivings. The chorus singers were arriving, eager to begin rehearsals. Apollonides helped me drag the basket of practise masks to the storeroom door and we began sharing them out.

The chorus men handed them round, laughing at the mismatched array of gurning caricatures drawn from a handful of different plays. As soon as they tied them on, though, I couldn't see anyone's face to see what they might make of Lysicrates and Hyanthidas ostentatiously ignoring each other. I wished I'd thought of that earlier. Some unguarded expression might have given us a hint of malice lurking in our midst, but there was no helping that now.

The first rehearsal wearing masks is always a test for a chorus, however well drilled they might be. Familiar moves become newly challenging, now that a singer's hearing is muffled and his vision's reduced to a narrow focus straight ahead. Since this chorus hadn't even had four days of rehearsal, we might as well be starting again from scratch.

I had to focus on my own performance in a way I hadn't needed to before. Wearing a mask means conveying your mood with gestures instead of expressions, stretching your whole body and lengthening your neck and arms. Extra care and effort is needed to control your breathing, and to project your voice clearly through the barrier of linen and plaster between you and the audience. All this comes as second nature to the likes of Menekles, Apollonides and Lysicrates, but it was several years since I'd last performed in a chorus. I'd forgotten how demanding it could be.

At least the need to concentrate took my mind off everything else going on down in Corinth today. Add to that, our singers had evidently performed in a theatre far more recently than me, and coped with the demands of wearing masks far better.

By lunchtime, we had mostly smoothed out our new missteps and stumbles. Fewer of the chorus were heading off to find food with each passing day. Everyone was keen to make the best use of our dwindling time before the performance. I spent the break discussing the finer points of the play's different songs and dances with a succession of the Corinthian singers. It wasn't until Telesilla arrived with a basket of food for me, Zosime and the actors that I was able to escape them.

'Arion says Tromes has been asking questions among our neighbours' slaves this morning,' she said quietly as she handed me a cheese pastry.

'Good.' Last night's distasteful pretence had been worthwhile. 'Have you seen Kadous?'

She shook her head. 'Not yet.'

So either everything was going to plan, or something had gone horribly wrong, and we would have no way of knowing until our sunset meeting out on the Sikyon road.

There was nothing I could do but turn all my attention to the afternoon's rehearsal. As a result, I became so ferociously intent on the play that it took Hyanthidas interrupting a dance with an uncharacteristic squeak of his twin pipes' reeds to break my concentration.

'So sorry.' Hyanthidas raised an apologetic hand.

Realising how late in the day it was, I called a halt. 'Thank you, everyone. We've made excellent progress. Let's continue tomorrow.'

I could only hope that we Athenians would be here tomorrow, and not locked up for defaming some noble Corinthian citizen, or for profaning a sacred site with our lies.

Chapter Fifteen

Hyanthidas made a swift departure, barely pausing to say his farewells. That was essential if our scheme was to succeed. He couldn't be seen with us this evening. He mustn't be seen heading out of the city. I could only trust his assurances that he knew how to lose anyone following him in Corinth's back alleys. Though I couldn't stop worrying that anyone working for our enemies would be just as well versed in the city's byways.

For the moment, I didn't think anyone in the chorus had even noticed the musician was gone. The singers were swapping observations and compliments as they returned their practise masks to Zosime. She thanked them politely as she stowed the battered and flaking caricatures back in their basket.

As the last Corinthian departed, she snapped her fingers to get my attention. 'Notice anything?'

She smiled sunnily, turning her face this way and that. That would normally be my cue to admire a new belt or some jewellery adorning her dress, or to comment favourably on the way she'd pinned and curled her gorgeous, raven-black hair. Try as I might, I couldn't see anything different. She looked exactly the same as she had this morning.

'Not particularly,' I said cautiously.

Her grin widened. 'I've been sitting in here wearing one of *The Builders*' masks all through your last two songs.'

'Really?' I stepped closer and ran my fingertips over her soft cheek, to convince myself my eyes weren't lying. Truly, there was no trace of the hellebore's venom searing her skin.

'A layer of clay and the extra linen did the trick,' she said with understandable satisfaction.

The actors had heard this good news.

'That's another head cut off the hydra, and the stump seared,' Apollonides said.

'Let's go and deal with a few more.' Lysicrates had a vengeful glint in his eye.

'You are as wise as you are beautiful.' I drew Zosime close and kissed her, long and deep. From dawn to dusk, in sunshine and in darkness, under the moon or beneath the stars, I hoped she would always see how utterly I adored her.

We locked up, Menekles returned the keys to the priestess, and we headed down the sloping road. Arion was waiting for us in the agora as previously arranged, sitting on the steps of the Peirene Fountain. I kissed Zosime again before entrusting her to his care. We'd agreed she'd be much better off with Telesilla if this evening ended with Perantas' men tearing apart our lodging to search for some clue that might lead them to Tromes.

She kissed me back. 'Good luck.'

We took the road that led past the theatre. I picked up the pace and the others fell into step with me. Once a soldier, always a soldier, in Athens or in Corinth or any other Hellenic city. I knew the actors and I were thinking the same, after so many frustrating days beset by enemies hiding in shadows and using other people to attack us. We all relished the prospect of meeting at least one of our opponents face to face. We might not have been wearing armour as we marched through that gate, but this was a fight we intended to win.

We passed out of the city proper and went by the burial ground where Eumelos had been laid to rest. I promised the guardians of the dead libations of oil and wine poured onto his grave, to console his restless spirit. I silently prayed to the gods below that we would learn who had murdered him before this night was out. Then the divine and fearsome Furies could pursue those villains through endless, sleepless nights until Corinthian justice exacted revenge on Eumelos' behalf.

Some way further down the road, Apollonides interrupted my dark thoughts. 'We're not too late, are we? What if they've got there before us?'

We were passing smallholdings and scattered houses by now, and there were only a few other people on the road.

'If they have, there's nothing we can do about it.' Lysicrates strode onwards faster all the same.

We soon arrived at the ruined temple, left alone amid a scatter of olive trees. The fire-scarred walls of the roofless inner sanctum were surrounded by blackened pillars, as broken and irregular as rotten teeth. The place had an ominous air as the dusk gathered around it.

'What happened here?' Menekles looked around, apprehensive.

'I wonder whose temple this is.' I couldn't see any indication on the long-abandoned altar.

A voice made us all jump. 'That depends on who you ask.' Hyanthidas appeared from behind a gnarled and ancient tree. 'Some say it was dedicated to Apollo, but Pyrros, son of Achilles, burned it down on his return from Troy, in revenge for the god killing his father. Others say it was a temple raised to Zeus, but a lightning bolt set it ablaze so he must have had some objection.'

Either way, this was an ill-omened place. I prayed fervently to both Zeus and Apollo that any misfortune lingering here would strike down our enemies, and not us. We had come to see justice served, and surely that deserved divine protection.

'Let's get out of sight,' I suggested.

No one made a move towards the ruined sanctuary. Instead we found hiding places among the olive trees, within sight of each other, and of the road. Birds tweeted and flitted in the branches. A few darted down to the ground to snatch up some morsel. Others wheeled above us, plucking insects from the luminous evening sky.

Apollonides was standing beside me. He chewed his lower lip. 'How long do we wait before we decide no one's going to come?'

My stomach hollowed as I realised that was one possibility we hadn't even discussed. We had been so certain that Tromes would take our bait, whatever he might do after that. I looked westwards to assess the sinking sun.

'Who's that?' Menekles shifted to get a clearer view past his chosen tree.

'Hard to say, at this distance.' Hyanthidas sounded hopeful all the same. 'Not the whole Council, obviously, but enough of them for our needs.'

Peering through the olive leaves, I saw a substantial group round a curve in the road. Broad-shouldered youths carrying vine staves flanked a knot of older men whose noble birth and civic dignity were suitably draped in voluminous cloaks.

'I can see Perantas,' Apollonides said quietly as the delegation drew closer.

I swallowed but my mouth was as dry as the scorched stones of the temple.

Hyanthidas had equally sharp eyes. 'There's Philolaos Kypselid.'

The Heirs of Hephaistos' paymaster. I wondered if the man who financed the Sons of Heracles was among the approaching Councillors, still confident that his plot to poison our masks remained undetected.

I recognised a couple of the others, from that day when Hyanthidas and I were hauled before Philolaos' selected members of the Council. Remembering the musician's impromptu lie about going to Sikyon had sown the first seed of our plot. With that suspicion already planted, we could hope that sufficient Councilmen would insist on coming to see for themselves, once Tromes had reported to his paymaster and our unknown enemy had slandered us to all and sundry.

I breathed a prayer of thanks to Athena, to Apollo, to Zeus and any other deity inclined to look favourably upon us. Then I reminded myself that we still had to bring this scheme to fruition.

The Councillors were still walking along the road but their escort was beginning to spread out among the tamarisks and juniper bushes scattered on either side of the highway. A small group were advancing on the temple, clearly intent on getting a look inside the ruined sanctum within the pillars.

'I'm not going to be hauled out to face them like some sneak thief.' Lysicrates strode forward, forcing the rest of us to follow.

His instincts were sound. Our unexpected appearance knocked these new arrivals onto the back foot. The Council members shuffled uneasily while their henchmen rallied around them.

We walked forward to stand beside the abandoned altar. I was in the centre of our battle line, flanked by Menekles and Hyanthidas, and with Apollonides and Lysicrates poised on each wing.

Corinth's elders warily advanced towards us. Their escort kept pace, their eyes darting from side to side in case we had allies hidden among the olive trees or lurking behind the ruined temple.

One of the Councilmen stepped forward as the rest halted. 'Who else is here?' he barked.

I recognised his bald head and weathered face. 'No one,' I said mildly.

'Who were you expecting?' Hyanthidas asked.

I searched the Councillors' faces for any sign of surprise at seeing the musician. Whoever had heard Tromes' tale today should be convinced that we were at each other's throats. If they'd had someone spying on us this afternoon, they'd know Hyanthidas had gone straight home. They should have no reason to think he'd slipped out again, climbing over his neighbour's walls to depart unobserved.

Philolaos Kypselid's expression betrayed him. So this was the man who thought it was his birthright to rule Corinth. I sincerely hoped this day's work would hole that ambition below the waterline, as well as frustrating his immediate plans to stop our performance.

He glared at Hyanthidas with barely suppressed fury. When he saw my grin, he spun around, beckoning to a heavyset minion. It looked as if he was about to leave. I wasn't having that.

I raised my voice. 'You were expecting to find us negotiating with men from Sikyon, perhaps?'

If the stocky man hadn't betrayed himself with a glance over his shoulder, the way the other Council members looked at him would have told us what we wanted to know.

'Honoured sir,' I addressed the leather-faced man. 'We never had any such intention, as you can see—'

'The Sikyonians must have already come and gone.' Philolaos Kypselid wasn't beaten yet. He gestured away down the road. 'These Athenians must have proved too greedy, asking a price they were unwilling to meet.'

I ignored him, keeping my gaze fixed on the bald Councilman. 'By all means, ask your business partners and trusted friends in Sikyon. They won't have heard so much as a whisper on the wind of us insulting your city so crassly.'

The weather-beaten man narrowed his eyes, as suspicious of me as anyone else here. 'Then what is the purpose of this farce, dragging us out here?'

'We have had a spy in our midst,' I said bluntly. 'He has been serving another master, one who wanted to put an end to our play. That man is out to serve his own interests, with no thought for the greater good of Corinth. He's a man heedless of your city's peace and prosperity. We have brought you here to unmask him.'

Perhaps I was exaggerating. A play can offer great insights alongside its entertainment, encouraging the audience towards moral and upright behaviour, and comedies can do that just as effectively, if not more so, than blood-soaked tragedies, whatever the gore-peddlers claim. But I grant you, sealing a city's fate is a lot to ask of any drama.

That didn't matter, out here on the Sikyon road. These Corinthian elders were looking at Philolaos with increasing suspicion and anger. I must find time to ask Hyanthidas what the Kypselid had done in the past to make these men so ready to believe his bad faith. For now though, I'd paused long enough.

'He is willing to entice another man's slave to serve him, whether through threats of violence or the lure of silver, I cannot say.' I shrugged before addressing Perantas Bacchiad for the first time. 'The only person we gave any reason to believe that we would dishonour you by abandoning our performance in Corinth is your slave Tromes. Believe me, it grieves me to tell you he is the only person who could have carried word to whoever made these accusations to bring you here.'

The flash of utter fury in Perantas' eyes came and went as swiftly as lightning. The contemptuous expressions of the assembled elders were more eloquent. Those standing closest to Philolaos edged away from him with sideways glances of disgust.

He glared at me, red-faced and irate in the fading light. Though I only saw his anger at being tricked. There was no hint of regret for what he'd done.

'You dare accuse me, Athenian?' He spat on the ground. 'Bring your proof before a full session of Corinth's Council, you scum! I will see you beggared—'

'You will see yourself censured if this ever comes before the whole Council,' snarled a man I didn't recognise. 'If you're not subject to worse retribution for humiliating us all like this. Your own words condemn you, fool.'

He waved a hand as though he wished he could wipe away the very sight of Philolaos. He turned for the road, shoving someone's hesitating henchman aside. 'Out of my way!'

Our unknown ally's departure prompted the rest to follow him as hastily as sheep hurrying after their bellwether. That left Philolaos Kypselid standing and glaring at me with his fists clenched. He was surrounded by ten or more burly men armed with vine staves. These must be the self-declared Heirs of Hephaistos.

Perantas Bacchiad hadn't moved either, and familiar figures flanked him. Thettalos and a dozen or so of his Brotherhood looked delighted at the prospect of a bloody brawl. Several had already unbuckled their belts, threading the leather through their hands, or winding the straps around their knuckles.

Wasn't that marvellous? All our subterfuge would be wasted if the day ended with broken bones and split heads littering the ruined temple, convincing the Council that our play was more trouble than it was worth. The Kypselid might still get his way, if he was prepared to shed enough of his henchmen's blood.

Perantas strode forward to demand Philolaos' attention. 'Don't. Just don't.'

Whatever the Kypselid was contemplating, the struggle was plain on his face. A few tense moments later, his shoulders slumped and he settled for sneering at us before turning towards the road.

Thettalos and the Brothers watched the Heirs go, as alert as dogs seeing unwelcome visitors safely away across their master's threshold.

As I breathed a quiet sigh of relief, I realised Perantas was looking at me, his expression unreadable.

I walked forward to meet him, to try and steer the conversation. 'Can we hope that Philolaos will draw in his horns, at least until we've performed the play?'

'Where is Tromes?' Perantas hissed, venomous.

'I have no idea.' I was close enough to the desolate altar to lay a hand on the weathered stones. 'I swear it, by Apollo and by Zeus and any other god here present.'

That was absolutely true. I had no way of knowing for certain whether the next act of our plan had succeeded.

Chapter Sixteen

I was telling Perantas the truth, though not the whole truth. I couldn't tell if he suspected some deceit.

He looked at me, contemplative, for a few long moments. 'Let's hope this evening's little performance sees an end to such nonsense, and we can all enjoy the play.'

'Let's hope so,' I agreed, 'though we'd be foolish to be complacent. Our storerooms should still be guarded until we've had our day in your theatre.'

That was perfectly true. The gods love to punish overconfidence. Once again, there was more to my request. I wanted to keep the Brotherhood as busy as possible for the rest of the night.

'Indeed.' As Perantas turned and strolled towards the road, the Brotherhood gathered around him. Thettalos hadn't been close enough to hear our conversation but that didn't stop him scowling in my direction, just on principle, before they headed for the city.

My hand was still resting on the abandoned altar. I prayed silently to Zeus and to Apollo that they would judge me when this whole day's work was finished, not merely for my calculatedly deceitful words thus far.

'Are we done here?' Lysicrates demanded.

'I'd say so.' Apollonides cracked his knuckles.

'Let's get to Lechaion before it gets too dark,' Hyanthidas suggested.

'Do we have to go back into the city to pick up the high road?' Menekles looked towards the Acrocorinth, a dark outline against the evening sky.

Hyanthidas shook his head. 'I know a shortcut.'

We followed the Sikyon road for some distance, then Hyanthidas led us down a donkey track threading through the olive groves. I didn't mind the extra walking. I could be certain none of the Brotherhood were loitering to insist on escorting us back, and asking where we were going. If Perantas did suspect I wasn't telling him everything, he could easily send someone to watch us, claiming concern for our safety. Refusal would as good as confirm our duplicity.

We passed storehouses, workshops and humble dwellings nestled among the olive groves, orchards and well-tilled gardens. Goats waiting to be penned for the night watched us, their black-slotted eyes incurious. No one busy about their evening chores paid us any heed.

When we reached the Lechaion Road, we made better speed and, though the night was drawing on, moonlight showed us our way. The lights of the port soon came into view. I hadn't lied to Perantas. I'd never been there before and I had no idea where Eumelos' property might be. Truthfully, I had no idea where Tromes was.

Hyanthidas on the other hand knew the little town very well, easily able to follow Nados' directions. Simias managed Eumelos' business here from a property not far from the dockside.

Aithon opened the gate to our knock. Storehouses flanked a narrow courtyard with a modest dwelling at the far end.

Nados was waiting. I looked back into the street, searching the gloom for suspicious figures, before he closed the gate behind the five of us. I saw no sign of anyone.

'You're sure you weren't followed?' I asked Nados.

'I'm certain.'

He had no doubts.

I could only hope he was right.

'What happened at the temple?' Aithon asked, tense.

'We learned what we needed,' I told him. 'Did you get him?'

'In here.' Nados headed for an open doorway where oil lamps shone bright.

We all went into the store. Amphorae were stacked high on all sides, and there was the distinct tang of pickled fish in the air.

Simias grinned at Lysicrates. 'You were right. He had no idea who we were.'

Tromes sat on a stool with his wrists and ankles bound, and his shoulders slumped in defeat. A gag ensured he couldn't yell for help, though seeing the despair in his eyes, I doubted he'd bother trying.

Traitor though he was, I was relieved to see he hadn't taken a beating, not yet anyway. Though he'd have been a fool to resist, outnumbered four to one once Kadous had led him into the alley where Eumelos' trio were waiting.

I glanced at the Phrygian. 'When did he start tailing you?'

'After I called on Telesilla.'

I could see my slave's veiled distaste for his part in setting this trap. I'd already made it clear this wasn't his responsibility. I had given him his orders and I would answer for the consequences, before the gods or men. For the moment, I was simply relieved that our plan was succeeding thus far.

'Let's see what he has to say for himself.' I nodded at Aithon who untied the rag stuffed in Tromes' mouth.

The slave stared at the earth floor.

'We know you've betrayed Perantas Bacchiad,' I began, conversationally, 'and that you've been telling tales to Philolaos Kypselid.'

That revelation prompted a stir among Eumelos' lads. I kept my attention on Tromes. 'How much did he pay you? Can any amount of silver be worth facing Perantas' retribution?'

Tromes looked up. I expected to see some desperate appeal, or perhaps a condemned man's defiance. The burning anger in his eyes surprised me.

'You—' A dry cough tore at his throat. He doubled over, still coughing and unable to catch his breath.

'Has he had any water?' I couldn't see a jug anywhere. 'Get him something to drink, for pity's sake.'

Kadous hurried out. I couldn't blame him for seizing his chance to get away.

'Philolaos Kypselid?' Aithon looked at Nados, incredulous.

'The Heirs of Hephaistos are as persistent as barnacles on a ship.' Nados could believe it. 'They dream of Corinth leading the Peloponnese, and lust after the profits they will accrue.'

Simias agreed with Nados. 'Philolaos and his cronies won't want the likes of us looking beyond these shores to Sicily, still less co-operating with Athenians who might infect us with foolish notions like democracy.' He surprised me with a sudden grin.

Kadous returned with a jug of water and a cup. The Phrygian held the water to Tromes' lips as the gasping slave struggled to drink. Most of it went down his tunic but he managed to swallow enough to curb his coughing. We waited until he sat, wheezing, his cheeks flushed and wet with tears.

'So what have you told Philolaos Kypselid?' I demanded. 'What else has he got planned to stop our play?'

'The Kypselid's man wanted me to stir up strife between you—' He broke off, his chest heaving as he fought to suppress another coughing fit. 'He didn't care if the play didn't go ahead,' he went on after a moment, 'or if the performance was simply a disaster. He wanted Perantas and his allies to look like fools. That's all. I swear it.'

'Tell us the truth,' I warned, 'if you expect us to show you any mercy.'

'I expect no mercy from anyone, least of all Perantas Bacchiad,' Tromes rasped with sudden fury that nearly set him coughing again. 'He sold the woman I loved, and my daughter with her. I begged Wetka to ask for the master's mercy, to keep us all together. Wetka said he didn't care. Perantas was only interested in the silver her weaving skills fetched, after one of his guests from Anaktorion admired her work.'

Now tears of grief streamed down his cheeks. 'The Kypselid man, he promised me her price, and the child's, and enough silver to get me to Epirus.'

I was sure the henchman had done. Whether or not he would have delivered the money was another question entirely. Promises are cheap, and Tromes could hardly complain to the Council that he'd been cheated.

Come to that, I didn't give much for Tromes' chances, even if Philolaos had been true to his lackey's word. Anaktorion was the first place Perantas would send someone to look for his runaway. That would be ten days travel by foot, by my best guess, heading across the Gulf of Corinth and beyond Aetolia to Epirus. Meantime the Bacchiad could put Thettalos on a ship and have him there in fewer than five, waiting for Tromes to arrive. I had no doubt that Perantas Bacchiad would consider his money and the Brotherhood's time well spent in pursuit of vengeance.

But how had Philolaos' man known about Tromes' grievance in the first place? Did the great and good of Corinth routinely spy on each other's households?

Simias had other concerns. 'Who is this Kypselid mouthpiece? Did he poison Eumelos?'

'He had no hand in that,' Tromes protested. 'If I ever

overheard you discussing it, if I got the least hint you'd discovered the guilty man, I was to tell him at once. He said that would earn me another fat purse of silver. He said that Philolaos was furious when he heard Eumelos had been poisoned so publicly. The last thing Philolaos wanted was the Council thinking someone was intent on wrecking the play.'

That had the ring of truth to me. So it seemed unlikely that a Kypselid henchman could have put that poison in Eumelos' hand, still less to have persuaded him to drink it. The mystery of this murder was a riddle that would frustrate a sphinx. Who had Eumelos trusted enough to accept that vial and empty it into his wine?

Tromes was staring at the ground again so I kicked his foot to get his attention. 'What does he look like?'

He looked up, his face hopeless. 'About as tall as you. Dark hair, brown eyes, a beard. A Corinthian.'

In other words, he looked the same as any ten men we might pass in the agora. This wasn't a play where such a character would have something helpfully distinctive about him, like a dragging foot that could be seen from the topmost seats in a theatre.

Simias shoved Tromes' shoulder. 'But you'd know him if you saw him.'

'We can hardly take him back to Corinth,' I objected, 'trussed like some fowl for the spit, and set up camp outside Philolaos Kypselid's gate to see who goes in or out.'

Hyanthidas waved that away. 'We already know Philolaos is guilty. He gave himself away in front of half the Council. We hardly need a slave's word that he's involved.'

'And Philolaos will never answer for this in court,' said Nados, resigned. 'The Council won't publicly disgrace one of their own.'

'We're the ones who could end up in court,' Menekles pointed out, 'if we're caught holding another man's slave captive.'

Hyanthidas agreed. 'Perantas could hardly keep the respect of his fellow Councillors if he declined to prosecute some Athenians caught red-handed with his stolen slave.'

'Especially after I swore to Perantas that I had no idea where he might be.' I looked uneasily at Tromes and wished the musician hadn't just said 'red-handed'.

I remembered Achilles striding onto the stage in Athens at the Dionysia the year before last. He stood with his hands swathed in crimson cloth as he justified cutting down Thersites, after the foolish hero mocked the dead Amazon queen Penthesilea.

'What are we going to do with him?' Apollonides looked at us all with misgiving.

'If we hand him back to Perantas, we have to explain where we found him,' Menekles said grimly.

The slave pleaded, desperate. 'I won't tell—'

'He will,' Hyanthidas assured us. 'Thettalos will beat everything that's happened out of him.'

'If we hand him over to Philolaos, there'll still be awkward questions.' Nados grimaced. 'And no guarantee that the Kypselid won't do some deal to hand him over for Perantas to punish.'

'We can hardly just let him go,' Lysicrates said reluctantly.

There was a moment's silence as we all acknowledged this unpalatable truth.

'Cut my throat and have done with it.' Tromes' whisper of despair was as dark as the shadows around us. 'That would be a mercy.'

We looked at each other, appalled, until I realised everyone was looking at me.

'What then?' I said slowly. 'We'll have a body to dispose of and we can hardly dig a hole in this floor to bury him under a year's supply of pickled fish. Does anyone want to volunteer to carry a dead man to the dockside and throw him in the harbour? How do we explain *that* to someone heading home from a tavern?'

I saw that Menekles, Apollonides and Lysicrates relished the prospect of killing the slave as little as I did. Yes, we had marched in Athens' armies and killed on the field of battle when our own lives were just as much at risk. But that was a world away from cold-bloodedly taking a bound and helpless man's life.

Nados, Aithon and Simias were more openly sickened by the prospect. For all their dutiful training, they were too young to have taken up spear and shield and marched to war. They would only have seen death at a bedside, or in some unforeseen accident.

'What happens when he's found? Because his blood will cry out for vengeance.' I had no doubt about that. 'My guess is Perantas will blame Philolaos, while Philolaos blames Perantas, and neither will believe the other's denials because, in truth, they're neither to blame.'

'We'll see the Brotherhood fighting the Heirs of Hephaistos in the streets,' Hyanthidas said sombrely.

'How much blood will be spilled?' I demanded. 'Do we want to answer for more deaths?'

I caught sight of Kadous standing silently by the door. His gaze was fixed on me, unblinking. He'd heard me often enough, castigating men who mistreated their slaves. The Phrygian expected me to live up to those words. I didn't want to forfeit his respect by failing.

'Killing Tromes solves nothing and risks making a bad situation worse,' I said, adamant. 'Besides, Philolaos Kypselid is the truly guilty one here. This—' I gestured at the slave '—is just his tool. If someone hits you with a rake, you don't throw it on the fire. You blame the man who picked it up.'

'Very true,' said Menekles forcefully.

'So where's a shed to stash him in?' Lysicrates demanded.

It wasn't much of a joke but we were all glad of an excuse to smile even for a moment.

Apollonides shook his head. 'Wherever he hides, Thettalos and the Brotherhood will be hunting him.'

'The length and breadth of the Corinthia,' Aithon confirmed.

'We need to get him beyond their reach.' I looked at Simias. 'What vessels are anchored in the harbour here? Do you know any captains who'd take on a passenger, no questions asked? Someone ready to sail first thing in the morning and heading a good long way.'

The youth looked thoughtful. 'There's a ship—'

'Don't tell me.' I wanted to be telling the truth when I told Perantas I had no idea where to find him. We were committing a crime, there was no doubt about that, but I wanted to limit my sins against the gods, if not against Corinth's nobility.

Tears of astonished relief ran down Tromes' face. 'Thank—'

I choked off his words with a ruthless hand, forcing his chin up so that he looked at me with terrified eyes. I did my best to emulate the ruthlessness of unrepentant Achilles.

'Run, far and fast, and believe me when I say that if any of us see you again, we'll kill you. Wherever you go, don't go near Anaktorion.' I shook him like a terrier with a rat. 'Perantas will expect you to run straight to this woman of yours and you'll betray us all if you're captured.'

'I won't,' he gurgled desperately.

'Make sure you don't.' I gave him another vicious shake before I released my hold and looked intently at Nados. 'Can you handle getting him out of here? You'll drop us all neck deep in the mire if you fumble it.'

'We won't, I mean, we will, we can do this.' Nados stumbled over his words but his resolve was plain to see. The same was true of Aithon and Simias.

I looked at Hyanthidas and my fellow Athenians. 'We'd better get back to Corinth before it gets too late for us to claim we lost track of time in a tavern. Perantas is bound to have his men asking questions and it's hardly

214

fair to leave Telesilla and Zosime to face Thettalos.'

'Agreed.' Apollonides shared my concern.

We left the storehouse and Nados closed and bolted the narrow yard's gate behind us. We headed for the road back to Corinth in silence. There was nothing more to say. As we walked through the darkness, I felt achingly weary, in body and spirit.

Whenever we discovered someone who might have killed Eumelos, we found good reasons to rule them out. I was ready to admit defeat and head back to Athens as soon as we'd performed the play, and the prospect of our day in the theatre brought me precious little joy. Apart from everything else, I still had those bloody rewrites to finish.

We reached the crossroads where Lechaion's streets met the highway running north, and I saw a familiar shape in the light of a doorpost torch. The others saw it too and we halted in unspoken agreement.

There's a Hermes pillar on pretty much every street corner in Athens; a square-cut stone topped with the god's head and with a jaunty jutting cock halfway down. They're fewer and further between out in Attica, and we'd seen fewer still since we'd arrived in Corinth. This was like meeting an old friend from home.

Apollonides ran his hand over the weathered stone curls in a gesture as natural as breathing to Athenians. Menekles followed, and Lysicrates made his own reverence. Even Hyanthidas had picked up the habit during his long stay in our city.

Hermes isn't merely the guardian of roads and

travellers. He understands that men must sometimes resort to trickery and subterfuge. I could only hope the wing-footed god would look sympathetically on what we had done. On what I had done.

'Watch over Nados, Simias and Aithon,' I quietly asked the god, 'as well as the unfortunate we left in their care. See him safely on his journey and forgive me if I went too far in frightening him. I only wanted to make certain he wouldn't do anything stupid and risk all our lives.'

As the others murmured their own prayers, I caught Kadous' eye. My slave gave an infinitesimal nod and I was relieved to think he understood my play-acting in the warehouse.

'Let's get back.' Menekles turned for Corinth, setting a challenging pace.

Chapter Seventeen

There were still a few Corinthians out and about as we walked swiftly through the streets. I didn't think we were being followed, though. Anyone dogging our steps would have been obvious.

Hyanthidas halted as we reached a crossroads. 'I'm heading home.'

'I'll come with you.' I was as concerned about Zosime was he was about Telesilla.

'Not on your own,' Menekles said firmly.

Lysicrates nodded. 'We stick together.'

So we all followed Hyanthidas through side streets and back alleys, on a route that would have shaken off any pursuit.

As we reached the quiet street where the tall musician lived, I saw the gate was firmly closed, with no light burning to welcome him home. Hyanthidas lengthened his stride. I had to scurry to keep up. His urgent knock echoed my heart pounding against my ribs.

Arion opened up, looking understandably sleepy. Zosime and Telesilla were sitting beside the brazier where the charcoal had burned down to glimmers of red amid dark, feathery ash. A jug and cups stood on a low table beside an oil lamp whose feeble flame was ready to give up.

I managed a smile. 'Have you had a good evening?'

'Very pleasant.' Zosime stood up. 'And you?'

'Everything's in hand.' I wasn't going to say any more. Hyanthidas had been adamant that his slave know as little as possible of our plans.

'We've had no visitors at all,' Telesilla assured the piper as the slave went to fetch Zosime's shawl.

I smiled at Telesilla. 'We appreciate your hospitality.'

Telesilla chuckled as she and Zosime shared a conspiratorial glance. 'Oh, you will, I can assure you of that.'

'What do you mean?' Hyanthidas looked apprehensive.

'Never mind.' I grinned, realising the women had been discussing the rewrites for the play.

Telesilla stood up to kiss Zosime farewell and then slid under the musician's arm. 'Come to bed. It's late.'

'Good night.' I offered my own beloved my arm and Arion barred the gate behind us.

Menekles headed for the agora, since none of us had a hope of following Hyanthidas' route back to the Lechaion road.

Zosime squeezed my arm. 'How did you get on?'

'Well enough, I think.' I related everything that had happened since we had parted.

'I hope they get him safely away.' She sighed. 'But we're still no closer to learning who killed Eumelos.'

'Unfortunately not.' I glanced up at the Temple of Apollo as we passed by, and silently asked the god for his help once again. I couldn't help feeling a little exasperated at his lack of assistance thus far.

We walked the rest of the way in silence. All I wanted to do was fall into bed, and judging by her yawns, Zosime felt the same.

No such luck. We got back to find upheaval. Before we reached the closed gate we heard the sharp crack of furniture knocked over on the paving within. Whimpering voices rose to terrified squeals as deeper shouts berated them. An attempt to answer was cut short with a ringing slap that provoked a chorus of wails.

Two burly men guarded the entrance. One was holding a blazing pine torch that struck a golden glow from a bronze Pegasus medallion he wore. The other was a man well built for throwing javelins or discus.

'What's going on here?' Apollonides fell into a loose-limbed stroll, his expression veering from amiable good cheer to vague concern.

Lysicrates drew himself up straight with a little too much determination, and was rather too careful to speak clearly. 'How can we help?'

The man with the torch glowered at us. 'Where have you been?'

Apollonides shrugged. 'Eating dinner.'

'Corinthian wine is very good,' Lysicrates confided with the wag of an upraised finger.

Since those two had the comedy well in hand, Menekles opted for the role of irritated elder. 'May we pass? You know who we are, and we have every right to be here. It's late and we have all had a long and tiring day.'

'It's hot work, rehearsing a play,' Lysicrates solemnly informed the Brothers.

'Thirsty work as well.' Apollonides beamed sunnily.

Menekles shot him an exasperated look. 'As I say, it's late, and we would like to go to bed. We all need a good night's sleep. Some of us more than others.'

Lysicrates looked indignant. 'We were only being sociable.'

I stepped forward before this improvised performance aroused suspicion. These Brothers might not be the sharpest spears in the phalanx but they couldn't be outright fools. They also made no move to step aside.

'If we're not allowed in here, where are we supposed to go?' I kept my tone reasonable. 'What are Perantas' instructions?'

A hint of anger sharpened Menekles' voice. 'I grant this house and household belong to Perantas, but I expect our personal property to be respected. Who is in charge?'

'Wait there.' The torch-bearer hammered on the gate with his free hand.

'All of you wait.' The discus thrower stepped forward, his gaze focused on Zosime in a way I really didn't like.

The gate behind the torch-bearer opened. I expected to see Thettalos. Instead the Nubian Wetka appeared. He nodded with satisfaction and I wondered uneasily what he had to be pleased about.

'Please, come in.'

I didn't move. If Perantas' man didn't like our answers, I didn't like the idea of being trapped in that courtyard with Zeus only knew how many Brothers of Bellerophon.

'Thank you,' Menekles said tersely as he walked forward.

Apollonides and Lysicrates followed, yawning extravagantly, and I had no choice but to do the same, though without the pretence of sleepiness. Zosime pressed close to my side.

A couple of lamps flickered fitfully in the courtyard, where the scene wasn't nearly as dramatic as I'd feared. The table had been dragged to one side and the fallen stools kicked underneath it, but nothing seemed to be broken. Amphorae and baskets of provisions had been dragged out of the storerooms, but they were carefully stacked rather than tossed aside. Everything here belonged to Perantas Bacchiad after all, just like the slaves.

They were huddled into a corner like sheep who'd caught the scent of a wolf. The girls were sniffing, damp-eyed with distress, but I couldn't see obvious signs that they'd been physically mistreated. One of the youths who had fetched and carried for Tromes was pressing a hand to a bloodied lip. From the defiance in his eyes as he stared at the closest Brother, I guessed he'd earned that slap, and didn't regret it.

The discus thrower and his mate with the torch went back to standing guard in the street, closing the gate behind them. A handful or more of the Brotherhood were still searching the stores and the slave accommodation. Their meagre possessions were trampled and torn by hobnailed sandals. A couple of blankets got stained as cosmetic jars were thrown out of a door to land hard enough to lose their stoppers. Several pallets spilled straw stuffing where a dagger had gutted them, and I guessed any carefully hoarded obols were now in some Brother's possession.

Menekles and Lysicrates pulled stools out from under the table. Apollonides set one on its feet, sat down and folded his arms on the table to make a pillow for his head.

I turned to Wetka. 'I didn't imagine you'd find Tromes here. I did tell Perantas I have no idea where he is.' The Nubian hadn't been at the temple on the Sikyon road.

He nodded. 'So the master said, but there is always the chance that the traitor left some clue as to where he might flee.'

They'd had plenty of time to discuss that. Perantas and his entourage would have got back to Corinth well before we reached Lechaion. I nodded and hoped this search would turn up some false scent to lead the hunters down any track but the road north to the port.

Menekles was still on his feet, indignant. He gestured up the steps to our accommodation. 'Can we go to bed?'

'Once we search those rooms. We have been waiting for you to return.' Wetka's smile was a meaningless courtesy.

I looked at Menekles and shrugged. 'I don't want to find a runaway under my bed in the middle of the night.'

The actor sighed. 'Very well, but be quick about it.'

Wetka snapped his fingers and two Brothers fetched lamps from the table. They went up the stairs, one on each side of the courtyard. Menekles strode after the first. I ushered Zosime to a stool between Lysicrates and Apollonides, before hurrying after the one heading for the rooms we shared with Kadous.

'Excuse me.' I pushed past him in the doorway and hurried through to the inner chamber. The last thing I needed was this clod spilling ink all over my half-finished rewrites. I gathered up the sheets of papyrus and made sure my pens and the ink pot were safely stowed in their box.

Hearing the scrape of furniture in the outer room, I returned to see the Brother holding the bag of Kadous' personal possessions. He had his dagger ready to cut the drawstring.

'You won't find Tromes inside that,' I said sharply.

He answered me with a faint sneer but dropped the bag on the bed.

'He's not through here either.' I waved a hand at the bed I shared with Zosime, at the table, the stools and our travelling chests. 'See for yourself.'

The man made a perfunctory search, and I followed him back down to the courtyard. Menekles was escorting the other Brother downstairs while Apollonides sat with an arm around Zosime's shoulders. Lysicrates looked to be genuinely asleep.

The courtyard gates opened and Thettalos strode in. Seeing Kadous standing by the storeroom door, the bull-necked man headed straight for the Phrygian.

'Where the fuck have you been?'

'You don't talk to my slave like that!' My loud rebuke echoed around the stone walls.

Hearing their leader's voice, the Brothers searching the lower rooms appeared in the doorways. All told, there were nine of them, as well as Wetka. Add the two on the gate and we'd be badly outnumbered if this situation turned ugly.

Lysicrates was sitting upright at the table now, and Menekles stood behind Zosime and Apollonides. Kadous was as still as a statue, his face a well-practised blank.

Thettalos turned on me as I crossed the courtyard. 'Where's he been? He wasn't with you on the Sikyon road.'

'He's been serving my companion today. What's it to you?' I matched his belligerence. That was taking a risk but I hoped Wetka could wield Perantas' authority over the Brotherhood.

'He's been in and out of the slave quarters here, ever since you arrived.' Thettalos' suspicious gaze searched my face. I could smell the stale garlic on his breath. 'If Tromes let anything slip, he heard it.'

I took a swift sidestep around the bull-necked man to stand between him and Kadous. 'You may speak freely,' I prompted.

The Phrygian clasped his hands behind his back, looking straight at me. 'I never heard Tromes say anything that hinted at betrayal. I have no idea where he might go.' His voice was strained but that was surely understandable in a slave facing such interrogation.

I turned to face Thettalos. 'You have your answer.'

'If I don't believe it?' His lip curled. 'I will find him, as Bellerophon is my witness.'

Wetka saved me from having to find a reply. 'What's the news from the city gates, Thettalos?'

At first I thought the bull-necked man wasn't going to answer the Nubian, but after a lingering stare at Kadous, he did so. 'None of our people saw him on the roads today.'

'And the Acrocorinth?' Wetka persisted.

Thettalos shook his head. 'No one's seen him.'

'Keep asking,' the Nubian ordered. 'There are a hundred places where he could be hiding but he will have to break cover eventually.'

I'd be very happy if their search stayed within the city walls, but I wasn't about to breathe easy just yet. It would only take a Bacchiad underling to find someone who'd seen Nados and the others hustling Tromes out of the city to bring disaster down on our heads. I wondered about putting Kadous on the next ship sailing from Kenchreai for Athens, for safety's sake, but doing that would arouse more suspicion.

'Excuse me.' Now Menekles was playing a reasonable man, polite despite severe provocation. 'If you are satisfied that this treacherous slave isn't here, perhaps you could depart? We would like to go to bed!' He let slip a calculated flash of anger.

Wetka bowed low. 'Please accept my sincere apologies.'

He even sounded as though he meant it. Perhaps he should take to the stage. Thettalos was unrepentant. He stood staring at us each in turn as Wetka told the Brotherhood that their work was done.

The Corinthians departed, taking their bright pine torches to leave the courtyard inadequately lit by its lamps. The slaves stayed cowering in the shadows.

'Should we make sure all's well at Eumelos' house?' Apollonides asked quietly. He and Lysicrates had abandoned their pretence of being overwhelmed by wine.

I looked at the huddled slaves and wondered who would report whatever we said to Wetka tomorrow in hopes of winning some favour, or from fear of retribution.

'Kadous!' I waved a hand at the stacked baskets and amphorae. 'Get them tidying up!'

The Phrygian immediately took charge. Now whatever we said should go unheard amid the bustle and whispered indignation as the slaves seized this chance to vent their feelings.

'Well?' Lysicrates prompted.

'I think we should leave well alone.' I'd been thinking about this. 'The last thing we want is to send the Brotherhood that way.'

Menekles nodded. 'Eumelos was Perantas' man and surely Thettalos will assume they're as loyal.'

I wasn't about to assume any such thing, given the suspicion I'd seen in Thettalos' eyes. Besides, Perantas had hardly rewarded Eumelos' allegiance. He hadn't attended his funeral, or made any effort to pursue his killer.

Before I could answer, there was an urgent knock at the gate. 'What have they forgotten?' I snarled.

But Kadous opened up to reveal someone I didn't recognise.

'Good evening,' the messenger said, composed. 'Chresimos sends his compliments, as well as his apologies given the lateness, but he has a patient you need to see.'

These past few days had been so hectic, it took me a moment to recall the amiable Cycladean doctor's name.

'Urgently?' The question was out before I could help it.

The man nodded. 'A man has been poisoned. Chresimos cannot say if he will live through the night.'

Apollonides, Menekles and Lysicrates got to their feet. 'Let's go.'

'Not you.' I pointed at Apollonides. 'Someone needs to stay with Zosime, and you need to suck on your pot of herbs.'

'I'll make sure he does.' Zosime kissed my cheek. 'Then I'm going to bed.'

'Sleep well.' I wished I could join her, but that didn't look like it was going to be an option tonight.

Chapter Eighteen

We made our way swiftly to the Asklepion. Our escort led us to the lower courtyard where the colonnade was as dark and still as it had been when Eumelos died. A single light shone to guide us to Chresimos and his patient.

A young man lay on a thin mattress, stripped of his tunic and draped with a rough blanket. His eyes were open but his expression was vacant as his head lolled from side to side. He didn't seem overly distressed, mumbling and giggling softly.

The Cycladean doctor stood by the bed, unfurling a scroll by the light of a lamp on a shelf. A young acolyte looked over his shoulder at the text.

'You were wise to look for a snake bite. However, since there's no sign of one, see here? All our observations agree with this account. When he arrived, he was able to talk but he could barely stand. He was convinced that the ground was shifting under him like a ship's deck in a storm. Then he began to complain of burning in his fingers and feet, but soon, he could feel nothing at all. His speech became slurred, and he collapsed.'

It sounded terrifying. I looked at the patient but I didn't recognise him.

'Good evening,' I said cautiously. 'Who's this?'

'I was hoping you could tell me.' Chresimos was clearly disappointed. 'This is the third poisoning I've seen inside eight days. Your enemies seem to have a particular fondness for such malice.'

'What's wrong with him?' At first glance I'd have said the boy was merely drunk, but the doctor clearly knew better.

'This particular affliction is known as "sweet madness", according to this physician's memoir.' Chresimos rolled up his papyrus with a brisk crackle and handed it to his apprentice. 'Please take that back to the library.'

As the acolyte left, the Cycladean continued as if we were all his pupils. 'You can smell a distinctive sickliness mingled with the wine on his breath. Please, go ahead.'

I was prepared to take his word for that. 'A poison caused this?'

'But not the same thing that killed Eumelos,' Menekles observed.

The doctor nodded. 'There's a particular honey found in Colchis, where the bees feed on rhododendron flowers growing up in the mountains. The locals take it in milk, in measured doses, as a restorative after illness, and apparently a spoonful adds quite a kick to a jug of wine. It's a hazardous pleasure though, as the potency of the honey can vary significantly. If it's too strong, such wine will induce euphoria that can slip into mania. Incautious indulgence can be very easily lethal.'

He gestured at the patient who was now muttering with more urgency, his arms and legs restless. 'This young fool has probably swallowed enough to lay him low for at least a day and a night. That's assuming it doesn't kill him outright. If he sleeps, he may yet recover. If he starts vomiting and purging, I'm far from hopeful.'

I still didn't understand what this had to do with us. Then the doctor reached under the mattress to pull out a bronze arm ring stamped with a familiar ragged club.

'He's a Son of Heracles. We treated enough of his friends after they tried to turn your chorus auditions into a riot, but we don't ask questions and they weren't inclined to identify themselves. Take another look. Are you sure you don't recognise him?'

'I'm sorry, no.' I glanced at the others, but they both shook their heads.

Chresimos looked down, regretful. 'If he has a family, they should be told, especially if he proves likely to die.'

I wondered if the stricken youth had heard the doctor. He started whimpering, and his wandering gaze fixed on something none of us could see. As his fists clenched like a man ready to fight, we all took a step away from the bed, apprehensive.

'He will suffer for some hours,' the doctor observed, dispassionate. 'Some men see enchanting visions, apparently. Others are besieged by horrors.'

'How did he get here?' Lysicrates asked.

'He was found wandering the streets by the agora by two men well known to the Asklepion. They had no idea who he was, but they could see he was in distress. They brought him here.'

I looked at my fellow Athenians, who were as clueless

as me. 'Who is the Sons of Heracles' patron? Presumably someone in that household might know who he is.'

'No one here can tell me whose silver currently funds that particular fraternity and their foolishness.' The doctor sighed. 'As a devotee of Asklepios, I steer clear of the hero cults, as do most of my colleagues.'

I raised a hand. 'Listen.'

The young man's thrashing had slowed to restless tossing, and his frantic whimpering had faded to a whisper. For the first time, I could make out words.

'Mother, help me. Help me, Mother. Mother, help me.'

Lysicrates moved swiftly to kneel by the bed. He stroked the matted curls from the youth's forehead with gentle fingers.

'I'm here, my poor boy, I'm here.' The actor spoke with the soothing tones of a loving matron. 'What's happened to you?'

The young man's wondering gaze fixed on Lysicrates but whatever he was seeing, it wasn't our friend's bearded face. 'Oh Mother, I'm so sorry.'

'I know, don't worry, but please, tell me what has happened.'

'They said not to drink the wine, but they didn't say why,' he babbled. 'They should have said it was dangerous. We had no idea . . .' His face twisted with concern. 'Don't drink the wine, Mother.'

'What wine, dearest heart? I don't understand.'

'At the theatre. Don't drink the wine,' he begged.

'I won't, don't worry, but what's wrong with the wine?'

Glassy-eyed, the boy stared. 'We're going to mix it with the wine for the theatre. They won't be laughing then. But you mustn't drink it, Mother, promise!'

'I promise, but tell me, where is this wine being kept?'

He smiled, lop-sided, as if the answer was obvious. 'At Demeas' house.'

I looked at Chresimos but the doctor answered with a shrug. He had no more idea than we did.

The boy was whimpering again, clutching Lysicrates' hand and begging his mother to save him from unseen terrors. The rest of us retreated. I don't know about anyone else, but I didn't want any malevolent spirits taking an interest in me.

Lysicrates stayed where he was as he hushed and comforted the youth. After a few unnerving moments, the frenzy subsided and the lad lay still, insensible.

Chresimos grunted inscrutably and drew the blanket down to uncover the young man's bony chest. He pinched a fold of skin between finger and thumb and twisted it viciously. Even though Lysicrates and I had seen him do the same to Eumelos, we still exclaimed as loudly as Menekles.

This time, so did the patient. His eyes opened and he moaned in wordless protest, trying to twist away from the pain, before sinking into unconsciousness again.

Chresimos grunted with satisfaction. 'That is a promising sign.'

'He's not going to die?' I hated to think of the bruise he'd wake up with.

The Cycladean raise a cautionary hand. 'It's far too

soon to be certain. Most likely, according to that scroll, he will linger for three or four days, until he either regains his senses or succumbs.'

Menekles shook his head. 'We can't wait that long to know what he knows.'

'We can wait until the morning to see if he's awake.' I stifled a yawn as I spoke.

'We've got to be at the Sanctuary for tomorrow's rehearsal,' Lysicrates reminded us.

'I suggest you take your discussion elsewhere.' Chresimos ushered us away from the bed and along the colonnade.

I stopped as we reached the stairs up to the hall of sleeping patients. 'Will you let the Sons of Heracles know he's here?'

The Cycladean looked at me. 'I take it you would rather I didn't?'

'We stand a much better chance of frustrating their plans if they don't know they've been betrayed.' I gestured back towards the lamp's glow. 'What do you suppose they'll do to him, if they realise he spilled the beans? Do you think they'll care that he was out of his mind?'

Chresimos nodded. 'Far better to wait and see how he fares. If he comes to his senses and can tell us his name, we can send for his family then. Of course, whoever he was with tonight must be wondering what's become of him. When someone goes missing, this is one of the first places people come to look.'

I remembered the boy had said 'we didn't listen'.

Hermes only knows how many of his friends were stumbling around the streets, raving.

'Could you . . . ?' Menekles hesitated.

Chresimos looked sternly disapproving. 'I will not lie and deprive this boy's family of a last chance to see him. He may still die.'

'That's only right and proper,' I said quickly.

The Cycladean nodded, his face a little less severe. 'I will not share anything he has said in his delirium. That can help no one.'

'Thank you,' I said fervently. 'We'll leave you to your duties.'

We walked quickly out and I glanced at the god's sanctuary to offer a prayer for the boy's recovery after a protracted sleep. Having him lie unconscious until the day after our performance would suit us. Though of course, that was in Apollo's gift, or Asklepios' and I dared not second-guess either deity's wisdom.

As we went out through the arched gateway, Menekles stopped abruptly. 'Does anyone really think the Sons of Heracles would try to poison our audience? To kill hundreds of Corinthians?'

Lysicrates glanced over his shoulder. 'Believe me, that lad wasn't faking.'

'I don't suppose they actually intend to kill anyone,' I said thoughtfully. 'Remember what he said about *mixing* the dangerous wine with the wine meant for the theatre? That would dilute this sweet madness to something less deadly, wouldn't it?'

'Getting the audience drunk against their will.' Menekles began walking again.

'More than drunk,' I pointed out as we all went with him. 'Feeling euphoria that can slip into mania.'

'The usual drunks in an audience are bad enough,' growled Lysicrates. 'Shouting and throwing things. Laughing like jackals in all the wrong places.'

I recalled my first play staged at the Lenaia festival in Athens. Finding courage in the bottom of too many wine cups, a couple of men in the upper seats had revived some old quarrel and began throwing punches. A handful of friends dragged them apart, adding to the cacophony as other audience members voiced their objections to such disruption. My whole chorus was distracted and their next song had been a ragged, feeble effort.

That chorus had been rehearsing for months, even though the Lenaia was only a city winter festival, nowhere near as prestigious as the Dionysia. After a mere eight days' practice, I wouldn't give a sixteenth of an obol for our Corinthian singers' chances of staying in tune and in step, if everyone in the theatre succumbed to this tainted wine. Whether the audience got ebullient or argumentative, *The Builders'* performance in Corinth would be remembered for all the wrong reasons.

'Where's the city's shrine to Dionysos?' I wondered aloud. 'We should ask the god to avenge this vile insult to his divine gift.'

If this was a play, I'd write a scene where the bastards responsible were strangled to death by grape vines. I didn't care that it wouldn't get a laugh.

As we reached the bottom of the ramp, two figures loomed out of the darkness. Thettalos was with a tall, heavyset man I recognised as one of the Brotherhood.

'So this is where you've hidden him.' Thettalos grinned unpleasantly at me.

It took a moment before I understood his meaning. It was hard to believe our trip to Lechaion had been earlier this same night. 'Tromes? Don't be an utter fool.'

'You're saying we won't find him tucked up in there?' the bull-necked man challenged me.

I spread my hands. 'Go and look for him, by all means. Go and insult another temple by starting a brawl. How many priests do you want complaining about your behaviour to Perantas Bacchiad?'

'You must know why we're here.' Menekles slipped instantly into the role of the voice of reason, counterpart to my antagonism. 'Whoever told you we'd been summoned to the Asklepion must have said someone had been poisoned.'

'Not just one idiot boy.' I gave Thettalos no chance to interrupt as I outlined this new threat to our performance. 'There's every chance his friends are still stumbling around the city, their heads filled with delights and nightmares. Make yourselves useful and go and find them. Someone called Demeas is behind this scheme apparently.'

'You'd like that,' Thettalos retorted. 'Sending us chasing shadows instead of looking for Tromes and finding out what he says about you.'

That had already occurred to me but I'd made sure no

one could read such thoughts on my face.

'You must know who Demeas is, surely?' Menekles was either genuinely puzzled or putting on the best performance I'd ever seen from him to provoke Thettalos. 'One of the Sons of Heracles?'

'Never heard of him,' Thettalos sneered, 'and we haven't heard a whisper of any plot to mess with the theatre wine.'

I suddenly realised why he was so confident. 'You've got your own spies, haven't you? Someone inside their patron's household is reporting to you. Who is behind the Sons of Heracles?'

Thettalos hesitated, but his desire to get the better of me won out. 'Alypos Temenid keeps that band of losers in cheap wine, and feeds their fantasies of being cocks of the dung hill. He'd be happy to see Perantas Bacchiad humiliated, but he threw his javelin when the Sons tried to smash up your auditions.'

'I'm sure he'd be delighted that you think so,' I countered. 'That'll make this scheme to wreak havoc so much easier.'

I saw a flicker of doubt in Thettalos' eyes. Menekles followed up our advantage.

'Why would we lie about this, when you can so easily check for yourself? Ask for a doctor called Chresimos. See what he has to say.'

I wished the actor hadn't said that. I reckoned Thettalos was perfectly capable of dragging that helpless boy out of his bed and trying to beat some answers out of him. Though it was hard to believe they'd get anything

237

out of the young Son without Lysicrates to play his doting mother.

Still, the Asklepion's slaves must be used to dealing with raving patients. I guessed they could easily deal with Thettalos and his hanger-on. That wouldn't do anything to stop this plot to dose our audience with madness though.

'Believe what you like. I'm going to bed.' I tried to walk around Thettalos but he sidestepped to stop me.

'You're lying about something, I know it.' He stared at me, before his gaze switched to Lysicrates. 'You sobered up fast, I see.'

Lysicrates met his gaze, glare for glare. 'Call me a liar, and you'll get a smack in the mouth.'

This time Thettalos stayed where he was as the two actors strode away. I quickly followed. No one said anything until we reached the main road to the agora.

Menekles spoke first. 'What are we going to do now?'

'We already know who peddles herbs to the Sons of Heracles,' I said grimly. 'We'll go and see Zopyros first thing tomorrow and find out whatever he knows. Meantime, we don't breathe a word of this where anyone can hear us. There's no way to know if Tromes was the only spy among Perantas' slaves. Someone could be carrying our every word to Alypos Temenid.'

The others murmured agreement and we continued on our way. We eventually reached our house, no longer the safe haven we had thought it, and found Kadous guarding the entrance with a club, which I guessed the

Brotherhood had left. I saw the silent question in his eyes.

'Let's get to bed.' I headed for the steps to the upper storey as the Phrygian bolted and barred the gates behind us.

Zosime was under the blankets, though she was still awake, stirring drowsily in the light of an oil lamp on the table as I opened the inner door. 'What happened?'

I waited in the doorway until Kadous appeared and closed the outer door to the stairs. I told them both what we'd discovered at the Asklepion, keeping my voice low to make sure my words didn't slip through the cracks in the floorboards to any slaves listening below.

'What are you going to do?' Zosime's eyes were dark and anxious in the dim light.

'I'm going to sleep.' I licked my finger and thumb and walked over to quench the lamp's wick. 'I'll tell you the rest tomorrow.'

Chapter Nineteen

I slept deep and dreamlessly, and woke still weary. The pale daylight told me it was still early morning, and I considered going back to sleep. Zosime had woken earlier still though. Dressed in a pale green dress, she was sitting at the table beneath the open shutters, diligently writing.

'Is that a letter home?' I didn't particularly want these past few days' events committed to papyrus.

There was no telling who might intercept a letter passing from hand to hand all the way to Athens. Such a document would be damning evidence for anyone accusing me of defaming a Corinthian noble.

Zosime's mischievous smile lifted my heart. 'I'm making some notes about the rewrites for the play that Telesilla and I discussed last night.'

'Oh, thank you, my beloved,' I said fervently.

Her tone was light, but as she sat there, pen poised, I saw concern in her eyes. 'I take it you have another busy day ahead of you?'

'I do, and I want you and Kadous to spend it with Telesilla and Arion. Take those notes with you,' I added.

Kadous had heard us talking. He knocked on the

inner door just as I heard familiar voices down in the courtyard. Apollonides and Lysicrates were awake.

Zosime stood up to peer out of the window. 'Time for breakfast.'

I threw back the blankets as she crossed the room and opened the door to let Kadous enter with a jug of washing water. By the time I was dressed and downstairs, Menekles had joined the others, and two subdued slave girls were setting out our breakfast on the courtyard table.

We ate in silence, apart from brief requests for someone to pass the fruit or some bread. No one needed reminding not to say anything that might be reported to hostile ears, and that list now included Wetka and Thettalos as far as I was concerned. We didn't tell any of the slaves where we were going and none of them dared ask.

On the plus side of the ledger, Apollonides' face was healing nicely, beneath the sheen of Chresimos' ointment.

As we reached the agora, people barely spared us an incurious glance. These Corinthians had their own concerns. I reminded myself how many ordinary citizens had no interest in the hero cults' rivalries. These were the people we'd come to entertain. These were the allies we were here to enlist, to join the Athenians founding the new city at Thurii. I mustn't lose sight of that, for Aristarchos' sake, if no longer for Perantas'.

'Are we all going to see Zopyros?' Menekles asked.

'Yes,' Lysicrates replied.

241

That was our sole conversation until we reached Hyanthidas' house, where only the briefest explanation was necessary. I told the musician how we'd uncovered yet another attempt to disrupt our play. Leaving Kadous with Telesilla and Zosime, the five of us headed up to the Acrocorinth.

Passing the Sanctuary of Demeter and Persephone reminded us that we needed to be back in time to greet our hard-working chorus. It wasn't only that we had no time to waste rehearsing our performance, we didn't want any awkward questions from our singers wondering where we might have been. There was still the possibility of a spy or merely some unwitting tattle-tale among their ranks.

The guards at the Acrocorinth's ever-open gates were lounging idly as usual. 'You won't find many places open for business just yet,' one called out.

Lysicrates acknowledged him with a casual wave. The rest of us soon saw that the guard was right. This fabled citadel of carnal delights had a mundane air in the morning. Gaggles of children were being escorted to their lessons. Household slaves were busy carrying baskets of charcoal, heavy jars of water, and the day's provisions from some market up here or down in the city.

Above our heads, women who could have been anyone's mother, sister or wife were opening shutters and shaking out bedding.

Tavern and brothel doors stood open as floors were swept and mopped. A couple of gangs in the uniform tunics of temple slaves were clearing up shattered pottery and more noxious refuse clogging the streets' gutters.

As we reached the small square overlooked by close-packed houses, we saw Zopyros sitting on his doorstep. The herbalist was sharing a jug of something and a loaf of barley bread with his brother. He looked far from sleek this morning, wearing a homespun tunic and with his hair yet to see a comb, never mind scented oils. His brother was tossing crumbs to drab little birds pecking about in the cracks of the paving. There was no one else around, though various windows were unshuttered and a door opposite stood ajar.

Zopyros stood up as soon as he saw us. We weren't close enough to hear what he said, but I'd put good coin on it being obscene. He looked at his door and I could see him debating the wisdom of hiding inside, with the two of them trying to bar our entry. That would be all well and good if they succeeded, but if the five of us forced our way in, he could expect more costly breakages. Staying out here at least offered the chance of his neighbours standing as witnesses if this encounter turned violent. Who knows, someone might even come to help.

'Good morning.' Still apprehensive, he greeted us. 'What can I do for you today?'

His brother got to his feet, still chewing and with drops of milk clinging to his beard. I saw a bruise on his face from our last encounter. He seemed slower to recognise us, and I wondered if he had all his wits. He was certainly content to let Zopyros do the talking.

'That depends.' I halted to keep more than an arm's

length between us in case the herbalist had another knife hidden in the folds of his russet tunic. 'Do you sell Colchis honey? The kind that causes what they call the sweet madness?'

'I don't touch that shit. It's far too dangerous, too unpredictable. I want satisfied customers coming back, not clawing out their own eyes to stop seeing the monsters, or jumping off the citadel ramparts because they think they can fly.'

His shudder convinced me he was telling the truth. I hated to think of the chaos this stuff could cause in the theatre, even diluted in the wine offered to the audience.

'Who sells it?' Menekles asked. 'Here in Corinth, or maybe in one of the ports?'

Zopyros looked at him warily, clearly wondering if this newcomer shared the talent for violence that the three of us he'd met had displayed. 'How by Hades should I know?'

Lysicrates took a step forward, cracking his knuckles. Slow-witted or not, the herbalist's brother stepped forward, scowling, and with his fists clenched.

'It's all right, Kittos,' Zopyros said hastily. He looked at me warily. 'There's a man I'd go to, if I had a need for Colchis honey. There may well be others,' he warned. 'Don't blame me if he's not who you're looking for.'

'Just give us a place to start,' I told him.

'What's it worth?' He challenged Apollonides with an unrepentant glance. 'Since we've already settled accounts for the hellebore lotion.'

'If your information is sound, we'll be back with a fat

244

purse for you.' I had no problem promising him Peran-tas' silver in return for saving our play. 'And we'll most likely be removing a rival in your trade. You said you were a businessman, didn't you?'

'That's true.' Zopyros' laugh told me I'd read the herbalist's motives right.

'I suggest you make enquiries of Hermaios Hygestra-tou,' he went on after a moment. 'He sells a whole lot of nasty things.'

'Where do we find him?' I asked.

'Three doors down from a brothel called the Hal-cyon.' Zopyros waved vaguely westwards. Then he paused, pursing his lips. 'I'll give you this titbit for free. The Sons of Heracles favour the girls at the Halcyon, so watch your step.'

'We'll bear it in mind.' That was a two-edged blade.

It probably meant we were on the right track, as the Sons of Heracles had already used poison on our masks. It also significantly increased the odds of passing some-one on that street who knew we were the actors from Athens. Someone we had scant chance of recognising, unless they were carrying scars and bruises from the fight at the Sanctuary.

'Well?' Zopyros was impatient, now that he was con-fident we weren't about to smash up his shop. 'Can I get on with my day?'

'By all means,' I said, obliging.

'Don't forget that fat purse you'll owe me,' Zopyros called out as we headed back towards the citadel's busier districts.

Once I was confident we were out of earshot, I turned to Hyanthidas. 'Do you know the Halcyon?'

He nodded. 'Are we going there now?'

'We've got time before we need to be back at the Sanctuary.' I saw the same thoughts on everyone's face. 'We may as well scout out the ground. If we come back after the rehearsal, I imagine the brothel will be open for business and that makes it far more likely we'll run into trouble if that's where the Sons of Heracles dip their wicks.'

We soon reached the main street leading towards the Temple of Aphrodite.

'Finding their honey seller won't tell us where they're keeping the tainted wine,' Menekles observed.

'Maybe this Hermaios knows who Demeas is.' I wondered what we might have to do, to persuade an unprincipled narcotic seller to tell us what we wanted. I didn't imagine he would be as obliging as Zopyros.

Hyanthidas took us to a district of this lofty city within a city which lay to the south of the great gleaming marble temple. He turned down a lane that ran close by the citadel walls topping those fearsome sheer cliffs. The gates to courtyards and houses on either side were still closed, with little to distinguish them from each other. At the far end of the lane a tavern stood on the corner of a street cutting back towards the heart of the citadel. A nondescript workshop faced it.

The musician halted, counting off the gates on the same side as the workshop. He pointed. 'That's the Halcyon.'

'So that's the honey seller's place on the corner.' This was a far less salubrious street than the route to the House of Pearls. There was filth in the gutters, and I could see chips and stains on the walls. Some rusty brown smudges looked ominously like dried blood.

'Are we all going in?' Menekles asked.

'Strength in numbers,' Lysicrates observed.

'Not everyone's as easily intimidated as Zopyros.' Apollonides voiced my own doubts.

'Let's see if he sells Colchis honey at all, before we ask who he sells it to.' I pointed at the tavern on the opposite corner, and looked at Hyanthidas, Apollonides and Lysicrates. 'You three wait there while Menekles and I go and get the measure of this Hermaios. Once we're sure he's our man, we can go back in with a show of force.'

'Once we know who else might be in there with him,' added Menekles.

'We'll keep watch for any Sons of Heracles.' Hyanthidas was already alert for approaching strangers.

'That sounds like a plan.' Lysicrates approved.

'Let's not ask for sweetened wine though,' Apollonides said in a vain attempt at humour.

'Give us a sign when that street yonder is empty.' I reckoned the fewer people who saw us visiting Hermaios in his dubious emporium, the better.

Menekles and I waited as the others took seats outside the tavern. A few moments later, Hyanthidas got up and went inside, presumably in search of someone to serve them. Lysicrates sat upright on his stool and stretched his arms high, interlaced fingers arching backwards.

I glanced at Menekles. 'Do you suppose that means it's all clear?

He laughed briefly. 'It did in Callias' *Ditch Diggers*.'

I couldn't remember if that comedy had come second or third in the Dionysia five years ago. I shook off the distraction and began walking.

Menekles fell into step with me. 'Who's doing the talking?'

'Just follow my lead.' We were going to have to improvise and, once again, I thanked Dionysos for an experienced actor at my side.

I knocked on the weather-beaten door and a voice inside snapped less of an invitation and more of a command. 'Enter!'

I pushed the door open. 'Hermaios Hygestratou?'

A hard-faced man with stained hands stood behind a table, grinding something in a mortar and pestle. He looked up, his eyes suspicious. 'Who wants to know?'

'Oh, come now.' Menekles smiled, sly as a fox skulking along the Piraeus docks. 'Isn't what we want to buy more important?'

'As long as we can find that,' I agreed, 'who cares if we don't find Hermaios?'

Menekles hooked his thumbs in his belt. 'Then we can't say who we bought it from. No matter who asks.'

'Any more than an honest trader could have any idea who we were or where we might have gone.' I smiled cheerfully at the man behind the table.

He didn't smile back. 'What might you be looking for?'

'A friend of ours told us you were the man to give us a special something to add to a cup of wine,' Menekles began, conspiratorially.

'I told him it would do the trick.' Unexpectedly, Hermaios grinned with all the charm of a month-old corpse. 'As long as his stupid little whore played her part.'

'Oh, she certainly did that.' Menekles was wonderfully convincing. No onlooker would know he had no idea what this villain was talking about. 'So what's the going rate for a little sweet madness these days?'

'What?' Hermaios laid down his pestle amid the clutter on the table.

I just stood there, as frozen with shock as one of Medusa's victims. We'd found the bastard who'd sold the dose that killed Eumelos.

'Colchis honey.' Menekles realised something was wrong but tried to brazen it out. 'Our friend told us you could supply it.'

I found my voice and tried to tell the actor what I'd realised. 'We're not looking for anything in a blue glass bottle today.'

I saw a flicker in the herbalist's eyes. It was as fleeting as lightning on the horizon, but it was there. It was enough to convince me that we'd found our poisoner.

'I don't know what you're talking about.' Hermaios had a wickedly pointed knife in his hand and he was coming around the table. 'Fuck off out of here. I know who you are now. Fuck off back to Athens, if any of you can reach Kenchreai without having your throats cut first.'

Menekles took a step back towards the workshop door. 'No problem.'

'You can't kill both of us.' I was retreating at his side, shoulder to shoulder.

'You want to bet on that?' The gleam in Hermaios' eye told me he fancied his chances.

I reached behind me with one hand as I watched for any sign that the bastard was about to attack. My fingers found the rough wood of the door. Thanks to Hecate, goddess of entrances and poisons alike, I hadn't latched it shut. I dug my fingernails into the edge of the timber and managed to drag it forward to get a firm hold.

'You don't want to be explaining two dead bodies.' I hoped to give him pause for thought, because I was going to have to take a step forward to get the door open wide enough for us to slip through.

His chuckle was chilling. 'You think anyone will wonder what killed you, when you're found broken at the foot of these cliffs?'

'You think we were fool enough to come here without our friends knowing where we are?'

Menekles' defiance gave me the chance I needed to get the door open. I slid through the gap and braced myself, ready to wrench it closed as soon as the actor was through, or to use all my weight to slam it into Hermaios if he lunged at Menekles.

We got out without him knifing either of us, and pulled the door closed. As we ran across the street to the tavern, the others sprang to their feet.

'What happened?' Apollonides demanded.

'What's he doing?' Lysicrates said in the next breath.

Menekles and I spun around to see the poisoner leaving his workshop. Hermaios was running away like a rat scurrying along a gutter.

Hyanthidas went after him, long-legged strides quickly closing the distance between them. Not quickly enough. Hermaios was only going three doors down. He hammered on the gate of the brothel. As the Halcyon's doorman opened up, Hyanthidas skidded to a halt. For a long moment, everybody stood motionless.

A familiar, wiry man appeared on the brothel's threshold. As our gazes met, there was no question that he recognised me.

'I'll wager all the silver in Perantas' strongboxes that's Demeas.'

The gate slammed shut before I finished speaking.

'Get back here!' I shouted at Hyanthidas. 'We need to leave!'

Chapter Twenty

Hyanthidas led us away down the broader street that ran towards the heart of the citadel.

'What happened?' Apollonides asked.

'He's the honey seller.' I had no doubt about that, even if we had nothing like proof. 'And he sold the poison that killed Eumelos.'

'What?' Apollonides stopped dead in the middle of the road.

'He thought we were there to buy another of those blue glass vials. He knew that someone somehow persuaded that little whore Arete to give the dose to Eumelos.' I shook my head. 'Whatever she said convinced him to put it in his wine. Why should he suspect any harm would come of it?'

I remembered the brothel keeper Eirene saying he knew full well the girl was devoted to him. Her hysteria hadn't been overwhelming grief. It had been guilt.

'Can we discuss this somewhere else?' Lysicrates demanded. He shouted at Menekles who was standing watching the lane where the brothel and the workshop stood. 'What are you waiting for?'

He sprinted towards us. 'A dozen or more men just

left the brothel. Five are coming after us. The rest headed the other way.'

'The wiry man,' I demanded. 'Not the poisoner or the doorkeeper. Which way did he go?'

Before Menekles could reply, our pursuers appeared by the tavern corner. I couldn't see any weapons but that meant nothing. There are more ways to kill a man besides knifing him. Hurling him off the top of these cliffs would do nicely.

'Come on!' Hyanthidas was striding on ahead.

We had to run to catch up with him. I heard Apollonides wheezing from the exertion.

'What's our plan?' Lysicrates looked back at our pursuers. 'What's their plan, come to that? Murder in broad daylight?'

'They're going to stop us reaching the gate,' I said grimly, 'while those bastards cut off our retreat.'

Our unseen foes must be cutting through alleyways and lanes to get ahead of us. Demeas doubtless knew the Acrocorinth like the back of his hand. I could only hope Hyanthidas was as familiar with these streets. The citadel was unknown territory to the rest of us.

'Should we make for the temple?' Lysicrates gestured towards Aphrodite's gleaming marble shrine as we walked quickly along. 'Tell the priestesses what's going on? Enlist some temple slaves as an escort down to the city? The Sons wouldn't dare attack us.'

I was torn. That was a sound idea, if our only aim was getting away unharmed, but other considerations applied. 'How long will all that take? We'd need to explain everything that's happened, and convince whoever's in charge that we're not raving mad. By the time we've managed that, Demeas and his henchman will have told Alypos Temenid that we've discovered their plot. They'll pour that tainted wine into a cess pit.'

'I'll settle for that,' Menekles said, forthright. 'Then our audience can enjoy a free drink with no need for us to worry.'

'But we'll have no proof.' Hyanthidas made a swift left turn down a side street. 'The Sons of Heracles won't be held to account.'

'What were you saying about Eumelos' death?' Lysicrates shot me a glance as we hurried faster. 'Can you prove Alypos Temenid ordered that murder?'

'It's complicated.' I realised how much depended on poor, foolish Arete. *If* she could be persuaded to admit her unwitting part in the plot. *If* the Corinthian Council would give any weight to her words.

My blood ran cold as Hyanthidas led us through a paved yard. Arete had to stay alive long enough to explain how she'd been duped into giving Eumelos the poison. Hermaios hadn't mentioned her by name. I wondered if Demeas and his fellow brutes knew who she was? If they did, there was every chance that a Son masquerading as a client would snap her neck before the end of the day.

I stifled an impulse to tell Hyanthidas to take us to the House of Pearls, to warn the brothel mistress, Eirene. Such heroics make for fine drama, but reality is more complicated. That detour would take up time we couldn't afford to lose. Besides, if the Sons of Heracles didn't know who Arete was, going there would be as good as telling them where to look for Eumelos' favourite whore.

Feeling sick with apprehension, I glanced up at the glorious Temple of Aphrodite as we reached a wider road. I begged the immortal goddess to stretch out a protective hand over her handmaiden. If I was wrong, I pleaded for her divine forgiveness. I prayed that she would sharpen every instinct that Mistress Eirene had honed over the years plying her trade. Let that slave Sekis be alert as never before, scenting danger like the good guard dog he was. As soon as I got the chance, I swore fervently, I would send them a warning.

Menekles slowed as we approached a junction. 'Those two just left the Halcyon.'

A couple of men appeared. They recognised us, and headed our way.

Lysicrates had taken over the rearguard's duty. 'Our escort's getting closer,' he warned.

These streets were getting busier, but there were nowhere near enough people out and about for us to lose ourselves in a crowd.

'Hyanthidas?' We needed a way out before we were caught like a shrimp in a crab's claw.

He hesitated an instant too long for my peace of mind. 'Down there.'

We cut down a winding lane. Our pursuers lost sight of us, though we also lost sight of them, so I wasn't sure who got the best of that bargain. We took one turning, then another, passing back exits and storage yards.

'How far to the citadel gate?' I asked Hyanthidas. I had lost my bearings completely.

'Follow me.' He strode along a narrow street.

I looked at Apollonides, concerned to see him increasingly short of breath. That left me and the musician to fight anyone in front of us. Menekles and Lysicrates were bringing up the rear.

'Shit.' Hyanthidas stopped as three men appeared from some unknown property's rear door. 'This way.'

We followed him down an alleyway. Now Hyanthidas was running and Menekles was pushing Apollonides forward to take my outstretched arm. The alley was barely wide enough for the two of us to run side by side. That meant I crashed right into Hyanthidas when he skidded to an abrupt halt.

We had stumbled into a small square surrounded by shuttered houses. One familiar face and three unknown men were waiting for us. They'd herded us here like hunters running deer to ground.

I nodded to the wiry man. 'You're Demeas, I take it?'

His grin was all the answer I needed.

I took a step forward. 'So what happens now?'

'We escort you to Kenchreai and put you on the first boat back to Athens,' he said cheerily, 'or your loving families get the tragic news that you died in a street robbery in Corinth.' He shrugged. 'It's all the same to me, as long as none of you set foot in the theatre.'

He sounded confident, but I could see tension in the men beside him. 'How long have we got to choose?'

Demeas laughed. 'Take all the time you need.'

I saw more unease among the men with him. I stepped backwards, still watching for any hint of an attack, but close enough to talk to my friends without being overheard.

'Menekles, can you hold that alley entrance on your own?' I asked quietly.

'I can try.' He sounded reasonably certain.

'He keeps looking around. So do his cronies. They're waiting for the rest of their phalanx to find us.'

'Tell me,' Demeas shouted. 'Where would you like your bodies found? In the house fire that will unaccountably consume Perantas' property, or floating face down in Kenchreai harbour?'

'See how happy he is to keep talking?' I murmured. 'Apollonides, are you fit to fight?'

'If we're quick about it.' He was wheezing like a blacksmith's bellows, but his colour was good and his eyes were determined.

'We're not going to get another chance,' I said. 'That man Demeas has a hand in all their schemes.'

'Let's shut his mouth, and see how well they cope without their chorus leader.' Lysicrates cracked his knuckles.

I took a step forward with him at my side. Apollonides was at my other shoulder, flanked by Hyanthidas.

'Oh, come now.' Demeas laughed, less convincing. 'You can't expect . . .'

We kept walking, our pace increasing. The gap between us closed. I was pleased to see Demeas' lips narrow and a frown crease his brow. The three men with him were scowling, fists clenched. Their eyes were darting this way and that, still looking for reinforcements.

'They're coming,' Menekles shouted behind us.

I could only trust that the alley's narrow mouth meant he only faced one attacker at a time. With his long reach, I could hope he'd have the advantage. I hurled a prayer at Ares as Lysicrates flung himself on the man at the end of Demeas' line.

'I'm going to rip your ears off, shithead!' He knocked the Corinthian clean off his feet and they wrestled in the dust.

Apollonides was saving his breath to fight. His opponent swung a wild punch. The stocky actor ducked, and drove his own fist into the Corinthian's ribs. Right hand and left struck in swift succession. The Corinthian staggered back.

I had no idea what Hyanthidas was doing, and taking a look would be utter folly. As fate would have it, Demeas was straight ahead of me and I relished my chance at revenge for the grief he had caused us.

'Stupid fucking Athenians. You have no business in the Peloponnese.' He was backing away. For all his belligerent words it seemed he wasn't so keen on fighting face to face, preferring to punch a man in the kidneys from behind.

I wasn't fooled. He unbuckled his belt, and started wrapping the leather around his knuckles like a wrestler.

'Come on,' he taunted. 'Let's see your dance steps.'

I made a move, as if I was about to rush him, only to recoil at the last instant. That meant I avoided the heavy bronze buckle hitting me in the face as he lashed out with his belt, the leather snapping like a striking snake.

Maybe he'd picked up that trick from the Brotherhood in that fight at the Sanctuary. Maybe it was a common Corinthian tactic. It didn't matter. I was ready. In the same breath, I lunged forward with my hand outstretched. The leather smacked into my forearm, burning like a whip lash. I didn't care. I closed my hand, too quickly for Demeas to realise I had a firm grip.

I planted my feet, bent my knees and hauled. He let go. It was still too late. He'd been dragged off balance, staggering towards me.

Now I had the belt in both hands. I dodged behind him, as light on my feet as any chorus singer. I flipped the leather over his head. Instantly seeing the danger, he got one hand up. That wasn't enough. I drew a loop tight around his neck. With his hand trapped, and me behind him, he could only flail wildly, unable to land more than ineffectual buffets with his other elbow.

His hair was close-cropped. I could see the skin below his ear, behind his beard, growing dark with blood. As his knees buckled. I hooked my heel around his shin to sweep his foot out from under him. As he collapsed, I leaned forward to make sure I kept the belt tight around his neck until he lay face down on the paving.

'Are you going to kill him?' Lysicrates was sitting on his victim's belly, his knuckles bloody. The man waved his hands feebly in surrender, his face cut by Lysicrates' rings. His anguished mumbling made me wonder if his jaw was broken, to go with his bloody nose and two blackened eyes.

'It's probably best if he lives.' Halfway across the square, Hyanthidas stood over a man lying huddled and weeping, hiding his head in his arms. I've no idea what the piper had done, but just the sound of his voice made the fallen man flinch and curl into a tighter ball.

I slackened the strangling loop of leather. I had no wish to stand before Corinth's Council accused of murder by Alypos Temenid. This wasn't Athens, where I could trust in a citizen jury's wisdom, where the law insisted on a panel of hundreds chosen by lot to pass judgement. Our democracy negates attempts at bribery or coercion by men of wealth and influence.

Besides, I wanted to know what this bastard knew about Eumelos' death. Moving quickly before Demeas regained his senses, I buckled his wrists together behind his back. Stepping to one side, I reached for his feet. The belt was just long enough for me to knot the leather loosely around one of his ankles, drawing it up behind his arse. That left his other foot free, but if he wanted to come hopping after us, he was welcome to try.

'That won't hold him for long,' Apollonides observed, breathless.

'Long enough.' I looked at the actor, who was standing hunched over with his hands on his thighs, his chest heaving. 'Where did your brave Son go?'

Apollonides managed a grin. 'He couldn't get away fast enough when he saw that bastard go down.'

'Let's get out of here before he comes back with some

friends.' I glanced across the courtyard to see Menekles smacking a man's head into a wall. The Son reeled backwards, only to trip over one of his fallen allies. A third man was lying moaning in the mouth of the alley. I wondered how many others had fled in search of reinforcements.

As the actor hurried towards us, he pressed a palm to his side, and blood trickled from his split lip.

'Well done, Leonidas,' Lysicrates said lightly. 'You'd think they'd remember Thermopylae if they admire the Spartans so much.'

He stood up and I saw he'd taken a few blows to the face. I also noticed him grimace as he cautiously flexed his bloody hands. There was no time to ask how much damage he'd done to himself. At my feet, Demeas was starting to stir. I kicked him in the groin to give him something else to think about.

I looked at Hyanthidas. 'Which way?'

'Follow me.' There wasn't a mark on him.

We left the square with Demeas spitting incoherent insults, unable to free himself with his wrists buckled together behind his back. None of the other Sons were in any condition to help him, and they wouldn't be any time soon. We walked along a side street to arrive at the main thoroughfare leading to the citadel gate.

'How do you know your way around this labyrinth so well?' Menekles asked Hyanthidas.

'I learned my trade up here. There's always plenty of work for musicians in these taverns and brothels and they're forgiving audiences, with so much else around to distract them. Generous, too.' The piper's face hardened. 'Bullies like the Sons and the Brotherhood are always hanging around, ready to demand half your earnings in tribute to whatever hero they're flattering.'

I guessed that was when he'd learned his fighting skills, but that was a conversation for another time. We were approaching the open gates and the road winding down the mountainside.

Apollonides was breathing easier by now, and Menekles was striding along without any obvious sign of pain. Lysicrates was the one of us who'd most clearly been in a fight. Bruises on his face were darkening and he held his blood-stained fingers loosely curled. Anyone who came close enough to risk jostling him was warned off with a glare.

The gate guards seemed their usual indolent selves as we drew closer, but we hadn't given them cause to be curious about us before.

'Are there going to be awkward questions?' I asked Hyanthidas.

'If you swear out a complaint, they'll investigate, and they're pretty good at sniffing out answers.' He shrugged. 'If you don't say anything, they won't ask. People come up here to get their fun in all sorts of ways.'

We went on our way unhindered, and had an easy enough walk to the Sanctuary. Unsurprisingly, Zosime, Telesilla and the two slaves were startled by our battered appearance.

'What happened?' Zosime demanded. 'The chorus will be here any time now. How do we explain that?'

She gestured at Lysicrates and Menekles.

'We wear the practise masks,' the tall actor said tersely.

'Let's wash and wrap your hands.' Telesilla directed Lysicrates towards the dining suite where we were storing our supplies.

Zosime narrowed her eyes at Apollonides. 'You look as if you could use a cup of wine.'

'I need papyrus and ink.' I headed for the other door. 'Hyanthidas, does Arion know the way to the House of Pearls?'

'Yes.' The musician had fetched a jug of water and was pouring drinks for us all. 'Here.'

I took the cup he offered and emptied it in one breath.

'More?' He raised the jug.

'Later.' I handed Menekles the cup and went to the table inside the costume store where writing materials lay ready to hand.

'What is going on?' Irritation was starting to outstrip Zosime's concern.

'I'll explain, I swear, but later.' I wrote a swift note to the brothel keeper Eirene. 'Forgive me, but lives may depend on this.'

I rolled up the crackling papyrus and handed it to Arion. 'Give this to the gate guard, Sekis. Tell him it's for his mistress and no one else. As quick as you can.'

As he scurried off, I looked at the actors. 'It only takes one of us to tell Perantas what's going on. Can you manage the rehearsal between you until I get back?'

'You're not going alone,' Lysicrates said, forthright.

'Of course not. Kadous!' I beckoned to the Phrygian.

Zosime wasn't going to waste her breath. 'We'll tell them you're still working on the rewrites,' she said sardonically.

I really wished she hadn't reminded me about that. 'I'll be back as soon as I can.'

Kadous and I left the Sanctuary and headed down the road to Corinth. 'Keep your eyes open,' I warned, before I told him the tale of our morning's adventures.

Chapter Twenty-One

We arrived at Perantas Bacchiad's house safely. I didn't recognise the Brothers guarding the gates but they knew who I was. One of them went running to fetch Wetka.

The Nubian was his usual imperturbable self. 'Good day.'

'Is your master at home?' I had no time to waste on pleasantries.

He nodded. 'He needs to see you both.'

As we followed him through the outer courtyard to the shady inner sanctum I wondered why. I had more time to ponder the question than I expected. Perantas wasn't sitting amid his painted olive trees. Wetka pointed to stools in the empty porch. 'Please wait here.'

'Take a seat,' I told Kadous, thankful for the chance to take the weight off my own feet.

The Nubian disappeared through a nearby door, and I wondered what lay beyond it. I had no idea if Perantas had a wife or children, whether he had an acknowledged lover or used slaves to warm his bed and slake his lusts. Somehow, he didn't strike me as the type to visit the Acrocorinth's brothels.

He soon arrived, narrowing his eyes at Kadous who

was already rising to stand behind my stool as a good slave should.

'I told him he could sit,' I said quickly.

'That's of no consequence.' Perantas waved a hand but his tone implied that something else was.

I got straight to the point. 'I take it Thettalos told you what we discovered last night? There's a Sons of Heracles plot to cause chaos at our performance with tainted wine?'

Perantas nodded. 'He did.'

'We think we've discovered who supplied the Colchis honey. He's a trader in dubious herbs and worse, up on the Acrocorinth, Hermaios Hygestratou. Unfortunately, he has close ties to the Sons of Heracles, and he realised who we were. They know we've discovered their plot. Whoever's storing the wine will destroy it as soon as they get word.' I spread apologetic hands. 'It couldn't be helped, I'm sorry.'

Perantas nodded, not unduly perturbed. 'That's unfortunate, but Thettalos and his Brothers are keeping watch outside Alypos Temenid's house. Hopefully they'll pick up a scent that will lead them to those responsible. Regardless, now that we know, the Brotherhood will guard the wine I'm supplying for the theatre like Cerberus guarding the Underworld.'

He broke off as a slave approached, carrying a tray with two fine ceramic cups and an equally expensive jug. Wetka poured aromatic amber wine and Perantas raised his drink to his lips.

'There's more.' I waited until the slave had set the

tray on a table and retreated. I leaned forward to take my wine. 'Hermaios let something else slip. He supplied the poison that killed Eumelos.'

'To whom?' Perantas looked at me intently.

'As yet, I don't know, but they must be Athenians.' On the walk down the mountain, I'd realised what was chafing me about that encounter. 'I was with Menekles who was hinting we were up to no good. When Hermaios heard our accents, he assumed we were part of that earlier conspiracy, not this plot to poison the wine.'

I saw no reason to mention Arete's involvement, and not just because she didn't deserve to be interrogated by the likes of Thettalos. There was no knowing who might overhear her name mentioned here. There was no knowing which conniving oligarchs on Corinth's Council might have their own spies in Perantas' household.

The Bacchiad's face was impossible to read as ever. 'Alypos has no allies in Athens, as far as I am aware.'

'It's hard to imagine Athenians conspiring with such a staunch supporter of the Spartans,' I agreed, 'but we know Aristarchos' rivals back home are opposed to the Thurii colony.'

'Indeed,' Perantas allowed.

'Surely that means they're opposed to our play,' I continued.

That also meant I wanted to know about any Athenians whom Arete had had dealings with. We needed to talk before anyone had a chance to silence her. I'd take whatever I learned back to Aristarchos. This could be our chance to discover who had paid the Peloponnesian killer Iktinos to do their dirty work back in the spring.

Perantas smiled. 'How are your rehearsals going?'

'Very well, and I had better get back.' I drank my wine and stood up.

Perantas raised a hand. 'There is something else we need to discuss.' He glanced at Kadous. 'Your slave is accused of theft. Apparently he stole a valuable belt buckle as well as sundry rings and brooches, and sold them to a trader in the agora.'

'Who says so?' I demanded.

'A sewer rat who rents a charcoal storehouse on the Kenchreai road, built on land that Alypos owns. He swears he can identify the belt buckle as his own. It's stamped with the Sons of Heracles' insignia,' Perantas explained, sardonic. 'A valuable family heirloom.'

I realised what this was about. 'They're talking about the bits and pieces we swept up after that fight at Demeter's Sanctuary, when the Sons tried to wreck our auditions. We had no way to know who that lost property might belong to.'

'Did you make any effort to find out?' Perantas asked.

'No.' I stared at him. 'Are you saying we should have?'

He shook his head. 'No, but that's what Alypos and his cronies will say, if they get a chance to drag you and your man before the Council.'

'That decision was mine,' I said firmly. 'I told Kadous to dispose of the rubbish and see if he could sell the rest, to use the silver to buy some treats for the slaves you've been lending us, as a reward for their diligent service.'

'Is that an Athenian custom?' Perantas didn't wait for

me to answer. 'Alypos and his allies will choose not to believe in such generosity, and many others will find it hard to credit.'

So did he, I suspected. 'I have witnesses to the instructions I gave my slave, all of them free men of Athens, as well as Hyanthidas, and he's a Corinthian citizen.'

'Your fellow actors and your musician.' Perantas smiled without humour. 'Leaving your chorus utterly bereft if Alypos persuades the Council to summon you when you should be singing your first song in the theatre, keeping you answering questions all day.'

'Could he do that?' I asked uneasily, remembering the temple slaves arriving at Eumelos' funeral.

'If he can muster enough allies, and I hear he's made common cause with Philolaos Kypselid, at least for as long as it takes to stop our play.'

Perantas' smile took on a cruel twist. 'Though they will have to find a new complainant. I gather your accuser cannot be found this morning. But that will only take Alypos a few days,' he warned. 'A fat purse of silver will outweigh someone's fear of the consequences. I suggest you make arrangements to sail back to Athens as soon as possible after your performance.'

'Indeed.' We'd all be ready to leave this city where we had been beset by malice at every turn. Even so, I would make sure to learn all I could from Arete before we took the road to Kenchreai.

Perantas was still occupied with his own concerns. 'Keep your man off the streets as much as possible. Alypos won't order the Sons to snatch you or any of the actors, for fear of insulting an Athenian as influential as Aristarchos. A slave will be fair game though, especially one who's clearly a favourite. Who knows what they might demand in return for sending him back.'

I was learning to read Perantas. He thought my loyalty to a slave was as foolish as it was distasteful.

I rose to my feet. 'We'll be careful.'

'I look forward to seeing you all at the theatre.' Perantas glanced at Wetka, who stepped forward to escort us out.

I turned to the Nubian as we reached the outer gate as casually as I could. 'Talking of slaves, have you had any success hunting down Tromes?'

I'd like to think that we'd know if they'd caught him, not least because we'd be neck-deep in the shit alongside Nados, Aithon and Simias, but I had to consider the possibility that Perantas would ignore our complicity in the slave's escape, at least until the play was over. Meantime, I had no doubt the slave's death would be ugly and painful if he had fallen into Bacchiad hands.

Wetka let slip a hiss of exasperation. 'Not yet.'

I shrugged. That seemed safer than saying anything. We walked through the gate, Kadous a few paces behind me, and I offered a meaningless smile to the Brotherhood boys loitering in the shade.

When we drew level with the theatre, I slowed to let Kadous walk alongside me. 'It looks like Tromes is well away. Let's hope he's still running.'

The Phrygian allowed himself a grin. 'If he's got any sense.'

270

'I made a bad mistake with those buckles and brooches,' I acknowledged. 'You're going to have to stay out of sight. I won't have some Corinthian oligarch thinking he can get to me through you.'

Kadous scowled. 'I'm not—'

'The same goes for Zosime,' I continued as if he hadn't spoken. 'She's not an Athenian citizen, and one of these bastards may think they can attack her without fear of legal consequences. I need you to stay as close as her shadow, on or off the streets.' With luck, they'd both stay safer that way.

'Now let's head back up this sodding mountain.' Not for the first time on this trip, I felt as if I'd already put in a full day's toil before we'd even started on the work we were actually here to do.

The effort was worth it. Thanks to Apollo, Dionysos, Athena, and any other god looking favourably on our efforts, the day's rehearsal went really well. The chorus were nigh on step and word perfect. The actors were well satisfied with the changes they'd made to keep Apollonides' exertions to a minimum. The challenge of the marketplace scene still lay ahead, but all I could do about that was trust in Chresimos' steamed herbs.

Menekles and Lysicrates kept their masks on until the last of the chorus had left, convincingly busy with something or other. When they took the masks off, I was relieved to see their faces weren't too badly marked by this morning's misadventures. Lysicrates' knuckles were discreetly bandaged but he had no problem holding a jug as he quenched his thirst, so I could hope no bones were broken.

'What did Perantas have to say?' Apollonides poured his own drink.

As everyone gathered, dragging stools into a circle, I related my conversation with the Bacchiad.

Lysicrates shook his head. 'Corinthians—' He pulled up short with a guilty look at Hyanthidas.

The musician shrugged. 'You may as well go ahead and say it. Our noble Council can hardly be called great or good at the moment.'

He tried for a rueful smile and failed. Telesilla slid her arm around his shoulder and drew him close to plant a comforting kiss on his cheek.

'A handful of the Council, perhaps,' I countered, 'but we're not here to perform for them. We're here to entertain the men and women who we've met in the agora, and in the taverns and temples. They're not to blame for a couple of oligarchs' scheming.'

Apollonides backed me. 'We can all see how much the chorus are enjoying themselves. Their families and friends will have a great time.'

'That's true enough.' Hyanthidas looked a little happier.

'All we need now are those rewrites.' Menekles looked at me, expectant.

'You'll have them tomorrow, at first light,' I promised. 'I'll get them done, if I have to work all night.'

I really should know better than to tempt some listening deity with promises like that.

'Philocles!'

We turned our heads to see Thettalos and a gang of the Brotherhood approaching. The bull-necked man looked at me. 'I need you to come with me.'

'Why?' I said warily.

'We may have found Demeas.' Thettalos looked grimly satisfied. 'We need to see if you recognise him.'

I hesitated, but it wasn't as if I had any real choice. Leaving the others to pack away and lock up, I headed down the mountainside with him.

'We're still hunting Tromes,' Thettalos said, un-prompted and belligerent, as we reached the agora. 'We will catch him.'

'So I would hope,' I lied with all the sincerity I'd ever seen Menekles display on stage.

Thettalos glanced at me, his suspicions plain. I smiled sunnily back, and we went on our way to yet another unfamiliar part of this city. The size of the houses and the cleanliness of the broad, gravelled street indicated this was another enclave of the wealthy. A gate guard watched us pass, a slave from some northern barbarian land with pale eyes and hair the colour of old straw. Thettalos was a big man but this doorkeeper could prob-ably take him with one hand.

We turned a corner and the Brotherhood leader led me down a narrow lane running between two high walls. The gravel gave way to earth underfoot, still swept scrupulously clean, and the lane was wide enough for the two of us to walk side by side. Subtle changes in the masonry and narrow iron-banded gates were the only indication that one luxurious property had given way to the next. Finally, the end came into view and I saw a skinny youth lurking an arm's length from the corner.

Thettalos snapped his fingers in front of my face. 'Stay out of sight of the street.'

'All right,' I said mildly. 'Are you keeping watch on Alypos' house?'

'Hardly.' He looked at me, scornful. 'There's half a phalanx of the Sons standing guard over there.'

'So what are we doing here?'

He didn't answer, his stride slowing as we approached the youth.

'Well?' Thettalos demanded.

'No one in or out.' The lad could rival the Spartans for brevity.

Three could play at this game. 'Well?' I asked.

'We wait.' Thettalos hunkered down, leaning his back against the wall. 'For as long as it takes.'

Since he'd forestalled my next question, I asked a different one. 'For what?'

I could see he was tempted to keep me guessing, now that he had the upper hand, but our task here was more important.

'Of course we watch Alypos' house. We've done that ever since we realised he was funding the Sons. The man we've followed here is the only new face we've seen go in and out of the Temenid residence, and he's someone we can't put a name to. Add to that, he paid a grain merchant to let him help with a delivery of wheat to get him inside the gate. He didn't know we have a man in

274

that merchant's yard who slips us interesting news.'

'I see.' How exhausting a hero cultist's life must be, perpetually conniving to ferret out secrets, and endlessly suspicious of everyone else.

I slid down the wall to squat beside him and leaned my head back. I wondered idly about writing a comedy for next year's Dionysia with a chorus of hero worshippers. Maybe not, if that risked me getting a thrashing from some Athenian devotees with no sense of humour. I'd have to ask the others.

Thettalos nudged me so hard I nearly lost my balance. 'Don't go to sleep.'

'I'm just resting my eyes.' Though if we were still here when dusk deepened, I wouldn't take any bets on me staying awake.

Before he could challenge me again, we heard two things. Bolts rattled, and the lad snapped his fingers to summon us as he peered around the corner. I didn't need Thettalos' shove to tell me this was my cue.

I crept forward, crouching low. I saw a man emerge from a gate. He scanned the street before turning to pull on the thong that secured the lock. Like every man since Deucalion survived the Flood, he looked this way and that, but only at head height. More than one comic writer has made good use of that perpetual human failing.

I ducked back. 'That's him. Demeas.'

The lad who'd been keeping watch took to his heels, heading back down the lane fast enough to win a victor's wreath at the Nemean games.

Thettalos stepped out into the street with a shout that cut through the peaceful early evening. 'Demeas!'

Our quarry made a convincing show of surprise, half-turning as if he imagined we were talking to someone behind him.

'Yes, you.' Thettalos strode forward.

I followed, for lack of anything better to do. Demeas realised that play-acting was pointless when he recognised me. As we drew closer, I saw the vicious welt I'd left on his neck with that belt. I'd come closer than I realised to killing him. Perhaps that was why he'd taken the risk of going to Alypos' house in person.

'Give me your key to that gate.' Thettalos held out a hand.

The plaited leather thong around Demeas' neck disappeared beneath his loose tunic. We could both see the characteristic dog's leg shape against his chest beneath the thin wool.

'You want to say hello to my friends?' Demeas raised his voice as though he was alerting some hidden allies.

Thettalos mocked him with a harsh laugh. 'If there was anyone inside there, they'd have bolted the gate, and you wouldn't need a key to get in.'

That didn't mean the bastard didn't have friends elsewhere. I heard the crunch of running feet on gravel, and turned, braced for trouble.

I need not have worried. The fleet-footed lad was approaching with a handful or more men. I recognised several faces from the Brotherhood's evening stints on guard at the Sanctuary. Wherever they'd been waiting for me to confirm that this was Demeas' lair, they hadn't been far away.

Thettalos waved a welcoming hand. 'Besides, I've got plenty of friends of my own.'

Demeas was already drawing the loop of plaited leather over his head. He reached inside his baggy tunic, his expression rueful and resigned. Thettalos chuckled, triumphant.

At the very last instant before his hand emerged, I saw Demeas' gaze cut from the bull-necked man to me. There was no hint of defeat in his eyes.

He'd had a knife hidden in his tunic. He ripped off the sheath in one fluid movement and the blade was coming for my chest. Thettalos moved but Demeas could reach me before the big man could intercept his thrust.

So he thought, anyway. As he lunged forward to bury his dagger in my entrails, I took a sidestep and spun around on my front foot. Now we were standing hip to hip, with his knife hand outstretched between us, and both of us facing the approaching Brotherhood.

I had my fist between us drawn back. Before Demeas could withdraw his blade, I punched him in the jaw and as he staggered, I straightened my arm. Using my forearm under his chin, I forced his head up and backwards. My other hand had already seized his knife arm at the wrist. Now his back was bent, arched like a bow from head to heels. As he lost his footing on the gravel, I dropped to one knee. Demeas fell backwards, unable to save himself since I still had firm hold of his knife hand.

I dropped to one knee rather than both. My other

foot, the foot that was between us, was still solidly planted. The back of Demeas' elbow struck my thigh as we
both went down and I bent my leg. With his wrist still
held firm on the inner side of my thigh, all the weight
of his falling body dragged his upper arm down on the
other side. An elbow is only supposed to bend one way
and this wasn't it. The joint tore apart with a sickening
crack and he screamed like a slaughtered pig.

The knife fell from his nerveless fingers as I threw
down his arm, stood up and stepped back. I'd practised
that move before, but never had occasion to use it. I
wondered if the veteran hoplite who'd taught it to me
was still alive, and if he'd be impressed to know it saved
my life. He'd insisted new conscripts needed to know
how to survive in a knife fight, as well as how to use
spear and shield in a phalanx.

Demeas sobbed in agony, writhing from head to toe
apart from that arm lying motionless on the gravel, bent
at an angle nature never intended. Thettalos looked
down and planted a merciless foot on the injured man's
chest, forcing him flat on his back.

He stooped to hook a finger in the plaited leather to
pull the angled brass key free. 'I'll take that now, thanks.'

I don't think Demeas heard him, now whimpering
breathlessly. His eyes were glazed with unimaginable
pain.

As Thettalos stood up, he glanced at me and for the
first time, I saw a measure of respect. All I had to do to
win his approval was maim a man for life. A man who'd
tried to kill me twice today, I forcefully reminded myself.

Thettalos tossed the key to the lad who'd stood watch. The gate was soon open and the Brotherhood surged inside. Thettalos and I watched and waited. It wasn't long before his men dragged a handful of amphorae outside, all identical and stamped with a seal depicting a bee.

'Open it.' Thettalos nodded at the closest one. 'Hold it up.'

A Brother used his dagger point to lever out the stopper and offered up the amphora. Thettalos took a cautious sniff. He dipped a finger into the broad neck of the vessel and licked it, before instantly spitting on the ground.

'I reckon that's that,' he said with satisfaction, before taking hold of the amphora and ramming its stopper back in. 'Is this all of them? Go and search again.'

As the brothers went back inside the gate, I gave thanks to Dionysos. Of all the plots we'd faced in Corinth, this was surely the most subtle. No one would have remarked on these few amphorae turning up at the theatre alongside all the wine Perantas was providing for free. No one would have known what was happening as the audience succumbed to the effects of innocent cupfuls dosed with a slosh of sweet madness.

'Have you any idea who was supposed to mix this into the refreshments during our play?' I asked Thettalos.

'I have a few ideas.' His grim expression promised no good for whomever he suspected. 'All right, boys,' he went on as his Brothers reappeared. 'Smash them.'

I turned away as the gleeful men shattered the earthenware against the house wall, and let the poisoned wine soak into the gravel. The heady, sickly scent nearly made me vomit. I was already feeling nauseous as the sound of Demeas' arm breaking echoed inside my head.

I cleared my throat and forced myself to speak. 'Hermaios may have more Colchis honey.'

'If he has, he won't be selling it to anyone else.' Thettalos' good humour vanished like early snows on Mount Olympos. 'His body was found at the foot of the Acrocorinth's cliffs this afternoon.'

I guessed that his scowl meant the Brotherhood weren't responsible. I wondered if this was another death Demeas would answer for in Hades. Well, until he faced divine judgement, he should find it harder to kill anyone else with only one working arm. That was some consolation to balance my revulsion at what I had done.

'I need to get back,' I said resolutely, 'and Perantas won't want me walking these streets on my own. The Sons of Heracles aren't the only ones out to wreck our play.'

'The rest of them will think again once word of this gets around.' Thettalos used the amphora he was still holding to gesture at the smashed pottery and wine stains disfiguring the threshold. 'But we won't take any risks. Kyros!'

He told the skinny lad to take me home. By the time we arrived, my nausea had receded and I was focusing on the hope that we would be able to stage *The Builders* without any more fear of disruption.

Kadous opened the gate to my knock, his face anxious. 'All's well?'

'Very well,' I said emphatically. I looked past the Phrygian to see the others, Hyanthidas and Telesilla included, sitting around the table with the remains of a meal between them. 'The poisoned wine's been destroyed.'

'Excellent news!' Menekles poured a splash of wine onto the ground. 'Thanks to Dionysos.'

As everyone else made their own libations, I decided not to spoil the triumphant mood with the brutal details of what I'd done to Demeas. As I pulled a stool up to the table, I made my own libation to Athena and silently prayed that she'd honour Thettalos' devotion to Bellerophon by making sure his confidence that the plot was foiled wasn't misplaced.

Kadous provided me with a bowl and I put a meal together. I suddenly realised I was ravenous.

Zosime offered me a plate of seared lamb's liver. 'So we can concentrate on tomorrow's final rehearsal?'

'All we need is those rewrites,' Lysicrates said.

I looked up, chewing a mouthful, and saw all three actors looking at me, expectant. Swallowing, I realised the day was still far from over.

Chapter Twenty-Two

Zosime and I didn't work *all* through the night, but only because she insisted we go to sleep after I made a pass over the rewrites that changed the amendments we'd just made back to the version we'd had before that. Though I didn't believe that until she fetched the discarded sheets of papyrus and invited me to see for myself. I apologised, meekly wrote out two fair copies of the scene as it now stood, and we went to bed.

'What else happened while you were with Thettalos?' Zosime asked as she snuggled close beneath our blankets. 'What didn't you want to talk about over dinner?'

'Can I tell you later, after the performance?' Hearing Demeas' arm snapping in my dreams was the last thing I needed.

'Whenever you're ready.' Zosime kissed my cheek.

'I love you.' As weariness washed over me, I vowed to put everything else aside until the play was over.

Hypnos must have decided that warranted his favour. The god of sleep blessed me with deep and refreshing slumber, though we only got a few scant hours before Kadous knocked apologetically on our door. When we got back to Athens I'd sleep in for a month.

Lysicrates and Menekles were pacing something out in the courtyard as Zosime and I came down the stairs. Apollonides looked on, sucking steam from his pot of steeping herbs. I laid one copy of the rewrites on the table for him and handed Menekles the other. Lysicrates peered over his shoulder.

For what felt like roughly half a year, the only sound was the subdued murmurs of the household slaves as they served us breakfast at Kadous' direction.

'Are you sure about this?' Menekles' expression made it clear that he wasn't.

'It would go down like a cup of vinegar at home, but we're not in Athens, are we?' Though Lysicrates was reserving judgement rather than offering whole-hearted support.

'Telesilla had a hand in this?' Apollonides looked at Zosime for confirmation. When she nodded, he shrugged. 'Let's see what the chorus make of it.'

I'd have preferred more outright enthusiasm, but I'd take what I was offered. 'If we set off early, you can try a few runs through it before the singers arrive.'

Menekles was already silently trying his lines, looking for the most effective emphasis. As he looked up, half his thoughts were on the new text. 'Let's go.'

As we prepared to depart though, I realised I couldn't put all yesterday's alarms behind me. Alypos Temenid had more henchmen to whistle up than merely Demeas.

'Kadous, you'd better come with us. Find someone you trust to bring us food at midday.'

As soon as I said that, I was struck by sudden doubts.

Would this give some hidden enemy their chance to poison us all? But everyone else was ready to go, so I gave up, commended our lunch to Apollo's vigilance, and we headed for the agora where we met Hyanthidas, Telesilla and Arion.

By the time the chorus arrived at the Sanctuary, Menekles and Apollonides were well on their way to learning their new lines. Hyanthidas and I led the singers through their songs and dances while the three actors went out onto the hillside. I saw them devising the gestures and movements around the stage that would get the very best out of my work.

I wished I could be out there, offering my own observations, but that wasn't my place. I was also feeling the effects of so many late nights. The third time I yawned and stumbled over my dance steps, I didn't need Hyanthidas' pained glance to remind me that I was supposed to be leading the chorus. I concentrated on doing just that.

When a trio of Perantas' slaves brought us baskets of food for the midday break, it became apparent that none of the chorus were leaving in search of refreshment today. My spirits rose as I ate cheese pastries and watched our singers sitting in small groups in the shade. They were all discussing some particular lyric or dance sequence to make sure they had a firm grasp on the vital details.

As I reached for a date and nut cake, I belatedly remembered I'd been worrying about some ill-wisher striking us all down with poison. Since no one was raving or vomiting, I decided it was too late to worry about that now.

Zosime came over to give me a cup of well-watered wine. 'Are we going to rehearse in the performance masks and costumes this afternoon?'

'Yes.' I brushed crumbs off the front of my tunic and poured the first sip of my wine in a libation to Apollo before I stood up.

The chorus weren't the least hampered by their costumes, confirming their experience as performers. The quality of the workmanship helped. The stage-skins covering them from neck to foot were closely woven and well stitched. The tunics that went over the body-stockings were simple and straightforward, little different to everyday Corinthian wear. Settling and adjusting the leather phalluses that distinguish every comedy from a tragedy took a little longer. Finally everyone was satisfied with his own particular angle of dangle, and I was glad that we'd decided to limit the more complicated comedy cocks to those of us already in the know.

Zosime brought out the basket of performance masks. My mouth went as dry as the sun-baked hillside as the singers tried them on and swapped them around, everyone looking for the best fit. No one complained of any discomfort, still less any burning sensations, and I silently offered Apollo fervent thanks that Zosime's ingenuity had foiled the hellebore's malice.

By the time we had finished our first complete run through and everyone temporarily shed their masks to take a drink, I was pleased to see Menekles and Apollo-nides smiling broadly. If this Corinthian chorus' reaction was any guide, that rewritten scene would be one of the highlights of the play.

I must ask Hyanthidas what gift would show Telesilla our gratitude for her invaluable assistance. Later, though. Satisfied that everyone had quenched their thirst, I clapped my hands. 'Right, let's go again.'

We called it a day when Zosime informed us that the Sanctuary sundial showed the eleventh hour of the day had gone by. A contingent of the Brotherhood arrived to stand guard for one last night. None of the Brothers said where Thettalos might be and I didn't ask. I didn't want to think about anything at all except *The Builders* until the sun had set tomorrow.

The day of the play dawned fine and fair, with a breeze to keep our audience comfortable in their unshaded seats. A few keen families were already claiming the best spots available when we arrived well before the second hour of the day. A handful of the Brotherhood were guarding the seats of honour in the centre of the first three rows from encroachment, deliberate or accidental.

'I suppose we need them here.' Lysicrates was torn between resigned and resentful.

'I'm more concerned with who else might turn up.' Menekles was watching the road. 'Sons of Heracles or Heirs of Hephaistos.'

'No one will start any trouble today.' Hyanthidas was certain. 'Not with everyone here to see who's to blame.'

Telesilla backed him up. 'The hero cults want everyone to believe they're devoted to their chosen patron and to serving their members' interests.'

'Everything they've tried so far has been mischief behind the scenes,' I agreed.

'Talking of which, let's get a feel for the place.' Apollonides looked at the stage building offering a backdrop to performances here. It was raised up above the dancing floor on a broad wooden platform. Ramps led to the stage on either side and we made our way up in unspoken agreement.

With the stage building behind us, and the dancing floor with its altar to Dionysos below, we looked out at the broad half-circle of tiered seats built into the gentle slope of the land. So far, so familiar. The view when we looked beyond the seats was entirely new though, and I found it oddly disconcerting. We were so used to performing in Athens where the theatre seats rise in far steeper ranks, backed by the golden crags of the Acropolis, crowned by our city's most sacred temples.

Here the Acrocorinth loomed, grey and forbidding in the distance, while the great Temple of Apollo gleamed white in the strengthening sunlight towards the southeast. The road heading northwards from the agora towards Sikyon ran right beside the theatre and the lie of the land meant I could see passers-by coming and going.

I wondered what the actors would make of such distraction during the performance but decided against asking. If they hadn't noticed, the last thing I should do was draw their attention to something that might throw them off their stride. As it turned out, their thoughts were elsewhere.

'There are our costumes and masks,' Menekles said with relief.

I saw the Brothers who'd been standing guard at the Sanctuary were carrying the heavy baskets between them. Kadous and Arion hurried to meet them.

'And Wetka.' Zosime pointed at a cluster of figures just passing Glauke's shrine.

I left the others to take charge of directing the Brotherhood to take the costumes around behind the stage and the scenery building. I walked down the ramp to meet Wetka who had gone straight to Dionysos' altar. He was directing a slave to scour the limestone with a block of chalk to render it immaculate, and he had a basket, which held an elegantly painted pouring dish and an equally exquisite flask of wine.

'Good morning.' He greeted me with his customary half-smile. 'Perantas Bacchiad will be here shortly. Once the rest of the Council have arrived, he will commence the day's proceedings with appropriate prayers and libations.'

'Naturally,' I said politely. Perantas was paying for this entertainment, so it was only fair that his fellow Corinthians get their chance to applaud his benevolence.

Wetka continued. 'After the performance, there will be fifty cattle sacrificed to Apollo and to Athena, and feasting in the agora at my master's expense. You are invited to the private celebrations in the colonnade to the north of the temple, along with your chorus and their families.'

'Your master is most generous.' Corinth would remember our play and this day's bounty for a good long while, whether or not they paid any attention to the plans for the Thurii settlement.

I wondered if it was really the colony in Sicily that prompted such enmity from Alypos Temenid and Philolaos Kypselid, or concerns closer to home. They would have to pour out their own silver to match Perantas' largesse, or watch him reap a substantial harvest of immediate popularity and lingering allegiance.

Movement at the rear of the seats caught my eye. Brawny men were wrestling heavy amphorae from a series of handcarts. 'The wine for the audience—'

'—has been strictly guarded. The seals have been double-checked, and slaves have drunk samples taken at random without any ill effects. We are fetching fresh water direct from Glauke's Spring.' Wetka was looking past me towards the road. 'Your chorus is here.'

I turned to see familiar faces saying their farewells to knots of friends and relatives by the entrance to the theatre's seats. Other singers were already heading for the rear of the stage. 'If you'll excuse me . . .'

The Nubian surprised me with a broad grin. 'Good luck!'

'Thanks.' I hurried after the latest arrivals.

The space behind the stage was bustling. Hyanthidas was checking over his twin flutes and their vulnerable reeds while the chorus helped each other into their costumes, with Kadous and Arion on hand. Apollonides and Menekles were doing the same for each other while Zosime and Telesilla assisted with Lysicrates' transformation into the luscious, golden-gowned Egeria. The Etruscan matriarch's wig, in particular, was a towering extravagance of chestnut curls and braids.

As I shed my own tunic and dragged on my stage-skin, I felt uncomfortably exposed in this open space in full view of passers-by, with a handful of the Brotherhood shooing away anyone looking too avidly curious. But the Corinthians were unconcerned and they were more familiar with performing in this theatre than any of us. I put my costume on and found the mask I'd earmarked as mine.

'Before we begin!' I shouted to get everyone's attention. 'After the play, we're invited to dine with Perantas in the North Colonnade, together with your families, as a reward for all our hard work.'

The singers cheered, giving me reason to hope this new incentive would inspire their performance to new heights. Then I noticed Zosime standing still, a few paces from Telesilla and Lysicrates. My beloved was frowning, and my blood ran cold.

I went over, my mask in hand. 'What is it?'

'Two of the chorus aren't here.'

'What?' I tried to count heads but that was impossible with everyone moving about. I clapped my hands. 'Stand still!'

The chorus complied, and I swiftly tallied their faces against the roster in my head. I felt sick. Zosime was right. Two of our builders were missing.

'Does anyone know where Eupraxis and Parmenon are? Does anyone know where they live?'

The singers looked uncertainly at each other and answered with headshakes and shrugs. I felt the breath catch in my throat. I tried to swallow but it seemed as if my chest was burning. I looked with horror at my mask, dangling from its straps. I hadn't even put it on yet, so how could any lingering poison already affect me? I tried to take another breath but it was no good. Light-headed, I wondered whether I would pass out before my knees gave way. My legs felt as weak as a newborn lamb's.

I wondered if the missing men had been bribed or threatened or worse to leave us so thoroughly stuck in the mire. Because this was a disaster. We had rehearsed every dance, every song, with a full complement of twenty-four. Everyone knew their place, and relied on the man beside him, just as every hoplite in a phalanx depends on the warrior at his shoulder. Gaps in either ranks, on the dancing floor or on the battlefield, could only mean disaster. Despite all our efforts, despite all our vigilance and contrivances, our enemies had finally succeeded in ruining my play.

Lysicrates was at my shoulder, forcing a cup of wine into my hand. 'You've gone a very odd colour. Drink this.'

I gulped down a mouthful and as Dionysos is my witness, I didn't even care if it was dosed with Colchis honey. Whatever horrific visions might follow, they couldn't compare to this nightmare.

Kadous was standing watch by the corner of the stage building, to get a clear view of the road. He turned and called out. 'The Council members have arrived.'

'Telesilla?' Zosime turned to the Corinthian woman and, to my utter disbelief, I saw a mischievous glint in my beloved's eye.

Telesilla pressed her palms to her cheeks. After a moment's stillness, she nodded. 'I think so. Yes,' she went on with more certainty, 'we can do this.'

'Do *what*?' I demanded.

No one was listening to me.

'All of you, into a ring,' Lysicrates ordered the chorus. 'Facing *out*wards,' he scolded.

I don't know if it was because he looked like their mother, but they obeyed with impressive alacrity.

'Mind your backs.' Apollonides dragged the costume basket into the centre of the circle. Menekles followed, carrying two masks.

'You cannot be serious.' Incredulous, I realised their plan.

'What else do you suggest?' Hyanthidas was already unpinning the shoulder brooches that secured Telesilla's dress.

'We know the songs. We know the steps.' With Lysicrates helping her, Zosime was already half dressed in a spare stage skin. 'We've watched enough rehearsals.'

'It's not the same,' I objected.

'No, it's not, but no one's going to know.' The Corinthian nearest to me was deadly serious behind his hilariously gurning mask.

The man beside him agreed. 'It's the only way to save the play, and I'll be cursed before I see our hard work go for nothing.'

Resolute agreement ran around the circle, with an ominous undertone that promised nothing good for the missing singers when their erstwhile allies caught up with them. I almost hoped they had been cornered in an alley and beaten up. They'd need that sort of excuse for their absence.

I wondered if Kadous had seen enough rehearsals to play a part. No, that was a stupid idea. Corinthians were used to seeing women perform, even if there would surely be uproar if our stratagem was discovered. Putting a slave on stage would be something else entirely. That would be a scandal to render this surge of goodwill for Perantas worthless.

'Will you help me with this or not?' Zosime held out the straps and buckles of a red leather phallus.

A roar went up from the theatre seats on the far side of the stage building. People were cheering and shouting and stamping their feet.

Kadous called out again. 'Perantas has arrived.'

A few moments later a cheer went up that could surely be heard in Lechaion. Someone must have announced the public feasting to follow the play. The uproar was followed equally swiftly by urgent shushing like waves breaking on a shingle shore. Silence fell and we heard Perantas making his prayers and libations to the gods.

In the stillness that followed, we heard the first notes of Hyanthidas' lyrical, beautiful music inviting us onto the dancing floor. Lysicrates had secured Zosime's comedy cock and someone else had done the same service for Telesilla. With their bewigged masks and baggy costumes, there was no telling the women from the rest of the chorus.

I tied my own mask on with shaking hands and turned to lead the singers out in front of the audience, to wait for our cue from the stage.

Chapter Twenty-Three

Menekles as Meriones, and Apollonides as Thersites, got our play underway. Meriones was tall and broad-shouldered in his armour, with a Corinthian helmet (naturally) tucked under one arm as he made commanding gestures with his spear. We've all seen such Homeric heroes immortalised on a thousand pots.

Thersites was altogether an earthier character, shorter, scruffier, and constantly interrupting Meriones' ambitious plans for settling in this fertile new land with persistent demands to know exactly where their shipload of Achaeans had washed up. His sly asides made it clear that Meriones was responsible for getting them so thoroughly lost on their way back from the Trojan War.

'You kept sticking your oar in! You told the steersman to stick the ship's prow between those inviting headlands and swore we'd find some nice snug anchorage.' Half-crouched, Thersites ran his hands suggestively up and down his thighs. 'You do recall it was Paris sticking his prow in Helen's harbour that got us dragged away from home in the first place?'

The audience's laughter suggested there wasn't much local sympathy for Sparta's straying queen. I desperately wanted to make a proper assessment of their reactions through this opening scene, but my vision was narrowed to a tight focus by my mask, so I could only pick out individual faces in the avid crowd. Besides, I was the leader of these singers today, and the bickering on stage demanded all my attention if the chorus and I weren't to miss our cue.

Finally, Thersites forced Meriones to admit they would be staying here, even if neither of them knew where 'here' might be.

I raised my arms to the heavens and led the chorus in Hyanthidas' first hymn of praise to this unknown land. Half the singers followed me in a half-circle heading away to the left of the stage building, while the others danced off to the right. Striving to stay light on my feet as we approached the audience, I swung back around to the centre of the dancing floor. The rest of the singers were heading towards me. Our two lines crossed, each man slipping deftly past his counterpart, turning one way and then the other. As the last pair went their separate ways, the chorus divided again, into four circles of six. Now our steps mimicked a country dance, before we all came back together for the hymn's triumphant conclusion.

Everyone was word-perfect and immaculately in step. That was a relief because I very nearly lost my own rhythm when our dance's sweeping gestures proved so well-suited to words I'd written long months ago and so far away.

As we praised seas full of fish, lush olive groves all around us, and well-watered heights offering timber and stone for building a new city, an Athenian audience needed to use their fertile imaginations to replace the city rooftops spread out below the theatre. Here in Corinth, in this shallow hollow of a theatre with unobstructed views in all directions, our outstretched hands pointed towards the sparkling blue waters of the Gulf, and to the well-tilled plain of the Corinthia. As we wheeled around in the dance, chorus and audience alike saw the mountains of the Peloponnese rising up beyond the Acrocorinth.

The Corinthian chorus' devotion to their city lent resonant fervour to their song. I felt a surge of pride in their performance as well as humble gratitude to Dionysos for bringing my play to this audience.

The cheers and applause died down as Egeria appeared, full-bosomed and sensual. Lysicrates was utterly convincing as the Etruscan noblewoman, who explained that the Achaeans had arrived in the notoriously licentious wilderness of Northern Italy. She welcomed them warmly, blithely unaware of Meriones' shocked reaction as she explained the sexual services that the local women would expect in return for granting the Achaeans land for their city.

'You look as if you know how to use your plough.' She stroked a tantalising hand down Meriones' breastplate and fluttered teasing fingers just below his belt buckle. 'You'll find we appreciate a good, deep thrust into our moist, soft furrows.'

'As for you—' She spun around to startle Thersites. 'You may not stand as tall and proud as your brother in arms, but a humble ass can serve just as well as a mighty stallion. Did you know that Etruscan women like to ride?' she cooed as she pressed herself up against him. 'To ride, and ride, and ride . . .'

She sighed winsomely as their hips moved in unison, and the audience chuckled appreciatively. This is where comedy always wins out over tragedy as far as I am concerned. Whatever a play's underlying message might be, a few bawdy gags ease it along like a splash of olive oil in a lover's hand.

Thersites protested, proclaiming his unsullied virtue, until Egeria pursued him off stage. Meriones turned to the chorus, aghast at this unexpected encounter with such unabashed, self-confident womanhood.

'We need to decide how we're going to rule ourselves, and quickly,' he told the Achaeans. 'Before I – before we – I mean you—' Meriones hastily corrected himself. 'Before *you* find yourselves trapped under Egeria's . . .' His voice trailed off, his hand straying towards his red leather cock. Then he shook his shoulders, like a dog coming in from the rain, and cleared his throat. 'Under her – her thumb, yes, that's it, her thumb.'

Meriones' first suggestion was adopting the rigorous Spartan system of discipline: all drill, and no sex. As the chorus leader, my role was to encourage the protests of these men eager to put all thoughts of war behind them, and to enjoy the fruits of this new land with their new Etruscan friends.

'I'm looking forward to splitting a nice ripe peach with my little fruit knife,' I told the audience, with a suggestive thrust of my hips. 'Or maybe a juicy pomegranate.'

So far, so well rehearsed. Menekles and I had been

repeating these lines since I'd first written my first draft back in Athens. If I hadn't played this part before, I knew the words as well as any of the actors, and from the audience's vocal support for the chorus, advocates for Sparta had few friends in this theatre today.

As Thersites came back on stage, we were into, dare I say it, virgin territory. I retreated with the rest of the chorus as the actors embarked on their rewritten and so recently learned scene. My mouth dry, I reminded myself that Hyanthidas and Telesilla had approved this new version, and that Zosime had lent me her wits to polish it up. It made no difference. All I could remember was that old saying about success having many fathers while failure has only one. That would be me. *The Builders* was my play. For the first time, I was glad I was safely anonymous in my mask and costume in the midst of the chorus rather than sitting in the theatre for unimpressed Corinthians to stare at.

Meriones was proclaiming his intention to rule as a king, and to bequeath this new kingdom to his sons. Thersites was pointing out the flaws in this plan, with a whole new set of arguments to replace the play's original praise for Athenian democracy.

'You don't think the Etruscans will have something to say about this? You did meet Egeria? That beauty with such great—' he mimed cupping ample breasts '—personal attributes?'

'We will put these Etruscan women in their place,' Meriones asserted loftily. 'Never fear.'

'How?' Thersites demanded.

'We will explain that we are stronger and thus naturally born to rule.'

'All right. You do that. What else?'

'We will explain that we are wiser, and obviously better suited to making decisions.'

'All right. You do that. What else?'

'We will explain that we are calmer and less easily swayed by our emotions.'

'All right. You do that. What else?'

'We will explain—' Meriones broke off. 'Why will I be the one saying all this? Where will you be?'

'Oh, I'll be right behind you,' Thersites dodged to stand with Meriones between him and the audience.

Meriones stepped aside. 'We should be standing shoulder to shoulder.'

'Not a chance!' Thersites instantly took cover again. 'They might start throwing things.'

Meriones clapped a hand to his breastplate, wounded. 'Have you so little faith in me?'

'When did you last win an argument with a woman?' Thersites demanded.

'Well, I—'

'You can't ever win. You know that. If you ever even come close, they change the subject and walk away.'

Now Thersites addressed the audience. 'They remember everything you've ever said, and every detail of every mistake you make. They remember these things for years and then they use them against you. Don't believe me? Ask Agamemnon. Oh, you can't, can you? His wife killed him.'

'Clytemnestra used an axe, not cutting words,' protested Meriones.

Thersites nodded sagely. 'Proving a woman can hold a grudge for ten years, keeping it sharp as ever. I'm not getting on the wrong side of that.'

'Oh, come now,' Meriones objected.

'Haven't you heard about the women here?' Thersites gestured vaguely off-stage. 'I've been asking around.'

This was where Hyanthidas and Telesilla had proved invaluable. Back in Athens, the lengthy scene debating democracy had included not-so-veiled references to recent successes, failures and scandals of local politicians. That gave the audience plenty to laugh at, and reminded the great and the good that they will always answer to the people. It wouldn't work in Corinth, so we'd taken a different line.

'Did you hear about the priestess and the doves?' Thersites invited the audience into his confidence. 'When that grain trader thought he could cheat her?'

I wasn't clear on the details, but Telesilla had assured me that Demeter's formidable handmaiden had made a local merchant look very foolish last winter. Having got on the wrong side of the woman who ruled the Sanctuary, I could well believe it. Judging from the audience's appreciative laughter as Thersites told the story, they'd heard it too.

'I did hear a rumour,' Meriones admitted uneasily. 'There's a town not so far away whose men were slaughtered in battle, leaving greybeards and boys to defend their walls. Apparently the women marched out to fight and the invaders ran away!'

301

That was of course a swift summary of the way that the renowned poet Telesilla of Argos had led the defence of her home town in our grandfathers' day. Hyanthidas' beloved had been named to honour the famous and formidable woman who had humiliated the Spartans so thoroughly. Refusing to fight females, the fearsome red-cloaked warriors had no option but turn around and go back home.

Thersites and Meriones swapped a few more stories of redoubtable women, which the audience cheered loudly. They were forced to conclude that any man trying to rule this new city alone would face more challenges from Egeria and her sisters than any single warrior could handle. Consultation and consensus was surely the way to ensure peace and prosperity, giving all voices a hearing.

That philosophy should be just about acceptable to Corinth's oligarchs, as well as assuring these ordinary citizens that Athens wouldn't have a whip hand over the new colony at Thurii. As far as the play was concerned, these tales were in keeping with Etruscan women's reputation for shameless behaviour. As far as the audience was concerned, they also enjoyed a good-natured laugh at Athens' expense.

The implication was clear. With our own wives and daughters so excluded from public life, as so many exaggerated travellers' tales claim, Athenian men simply couldn't cope if they met an assertive woman. Menekles and Lysicrates were right. We'd get pelted with nuts and worse if we ever played this scene in Attica, but this was

Corinthia and so the new scene went down as smoothly as Perantas' free wine.

As Meriones and Thersites agreed to work together, I felt like Sisyphus reaching the top of his mountain and realising that bloody boulder was actually going to stay there for once. With a spring in my step, I led the chorus across the dancing floor once again, to celebrate the benefits of cooperation. This time we turned and stepped and twirled in unison, as our song remembered the Hellene forces standing united against Troy.

After that, the play proceeded much as it had originally been written. Everyone's thoughts turned to building a shrine and a marketplace. We'd rewritten a few lines so this scene honoured Apollo in place of Athena. That was only courteous when we were performing within sight of his glorious temple.

First, the question of tools arose. Thersites and Meriones made the most of the resources to hand; that helmet, a shield, the spear. Then they faced the challenge of establishing a standard measure. With one good tug, Meriones' comedy cock unexpectedly tripled in length, and he proudly proclaimed that was clearly a foot long. Naturally Thersites outdid him by suddenly yanking out a still more ludicrous phallus.

Of course, back in Athens, the entire chorus had been similarly equipped, and I was still a little sorry we'd decided against that here, but since the Corinthians didn't know what they were missing, the audience laughed themselves hoarse.

Egeria slipped back on stage in time to lavish praise

on Thersites' impressive equipment and express her will-
ingness to give him a hand deploying his measuring rod.
Thersites fled, with Egeria in pursuit, leaving Meriones
alone on the stage, and the Chorus in lyrical mood, en-
visioning the fine city they would build and its cultural
riches they would bequeath to their sons.

More tangible riches were the focus of the next scene,
and once again I had to force myself to focus on the words
and dance steps that were my immediate responsibility. It
wasn't easy. There was still so much that could go wrong
on stage. Lysicrates and Apollonides had to make a series
of swift costume changes, to reappear as a multitude of
eager merchants looking to trade with Menekles. With
Zosime and Telesilla out on the dancing floor, only
Kadous and Arion were left to help behind the scenes.

The scene started slowly enough, with Meriones
seduced into banter and barter as he realised he could
make himself rich, but by the time Lysicrates appeared
with a ruddy-cheeked mask and a Sicilian accent, he
was apparently breathless with haste. 'Good day to you,
honoured sir, tell me, are you interested in gold—'

'Ooh, yes,' Meriones said greedily.

'—en grain?' the Sicilian concluded.

'Oh, no' said Meriones, disappointed, and then af-
fronted. 'Do I look like a baker to you?'

'You look like a man—' the Sicilian pointed at the
expectant chorus '—with plenty of mouths to feed.'

'Oh . . . yes . . .' Meriones said, apprehensive, as we
all raised pleading hands or hugged our empty bellies.

'Leeks! Firm, fresh leeks to trade!' An eager Phoenician

appeared on the other side of the stage, equally breathless.

Meriones planted his hands on his hips. 'Do I look like a greengrocer to you?'

'You look like a man—' the Phoenician mimicked a rising erection with the vegetable in his hand, before peering at the cock dangling to Meriones' knees '—who could use a good dish of leeks.' He paused before continuing with salacious emphasis. 'To give you an appetite for the local delicacies.'

The audience's appreciative roar gave Apollonides a chance to catch his breath. Even so, I could hear the increasing toll all this coming and going was taking on him. It was all very well Lysicrates pretending to pant with exertion so the audience thought this was part of the play, but I began to worry that Apollonides might not make it to the end of the scene.

Menekles clearly thought the same. There were still two more merchants to come and go when he cut the action short by striding to the front of the stage where Meriones gloated over his newly acquired goods.

'Mine. All mine.'

'Really?' I seized on the chorus' cue to challenge him, asserting the rights of the men who were building this city to share in the profits to be had. The cheers of support from the audience made me think there'd be plenty of interest in Thurii after this.

Hyanthidas' music led us into our next song and dance. The chorus stepped forward in twos and threes as the rest of us clapped and danced in place. Each couplet cheerfully anticipated the sumptuous meals we would now prepare, and the comforts that would furnish our new homes. Above us on the stage, Menekles conveyed Meriones' anguish at losing his hoard with extravagant gestures.

When we were about to finish our dance, though, there was no sign of Egeria and Thersites. They should have been at the side of the stage, ready to make their next, and final, entrance. Thankfully Hyanthidas didn't miss a beat. His pipe swooped seamlessly into a repeat of our last caper around the dancing floor. With my heart racing, I strode forward, praying fervently that the rest of the chorus would follow me. As I turned in front of the stage, I saw that they had done so. By the time we'd reprised our final steps, Apollonides and Lysicrates had appeared.

'Oh! Meriones! You shouldn't have!' Egeria fluted as she dragged Thersites onto the stage, his arm firmly locked in hers. 'A wedding feast for us? How generous. Truly, a noble gesture!'

As originally written, those were Thersites' words, but I wasn't going to argue with whatever stratagem got us to the end of the play without the audience noticing anything amiss.

'What? Wait! No—' As Meriones protested, I led the chorus forward into a rousing rendition of a bridal hymn. Once we had looked forward to Egeria and Thersites raising a fine family of noble sons and beautiful daughters, a wedding ballad ushered them off stage to their waiting marital bed, escorted by the gleeful Achaeans.

Cheers and applause were ringing around the shallow bowl of the theatre as we disappeared behind the stage building. Glad as I was to hear it, I was more concerned about Apollonides.

Ripping off my mask, I saw him lying flat on his back, his own mask discarded. Zosime knelt beside him, lifting his head with one hand as she held a cup to his lips. I hurried over.

'Let me do that. You and Telesilla get dressed before anyone comes around to congratulate us.'

Zosime saw the sense in that. As I took her place, I saw Kadous and Arion were standing ready with both women's clothes. They disappeared into the milling throng of singers. I had to leave them to it. Apollonides' face was ominously pale and his lips were a sickly hue.

Menekles knelt opposite me. 'Do we carry him to the Asklepion, or send someone to fetch Chresimos?'

'Neither,' Apollonides said, more forcefully than I expected. 'Give me a moment, and give me that.'

He took the cup of wine and though he spilled some, he drank plenty, and I was reassured to see his colour improve. His chest was still heaving but I could barely hear him wheezing.

Menekles was equally relieved. 'We'll get you back to the house and boil some water for your herb pot.'

'After we've eaten.' Apollonides was adamant. 'I've earned a decent feed at Perantas' expense.'

'We all have.' Lysicrates appeared, out of his costume and dragging a comb through his curls. 'Are you getting changed, or are you going like that?'

Looking around, I saw Zosime was respectably dressed once again. She and Telesilla were tidying each other's hair while Kadous and Arion were putting all the costumes and masks back in the baskets. Our chorus were greeting friends and proud family members who had come around to the back of the stage to congratulate them on their superb performance.

We had our own visitors. I saw Nados, Simias and Aithon making their way through the swelling crowd. All three young men looked happier than I had seen them since our first unfortunate introduction.

'That was hilarious.' Aithon grinned.

'I'm glad you enjoyed it. I hope you've been invited to dine in the North Colonnade with us all?' If they hadn't, I'd be having words with Wetka. It was little enough recompense for all that they had suffered these past ten days.

'We have,' Nados assured me.

'Oh, and that pickled fish you were asking about,' Simias said, guileless. 'We shipped it to Zakynthos yesterday morning, with a captain we can trust absolutely.'

The glint in his eye told me he was talking about Tromes. 'Good to know.' I meant it. There had been enough pain and suffering caused by Perantas' rivals attempting to wreck our play.

Now we could put all that behind us and pursue whoever had bought the poison that had killed Eumelos. Though I would tell Nados and the others about that tomorrow, I decided, rather than cast a blight over this evening's celebrations.

We entrusted Kadous, Arion and the baskets to a contingent of the Brotherhood who would escort them back to our lodging, and made our way to the agora and the paved precinct in front of the Temple of Apollo.

Priests with deft knives and muscular slaves to assist them had begun sacrificing bullocks grown fat on summer grazing. The crowd of Corinthians ready to praise the god by claiming a share in this bounty was growing ever larger.

When we reached the North Colonnade, Wetka was in charge of approving who was, and who was not to be admitted to the sumptuous feast that Perantas' silver was paying for. We were escorted to one of a series of spacious dining rooms, where I admired the fine mosaic floor of interlaced vines and the painted orchard adorning the walls.

It still struck me as strange to be dining in this semi-public fashion, with men and women sharing the cushioned couches, but Zosime and Telesilla looked entirely at ease, so I did my best to emulate them, turning my attention to the excellent food and even better wine being served.

By the time the soft-footed slaves were removing the last tables strewn with the remnants of our dessert course, I was unable to stop myself yawning. At my side, Zosime was looking equally heavy-eyed.

She leaned over to kiss my cheek. 'Do you think we can leave without causing any offence to our host?'

'I imagine so.' We'd barely seen Perantas. He'd paused to thank us and then gone to a different salon, doubtless to dine and share his triumph with his allies among the city's great and good.

He was welcome to his celebration. I looked around for my friends. Hyanthidas and Telesilla were deep in conversation with some people I didn't recognise while Apollonides and Simias were chatting on the couch they were sharing and looking at each other in a way that hinted they'd be sharing a bed later on.

Lysicrates and Menekles were playing a drinking game with Aithon and Nados, and there was no way I was going to get dragged into that. Back at the Dionysia, I'd learned the folly of matching actors cup for cup the hard way, especially when they were celebrating a successful performance.

I kissed Zosime. 'I don't think anyone will miss us, but we should say our goodbyes.' We also had to be paid before heading home. 'Let's go and make our farewells to Wetka.'

The Nubian was outside in the colonnade, accepting thanks from departing guests. I approached him with a polite smile, but he spoke first.

'I take it you're ready to say good night? Sleep well, and I'll see you in the morning.'

I nodded, trying to stifle another yawn. 'We must discuss arranging a ship back to Athens.'

Wetka looked at me. 'After you've given your evidence to the Council. Alypos Temenid has been called to answer for his crimes at noon tomorrow.'

Suddenly I was extremely relieved that I hadn't been tempted into the actors' drinking games.

Chapter Twenty-Four

At least I got a good long lie-in the following morning, and that was welcome after so many long days and late nights. When I finally woke, I heard Kadous moving around in the next room, presumably making preparations for the trip home. I stayed where I was, taking some time to savour the recollections of yesterday's success, achieved despite all the foes arrayed against us. When I felt Zosime stir beside me, I rolled over to kiss her.

She put a stop to my caresses with a firm hand. 'If you're giving evidence to Corinth's Council at noon, you need to visit a barber and a bath house.'

She was right. This would be as much of a performance as my role yesterday, and appearances would matter, as they always did on the stage. More than that, this was my chance to see someone held to account for Eumelos' death. If Alypos Temenid hadn't directly ordered his murder, he'd instigated the campaign against our play that had caused it.

I found yesterday's tunic and went to tell Kadous we were ready for breakfast. Down in the courtyard, there was no sign of the others, but the Phrygian assured me they had all arrived safely back in the early hours of the morning, accompanied by Simias.

'I assume it's a good thing none of them are called before the Council?'

'They'll be hard pressed to remember what city they're in when they wake up,' Kadous confirmed.

I glanced at the sun, and realised that I didn't have time to waste. Fortunately it wasn't far to a decent bath house, with a charming mosaic of a donkey on its pebbled floor. Kadous kept watch over my clothes while a slave rubbed me down with olive oil. As I lay on his massage table, to be scraped clean with brisk strokes of a strigil, I wondered what to tell the Council about recent events.

Like pretty much every poet and playwright, I put bread on the table between festivals with funeral elegies, celebratory odes and routine business agreements. I've written plenty of speeches for other people to deliver in Athens' courts, but at such short notice, there was no time to craft and hone such eloquence, let alone practise the rhetorical gestures that my brothers and I had learned as boys at the Lyceum. All I could do was tell the truth as straightforwardly as I saw it, and trust that divine justice would follow.

This establishment wasn't large enough to have a bathing pool but the stone-built tubs were more than adequate for a satisfying wash in warm water. Getting out, I tipped a final cold bucketful over my head and briskly rubbed myself dry. A barber that Hyanthidas recommended was close by, and I emerged with my hair and beard neatly trimmed. Wearing one of my best tunics, belted with a piece of my family business' finest leatherwork, I felt ready to represent Athens before Corinth's oligarchs.

'Good day to you, Philocles.' Wetka hurried up to us, with one of the Brotherhood a few paces behind him. 'Your delightful companion told me where to find you,' he explained smoothly. 'We're here to escort you to the Council.'

'Thank you.' I could hardly object. 'My slave—'

'Will not be required,' Wetka said firmly. 'The fewer opportunities our opponents have to make mischief the better, don't you agree?'

'Then we walk to the agora by way of our lodging, to see him safely back,' I said with equal determination.

Once we had delivered Kadous, we made our way to the Temple of Apollo. As we reached the paved precinct, I headed for the magnificent statue of the god seated with his lyre.

Wetka scurried after me, caught unawares. 'The Council—'

'One moment.' I took a knee and thanked the god for our successful performance. I vowed to tell the truth before these oligarchs, so that Apollo could see justice done.

Wetka shifted from foot to foot. Since a sundial indicated we had time in hand before noon, I wondered at his agitation. Then I saw some Sons of Heracles escorting an expensively cloaked man towards the temple entrance. He was of middling height and build but carried himself like an athlete. There was barely a touch of grey in his close-cropped hair and beard, and his legs were leanly muscled. 'Is that Alypos Temenid?'

The Nubian nodded, his face taut. He led the way to the temple, and I was relieved to see Alypos leave his escort at the bottom of the steps. Though I could also see other knots of men around the precinct scowling at them and I recognised one group from the Brotherhood of Bellerophon. I hoped those burly temple slaves who'd been wrestling yesterday's sacrificial bulls were ready to intervene if one hero cult's belligerent glares provoked violent retaliation from another.

As Wetka and I went through the temple colonnade to the inner chamber, I saw that Perantas Bacchiad was already here. I glanced at the man I now knew as our foe. Alypos couldn't hide his scowl when he saw Perantas was speaking to Philolaos Kypselid, with his paunch and fussily combed hair.

I laid a hand on Wetka's arm. 'Why is Perantas only calling for Alypos to answer before the Council? Philolaos tried just as hard to wreck our play.'

I felt the Nubian stiffen, and an instant's hesitation betrayed him. 'None of his schemes came close to succeeding, thanks to your quick wits. It is hard to accuse a man over something that never happened, so let's not raise distractions that Alypos can hide behind.'

That was undoubtedly true, but looking at Perantas' confident smile, I concluded it wasn't the whole truth. There were potential witnesses to both those conspiracies, including Corinthian citizens. Even if a prosecution didn't succeed, Rumour rushing around with all the juicy details would do neither man's reputation any good.

Philolaos looked as happy as a man with a cock hair caught under his foreskin and no opportunity to do anything about it. I wondered what concessions Perantas had extorted from him as the price of his forbearance.

That left a sour taste in my mouth when I thought how close we had come to disaster, thanks to these rich men and their selfish rivalries. On the other hand, Wetka had a point. The wise archer takes aim at a particular duck rather than loosing his arrow at a whole flock. The Heirs of Hephaistos' schemes had been disruptive and damaging but not potentially lethal. It was the Sons of Heracles who had opted to use poison.

Glancing at Alypos, I saw his expression had grown even more grim. I'd say he was assuming Philolaos was abandoning their prior alliance to save himself from accusation and humiliation.

I'd be glad to get back to Athens where justice is done in the open air, in full view of gods and men, not in back-room deals by secretive cliques. But home was two days sail away, and I was here in Corinth, facing the Corinthian Council with all the complications that entailed. How many allies could Perantas call on, and how many men would support Alypos, regardless of the evidence? A substantial number clustered around the lean man.

There must be twice as many Councillors present as there had been when Philolaos had tried to get our play stopped to secure public order. Each was sumptuously dressed as befitted his wealth and consequence. More were arriving, and conversation grew steadily louder. Mighty Apollo gazed over their heads, aloof.

The bald, leather-faced Councillor who'd shown himself to be a man of influence out on the Sikyon road, silenced the hubbub with a single clap. Corinth's rulers took their places on those elegant stools, arranged like a theatre's seats. I stayed standing with Wetka by the wall, along with a host of others. I had no idea if they were rich men's cloak carriers or potential witnesses. I had no idea how these oligarchs would handle proceedings. I only knew I must tread very carefully.

Perantas was sitting on one side of the half-circle while Alypos faced him from the opposite ranks. Many of the councillors between them were looking from one to the other, their expressions variously thoughtful, irritated, or studiously impassive.

If there was some signal, I didn't see it, but Perantas got to his feet and strode forward to stand beneath Apollo's outstretched, cloak-draped arm.

'Good day, fellow Council members.' He wasn't smiling now. He wasn't making some pretence of outraged sorrow either, or any other emotional display that advocates in the Athenian courts use to divert attention from some significant flaw in their argument. Perantas' poise spoke of absolute certainty.

'We meet to address the decision of Alypos Temenid to instruct the Sons of Heracles to prevent yesterday's performance in our theatre. The successive attempts he approved of included an initial attack that saw significant injury inflicted on innocent Corinthians. When that failed, he resorted to a vile deceit that could have seen any number of our citizens struck down in the theatre. This much, I can prove.' Perantas paused and glanced up at the god. 'As for my further suspicions, I am content to lay those before Apollo, and trust in his divine justice.'

This was the Perantas I had seen in Athens; a calm and confident orator, selflessly dedicated to public service. A worthy business partner for my patron, Aristarchos, and doubtless an equally virtuous man. I would have believed it, if I hadn't seen the man behind the mask, behind his own closed doors here in Corinth, as he constantly and ruthlessly calculated where his own best interests lay. Perantas was nothing like Aristarchos, but he could certainly play the role convincingly.

I had no time to work out what he was aiming for in today's performance, because he gestured towards me. Every Councillor and his cloak carrier stared, and I tried not to betray how unnerving that was.

'In attacking our honoured guests from Athens, Alypos foully besmirched our city's reputation. What tale will these actors take back home? What will they tell the great and good of their own city?' Perantas asked with a fine rhetorical flourish. 'Philocles Hestaiou, tell us what happened when you held auditions for your chorus.'

I didn't need Wetka's sharp elbow in my ribs to propel me forward. As Perantas returned to his stool, I walked out to stand in Apollo's shadow and drew a steadying breath. Looking at the Councillors in front of me, I decided to address the weather-beaten man with the shrewd eyes who'd called this meeting to order.

As unemotionally as I could, I detailed the brawl at Demeter's Sanctuary. I didn't downplay the Brotherhood's part in the violence. If Perantas didn't like it, that was not my concern. These Councillors weren't going to discount my evidence because they thought I was a Bacchiad mouthpiece. On the other hand, I didn't mention Eumelos' list warning us against various hero cults. Wetka had a point. It would do no good to muddy these waters.

As I concluded, I saw the Councillors facing me were looking at Alypos, clearly disapproving.

Perantas' stool scraped on the tiles. He stood up, sombre-faced. 'If I might clarify, you say insults were thrown on both sides, but the first punch was thrown by this man you know as Demeas?'

'That's correct.' I wasn't sure why I needed to repeat that.

'The arrangements for these auditions were made before you arrived in Corinth, by Eumelos, the pickled fish trader?'

'They were.'

I wondered if he wanted me to talk about Eumelos' list, but he'd moved on.

'Where did you next encounter Demeas?'

I hesitated. Strictly speaking, I'd seen the wiry man talking to Philolaos Kypselid's woolly-headed underling outside this very temple, but I guessed Perantas wouldn't want me mentioning that. I could also see Philolaos staring at me with an intensity that warned me not to make him my enemy. I looked for the best way to avoid sinking into this quicksand.

'I saw him in the gateway of a brothel called the Halcyon, up on the Acrocorinth.'

'What took you to the citadel?'

Now I was on surer ground. 'We were looking for a herbalist called Hermaios Hygestratou. He supplied the Sons of Heracles with Colchis honey. They intended to mix it into the wine to be offered to our audience at the theatre, in hopes of causing some sort of uproar, with so many people intoxicated.'

The assembled Councillors stirred with audible consternation.

'Please, explain,' Perantas invited,

'We were summoned to the Asklepion by a doctor, Chresimos,' I began.

'Excuse me,' Perantas interrupted. 'Is this the doctor who saw Eumelos when he was stricken by poison?'

'He is,' I confirmed.

Seeing Perantas had nothing more to say, I went on to tell the Council about the stricken boy, babbling about a plot to taint the wine for our play's audience. After explaining what Chresimos had told us about the dangers of sweet madness, I related our conversation with Hermaios, though I didn't mention how Zopyros had told us where to find him. I didn't mention the poor little whore Arete, either. They'd both been no more than tools used in these rich men's rivalries. If Perantas was going to pick and choose which people he would protect, I was entitled to do the same.

I described the Sons' murderous pursuit through the Acrocorinth's alleyways, and the fight before we escaped to the gates. That epic needed no embellishment. I could see the Councillors' shocked faces. This time I was ready for Perantas' question.

'At first, Hermaios thought you were there to buy more of the poison that killed Eumelos?'

'That's right.' I waited for Perantas to ask me where I'd next seen Demeas, and steeled myself to explain how I had maimed the man as he tried to kill me.

Instead the Bacchiad surprised me by walking forward and waving me back to rejoin Wetka by the temple wall. Perantas turned to address the assembled Councillors.

'I wish I could bring Hermaios before you all, to admit his undoubted guilt, but he was found dead at the foot of the Acrocorinth. We will never know if he threw himself from the citadel's ramparts, hounded by the Furies for his crimes, or if whoever procured these poisons from him took steps to shut his mouth. As for Demeas . . .' He paused, shaking his head regretfully.

With the assembled oligarchs' attention on Perantas, I could take a good look at Alypos without anyone noticing. I felt a hollow in my stomach as if I'd missed a step on a stair in the dark. He wasn't foolish enough to look smug or defiant, opting instead for a long-suffering air of being unjustly accused. It was the cold composure in his eyes when he looked at Perantas that betrayed him though. A truly innocent man would have shown more anxiety at being so perilously misunderstood.

Perantas cleared his throat. 'Excuse me. As for Demeas, he can answer for himself.'

Shock flashed across Alypos' face, followed by a blaze of fury. Inside a breath, he had mastered himself, but the damage was done. Other members of this Council had seen his reaction as Demeas was escorted into the chamber by Thettalos.

I swallowed hard, feeling sick. Demeas' useless arm was heavily bandaged and strapped across his body. There wasn't a mark of further violence on him, but his eyes were so darkly hollow with agony that he looked as if he'd been punched. His face was the colour of mud.

Thettalos had firm hold of his other elbow and brought him to stand in front of Apollo. Since I couldn't see any prospect of the injured man trying to escape, I hoped the bull-necked man was there to catch him if he passed out from pain.

Alypos was on his feet, demanding the Council's attention. 'Whatever this man might say, his words cannot be trusted. He has clearly been foully mistreated to compel false testimony.'

I pushed myself away from the wall, ready to explain my responsibility for Demeas' injuries. Wetka seized my wrist with a grip like an eagle's talons, and answered my questioning gaze with an emphatic shake of his head.

Alypos was still speaking, convincing in his outrage. 'I do not know this man. I know nothing of these fanciful plots. My association with the Sons of Heracles is in support of their charitable endeavours, and nothing more. If some devotees were provoked by these Athenians, for whatever reason, that cannot be laid at my door.'

I wondered how Perantas intended to prove the Sons were doing Alypos' dirty work. Doubtless Demeas was here to testify, and I hated to think what might have been done to his broken arm to ensure that he said what suited the Bacchiad, but it would still be this single, unknown man's word against one of Corinth's most powerful citizens.

Perantas snapped his fingers and another man appeared, carrying an amphora. A boy followed with a tray of cups. 'On your oath in Apollo's presence, Demeas, was this wine taken from your house?'

'It was,' the wiry man said through gritted teeth.

Perantas addressed Thettalos. 'On your oath in Apollo's presence, have you been in possession of this amphora since you seized it from Demeas' house?'

'I have,' the bull-necked man said calmly.

Perantas turned to Alypos, his expression enquiring. 'Will you drink a cup of this wine?'

'What?' Taken aback, Alypos rallied swiftly. 'No, I will not. I have no idea what might be in that amphora, or where it could have come from.'

I knew exactly where it had come from. I could see the bee seal stamped into the earthenware from here. If I could see it, so could Alypos. He knew it held the lethally honeyed wine, strong enough to cause delirium, and even death.

Perantas gestured at Thettalos and Demeas. 'These men have told you where it is from, on their oath before the god. Are you calling them liars in Apollo's presence?'

'That man is your creature.' Venomous, Alypos jabbed a finger at Thettalos. 'The gods alone know what he might do or say at your bidding.'

Such naked animosity didn't go down well. Nor did accusing the two men of lying in Apollo's own temple, judging by the disapproving rustle among the Councillors.

Perantas raised a conceding hand. 'It is true, Thettalos is a loyal member of the Brotherhood of Bellerophon, as am I. As Apollo is my witness, *I* do not deny my allegiances.'

The implication was obvious, since my evidence had already tied Demeas to the Sons of Heracles and Alypos' association with the hero cult was well known. I saw the first flicker of unease in Alypos' eyes.

'But you say you do not know this other man,' Perantas continued in mild and reasonable tones. 'So what reason could you have to call him a liar? Why should you imagine that any possible harm could come to you from drinking wine taken from his house?'

He looked at Demeas. 'We can see that your arm is broken, and I am sorry for it. Were you injured by any Brother of Bellerophon? At the hands of any Corinthian? On your oath to Apollo.'

'No,' the wiry man said, staring at the floor.

I wondered what the god was making of these answers that might not be lies, but certainly had the potential to mislead, even in overall service of the truth.

'So why won't you drink this wine?' Perantas challenged Alypos.

'Because I choose not to indulge your theatrics in this holy place, before this honoured Council,' Alypos said coldly. 'Besides, the ridiculous play you sponsored went ahead without any incident. How can I be accused of attempting some outrage that never even happened?'

Perantas stared back at him. 'Every bone in Hermaios' body was shattered by his fall from the Acrocorinth. Eumelos was poisoned.'

Alypos shrugged. 'Their blood is not on my hands.'

'Then let us share a cup of this wine,' Perantas invited, 'and pour a libation to Apollo as you testify to your innocence, and I will beg your pardon.'

I could see a good many Councillors looking expectantly at Alypos. If he had nothing to fear from the wine, or from perjuring himself in the god's presence, why would he refuse? Others were increasingly irritated, while a few looked apprehensive. I guessed their association with Alypos wasn't going to be so mutually beneficial now. Mud doesn't only stick. It gets smeared around.

The silence lengthened until Demeas broke it.

'I will drink the wine.'

The shock on Alypos' face was mirrored on Thettalos', and Perantas' too. Evidently Demeas wasn't following the script they'd prepared.

'It's the last amphora left of the wine we stirred the Colchis honey into, to take it to the theatre. He knows that as well as I do, because he supplied it,' Demeas said tightly. 'I know it will strike me down with sweet madness, and if that will give me some relief from my pain, I will welcome it. Whether I live or die?' He shrugged. 'I leave that in Apollo's hands. He can condemn me for my crimes or pardon me, for the sake of my loyalty to you.'

The hatred in his eyes as he looked at Alypos was greater proof of the Temenid's guilt than anything said so far. That's the thing about loyalty. When a man has truly sworn his allegiance only to find his commitment isn't returned, he will often repay such treachery with equally single-minded fervour.

Demeas turned to Thettalos. 'Open the wine.'

'No.' The weather-beaten Councillor stood up and looked at Demeas without much sympathy. 'We may yet have further questions for you, and this city has the right to see you answer for your crimes. We commend you to this temple's care for the present.'

He looked around and a priest I hadn't even noticed strode forward, backed by a couple of burly slaves. They escorted Demeas out and he went willingly enough. He was hardly in any condition to resist.

The weather-beaten Councillor turned to his fellow oligarchs. 'We must decide if there is a case to answer.'

Voices erupted around the half-circle of seated men. One man snapped his fingers and pointed at Thettalos. 'A priest must take charge of that amphora.'

Several Councillors agreed and one went further. 'Someone find a stray dog and pour a cupful down its throat! Then we'll know, one way or another.'

I didn't get a chance to see who agreed with that. Wetka took hold of my elbow and ushered me towards the temple's entrance. I would have resisted, but everyone else was leaving. This debate was only for the oligarchs.

'Why was Alypos so surprised to see Demeas?' I demanded.

'You're not the only ones who can let treacherous ears hear a lie.' He smiled, as smug as a fox who's caught a cockerel. 'We made sure that Alypos' man in the Brotherhood was certain that Demeas was dead and that all the tainted wine was destroyed.'

'Would Perantas really have drunk a cup, and risked the sweet madness?' I didn't doubt that Thettalos and Demeas had told the truth about that amphora in Apollo's presence.

'Yes, putting his faith in Apollo and Athena,' Wetka said steadily. 'The mistake my master's rivals so often make is to think he's as cowardly as they are. Alypos realised his error too late.'

'What happens now?' I shook off the Nubian's grip.

'Most likely, Alypos will flee the city before dark. It will be interesting to see where he seeks sanctuary.'

'Sanctuary? Not exile?' I was infuriated. 'You mean he won't face justice? Not for killing Eumelos or anything else?'

Wetka smiled at me. 'Justice is in the gift of the gods.'

Before I could decide if I was going to challenge him or slap him, the Nubian walked away. I turned on Thettalos instead, since the bull-necked man was approaching me.

'How long will Alypos quit Corinth for? How long before rumours and memories fade and he comes quietly back to pick up his life where he left off, with most people outside the Council none the wiser about his crimes?'

If this was Athens, Alypos would be ostracised by the People's Assembly, condemned to ten years' exile, and everyone would know exactly why. Such a man coming back to the city would never escape that stain on his reputation.

Thettalos ignored my furious questions. He had other things on his mind. 'We found that missing slave, on the road to Kenchreai last night.'

'What?' I stared at him, incredulous. 'Tromes?'

How could the fugitive have been so stupid? Come to that, how could the idiot have got off a ship bound for Zakynthos?

Thettalos studied my face, looking for some sign of guilt, since he was still convinced I'd helped Perantas' disloyal slave to escape. Thankfully, all he saw was my genuine astonishment. Regardless, he smirked with satisfaction at misleading me.

'We found Dardanis, while we were beating the bushes for Tromes.'

I was even more taken aback. 'Eumelos' slave? What has he got to say for himself?'

'Nothing much. He's dead.' Thettalos' smile faded and he looked grim. 'It seems he was killed the same night that Eumelos died.'

'Murdered by some Son of Heracles?' Now I glared at him. 'Another death that Alypos won't answer for?'

'Alypos didn't need Eumelos dead.' He looked levelly

at me. 'Why don't you go and help young Nados find out who did? Who wanted to silence his slave as well?'

He turned away, but I grabbed his arm. I had a thousand questions, but one clamoured louder than the rest. 'Why are you telling me this? Perantas won't like it. He wants everyone to think that Alypos had Eumelos killed.'

Thettalos shook himself free. 'He never accused him of it.'

That was true but the bull-necked man still hadn't answered my question. 'Why are you telling me?'

Thettalos raised his hand and I saw he was wearing the dead man's agate ring carved with the image of Bellerophon astride Pegasus. 'He was my brother.'

He strode away. I stood still as a temple pillar, trying to make sense of this as the Corinthian crowds swirled around me. Then I headed for Eumelos' house.

Chapter Twenty-Five

I could smell the lingering stench of putrefaction before I reached Eumelos' gate. It might have been years since I'd searched a battlefield's dead for a friend, but I'll remember that reek till I die. They had brought Dardanis home.

Thankfully, I hadn't stopped to eat any lunch on my way here, and I was very glad indeed that I hadn't stayed up late last night playing drinking games. When Simias opened the gate, he looked horribly hungover.

'You heard?'

'Thettalos told me.' I looked over his shoulder. 'Where is he?'

'On his way to be buried alongside Eumelos,' Simias said with undisguised relief. 'The body was vile.'

Presumably the silent litter bearers had been given that revolting task, and they had all my sympathies.

'Have you any idea how he died?' Though establishing that must be a vain hope after ten days.

Simias opened the gate wider. 'Come and hear what the doctor has to say.'

I went into the courtyard and saw Chresimos the Cycladean sitting with Nados in the portico's shade. The housekeeper Abrosyne and two other girls were scrubbing a grim stain on the paving, pouring vinegar onto handfuls of wood ash scooped from a bucket. A sharp odour rose above the stink of decay.

Chresimos raised a hand as I approached. 'It is impossible to tell if Dardanis was poisoned, still less if he died from the same concoction that killed Eumelos.'

'I can imagine.' Though it was an obvious question to ask, I guessed that's why the trio had sent for this particular doctor, with all the optimism of youth. 'Was there anything to be learned from his body?'

'He wasn't robbed. He still had his purse and his cloak and shoes.' Nados poured well-watered wine into four waiting cups as Aithon appeared from the house with another one. He must have gone to fetch that when Simias opened the gate.

'Theft may have been his killer's intention,' Chresimos observed. 'His arms had been slashed with a blade and his scalp was torn. That much was clear, despite the maggots.'

Aithon took a gulp of his wine, looking queasy. 'But he got away.'

'I'm reminded of something I saw during the fighting in Megara,' Chresimos mused. 'Several soldiers in the thick of a battle lost their helmets and suffered head wounds that broke the skin but not the skull. They seemed to be recovering but two fell into a stupor a day or so later. They could not be roused and died during the night. Dardanis' skull was intact . . .'

I really didn't want to think how the doctor had established that.

'If we assume he was attacked at night on the road,' the Cycladean continued, 'it's possible that he escaped his assailants, and hid where they couldn't find him in the darkness. Alas, he succumbed to that head injury before morning, and no one discovered him before he died.'

'He'd never have been found, most likely,' Nados said sombrely, 'if Thettalos and his brutes hadn't been tearing up every thicket between here and Kenchreai, hoping to flush out Tromes.'

The trio exchanged an eloquent glance. I spoke up before Chresimos could ask any awkward questions.

'He disappeared the night Eumelos died, so it's fair to assume he was attacked on his way to the port.'

'How did he know the master wouldn't recover?' Simias objected.

Chresimos set his wine cup down on the table, looking a little embarrassed. 'I believe I was the one who told him. A man called at the Asklepion in the dead of night and asked how Eumelos fared. He gave me his oath that he was one of this household. I told him his master would die before morning. I assumed you had sent him to enquire. He may well have been Dardanis, though I cannot say for certain, given the decay of the corpse. He was a man of the same stature.'

'Instead of coming to tell you, he took the road to Kenchreai.' I looked at Nados. 'Have you any idea why?'

Chresimos got to his feet. 'Perhaps you'll find some answers in there. I'll leave you to it.'

I followed his gaze to the far end of the portico where

a leather-bound package lay on the tiled floor beside a lumpy purse tied with a thong. 'What's that?'

'Dardanis had it tucked inside his tunic, against his chest.' Nados grimaced. 'Fortunately it seems maggots prefer fresh meat to tanned hide.'

Simias took a deep breath. 'Better yet, he was lying on his back when he died, so the worst—'

'I understand.' I didn't want to contemplate the consequences if whatever this was had been trapped beneath a decomposing corpse.

'His purse, on the other hand.' Simias grimaced and swallowed hard.

'We really had better see what's inside them.' Nados was still trying to convince himself as Aithon returned from escorting the doctor to the gate.

I went over for a closer look. Something had been placed in the centre of a large square of leather. The sides had been folded across it, and then the top and bottom flaps. Two leather straps had been knotted around it, crossing over each other. The package was gruesomely stained, though the reek of decay was mostly coming from the purse sitting in its noxious little puddle.

I found the prospect of investigating them nauseating, and I wasn't battling the after-effects of too much wine the night before. Still, someone needed to do it, and ideally someone who wasn't going to add vomit to the mix of odours.

'Abrosyne?' I called out to the housekeeper who was still scouring the paving. 'Please fetch me some meat skewers and your two sharpest knives.'

The old woman looked at Nados. When he nodded, she got to her feet and went into the house.

I saw the three lads looking at me uncertainly. I raised my eyebrows. 'Do you want to touch any of that?'

They were still shaking their heads when Abrosyne brought what I asked for. She retreated to the courtyard where the other household slaves were gathering. I supposed they had as much of an interest in this as Eumelos' boys.

First, I used a skewer to shove the stinking purse into the far corner. Then I knelt in front of the leather package and slid one knife under the strap that ran from top to bottom. I slipped the other beneath the strap running across it. Using both hands, and putting equal force behind both blades, I was able to cut the two straps without any need for someone else to hold the package steady. Thankfully Abrosyne kept her knives razor sharp.

'Neatly done,' Nados approved.

'Let's see what we've got.' I flipped the cut straps away and used the knife points to unfold the leather. That revealed another square of tanned hide, thinner and with a sheen that I recognised. I braced myself and leaned closer to pick out a familiar scent amid the fading odours of death. This inner layer was oiled skin.

I handed Simias the knives. 'Let me have those skewers.'

It wasn't easy but I turned the inner package over. This square of oiled leather had been folded in the same way as the outer layer. Placing it folded-side down on the larger square had ensured that the package's contents

333

were protected by equal thicknesses of leather on either side.

'Dardanis wanted this kept safe.' I carefully unfolded the oiled hide with the knife blades.

'Or Eumelos did,' Aithon said.

'He wouldn't do anything that Eumelos hadn't told him to do.' Simias was sure of that.

I flipped aside the last flap of leather to reveal an inner layer of linen, thankfully free of ominous stains. Belatedly, I realised it was the characteristic length and width of a sheet of papyrus. I looked up. 'Nados?'

He bent down to pick it up.

'Abrosyne, get the brazier lit and burn all this.' Nados kicked the discarded leather aside and returned to the table with the linen-wrapped documents.

I saw desperate hope on all their faces as we took our seats once again. 'Is it the missing will?'

Nados didn't answer, handing several sheets to Aithon, and studying the papyrus that remained in his hand intently. With nothing to read, Simias could only tap a frustrated foot on the tiles. I sympathised.

'It is the will,' Nados said slowly as he turned to the second sheet. 'We inherit equal shares in the business, and he divides up his property between us. I inherit this house.' He looked around, wide-eyed, as if he couldn't believe his good fortune, before nodding at Aithon and then at Simias. 'You get the Lechaion house, and you get Kenchreai.'

He read through both closely written sheets a second time and shook his head mystified. 'There's no mention of the silver reserve, or where to find any strongbox.'

Simias was dumbfounded. 'Where's the money gone?'

'To Isthmia.' Aithon had been so absorbed in what he was reading that I don't think he had registered he was now a man of property. 'Listen to this.

'From Eumares Demetriou of Leukonoion to Myrrhine, daughter of Pratinias Pharou of Paionidai. My honoured wife—'

'He was married?'

'He was Athenian?'

Nados and I exclaimed, half a breath ahead of Simias.

'What name did you say?'

Aithon ignored us all, picking up where he'd been interrupted.

'My honoured wife, if you are reading this letter, then the man who brings it has come to tell you that I am dead. I am sorry to burden you with such news and all that inevitably follows. I had hoped that you would receive these tidings after we had lived a long and happy life apart, as we never could together. I had hoped that our son would be a grown man we could both be proud of, married according to the law, and you would be delighting in your grandchildren.

'Since the Fates have decreed otherwise, please ask your father and your brother to take this letter and my messenger to my father so that they can inform him our son is now his heir according to the laws of Athens, and to see that this is recognised by the courts. The quarrel between myself and my

335

family must not deprive our child of his rightful inheritance.

'For my own part, I bequeath our son the strongbox safe-guarded in my name by the priests of Poseidon at Isthmia. I have no doubt that you have raised him to be a thoughtful, respectful boy, and that you and your family will use this silver to see him educated to become a dutiful citizen of Athens, equipped as befits a soldier sworn to fight for our democracy.

'I hope that this will win me some measure of forgiveness from the gods above and below for my undoubted failings as a husband, and my delinquency as an Athenian.

'Written and sealed by my own hand . . .'

Aithon looked up. 'It's dated at the start of this year, and this is his handwriting, I swear to Hermes.'

He showed us all the papyrus and Nados held the will beside it, clearly stating Eumelos' name, or rather the name he'd been known by here in Corinth. There could be no doubt that the same man had written both documents.

'He always updated his will at the new year,' Simias said faintly.

'Now we know where the silver went.' Nados looked less bothered about the money and more distressed to learn that Eumelos had kept something so significant as a wife and child a secret.

The will was endorsed with the Brotherhood of Bellerophon ring that Eumelos had worn. There was no mistaking the image of Pegasus taking flight on that seal. The letter bore some other symbol that I couldn't make out. 'May I see that?'

Aithon handed over the papyrus. I examined the image pressed into the oval of wax. Close to, it was clear enough; a lyre within an olive wreath. A suitable insignia for a man born into the voting tribe of Leontis, named for the hero Leos, son of Orpheus.

'Presumably his family will recognise this. Of course, it would be best to have the ring as well . . .'

I looked at the noisome lump of Dardanis' purse squatting like a toad in the corner of the portico. 'I'd dump that in a bowl of vinegar and let it soak for a good long while before you untie it. Coin won't come to any harm, or that seal ring, if it's in there.'

Nados shook off the thoughts taunting him, like a horse shaking off troublesome flies. 'But we still don't know who killed Dardanis.'

'The same man who murdered Eumelos?' Simias hazarded. 'Eumares, I mean.'

'Someone who didn't want him taking this letter to Athens,' Aithon said slowly.

'Maybe he had Eumelos' will with him, because he was going to give it to you in Kenchreai, before finding a ship.' Nados looked at Simias. 'But is it still valid, if that wasn't really his name?'

'It was the name he was known by in this city.' Aithon looked at us all uncertainly. 'Surely that will weigh in our favour with any court?'

'I suggest you continue to call him Eumelos,' I advised, 'and not just to avoid confusion over his will. He kept his former life secret for a reason, and until we can discover why, secrecy is our best protection. Someone murdered the only two men who knew the truth.'

'How did this killer know that Dardanis would be taking such a vital message back to Athens?' Aithon wondered aloud.

Nados had other concerns. 'What will happen to the child, if this woman never learns that her husband is dead?'

'They'll be a good deal poorer for one thing,' Simias observed.

'That depends on how old this boy is, and whether or not these two families can come to an agreement over who now serves as his guardian. Whatever this quarrel was, it must have been serious for Eumelos to cut all ties with his family and make a new life in Corinth.'

I couldn't imagine what could make a man abandon his duty as a father, as a husband and as a citizen of Athens. I offered the letter back to Nados, but he wouldn't take it.

'Someone needs to tell these families what's happened,' I pointed out.

'I wouldn't know where to start,' he protested. 'I've been to Piraeus twice and walked up to see the Acropolis once. That's all I know of Attica.'

'That's more than me,' said Aithon.

'It'll be simple enough to find them.' I gestured with the letter. 'This gives us Eumelos' true name along with his father's and the city district where he must have been enrolled as a voter. Find the district officials and they'll tell you where to find his family. Paionidai is some way outside the city, so that'll be more of a journey, but the local officials will be able to introduce you to this Myrrhine's father.'

'Three Corinthians they've never met before, claiming to bring news of a man they haven't seen for, what, ten years?' Nados challenged me.

'Bringing news of a strongbox filled with silver?' Simias shook his head. 'They'll expect us to demand a share.'

'We don't want a clipped obol,' Aithon said quickly, 'but that conversation could still turn ugly.'

'What if they accuse us of having a hand in Eumelos' death?' Nados' voice cracked with emotion. 'To get this silver? You said it yourself. Someone he trusted gave him the poison that killed him.'

I realised he had a good point. Such suspicion was unfortunately a very real possibility. Lysicrates wasn't the only Athenian whose first instinct was to mistrust Corinthians. Out in rural Attica, reactions could well be even more hostile. I remembered youthful summers helping my mother's brothers, raising sheep out by Mount Pentelikos. They would whistle up their dogs if they found they were dealing with someone from more than a day's walk away, wary of any man whom no one they knew could vouch for.

Then I saw all three youths were looking at me with the same eager expectation as my uncles' dogs when we sat down to eat our midday bread and cheese.

'You're an Athenian citizen,' Aithon pointed out, 'well known and respected. Any number of people can attest to your honourable reputation.'

'You have no personal interest in this,' added Simias. 'You won't profit in any way. No one can accuse you of doing anything underhand.'

339

'We have a duty to Eumelos, to see this family matter resolved.' Nados was sorely troubled. 'But we also have a duty to tend to his business affairs here. These past ten days have been a real challenge as it is, with no one knowing who would inherit his property, and unsure about entering into contracts with us. Now that we have his will, we can take it to the Council and those we trade with can be confident in our future dealings, but what will they think if we disappear to Athens for however long it could take to find his son?'

'It wouldn't take all three of you.' Though as I spoke I imagined the scepticism that would greet a solitary, youthful Corinthian arriving with this unlikely tale, certainly until someone could be found to verify Eumelos' seal ring. Who knew how long that could take, if he'd left the city a decade ago?

'What if his family decide to challenge our right to his property here?' Aithon wondered uneasily. 'Could we be called before an Athenian court?'

I had no answer to that. I could think of men who would gladly give these three a share in whatever silver was held in trust at Isthmia as a reward for them bringing this news of a lost husband, father and son. Equally, I knew a few who would seize such an opportunity to try claiming everything Eumelos had owned in Corinth, down to the last amphora of pickled fish.

Simias broke into my thoughts. 'You'll be going back to Athens in any case, and soon. Is it asking so much for you to deliver this letter?'

That was also unfortunately true.

'I will consider it,' I said reluctantly. 'I will need to talk to the others.'

'Of course.' Simias was already smiling. 'And as Athenians, they can stand witness to everything you say.'

I got to my feet. 'Find a scroll case and keep that letter safe. I'll let you know what we decide once Wetka's made our travel arrangements.'

That was another consideration. Perantas Bacchiad, not to mention Thettalos, would expect me to do what I could to help settle Eumelos' affairs. Come to that, I didn't relish the thought of going home and telling Aristarchos that I had neglected such an obvious duty to a fellow Athenian citizen, even one who'd absented himself for so long. I liked the idea of answering to Athena for such dereliction even less.

Then there was my duty to the Furies, the avengers of the unjustly dead. If I learned why Eumelos had left his old life behind, perhaps that would tell me who had murdered him, and we could see justice done for both these dead men.

I pointed to the noxious purse in the corner of the portico. 'You lot deal with opening that before I get back, and see if the seal ring is in there.'

Chapter Twenty-Six

When I got back to our lodging, Hyanthidas and Telesilla had stopped by to relax with the actors and Zosime. Everyone was sitting in the courtyard as Kadous served dishes of olives and other dainties.

'How did it go?' Menekles asked.

'They found Dardanis' body on the Kenchreai road yesterday.' I took a seat and reached for a hunk of bread.

'We know,' Apollonides interrupted. 'Aithon told us when he came looking for Simias.'

'What happened with the Council of Oligarchs?' Zosime demanded.

'Oh.' My head was so full of Athenian concerns that Perantas taking his revenge on Alypos seemed irrelevant. I looked around but there was no sign of any Bacchiad slaves, not that it mattered if they overheard me. I quickly related the events in the Temple of Apollo in between mouthfuls of bread and salad leaves.

Lysicrates glowered. 'So he won't answer for his crimes.'

'And Philolaos won't even have to leave the city.' Apollonides wasn't about to forgive him any time soon. 'Did anyone mention that his henchman paid off

Parmenon and Eupraxis? To leave our chorus two short on the day of the play itself. Hyanthidas was just telling us.'

The piper nodded. 'Offered them the choice of enough silver to settle their debts, or a lifetime of living on soup after getting their teeth kicked in.'

I hoped the two singers thought the bargain they'd made was worth it, once Thettalos and the Brotherhood turned up to collect whatever vengeance they reckoned was owed.

'Oligarchs.' Zosime was still scowling about the Council. 'They always look after their own.'

Menekles' thoughts were elsewhere. He had been paying close attention as I repeated the evidence set before the Council. An actor always looks for hidden meanings. 'Perantas never accused Alypos outright of killing Eumelos.'

'With Hermaios dead, there's no way to prove it, one way or the other.' Hyanthidas shrugged. 'People will draw their own conclusions.'

'Assuming that if he was willing to use poisons twice, he surely used them three times?' I shook my head. 'People thinking that may very well be wrong.'

I explained what we had found in the leather-wrapped package that Dardanis had been carrying. I kept my voice low, alert for any Bacchiad slaves unexpectedly appearing. 'Until we know what lies behind this, I suggest we keep it to ourselves. We don't want to cast unnecessary doubt on his bequests to Nados, Aithon and Simias.'

Telesilla looked at Zosime. 'That explains why he never married.'

My beloved was shaking her head. 'Poor woman.'

'It obviously wasn't a happy marriage,' Apollonides pointed out. 'Perhaps she asked him to leave.'

'Why didn't he simply divorce her?' countered Zosime. 'Setting her free to find happiness with someone else?'

I kept quiet. Someone else could point out an Athenian wife's right to petition for divorce, difficult though that might be in practice, if they wanted to risk Zosime's ire.

'At least he was determined to see his son's rights protected.' Lysicrates looked disapproving all the same.

'No one could think of a Corinthian with a reason to kill him,' Menekles said slowly, 'but surely this means he could have had Athenian enemies.'

I agreed. I'd examined this puzzle from every angle as I walked back from Eumelos' house, or rather Nados' house. 'You remember what Hermaios said to us?'

Menekles nodded. 'He thought we wanted the same poison that had killed Eumelos, on the recommendation of a friend.'

'He could tell we were Athenians,' I explained to the others. 'I assumed that meant Athenians were working with whoever was out to stop our play. We know there are would-be oligarchs back home who oppose Aristarchos' support for the Thurii colony.'

In the light of this morning's revelations, that

conversation now suggested very different possibilities.

'If an Athenian killed Eumelos, it makes sense to kill Dardanis, to stop that news reaching Athens,' Menekles agreed.

Lysicrates was puzzled. 'If whoever did this intends to profit by Eumelos' death, surely he would want that known?'

None of us had an answer for that.

Telesilla wasn't convinced. 'Surely it's just as likely that some Corinthian who knew who Dardanis was wanted Eumelos' will lost, in order to profit from the confusion that followed?'

'Has there been any word of someone laying claim to his property here?' Apollonides wasn't challenging her, merely curious.

'Not that I've heard.' She exchanged a glance with Hyanthidas. 'Though we have been too busy to follow the latest gossip.'

The musician pursed his lips. 'We can ask around. See if anyone's looking particularly sour at the news that his will has been found.'

'The killer must have known Dardanis by sight,' Lysicrates pointed out. 'To be certain of killing the right man.'

I nodded. 'Everyone says that Dardanis had been with Eumelos for longer than anyone else. Since before they came to Corinth.'

Unfortunately, that was as much as anyone knew. Perhaps he had shared something about his former life with a fellow slave. I looked across the courtyard at Kadous.

He would be far better suited to making such enquiries than me.

'There's someone else we should talk to,' I realised. 'Eumelos' favourite whore, Arete. Hermaios said she gave him the poison. We should ask who gave it to her.'

Apollonides was doubtful. 'Whoever it was will be long gone by now.'

'I should come with you.' Hyanthidas had other concerns. 'If she says that was a Corinthian, Nados and the others will need a Corinthian witness, if they ever bring him to justice.'

'We could all go up to the Acrocorinth,' Lysicrates said with a gleam in his eye. 'It would be a shame to go home without sampling such famous entertainments.'

Apollonides grinned. 'We have earned some reward after all our hard work.'

'I would say so,' Menekles agreed.

I could see Zosime looking at me quizzically. Hyanthidas was looking to reassure Telesilla. 'We will go and see what this girl knows and come straight back.'

'Take all the time you need,' she said obligingly. 'My poetry circle is meeting tonight, so Zosime and I will be well entertained.'

My beloved smiled sweetly. 'Arion can escort me back here, however late that might be.'

'Of course.' I was tempted to insist that Kadous went with her, but I wasn't about to insult Hyanthidas by implying I didn't trust his slave. Besides, I wanted the Phrygian seeing what he could learn about Dardanis from Nados' household.

Lysicrates and Apollonides were already on their feet. As they went to fetch enough silver to buy plenty of entertainment, and Zosime went upstairs to choose a shawl, I took Kadous aside to explain what I wanted from him.

He nodded. 'Perhaps they'll be more willing to talk with their tongues loosened by grief.'

'Let's hope so. Dardanis' loyalty deserves the reward of seeing his killer brought to justice.'

The others were returning and we set out together. I still felt a qualm when we reached the agora and Zosime and Telesilla went on their own way together. Hyanthidas was clearly unconcerned so I told myself not to worry about their safety as they walked through the city without an escort.

That didn't stop me wondering how my beloved would feel about returning to Athens where such behaviour by a citizen woman and her resident foreigner friend would draw disapproving stares.

I hadn't come to any comfortable conclusions by the time we had made the long climb up to the Acrocorinth's gates yet again. On the other hand, I was pleased to think this was the last time I'd be hiking up this bloody mountain if I could possibly help it.

The citadel was as busy as we had ever seen it. Finding a place to pause together without impeding passers-by wasn't easy.

'You're sure you don't want us to come with you?' Though Menekles was already assessing the delights on offer on either side of the street.

'Only if you want to take your pleasures at eight obols a time.' As I suspected, that gave the three of them pause for thought, and Hyanthidas and I made our way to the House of Pearls alone.

The brothel was evidently doing good business, high prices notwithstanding. Young girls in translucent linen dresses served cups of wine to waiting customers. Two older women played a flute and a lyre and their tuneful music was accompanied by equally well-practised giggles and murmurs of delight floating through the shutters.

The slave Sekis had three well-muscled underlings to assist him today. Hyanthidas and I stood aside as two of them escorted a drunk who'd overstayed his welcome out through the gate.

'Good afternoon. I wonder if we might have a few moments' conversation with Arete?'

Sekis shook his head, so I reached into my tunic for my purse, about to assure the slave we would pay.

His next words surprised me. 'Madame Eirene will want to speak to you first.'

'By all means.' I guessed the slave had been told to keep an eye out for us. A memory for faces must be essential for him as he kept troublemakers and reluctant payers out.

'Take a seat.' He gestured to a bench where visitors sat in varying states of inebriation and anticipation.

We did so as Sekis went into the house. I barely had time to wonder how long we'd be kept waiting before Eirene appeared in the doorway to summon us with a peremptory hand.

She led us up the stairs to the house's upper storey. These white-plastered walls were as plain as the furnishings in her sitting room. There was no sign of a water clock, so I hoped we were going to be spared a request for payment.

'May we speak to Arete? Briefly,' I added as Hyanthidas and I found ourselves stools, 'when she's not otherwise engaged.'

'She has precious few clients at the moment.' Eirene clicked her tongue with exasperation, taking her seat in a cushioned, high-backed chair as befitted a matriarch. 'Some men find consoling a weeping woman arousing, but most come here to escape tears and such inconveniences. But I must thank you for your warning,' she continued. 'We have kept her safe.'

We heard footsteps in the corridor and Arete appeared in the doorway. Sekis must have summoned her. She wore a plain wool dress and her hair was simply braided. Her doleful expression was as far from seductive as I could imagine.

Arete looked at Eirene and at the older woman's nod, she took a stool beside the high-backed chair, her shoulders hunched and both hands folded in her lap.

I chose my words carefully. 'We believe you may be able to help us find Eumelos' killer.'

Arete's eyes brimmed with tears. 'But I—'

'We are pursuing the man who gave you that vial to give to him,' I said firmly. 'Who lied to you about its purpose, knowing full well that it was poison. Who deliberately procured it, intending to use your love for

Eumelos to deceive him. He is the murderer here. You bear no guilt in the eyes of gods or men.'

'As I have told you,' Eirene agreed.

Though I could see that her sympathy for the girl was finely balanced with exasperation that Arete could have been so gullible.

Hyanthidas chimed in. 'What can you tell us about this villain?'

'He was an Athenian.' A tear spilled from Arete's lashes, but thankfully she didn't start sobbing.

'Was there anything noteworthy about him?' I had to ask.

Arete shook her head, bemused. 'He was ordinary, like any other man. He said he was Eumelos' friend, an old friend from years ago.'

'He was very clear as to what he wanted,' Eirene added. 'He asked to be introduced to Eumelos' favourite companion.'

'He told me he wanted to see him married and happy.' Arete's chin quivered.

'Eumelos wasn't free to marry you, even if he had wished to,' Hyanthidas said gently. 'He had a wife in Attica.'

Arete stared at him, aghast, and choked on a wail of protest. Eirene leaned forward and laid a quelling hand on her shoulder.

'No different to half the men who visit us, then.' She had been more observant than the girl though. 'When this liar came back, his forearm was bandaged. Perhaps that will help you find him.'

'You saw him again?' That caught my attention more than mention of his injury. 'After he tricked Arete into supplying the poison?'

'Of course.' Eirene looked at me, puzzled. 'As you feared. We didn't let him through the gate, as you warned.'

'Of course.' I'd sent that note when I still thought some unknown Athenians were conspiring with the Sons of Heracles. 'When exactly did you see him?'

Eirene took a moment to think. 'He first returned three days ago, and then yesterday evening, very late.'

'When was he injured?' Hyanthidas asked.

Eirene shrugged. 'His arm was bandaged when we first saw him again, but I have no way of knowing when he was hurt between the day before Eumelos died and then.'

'Which arm was injured? What more can you tell us?' Belatedly, I realised a whore used by countless men would find their faces indistinguishable after a while, but I had higher hopes of Eirene, who needed to keep undesirables out of her house.

'His knife arm was hurt. He was nothing out of the ordinary to look at; dark of hair and eye, stocky and broad-shouldered.' She looked at me. 'He was insisting on seeing Arete. Sekis had to threaten to call the citadel guards to make him leave last night. How long must we stay watchful?'

'I don't know.' Though if my growing suspicions were correct, the little whore should be safe enough now. I rose to my feet. 'Thank you. With Aphrodite's blessing, and Athena's, we will see this man pay for his crimes.'

I've no idea why, but that did make Arete burst into tears. As Eirene sought to console her with bracing words and a gentle embrace, Hyanthidas and I made good our escape. Sekis was waiting at the bottom of the stairs, but with no shouts of alarm from Eirene, he allowed us to pass. The younger man guarding the gate wasn't interested in anyone trying to leave, more concerned with those overeager to enter this house of delights without proving they could pay for their pleasure.

By the time Hyanthidas and I had reached the end of the street, I had come to some conclusions. 'Dardanis was in a knife fight before he was killed. That much was obvious from his body.'

'With luck, he left his own mark on his killer.' Hyanthidas clearly hoped so.

'More than likely,' I agreed. 'Surely, this unknown Athenian must have killed him. That may not be the only blood on his hands, if he was here in the citadel on the same day Hermaios died.'

Hyanthidas was startled. 'Do you think he killed the poisoner?'

'If he saw us visit that shop. If he thought we were on his trail. That would make sense, as well as killing Arete if he could.' I spared a moment's thanks for whatever deity had used my mistaken message to protect the unfortunate girl. Aphrodite most likely.

'But why would he still be here?' Hyanthidas wondered. 'If Eirene saw him yesterday?'

'He didn't know that Dardanis was dead. As long as there was some possibility that the slave might reappear, my guess is he hung on in the hope of getting another chance to kill him. Look how many times he tried to get at Arete.' I cursed under my breath. 'I bet he was on the first ship out of Kenchreai after word spread that Dardanis had been found to get back to Athens ahead of the news.'

Hyanthidas looked towards the citadel gates, and then at Aphrodite's temple. 'So what are we going to do now?'

'I have to see Demeas.' The realisation startled me nearly as much as it surprised the musician. 'If I'm making a tally of this Athenian's crimes, I want to know everything that's owed to his account. Add to that,' I went on, 'Demeas may be able to tell us something to help us identify him.'

Hyanthidas snorted. 'He could hardly be less use than Arete.'

We made our way down the mountainside. As we passed by the busy Sanctuary of Demeter and Persephone I guessed that no trace of our presence remained, any more than it did at the theatre.

I wondered how long memory of our play's performance would linger. That joyous entertainment was what I wanted Corinthians to remember, not some garbled gossip that my play had somehow got Eumelos killed. If we could track down this murdering Athenian, Nados and the others could spread that news. If the true sorry tale didn't reflect well on Athens, at least our determination to see no Corinthian was unjustly accused should count for something.

As we reached level ground, I picked up the pace. We soon reached the Temple of Apollo, and found an elderly priest sweeping the day's dust out of the pillared porch.

'Excuse me,' I said politely. 'A man was given into the keeping of the priests earlier today, by order of the Council—'

'He was taken to the Asklepion.' The greybeard didn't even look up, intent on his work.

'Thank you.' I looked at Hyanthidas as the old man went on his way, his broom whispering on the stones.

'I'm coming with you,' the piper assured me. 'You'll want a Corinthian witness to whatever he says.'

'He may not be willing to talk.' It wasn't as if Demeas owed me any favours after I'd maimed him for life.

Hyanthidas shrugged. 'There's only one way to find out.'

We took the now familiar road to the Temple of Asklepios. I half-hoped we would find Chresimos on duty, to save endless explanations. On the other hand, I shrank from the prospect of seeing the look in the Cycladean's eyes when he realised I had crippled his patient. No, I refused to feel guilty. It had been Demeas or me, after all.

When we reached the Infirmary, the temple slave took us to the hatchet-faced Arkadian who sat patiently mixing his medicines. At least he was aware of Eumelos' death. I explained that Demeas might know something to help us find his killer.

'The Council is gravely concerned,' Hyanthidas assured him.

The Arkadian looked at us, his expression unreadable. The silence lengthened, and I had decided this was a fool's errand, when the doctor stood up.

'This way,' he said, austere.

He led us down to the lower courtyard and past the fountain, to a cluster of individual rooms with solid wooden doors secured with bolts on the outside. I didn't like to imagine what afflictions saw patients sequestered here for their own, and others', safety.

A burly slave sat on a stool outside a door that wasn't bolted. With only one good arm Demeas was hardly going to fight his way out past a man that size.

The slave looked at the Arkadian. 'Doctor?'

'They wish to talk to our patient. Observe their conversation. I'll be back with his sleeping draught.' He walked away without another word.

I had no idea how long he was going to allow us. 'If you please,' I prompted the slave.

As he opened the door, the lamp in a niche high up in the wall showed us Demeas lying flat on his back on a bed. His face was turned away from us and his injured arm was bandaged and splinted, half-bent, and strapped across his belly.

Hyanthidas was startled. 'What happened to him?'

Before I could answer, Demeas looked at me and spat. His face was drawn with pain, and loathing glittered in his eyes. 'They say the best I can hope for is a stiff arm for life. If the feeling in my fingers doesn't return, my whole hand may wither.'

I had decided on the walk here to take my cue from his attitude. 'Do you want to live long enough to find out?' I demanded, as merciless as any tyrant. 'Eumelos' slave has been found dead, so someone must answer for two murders.'

'No!' That startled Demeas into an incautious move that jolted his ruined arm. 'Perantas swore—' He gasped as the pain was too much for him to continue.

It didn't matter. I could guess the deal that had ensured his cooperation in front of Corinth's Council. 'Perantas Bacchiad promised you wouldn't be accused of killing Eumelos. I'm sure he's a man of his word. But can you trust Alypos Temenid, now that you've betrayed him? He'll want to scrub any stain of suspicion from his noble name. You don't think he'll be busy finding witnesses willing to say you killed both men, while you're in here, helpless and friendless?'

Demeas drew a long shuddering breath. Now the burning hatred in his eyes encompassed men far beyond this room.

'I believe an Athenian killed Eumelos as well as his slave,' I said bluntly. 'He may also have killed Hermaios, unless that was you?'

'Why would I?' Demeas forced out the scornful question. 'I valued him—'

He broke off, though I couldn't tell if that was due to his anguish or belated discretion before he confessed to some other crime. He drew another breath, and managed to continue through gritted teeth.

'That day, when we followed you, after you got the better of us, we went back to the Halcyon. Hermaios wasn't in his shop. No one saw him again until his body was found at the foot of the cliffs.'

That wasn't how I would have described that murderous pursuit through the Acrocorinth, but I guessed Demeas was mindful of the listening slave by the door. I let the evasion stand.

'When you were following me around Corinth, did you see another man dogging my steps? A man with a bandaged arm?'

Demeas lay very still. 'What's it worth?'

I was suddenly tired of this feinting and parrying. 'We have reason to believe Eumelos had old enemies in Athens. We think that one of them killed him. We have names that might lead us to answers, but if we can't recognise the guilty man, we can't see him brought to justice. If you help us do that, I swear by Athena and Apollo that we will stand witness before Corinth's Council and lay out the proof to clear your name.'

'On my oath to Apollo and Athena,' Hyanthidas said firmly, 'as a citizen of Corinth.'

I heard footsteps and turned to see the hatchet-faced Arkadian crossing the courtyard with a cup in one hand.

Demeas began speaking swiftly. 'I saw him. I didn't know him, but I assumed he was working for Perantas, watching your back. He's two fingers shorter than you—' he jerked his head at me '—with dark hair and

357

eyes. His knife hand was bandaged just below the elbow and I saw a bloodstain on it once, in line with his thumb. There's a mark on his face, just below his eye.' He used his good hand to point to his own cheekbone. 'Someone wearing a ring punched him hard, a long time ago.'

I had been right to come here. A man who spent his life sneaking around would pay close attention to any other spies he saw.

'Thank you,' I said sincerely.

Demeas bared his teeth. 'Just keep your word.'

'I will.' I would, for my own sake and for Eumelos.

'Well?' the doctor demanded, standing in the doorway.

'He has told us all that he can.' I had no doubt that the attentive slave would repeat our conversation, most likely word for word, and that meant this Arkadian could attest to our visit here, should the need arise.

'We can find our way out,' Hyanthidas assured him.

'Good.' The doctor went into the room to attend to his patient as we left.

Once we were outside the Asklepion, Hyanthidas looked at me. 'What happened to his arm?'

I rubbed a hand over my face and began to explain as we headed back to the heart of the city. Barely half my mind was on the sorry story. I was more concerned with what we had to do next.

Chapter Twenty-Seven

The next morning began with a succession of visitors whose news made my decisions much simpler. My first useful conversation was with Kadous as he served me a solitary breakfast.

Zosime was still sleeping upstairs. It had been her turn to come back late at night, bright-eyed and cheerful after an evening of poetry and wine. I didn't begrudge her such fun after all her hard work. I definitely had no objection to her amorous embraces waking me as I drowsed in our bed. I made very sure to remind her of the pleasures we shared, whether that was in Corinth or Athens.

Kadous put a bowl of figs on the table. 'Abrosyne was more willing to talk, now that she wasn't betraying Dardanis.'

'What did she say?' I gestured for him to take a stool as I ate.

'Eumelos came to Corinth seven years ago. She was the first slave that he bought here.'

That surprised me. 'Everyone at the funeral was talking as if he'd been in business for at least a decade.'

Kadous nodded. 'That's what they told everyone, him

and Dardanis. He let people think he'd been trading around the Corinthia for several years before he set up his premises in the city and both ports.'

I was mystified. 'Did she know why?'

'He'd had a serious falling out with his family, though she had no idea he was Athenian. When they first arrived, Dardanis told her they were from Boeotia, and swore her to secrecy about that, even though it was another lie. Eumelos wanted to be hard to find.'

'If anyone came asking for Eumares Demetriou who left Athens seven years ago, no one would think of pointing them towards Eumelos the Boeotian because everyone knew he had been in Corinth for ten years or more.'

I guessed he'd adopted a name so close to his own to make sure of answering to it, at least until the new one bedded in. I'd heard no trace of an Athens accent, but I imagined he'd shed that as soon as he could. It's not only actors who can do such things. Meantime, a slave like Abrosyne, Peloponnesian born and bred, would have little opportunity to learn how Athenians speak.

She was already an old slave, I noted, when she had been sold on seven years ago from whatever household had no more use for her. A woman with nothing, and no one to save her if she was cast out onto the streets. Abrosyne wouldn't have asked awkward questions or done anything else to betray the kind and considerate owner who'd saved her from such a dreadful fate.

In as little as a year, most likely, Eumares would have shed his old life as smoothly and completely as a snake sheds its skin. With every passing season, the chances of him coming face to face with someone who'd known him in Athens would surely grow less and less.

I shook my head. 'If he wanted to be hard to find, he should have gone a lot further away.' Somewhere like Zakynthos, where I fervently hoped no one would ever find Tromes.

'He hadn't fallen out with *all* of his family,' Kadous reminded me.

'He wanted to be close enough to get news of his wife and son?' I supposed that made sense.

Kadous nodded. 'Abrosyne said that Dardanis made a lengthy trip every year, though she swears she has no idea where he went or why.'

'I'd say it's a fair bet that he was taking caskets of silver coin to the Temple of Poseidon at Isthmia.'

That had been a smart move. Since that temple is a Pan-Hellenic sanctuary, the priests wouldn't yield jurisdiction over this bequest to either Athens or Corinth. Since the whole Isthmia complex was in the final stages of rebuilding after fires ravaged it a generation ago, I'd also wager that Eumelos had made generous donations to ensure that his wishes would be honoured. I'd bet there was another signed and sealed letter safeguarded there, identifying his son and heir.

A knock on the gate turned our heads. Kadous opened it and Nados entered. He looked surprised to see me sitting alone. I grinned and pressed a finger to my lips.

'Everyone else went up to the Acrocorinth yesterday, and I have no idea when they got back last night.'

'I hope they had a good time.' Nados' thoughts were elsewhere. He reached into the neck of his tunic and pulled out a gold ring with a garnet seal stone secure on a leather thong.

'Who dealt with the purse?' I asked.

'Aithon.' He handed me the ring with a grin. 'We rolled dice and he lost.'

'I hope he got to keep the coin.' I studied the olive wreath and lyre insignia.

It was expert, expensive workmanship, a piece made to order, or a family heirloom. This wasn't some briskly incised eagle or owl picked up from a Piraeus jewellery workman's tray, bought for show and hard to tell apart from a handful of others.

'I never saw him wear it,' Nados said, mystified.

'It's from a life he left behind.' I ran a finger around the stone and wondered if this had left the mark that Demeas had seen on the killer.

'Have you made up your mind?' Nados looked at me anxiously. 'To take the letter back to Athens?'

I hesitated. 'We still have to decide.'

Strictly speaking, that was true, if I was prepared to slice my words as finely as Perantas Bacchiad. Realistically, I was sure the others were assuming that's what we'd be doing. If not, one of them could tell Zosime we were abandoning a deserted wife to whatever uncertain fate awaited her in widowhood without proof of her orphaned son's claim to family and citizenship.

I wasn't any more eager to face whatever retribution Athena would deem fitting, nor Demeter's wrath, or

Hera's, or any other outraged goddess with an interest in matters of hearth and home.

'You have it safe?' I saw Nados didn't have a scroll case with him.

As he nodded, there was another knock at the gate. My morning was starting to look like the opening act of a play.

Kadous opened up and I glimpsed Wetka on the threshold. I scooped up the seal ring and dropped it down the neck of my tunic, leather thong and all.

The Nubian entered, followed by a slave carrying a promising-looking coffer, its hasps secured with lead seals. Another slave walked a few paces behind, armed with a warning scowl and an olive wood club.

'Good day to you.' Wetka smiled as the slave put the coffer down on the table with an encouraging thud and the muffled chink of coins. 'Perantas Bacchiad sends his sincere regards, and this tangible expression of his appreciation. I have arranged passage back to Athens for you all on a ship that sails at midday tomorrow. I will call here in good time to see you and your belongings carried to Kenchreai by cart. Meantime, Perantas invites you all to dine privately at his house this evening.'

'Thank you.' I hoped the actors would be sufficiently recovered from last night's debauches by then.

'Excuse me.' Nados raised a hand. 'Could you carry a message to your master for me, and for my business partners.' He was clearly still getting used to saying that. 'We have discovered that Dardanis, Eumelos' missing slave, was carrying our master's will—'

'I take it these young men can rely on Perantas' support?' I interrupted before Nados could mention the letter and Eumelos' former life and name. I had no idea what use Perantas might make of that information, but I had no doubt he would try. 'In getting their rights to his property recognised by the Council of Corinth?'

'The will bears his signature and his seal,' the lad said earnestly, 'as a Brother of Bellerophon.'

'I gave that ring to Perantas myself,' I added.

Wetka nodded with a reassuring smile. 'His bequests will be respected. Perantas will make certain of that. Now, I must ask you to excuse me. I have other errands to run.'

'By all means, and thank you.' I smiled, equally obliging.

As Wetka and his retinue departed, I looked across the table at Nados. 'Will you be joining the Brotherhood of Bellerophon?'

'Not if I can help it.' Nados grimaced. 'Though I think Simias might.'

Before I could pursue that, a door up above opened, and Zosime appeared. She waved a cheerful hand.

Nados stood up. 'I should go.'

'No, wait.' Zosime hurried down the steps. 'How are you? All of you?'

I signalled to Kadous to fetch more food and cups as Zosime enquired after all the household, slave and free, whom she'd met as she'd assisted with Eumelos' funeral.

By the time she was satisfied that all was as well as could be expected, and markedly better now that

Eumelos' will had been found, Menekles had appeared, shortly followed by Lysicrates and Apollonides. Where Zosime was clear-eyed and fresh-faced, the actors most assuredly weren't.

'What's that?' Menekles pointed at the coffer on the table.

'Payment from Perantas Bacchiad.' I lifted one end and let them hear the thud and chink of coin as I dropped it.

'Excellent.' Apollonides poured himself a cup of spring water, drank it down, and poured another. 'You know they say a man should visit the Acrocorinth once in his life?'

'Yes?' I waited for him to empty his second cupful.

'Once is as much as most men will be able to stand,' he said with feeling.

Lysicrates was contemplating some cheese. Deciding against it, he greeted Nados with a nod. 'Any more news for us to take back to Athens?'

'Any more secrets?' Menekles asked.

The lad's expression brightened, as well it might. 'We found Eu – Eumares' seal ring.'

Lysicrates stretched out a hand. 'Let's see?'

'I've got it.' I fished the leather thong out of the front of my tunic.

Lysicrates studied it, before passing it to Menekles who took a close look and handed it to Apollonides.

Zosime cupped her hand to receive it next. 'Someone should recognise this when we get home.'

'Are we taking the news to Eumares' family in Athens

first?' I decided this was as good a time as any for this conversation.

'That letter is addressed to his wife and this ring belongs to his son.' Zosime set it down on the table with a decisive click.

'He clearly felt an enduring obligation towards his wife and child, if not much true affection,' Menekles pointed out.

Apollonides yawned. 'All we know about his family in Athens is there was a quarrel of such enduring bitterness that this man cut himself off from his father and discarded his name and citizenship.'

I nodded. 'Whereas we know Eumelos of Corinth was a well-respected and prosperous merchant who was as good as a father to three young men. A man whose friends and business acquaintances sincerely mourn his death. We saw that at his funeral.'

'There are invariably faults on both sides in any family row,' Nados ventured, 'but I find it hard to believe that Eumelos was most to blame.'

'If he was the more injured party, that doesn't augur well for his father's character,' Apollonides mused.

'Unless he had done something he was so ashamed of that he fled and hid, and spent his life since atoning for it?' countered Lysicrates.

'Spinning yarns out of speculation will get us nowhere.' Menekles picked up the ring and studied it again.

'If we take the letter and the ring to his wife first of all, we can get her side of the story,' I suggested. 'Then we can see what Eumares' family in Athens have to say.'

'The truth will lie somewhere in the middle,' prophesied Lysicrates.

'I don't doubt it,' I agreed, 'but he must have had some reason to send Dardanis to his wife and her father with this news, instead of trusting his own family.'

'Some good reason.' Apollonides was sure of that.

'So as soon as we get home, we set out for sheep-shagging country.' Menekles wasn't thrilled at the prospect.

'All of us?' Apollonides looked keener.

Lysicrates shrugged. 'We may as well. The more witnesses the better.'

I reached for Zosime's hand. 'I'll see you safely home, and I'm sure your father—'

'I'm coming with you.' She was adamant. 'What secrets do you think a newly widowed woman will share with four strange men, and in her father's presence?'

I looked at the others and saw I was going to get no help there. Far from it.

'It's a fair point,' Menekles conceded.

Apollonides was grinning from ear to ear. 'That's agreed then.'

'When are we going home?' asked Lysicrates.

I realised I hadn't shared the message Wetka had brought us along with our money. 'Tomorrow.' I explained the arrangements, and said that Perantas had invited us to a private dinner.

Zosime stood up. 'If this is our last day, I want to go shopping.'

'Me too.' Apollonides joined her.

Menekles grimaced, though without real displeasure. 'My mother will expect a present from Corinth to impress her neighbours.'

Lysicrates chuckled. 'My sister's kids won't care where a new toy comes from, but she'll want to know I remembered them.'

I thought of my own nephews and niece. 'Then let's visit the markets.'

'It'll be my pleasure to show you around,' Nados said eagerly.

So that's how we spent our last day in Corinth. I finally got to see the sights of the city, and Nados helped us bargain the traders down to local prices, not the usual visitors' mark-up. I bought gifts for my own family and some of the finest Corinthian pottery for Zosime's father.

We had gifts pressed upon us when merchants in the agora realised who we were. They assured us they'd enjoyed our play and most mentioned enough specifics to convince me this wasn't mere flattery. We encountered several of our chorus singers on our wanderings, and it was a pleasure to thank them once again.

As evening was approaching, we bathed and dressed in the finest clothes we had left clean in our luggage. When we arrived at Perantas' house, we were ushered into the most elegant dining room I had ever seen. We were exclaiming politely at the wall paintings of mountain vistas, and the intricate floral mosaic underfoot, when Hyanthidas and Telesilla were announced.

More dinner companions arrived; three elegant women and a clean-shaven young man with a face to

368

rival Ganymede, who was happy to share Apollonides' cushions. Someone, most likely Wetka, had been paying attention to whatever the Bacchiad slaves had learned about us while we lodged in Bacchiad property.

I was apprehensive as we took our couches. I didn't want to have to lie or evade awkward questions about the discovery of Dardanis' body. I need not have worried. The Bacchiad was intent on relaying the praise lavished on him on our play's account. He went on to list those among Corinth's rich and powerful who were now far more favourably inclined towards the Thurii colony.

As I committed those names to memory, to tell Aristarchos back in Athens, I wondered if Perantas was ever going to spare Eumelos another thought. I doubted it. The Bacchiad was always going to be looking forward not back.

Not that he monopolised the conversation. He was interested in the actors' stories of taking different plays to other theatres, within Attica and beyond. Since any actor has plenty of amusing anecdotes, there was more than enough chat and laughter to allow me to say very little.

Excellent food and superb wine was followed by music and poetry from hired entertainers. We all enjoyed being an audience applauding skilled performers for a change. An escort of torch-bearers saw us safely home and I slept deep and dreamlessly.

Wetka arrived the following morning with two carts and a contingent of burly slaves to manage the costume and mask baskets, so we were soon on the road to Kenchreai.

A pleasant breeze softened the sun's warmth, and the sea sparkled beneath a clear blue sky when we arrived at the port.

Simias met us on the dockside, ostensibly to bid us farewell. If Wetka happened to see him pass me a scroll case, it was too late for the Nubian to discover what was inside it.

As we waved farewell to the young man, I couldn't help remembering our arrival, and our first meeting with Eumelos. I found it didn't matter to me why he had fled Athens. I wouldn't be able to consider this trip to Corinth over until we had seen his last wishes honoured, and, Zeus willing, seen his killer brought to justice.

Chapter Twenty-Eight

We stopped in Athens for one night; long enough to entrust our coffer of coin to the priests of Dionysos, to return our masks and costumes to Sosimenes, and for me to fail to persuade Zosime that she need not make the journey to Paionidai.

'I am coming,' she insisted, leaving our bedroom and heading for the storeroom.

Her father, Menkaure, was leaning against the door-post. 'I could come too,' he offered. 'I haven't been out to the country since the spring.'

That didn't surprise me. Resident foreigners coming to live and work in Athens rarely venture beyond the city walls into Attica.

'There could be bandits on the road, or even wolves.' He looked at me as we listened to Zosime satisfying herself that everything was in order.

'Those are just tavern tales,' I assured him. Though it might be a different story in the hungry depths of winter. 'We still need you watching our door here. The neigh-bours will have seen us come back and they know we've been to Corinth. Someone curious and finding the house empty might be tempted to see what we brought back.'

'I suppose so.' He let the matter drop, to my relief. I didn't want to arrive mob-handed, getting on the wrong side of this unknown Myrrhine's father.

The walk to Paionidai would mean a long day on the road, and we didn't want to arrive too late when we could not be sure of our welcome. So Zosime and I rose at first light, meeting the others in the agora so early that even the keenest merchants were only just setting up their stalls.

As we headed north, we passed the turn that could take us to Leukonoion. I caught Lysicrates' eye and could see he was thinking the same as me.

'I wonder what his father will say, when we bring him the news?'

Lysicrates shrugged. 'We'll find out, once his wife's had her chance to throw pots at our heads.'

Leaving the city, we paused around noon at Athena's temple in Acharnae, to eat and drink, and to seek the goddess' blessing on our endeavours until the heat of the day had passed. As we set out again, I had to curb my pace. I was consumed with curiosity about Eumelos' former life and the family he had kept so secret.

We found Paionidai at the foot of an outcrop thrusting southwards from the high ridge of Mount Parnes. That snow-capped rampart has long been an Athenian defence against Boeotian hostility. The village was like any other out in Attica, with a sprawl of modest houses surrounding a market place. A cluster of olive trees looked to serve as a sacred grove, with an all-purpose altar close by. A handful of women and girls were fetching water from the communal well.

'I'll get a drink while you talk to the local sages.' Zosime nodded towards two old men sitting on stools in the evening shade beside the village tavern.

They were both as wrinkled as raisins. One watched Zosime head for the well with evident appreciation. I could hardly blame him. As soon as we'd returned to Athens, she had swapped her long, pleated gown for a knee-length draped dress that revealed her shapely figure considerably more clearly.

Menekles led the way, and Apollonides, Lysicrates and I followed a few paces behind. Kadous brought up the rear as a well-trained slave should. I was doing my best to look like someone who'd never laughed at jokes about country bumpkins back in Athens, and certainly had never written such ridiculous characters to amuse a theatre audience.

Menekles addressed the old men formally. 'Good afternoon, honoured sirs. Please can you direct us to Pratinias Pharou's household?'

The old man sitting closest to the tavern pursed withered lips. 'What business do you have with him?'

Menekles ducked his head respectfully. 'Forgive me, but that is his business, and therefore is not mine to share with you.'

The old men exchanged an impenetrable look, before the other elder raised his stick in a shaking hand and jabbed it towards a gap between two long, low houses.

'Follow that road. You want the first farmstead outside the village.'

'Thank you very much,' Menekles said with scrupulous politeness.

We walked back across the market place like a well-rehearsed chorus. A piercing whistle cut through the golden calm. Looking back, I saw the old man with the stick had his fingers in his mouth. He whistled again, and several people appeared in doorways, to witness whatever might occur.

'What is going on?' Lysicrates wondered, wary.

'They are looking after their own.' Zosime left the women at the well and rejoined us, her face sombre. 'Myrrhine's brother died this past winter. Her father's health has been failing ever since.'

Apollonides winced. 'Now we've brought even more bad news.'

'Not all bad,' Lysicrates observed as we followed the path the old man had indicated. 'Remember what's waiting for her son in Isthmia.'

'Who can she trust to collect it?' countered Zosime.

I reached for her hand as we walked on. That old man's eyesight must be failing if he thought this was a road. I'd have called it a sheep track. Thankfully the farmstead was only a short walk away.

Menekles was looking at the groves and pastures. 'For a household beset by misfortune, they're keeping their land in good order.'

He was right. Several labourers paused to watch us approach. An itch between my shoulder blades made me want to look back and see if we were being followed.

The farmstead's entrance was firmly closed, and the solid wall was high enough to hide all but the roofs of the buildings within. Not that ill-wishers could sneak up. A watchman looked down at us from a vantage point by the gate.

'Good day.' He was thickset and weather-beaten, and his expression suggested we'd be ill advised to think that he hadn't seen most of what life had to offer.

'Hello.' Menekles tried for a friendly tone, shading his eyes with one hand as he looked up. 'We bring news for Pratinias Pharou and his daughter Myrrhine.'

'From Athens?' The watchman's face hardened, his voice distinctly unfriendly.

I stepped forward, suspecting the reason for this cool reception. 'We have come from Athens, but we have had nothing to do with Demetrios—' I abruptly realised I had no idea what Emelos' grandfather had been called, in order to give his father his formal patronymic '—of Leukonoion. We are not here on his behalf.'

The watchman's derisive snort puzzled me, but at least he looked more curious than hostile. 'Who do you speak for?'

I didn't want to shout about our connection with Eumelos, or Eumares as these people had known him. I reached into the neck of my tunic, drew out the seal ring on its leather thong and let it dangle. 'I have brought this for Pratinias' grandson.'

As I'd hoped, that prompted a stir on the far side of the wall. The watchman looked down and we heard a rasp as the bar securing the gate was withdrawn. A younger man slipped through the gap before the gate was quickly pushed closed behind him.

He reached us and held out a hand. I let the ring hang over his open palm but twitched it away as he closed his fingers. 'There is more. We have a letter, but we're only handing that over to Pratinias or Myrrhine.'

Zosime spoke up unexpectedly. 'I can do that, if Myrrhine doesn't wish to talk to these men.'

I wanted to say there was no way I was letting her go unaccompanied into a strange household, but muttering and shuffling on the other side of the gate interrupted me. A woman in a household matron's pleated gown emerged. She was a handful of years younger than me. Her long hair was simply braided, and her expression told of a hard life.

'I am Myrrhine,' she said briefly. 'Let me see that ring.'

I let the youth take it to her. As she studied it, I saw her mouth quiver.

'Where did you get this?' Her voice was hoarse with some tangle of emotions I did not understand.

'A man called Dardanis was supposed to bring it, with a letter that I have now,' I said cautiously. 'Things turned out – differently.'

I saw desperation as well as confusion in her eyes.

'My name is Philocles Hestaiou of Alopeke,' I said formally. 'I can return to Athens with someone you trust, so that our district's officials can confirm my identity, and witnesses can attest to my good character.'

Menekles, Apollonides and Lysicrates introduced

themselves with similar assurances, though I hoped Myrrhine didn't take us up on this offer, because that amount of back and forth would take up days.

Then I realised she was looking at Zosime, thoughtful as well as curious.

Zosime smiled. 'I only met him briefly, but he was a charmer.'

Myrrhine bit her lip, and then turned abruptly to address whoever was standing behind the half-open gate. 'They can come in.'

Whoever it was made some inaudible objection. Myrrhine overruled him with the firmness of a woman used to being obeyed. 'Do as I say.'

I glanced at Menekles as the gate opened wide. Apollonides and Lysicrates exchanged a shrug. Zosime looked at us all, amused, and walked forward. We hurriedly went with her.

The farmstead was a square of substantial buildings around a central courtyard. Over to one side, pillars supported a shallow roof over an altar and Myrrhine walked past that to an open door.

Menekles looked warily at the men and women standing, stony-faced, in the doorways to storerooms and other quarters. 'Are we invited in, do you suppose?'

'Yes.' The watchman looked down from his lofty post.

We entered a large room where day-to-day pots and cups were neatly stacked on shelves, and the lady of the house's distaff was propped in a wool basket in a corner alongside a heap of carved wooden animals. Sturdy chests against the walls doubtless held other household goods.

Against the far wall, an old man lay on a high-backed couch softened with sheepskins. Though the weather was mild, he clutched at his brightly coloured blanket as though we were in the depths of midwinter. His eyes were blurred with cataracts and his expression was vague. Myrrhine sat on a stool by his head. Her gaze was as sharp as a razor.

'My letter?' She held out a hand.

I pulled the scroll case from the centre of the blanket I was carrying, rolled and secured with a strap. Handing it to her, I retreated to stand with the others. Shadows passed by the door. Help would arrive before Myrrhine finished calling for it.

We stood in silence as she read the letter. As she finished, she sighed and rolled it up. We waited for her to ask some question, but she sat still, her eyes distant and her expression grim. She certainly didn't look like a woman who'd just learned that a handsome bequest awaited her son. The old man said nothing. I wasn't even sure that he knew we were there.

'Eumares had a thriving business in Corinth,' I ventured. 'His business partners have every reason to believe his silver reserve was substantial.'

Myrrhine looked at me, diverted from whatever dark thoughts beset her. 'He was in Corinth?' She shook her head. 'Dardanis never said.'

'You knew Dardanis?' I prompted.

'Knew him?' Dread shadowed her eyes. 'He's dead as well?'

'I'm so sorry, he is.' I hesitated, trying to find the words to explain the dreadful circumstances that had brought us here instead of her husband's trusted messenger.

Myrrhine forestalled me, clapping her hands and calling out, 'Bring refreshments for our guests!'

An older woman appeared with jugs of wine and water with such swiftness, she must have been waiting outside the door. The watchman and his young underling brought stools and a small table.

Once we were settled, a spark of curiosity was lightening Myrrhine's dour expression. 'You had better begin at the beginning.'

Menekles took up the challenge, his words as clear and concise as the prologue for a play. 'We are actors, and we were invited to perform a comedy in Corinth.'

We took up the tale, turn by turn, as fluently as if we'd rehearsed it. Myrrhine's eyes widened as she listened, and I heard exclamations stifled outside the door. Finally, I explained how the gods had apparently chosen us to fulfil Eumares' final wishes.

'I see that your father is too infirm to travel to Athens, and I understand that your brother has died. We are truly sorry for your troubles. If we can help in any way, to carry a letter to Eumares' father, we will gladly do so.'

As the others echoed my condolences and assurances, Myrrhine surprised us with a mirthless laugh. 'If you want to speak to Demetrios, you will need to follow Odysseus down to the Underworld. He died on the first of the month.'

'Who . . .' I wanted to know who had told her. I

wanted to know who the dead man's heir might be, now that Eumares was dead. Asking any of these things would be hideously bad manners, though.

Myrrhine tapped the rolled-up letter against her cupped palm. 'I suppose it's my turn to begin at the beginning.'

Chapter Twenty-Nine

Myrrhine sat straight-backed on her stool, with her ankles demurely crossed and her hands in her lap. 'This sorry tale begins before I ever met Eumares. His family live in Athens, although they own substantial property not far from here, and live well on the proceeds of selling the harvests from their olive groves and vines. He was the eldest son, the only child who lived to adulthood, and his mother died when he was barely twenty years old. I believe it was grief for their losses that first soured relations between him and his father. That may explain why Eumares married young, to a woman from Rhodes. Her name was Kleoboulina. They had a child, a daughter, and I've every reason to believe they were happy. He certainly adored them both.'

As Myrrhine paused, I saw sadness in her eyes, though it was the old, cold ashes of disappointment rather than recent, still-smouldering pain. Abruptly brisk, she resumed her story.

'Then Pericles introduced his citizenship law and Demetrios realised he would not have a legitimate grandson to inherit his wealth as long as his son lacked an Athenian citizen wife. He said Eumares must divorce Kleoboulina, in order to marry again to secure their family property through citizen sons. When Eumares refused, Demetrios made their lives a misery. One day, Eumares returned to Athens from a trip to their property near here, to find his house deserted. Kleoboulina and the child were gone. It seemed she had confided her unhappiness to his cousin's wife and had decided to return to Rhodes.'

That would have been eight years ago, I swiftly calculated, around the time I was finishing my hoplite training. Eumares would have been a couple of years older than I was now. Myrrhine would have been half his age, a country girl trained to run a household by her mother and ripe for marriage by her fifteenth year.

She shook her head. 'He couldn't find any trace of her in Rhodes or anywhere in between. When he returned to Athens, Demetrios resumed his demands for a legitimate grandson. Eumares was ready to defy his father until he realised that his cousin Alkias was counting on him having no heir. Then all the family property would go to Alkias and his sons. More than that, he learned that while Alkias had been swearing he supported his marriage to Kleoboulina, encouraging him to stand up to his father, he'd been just as earnestly urging Demetrios to insist that his son did his citizen duty, as well as doing all he could to convince Kleoboulina to leave Athens while her husband was away. So Eumares decided that he would marry again, and start a family, purely to spite his cousin.'

She reached out to stroke her oblivious father's grey head. 'He never knew. He thought he was arranging a fine marriage for me, with a respectable, well-connected family. I knew none of this, not until later. Truth be told, we were happy enough, Eumares and I, at least at first. I was quickly pregnant, and we were blessed with a healthy son.'

Her face softened with love for her child, and I caught a glimpse of the sweetly biddable girl she had been, coming to the altar as a bride with such high hopes soon to be so cruelly disappointed.

'He thrived?' Apollonides asked hesitantly. 'The boy?'

'He did, and he does,' Myrrhine assured us, 'but Eumares refused to honour his father by naming his grandson for him. He's called Laches.'

I couldn't imagine how much Eumares must have hated his father to insult him so viciously.

Myrrhine looked at us, her expression wry. 'As you might imagine, Demetrios was furious. I don't know all the details, as their final argument erupted only a few days after Laches was born. Demetrios did let slip that he had paid Kleoboulina to leave and to take their daughter. He said that proved she had only ever been a greedy whore. He and Eumares had to be pulled apart before they beat each other senseless.'

She shook her head. 'That was the last time Eumares spoke to his father. We left Athens and came here to live but, within the month, Eumares couldn't stand the torment of reflecting on all he had lost. He left me and our son in my father and my brother's care. He said he'd return to Attica when his father was dead and not before. I never knew where he had gone. Dardanis visited from time to time, to bring us money, and to make sure we wanted for nothing.' She gestured at the comfortably furnished room.

'Laches hasn't seen his father since he was born?' Zosime clapped her hand to her mouth, mortified. Clearly, she hadn't intended to utter that thought aloud.

Myrrhine managed a shaky smile, though tears were trickling down her cheeks.

'Once, when he was three years old. No one expected to see him but Eumares arrived at our gate one spring day. We travelled to Athens so that Laches could be presented to the Leukonoion District Assembly as Eumares' legitimate son and heir.'

'Good to know,' I said fervently, and the others echoed my relief. Upholding a citizen's rights in the courts, especially for a child, meant having witnesses to his participation in such civic rites. Eumares had been determined to do his duty as an Athenian by his son, however much he hated his family.

I still found it impossible to imagine such a vile family quarrel. Judging by everyone else's expressions, so did Menekles, Apollonides and Lysicrates. Sitting next to me, Zosime reached for my hand and held tight.

Myrrhine bit her lip. 'While we were in the city . . .'

'We're here to help, however we can,' Menekles prompted gently.

'I'm not sure that anyone can, but you may as well know it all.' Myrrhine took a deep breath and wiped her face with the back of her hand.

'While we were in Athens, Alkias' wife came to see

384

us. She was deathly ill, and desperate to unburden herself before she crossed the Styx. She warned us against Alkias. She said that she had lied about the supposed conversation when Kleoboulina had said she was leaving. Worse than that, although she had no proof, she was convinced that her husband had killed Kleoboulina and the little girl. Alkias had told Demetrios that he'd forced Eumares' wife to take his money and leave, but she said he'd really kept the silver for himself.'

Her voice shook. The rest of us were dumbstruck with horror.

'Eumares left as soon as he had brought us safely back here. He said my father and brother would protect us, but he couldn't stay in Attica. He couldn't trust himself not to knife Alkias or his father in the street. If he was provoked into violence, then he'd be exiled or executed and Alkias would get what he'd wanted all along.'

Myrrhine started weeping again. 'When Alkias was here a few days ago, when he came to tell me that both Demetrios and Eumares were dead, he told me that he is going to adopt Laches and manage this property alongside his own, since my father cannot and my brother is dead. Since Alkias' three sons are already grown, he will send one of them to live here. By the time Alkias dies, Laches will be lucky to see a quarter of what's rightfully his, and . . .' She doubled over, burying her face in her hands, unable to hold back her sobbing.

Zosime went to kneel beside the distraught woman, offering a comforting embrace. The four of us shared our dismay.

'This Alkias,' Lysicrates observed, 'he would have to bring such an adoption before the courts. It could be challenged.'

'Only if Eumares still has friends among the Leukonoion District Brotherhood with some reason to do so.' Apollonides sounded doubtful, and I didn't blame him.

Unless they knew this whole dreadful story, those Athenians would only see the son of a man who'd abandoned his family without explanation, presented by an honest citizen doing his best by his orphaned nephew, and fulfilling his obligations. Even if Myrrhine did try to tell her side of that story, she had absolutely no proof, and no standing in law.

The old woman who'd brought us wine spoke up from the doorway. 'Alkias said she had better agree, or he would go to the magistrates in Athens and accuse her of adultery with our slave overseer. Then there could be no possible objection to him adopting Laches, and taking the child to live in Athens away from her corrupting influence. He swore, if she crossed him, she would never see her son again.'

'Oh.' That made everything a hundred times worse, and not just for Myrrhine. She would be disgraced but the slave would be executed. That would warn all the others not to cross their new masters.

'How did Myrrhine's brother die?' Menekles asked the old woman.

I had been wondering that. If this Alkias truly was a killer, how many deaths could be laid at his door?

She shook her head. 'He had a bad fall on the mountain, and gashed his thigh on a rotten branch. The wound was long, deep and dirty. Despite all we could do, it festered. After he died, Pratinias took to his bed.'

She looked at the stricken old man who seemed to have fallen asleep, oblivious to his daughter's distress. Zosime was having no success soothing Myrrhine. Telling us her troubles and fears seemed to have let loose years of pent-up misery.

My beloved looked up at the old woman. 'Help me get her to her bedchamber.' Between them, they got Myrrhine to her feet, still weeping, and ushered her out of the room.

We sat in silence broken only by the old man's snores. I looked at the others. 'What do we do now?'

This time the weathered watchman answered from the doorway. 'Let me show you where you'll be sleeping.'

'We don't wish to intrude,' Menekles said politely.

The watchman snorted. 'It's a bit late for that.'

His tone wasn't hostile, though, and as we followed him out to the courtyard, we saw other members of this beleaguered household looking at us with not-so-covert hope. Then the gates opened and the farm labourers came in from their day's work. Slave or free, it was impossible to tell them apart.

A cheerful, well-grown boy of around six or seven years was skipping along among them, holding a broad-shouldered man's hand.

'Is that Laches?' I asked the watchman.

He nodded. 'This way.'

The watchman led us across the courtyard to some sort of storeroom. It was empty at the moment, apart from two girls unrolling plumply stuffed pallets. That's one good thing about sheep country. Waste wool makes for a much more comfortable mattress than straw.

Out to the courtyard we could hear rising voices amid the clatter of cooking pots and plates. The first smoky hint of charcoal burning in a brazier drifted through the open door.

I dragged two pallets close together and claimed them for me and Zosime with our rolled blankets. The others picked their own spots and we went back outside to find the assembled household looking at us with growing interest. The actors and I met their curiosity with expressions as blank as masked characters. Working in the theatre means we're well practised at keeping secrets.

On the other hand, a theatre audience invariably reads what they want to see into an expressionless mask. Ask someone at the end of a powerful tragedy and they'll swear that they saw Creon gape, astonished, and then scowl with fury as he condemned Antigone. Never mind that in truth, that actor's face has been the same immobile visage wrought of plaster and linen throughout the play.

The old woman and the two slave girls set out bread and freshly cut salads on trestle tables, along with the succulent meat of this year's lambs fat from summer grazing. Myrrhine appeared to take her seat of honour as the daughter of the house, and was able to greet her adored son with a fair degree of composure. Still, I noticed that

Zosime stayed close until the widow took the protesting boy off to bed.

Thankfully these country dwellers were all as early to sleep as they were early to rise, once the evening meal was cleared away. I was glad to be spared an evening of hospitable drinking and pointed questions that I had no idea how to answer.

We retreated to our storeroom, made ourselves comfortable, and Menekles snuffed the lamp. Zosime and I cuddled close, and I tried to go to sleep. I couldn't. As it turned out, nor could anyone else.

'Does Myrrhine really have no other male relatives who could speak up for her?' Apollonides asked the darkness, despairing.

'Not according to anyone I spoke to,' Menekles said glumly. 'This family is a withered vine.'

'The Paionidai District Brotherhood do all they can to help her,' Zosime assured us. 'For her father's sake, and in her brother's memory. He was well liked and respected.'

'It's not the same though, is it?' Apollonides countered.

No one challenged that, because he was undeniably right. I took a moment to silently thank Athena that both sides of my fruitful family would never leave my sisters so undefended.

'What difference would that make?' Lysicrates shifted with a rustle of his blanket. 'The issue is the child's inheritance and that's not in dispute. He inherits from his dead grandfather in Athens, through his father's rights. The next question is who becomes his guardian, and that's not up for debate either. Alkias' father was Demetrios' younger brother and he has been dead for a couple of years, so our new friend the watchman was telling me. That means Alkias is now head of that family.'

'And young Laches becomes head of this family when Pratinias dies,' Menekles said sombrely. 'Since he'll still be a child, no one will argue that Alkias shouldn't manage his affairs here as well.'

'If that bastard adopts the boy, does anyone seriously think that Laches will regain control of either inheritance when he comes of age?' Lysicrates growled. 'Give it a dozen years and he'll just be Alkias' fourth son, getting the last scraps from the table.'

I wanted to know something else.

'How did Alkias know that Eumelos – or Eumares as we should call him – was dead? Remember what Myrrhine said? How Alkias came to tell her that they had both died, Demetrios and her one-time husband? That's when he told her he was adopting her son. But how did Alkias know?'

No one had an answer. Silence and darkness wrapped around us.

'No one in Corinth knew that Eumelos was really an Athenian called Eumares, still less who his family might be,' I persisted. 'How could anyone have possibly sent Alkias the news of his death?'

'Dardanis knew the truth,' Apollonides said slowly.

Zosime shifted beside me. 'And someone killed him in Corinth to stop him bringing that letter to Myrrhine.'

'If Dardanis had been with Eumelos since his Athenian

days, there's every chance that Alkias knew who he was,' Menekles said with growing unease.

'But how did he know *where* the slave was?' I demanded.

'When *exactly* did Alkias come out here from the city, to bring Myrrhine the news?' Lysicrates asked. 'Does anybody know?'

The others realised they had no idea, and no one had thought to ask what she meant by 'a few days ago'.

I had one last thing to say. 'Do you remember that first night in Corinth, when we were all in the tavern? When Eumelos first succumbed to the thornapple and began seeing strange visions? When he thought Telesilla was his lost love, Kleoboulina? He called out another name too.'

Zosime remembered. 'Alkias! He was trying to get through the crowd to whoever he thought he had seen when he collapsed.'

'What if that wasn't some delirium caused by the poison?' I challenged them all. 'There was no one else in the tavern, but there was a window by the door. What if his cousin Alkias was standing outside, looking in to see his handiwork?'

Chapter Thirty

What could we do for Myrrhine and her son? All the way back to Athens, we worried at the problem like hounds trying to bring down a stag. No matter how we circled it, we always ended up facing the same insurmountable challenge.

'We can't hope to bring Alkias before the courts and win,' Lysicrates said, for what felt like the hundredth time. 'None of us can testify that we saw him in Corinth. Even if we brought that whore here, the girl who was duped into giving Eumelos the poison, even if she could identify Alkias as the man who gave it to her, no Athenian jury would give her a hearing.'

'Who would bear the costs of getting her here, or that man whose arm you broke?' added Menekles. 'Perantas Bacchiad? I don't see him doing anything that doesn't directly serve his own interests.'

'There's the Brotherhood of Bellerophon. They must have funds, and Thettalos is going to be interested in everything we've learned.' Apollonides didn't sound convinced though.

'I don't think we'd even get the case before a jury.' I'd been thinking about this as we walked. 'I can't see any examining magistrate agreeing that we have enough evidence to bring him to trial.'

As for expecting Demeas to testify to help us, I'd be more worried that the bastard would seize his chance to exact some vicious revenge. Whatever lies he chose to tell there and then, that day in court, would be all that the jury got to hear, right before they decided their votes.

'If we cannot hold Alkias to account for his past crimes, how do we protect Myrrhine and her child?' Zosime demanded. 'How do we stop him embezzling their income and appropriating their land before Laches comes of age to claim his inheritance?'

'Who do we know in the Leukonoion District?' Menekles demanded, equally determined.

By the time the walls of Athens came into view, the actors had thought of several acquaintances among the city's playwrights, musicians and their fellow thespians whose grandfathers had lived in that part of Athens when Cleisthenes united city, country and coastal districts into the voting tribes that underpinned our new democracy. I could think of a handful in the leather business, a couple of whom owed my brothers favours, and I was pretty sure our sister's husband, Kalliphon, could make some useful introductions.

'But who do we know who's influential?' Apollonides asked.

He had a point. The men we knew were unremarkable. They did their duty to the gods, to the city, and to their families, but unless the annual lottery for civic offices saw Athena hand one of them a magistracy or a Council seat, they played no part in directing Athenian affairs.

'Aristarchos might know someone who would take an interest in seeing a widow's rights defended,' I said thoughtfully.

These wealthy men of ancient lineages no longer have the unquestioned right to rule, which would-be oligarchs crave, but the honourable well-born like Aristarchos retain a sense of obligation to the less fortunate.

'Do we know what sort of influence Alkias wields in the district?' Lysicrates wanted to know. 'He's bound to hear, if people start talking about Eumelos – Eumares, I mean.'

'If he's as guilty as we think he is, do you suppose he'll run?' Apollonides didn't sound particularly hopeful.

'Opt for exile instead of execution?' Menekles spread his hands with a shrug. 'No idea.'

He had a point. We wouldn't even recognise the man in the street, so we had no way to know what he might do.

'If he did flee, how would that help Myrrhine?' Zosime was getting impatient. 'His eldest son would become head of the family, and I'll bet he believes everything his father has told him.'

'Myrrhine and Laches could well be worse off,' Menekles observed. 'If worst comes to worst, Laches can petition the courts as an adult to restore his inheritance when Alkias dies. He'll have to wait years longer if his cousin takes charge of the family holdings.'

Lysicrates had more immediate concerns. 'Or Alkias could call us before the courts, accusing us of defamation, if we're not very careful what we say.'

That was a very real possibility. Regardless, I grinned. 'Then we must be absolutely clear on every detail of what we're *not* accusing him of doing.'

At long last, I felt like Odysseus, able to see a safe course between the man-eating monster on the one hand, and the whirlpool on the other.

Apollonides was the first to take the bait. 'What do you mean?'

I explained what I was thinking, and then I reminded myself that Odysseus still lost six of his sailors to Scylla's ravening claws and teeth to avoid being drowned by Charybdis. 'We will be making an enemy, you know, most likely for life. An enemy who's willing to kill, if he's guilty of these crimes.'

'Which brings us back to the fact that we know nothing of the man,' Menekles said thoughtfully. 'There's a lot more we need to find out if we're going to try this.'

Lysicrates rubbed his hands together, bright-eyed. 'So who's going to do what?'

We paused outside the Dipylon Gate to assess the necessary tasks, and divided them up between us. I tried, and failed, to persuade Zosime that I should escort her to the pottery where she and Menkaure worked, and come to collect her when I was done.

'You can see who's left word of commissions for you, while we were away,' I suggested hopefully.

'Not a chance,' she said crisply. 'I'm coming with you to see Aristarchos.'

As we entered the city, I reflected how different Myrrhine's life might be if she hadn't been raised to always defer to male authority as a dutiful Athenian maiden. Though not necessarily for the better. Her marriage hadn't brought her much joy, but at least it had given her a child, and better yet, a son with an Athenian citizen's inheritance rights enshrined in law.

If she had still been the unmarried heiress of her father's property, spurned as headstrong by suitors who wanted a properly demure Athenian citizen wife, Myrrhine could have legally been forced into marriage with whatever cockroach had the closest provable link to her father's family. I'd be willing to bet there was some distant cousin of a cousin who would come scuttling out of the shadows if there was wealth and land on offer instead of the complications of standing up to Alkias on Myrrhine's behalf.

When Zosime and I reached Aristarchos' house, he was very happy to receive us in the elegant portico where he was accustomed to sit and deal his business and political interests. He was even more pleased to hear of *The Builders*' successful performance, and every detail of Corinthian enthusiasm for the colony at Thurii which we had prompted.

'And now you must be glad to get home, free to start work on your play for the Dionysia.' He paused to beckon to his personal slave Lydis. 'Still, that can wait until tomorrow at least. Please, stay and eat with me this evening, both of you.'

'I brought a few further obligations back from Corinth,' I said, resolute. 'Our success in the theatre was hard-won, and you should hear the full story.'

Telling him everything that had happened took us late into the evening. By the time I concluded our epic tale, Aristarchos had readily agreed to do all he could to help us.

Five days later, the elders and officials of the Leukonoion District called a meeting in a quiet colonnade on the southern side of the Academy. Whatever teachers should have been instructing reluctant pupils in mathematics, rhetoric or philosophy had gone elsewhere, and we were far enough away from the wrestling and athletics grounds not to be disturbed by grunts of exertion.

'Did we expect this many?' Apollonides was counting heads as still more men arrived to join the citizens milling around the pillars. Word had spread like wildfire sweeping through Attica at the height of summer.

'The more witnesses the better, to deter Alkias from coming after any of us with a knife in some alleyway.' I sought to reassure myself as much as anyone else. 'Is he here yet?'

I looked at Lysicrates, who had taken on the task of finding out where Alkias lived, and of learning all he could from the man's neighbours.

The actor shook his head. 'I haven't seen him yet.'

'Perhaps he won't come.' Apollonides looked around.

'Maybe he's sent a friend to report back, for fear of betraying himself somehow.'

'He'll come.' Lysicrates had no doubt of that. 'He never trusts anyone to do something, if he can possibly do it himself. Besides, he has no real friends to speak of, just men who are wary of offending him.'

A well-dressed man approached, with his attendant slave a few paces behind. 'The Leukonoion Treasurer has arrived, with the other officials. Shall we begin?' His apprehension was in sharp contrast to his genial goodwill when Aristarchos had introduced us.

'Of course,' I said politely, before turning to the actors. 'I have the honour to present Xenocritos Neleid, who has obliged us by vouching for me here.'

I couldn't help wondering how Aristarchos had persuaded this nervous nobleman to help, but that was a question for another day.

'If we could call this meeting to order?' Xenocritos snapped his fingers at his slave.

The keen-eyed youth hurried over to the Leukonoion officials who nodded, their expressions suitably grave for what they thought they were about to hear. I wondered how appalled they would look when they'd heard everything I had to say.

The slave clapped his hands, and he must have had palms like leather, because the sound echoed around the colonnade like a whip crack. The noise silenced all the quietly curious conversation.

I waited for Xenocritos to speak, but he gestured for me to step forward. I took a breath and tried to convince myself that this was little different to any other stage. That would have been a great deal easier if I'd been wearing a mask. On the other hand, without eyeholes limiting my vision, I saw a slight commotion at the far end of the colonnade. A late arrival.

'That's him,' muttered Lysicrates.

I wished I was close enough to get a good look at Alkias, but that risked alerting him to our particular interest in his affairs. We were here to talk about something quite different, as far as these Leukonoion officials were concerned.

I raised my voice to carry to all comers. 'Good morning, fellow citizens. I am Philocles Hestaiou of Alopeke. I am here by the gracious permission of your Brotherhood, to inform you of the untimely death of one of your own, Eumares Demetriou.'

I allowed a murmur of consternation to run its course up and down the colonnade. Apollonides had done a good job over these past few days, discovering where Demetrios had lived, and prompting his neighbours to wonder what could have become of his son. Those who remembered the uproar when Kleoboulina and her child had vanished were swift to recall their unease at the time. Such behaviour had seemed so out-of-character, even for a strong-minded woman from Rhodes.

Though Apollonides had learned that no one had suspected foul play, by Alkias or anyone else. Since the new citizenship laws had rendered the little girl illegitimate without an Athenian mother, it was surely reasonable for Kleoboulina to take her child back to her own family, or to some other city where the girl could make a good marriage in the fullness of time. Her prospects in Athens were now non-existent, after all.

Apollonides had also discovered that Eumelos – Eumares – had been well liked, far more so than his father. The best thing that could be said for the recently deceased Demetrios was that he wasn't Alkias. As for him, Myrrhine hadn't been exaggerating when she said that the man who threatened her so vilely had no friends. It also appeared he was raising his own sons to follow in his footsteps.

I cleared my throat as the noise faded to an expectant hush. 'Whatever quarrels caused such a rift between father and son are no business of mine. I only know that Eumares went to live in Corinth, where he established a flourishing business, trading in pickled fish to east and west. Those of you who knew him here will not be surprised to learn that he made many friends across the Corinthia and beyond. He was sincerely respected by all those with whom he had dealings.'

I paused for a moment to let those whose memories hadn't been jogged by Apollonides in some Leukonoion tavern exchange glances and nods of approval. Then I continued, sombrely.

'You will be accordingly shocked to learn that Eumares died of poison. I was there when he was struck down, as were three of our fellow Athenians. All of whom can stand witness to his appalling death, if your elders and officials ask.'

We fervently hoped that they wouldn't. As long as

Alkias didn't know who else could testify to these events, he was surely less likely to try cracking my skull.

'Eumares was dosed with a thornapple potion, according to the doctors at Corinth's Asklepion. Perhaps he thought it was an aphrodisiac.' I shrugged. 'We can surely understand any man seeking assistance to satisfy Aphrodite's handmaidens.'

That won me a few half-smiles, though most of the assembled men were already looking uneasy. They looked downright troubled when they heard what I had to say next.

'As the poison seized him, he was assailed by visions of his family. First, he mistook a Corinthian woman of impeccable reputation for his lost wife, Kleoboulina. Then he saw someone whom he insisted was his cousin Alkias—'

That caused considerably more than a murmur, and for good reason. There might not have been much speculation about Kleoboulina's disappearance, but Lysicrates had unearthed dark rumours about the death of Alkias' wife. A few, the most cynical, reckoned that once he had three well-grown sons, he'd had no more use for her. That made her supposed wasting disease extremely convenient, and quite possibly the result of poison.

The majority were prepared to believe that the unfortunate woman had truly been ill. Nevertheless, some thought that Alkias could well have hastened her end with some lethal potion. Opinion was divided as to whether that was to spare himself the inconvenience and cost of a nurse, or to spare the mother of his children undue pain.

Ordinarily I'd ignore such spiteful rumours, but Myrrhine had told us how the woman had confided her suspicions about Kleoboulina's fate. I was forced to acknowledge that a man who had killed once wouldn't hesitate to silence his wife if he feared betrayal.

'Please, please!' I held up my hands, appealing for silence. 'Eumares was out of his senses, thanks to some potion he poured into his own cup. The woman he thought was his lost wife was a well-known Corinthian musician. I have no idea who he was addressing, when he thought he saw his cousin.'

Hopefully that would make Alkias less likely to try silencing me, as long as he thought I had nothing more damning to say.

Though I wasn't about to go on and say that I had no reason to think Alkias had been in Corinth. One of the first things Lysicrates had established was that the man had been nowhere to be seen in Athens from four days before our own departure until two days before we'd returned.

I shook my head, sorrowful. 'Whatever befell Eumares in Corinth, those of you who were his friends will be relieved to learn that he remained true to his wife, Myrrhine, and mindful of his responsibilities to his young son. He had been sending them regular sums of money,' I explained, 'to support her as she cares for her ailing father in Paoinidai.'

Several men standing near me were pleased to hear

that. Rather more looked shame-faced as they realised they hadn't given Myrrhine and her child a second thought since they'd left the city. Out of sight, out of mind.

'Eumares made provision for them both, in case of his death.' I raised my voice as I unrolled the papyrus I was holding. I'd made a careful copy of Myrrhine's letter before we'd come back to the city.

'*My honoured wife, if you are reading this letter, then the man who brings it has come to tell you that I am dead . . .*'

I read out Eumares' measured, considered words in a ringing voice that carried to every corner of the colonnade. When I finished, I rolled up the letter and handed it to Xenocritos Neleid.

He held the scroll aloft. 'This will be held in the District Archive, and our Treasurer will take all necessary steps to secure this legacy for Eumares' widow and her son. The boy was duly presented as a citizen's son at the appropriate Anthesteria, as many of you will remember.'

He looked distinctly disapproving, but I hoped this gathering would see that as unspoken criticism of Eumares rather than guessing at his irritation with me, for embroiling him in all this. I was just glad to see enough nodding heads to reassure us that Alkias had no chance of claiming Laches' citizenship was somehow in question.

I reclaimed the crowd's attention. 'You may well remember Eumares' trusted slave, Dardanis. He should have been the one bringing this letter to Athens, but alas, he was found dead on the road between Corinth and

Kenchreai. Truly, a tragic end for a loyal slave who had long been the trusted messenger between Eumares and his wife and son.'

I shook my head sorrowfully to allow these assembled men a few moments to recall Dardanis, and to wonder who might have wanted to kill him. Then I continued with a hefty hint for those slower on the uptake.

'The Furies only know what befell him, since he was found with both his purse and Eumares' seal ring still in his possession. We can at least trust in the divine providence that saw his body discovered, in the hidden thicket where he crawled to hide after escaping his attacker. Great Zeus be thanked that this letter was re-trieved, so that Eumares' last message to his family could be delivered.'

I paused to allow a suitably pious murmur to rise and fall.

'There was also a will disposing of the property that he had amassed in Corinth. Neither Myrrhine or her father wish to make any claim on that, on behalf of Eumares' son,' I assured the crowd. 'She wishes to remain living quietly in Attica, raising her child with the support of her family, and grateful for the assistance of your brothers in Paionidai. When Laches comes of age, he will assume the rights and responsibilities of a citizen as he takes possession of the lands and interests that his grandfather Pratinias bequeaths him in Paionidai, as well as the property that he inherits from Demetrios here in Athens.'

With a cheery smile on my face, I flung out my

hand towards the far end of the colonnade.

'In the meantime, as you all know, that property will be safeguarded by Alkias Theocritou. I'm sure you all share Myrrhine's confidence that he will prove a faithful steward of her son's inheritance, to honour the memory of his late cousin, and of his late uncle, as befits the new head of such an honoured and respected family.'

Everyone turned to stare at Alkias. Since all I saw was the backs of their heads, I couldn't tell if these men were looking at him with mistrust, with some guileless promise of support for Eumares' sake, or with simple curiosity, to find out who he was.

What I did know was there were countless witnesses to everything I said here today. That meant plenty of men would keep an eye on Alkias' dealings with Demetrios' property. Whether they did that for Eumares' sake, or because they disliked Alkias really didn't matter. More than enough of them were young and sufficiently hale to stand as witnesses on the day twelve years or more from now, when young Laches came to Athens to take his place among them and claim what was rightfully his.

For the first time, I could see Alkias clearly. He was a stocky man, with a belligerent set to his shoulders, and an arrogant tilt to his head. I made sure that I would know him again, if he decided to take issue with anything I said. Though I couldn't say what he was thinking at the moment. His face was as emotionless as marble.

Xenocritos' slave clapped his hands once again, and the nobleman wound up the meeting with a few well-chosen words. I barely heard him, silently running through my speech, to be certain that I'd said everything we had intended, to be sure that we'd done all we could.

Now we could only wait and see if Alkias thought he could find a way through the walls we'd built around him. This wouldn't be over until we knew that he knew it was.

Chapter Thirty-One

Nine days later, Alkias made his move. It had taken him long enough. I'd been out and about in the city without Kadous at my side every day since that meeting at the Academy. I had called regularly on my mother as a good son should. I ran errands for my brothers around our family's leather workshops. I visited my patron for this year's Dionysia play, and made the rounds of the city's most noted choir masters to enquire about likely prospects for my new chorus.

Not that my faithful Phrygian was sitting at home twiddling his thumbs. He'd carried word of our meeting with the assembled men of the Leukonoion District to Myrrhine out in the country. He'd waited to bring back answers from her father's faithful friends to some crucial questions. We also asked if they'd had any enquiries from their own connections in Athens, asking how her family fared. Kadous returned, able to reassure us that the Paionidai village elders were ready to downplay the extent of Pratinias' decline, to protect young Laches, in case Alkias sent some allies from Athens to discover how frail the old man really was and to seek support for his plan to send a son to take charge of the household.

Alkias finally confronted me as I was walking down the road to Alopeke, out beyond the Itonian Gate and on my way home. He must have been waiting out here in the shade of that olive tree for quite some while, now that he'd been goaded into action by the gossip that was swirling around him.

'You need to shut your mouth, Philocles.' Words to start a tavern brawl, but Alkias was as sober as a statue on the Acropolis, and just as stony-faced.

I hooked my thumbs in my belt and challenged him with a thrust of my jaw. 'I notice you don't accuse me of lying.'

Alkias scowled, and I saw outrage kindle in his eyes. Lysicrates had learned from the man's neighbours that he wasn't used to being defied. As his sons had grown up, their bruises made that plain for all to see.

I cocked my head with the grin that always infuriated my older brothers. 'If you claim you're being defamed, call me before the courts to answer for slander.'

He took a step forward, and I retreated a pace. I wasn't surprised that he'd chosen to try browbeating me outside Athens' walls. The few passers-by weren't inclined to stop and stare as they would be inside the city. Indeed, the tall man who strode past, followed by an equally tall attendant, studiously avoided making eye-contact with either of us. There were no windows or doors close at hand for nosy people to gawk from, and if any concerned citizen sent word to the Scythian public slaves tasked with keeping civic order, they would doubtless be reminded that their writ ran as far as the city gates and no further.

In my favour, it was still mid-afternoon, and even if there weren't many people about, the ones that were would notice attempted murder in broad daylight. Now we were standing face to face, I could see the pale arc of a long-faded, ring-sized scar beneath his eye. I could be certain that Alkias was the killer that we sought, and I was very glad that he hadn't waited to corner me somewhere late at night.

'Go on,' I prompted. 'What are you going to do to shut me up?'

We'd made our calculations when we'd decided who was going to stand before the Leukonoion officials and tell our carefully crafted version of events in Corinth. I could call on the protection of my association with a man as influential as Aristarchos. My brothers' business was well established, and they had no dealings with anyone whom Alkias could bully. We had no unmarried sisters whose reputations could be smeared.

Alkias smiled nastily. 'You want to see what happens, the next time a play of yours is staged? You want your chorus pelted with muck? You want your musician's legs broken? You want your masks stolen and thrown down a well?'

Before we'd been to Corinth, these would have been threats to make me quail. After everything that we'd survived there, such menace seemed positively lightweight.

I smiled sunnily back. 'You want to see how many men stand by you, once I start going around the Leukonoion taverns and asking all the questions that I didn't bring up at the Academy? Let's start with your recent trip to see Myrrhine, when you threatened to adopt her son—'

'You think any jury will hesitate to hand the boy into my care,' Alkias scoffed, 'when they hear how her father's wits have gone begging?'

'They might,' I retorted, 'when someone asks exactly when you found that out. No one in Paionidai has seen you for years, not until your recent visit. We can bring witnesses to the city to swear to that.'

Kadous had brought back written testimony, with every detail and date of Alkias' visit precisely recorded.

'Why didn't you go out there to see her as soon as Demetrios died? Surely you had a duty to discover if she knew where Eumares might be, so you could get the sad news to him, and inform him of his inheritance?'

Now I saw uncertainty in Alkias' eyes. I followed up my advantage.

'Why did you wait until you could tell Myrrhine that Eumares was dead as well? Come to that, how did you even know that he was dead? Because you took her the news before we got back to Athens. Please, do tell me,' I invited, 'who sent you word from Corinth? Who do you know there, who knew he was your cousin?'

'Let's see how many questions you can ask with a broken jaw.' Alkias clenched his fists, his face ugly.

Intent on giving me a thrashing, he was about to take a long stride forward. Fortunately for me, Menekles' long arm slipped around his neck and pulled him up short.

This was something else we'd decided before we'd gone to that meeting at the Academy, when we devised this second half of our plan to convince Alkias we could condemn him in the eyes of his fellow citizens in the Leukonoion District, even if we couldn't convict him before a jury in the law courts.

If I was going to be strolling around Athens like a lamb left unattended in its pen to draw a jackal into an archer's line of sight, I needed someone Alkias wasn't likely to recognise watching my back. Lysicrates and Apollonides had been making enquiries around his home and neighbourhood, so there was every chance someone had pointed out two nosy strangers to him. Menekles, on the other hand, had headed straight for Piraeus when we'd gone our separate ways at the Dipylon Gate.

When he'd seen Alkias confront me just now, he'd walked straight past the pair of us, like several others on the road who'd all been intent on their own business. Once he was sure that I had Alkias' attention, he'd turned around and walked up behind him, as light on his feet as a dancer.

Alkias choked. He tried to claw at Menekles' arm, but the actor had seized his right wrist. So the killer had only one hand left free to scrabble ineffectually at the elbow steadily tightening around his windpipe.

Now I was happy to approach him. I ran my fingertip along the scar on the inside of Alkias' forearm. It was freshly pink and puckered and just where Demeas had said I would find it, in line with his thumb. Still tender too, judging by the way Alkias writhed at my touch, but Menekles held him tight.

I wasn't smiling now. 'What will happen when we

ask if anyone in Athens knows where you got this cut? Who remembers when they first saw it? What story did you tell to explain it away? Because you won't be able to call on any witnesses who can swear that they saw what happened, will you?'

Menekles loosened his hold just enough to stop Alkias passing out for lack of breath. He leaned forward to put his lips close to the killer's ear. His voice was as merciless as any wrathful god.

'We know a man in Corinth who saw you there, and remembers the wound you were carrying. We can call up witnesses from Piraeus, who can swear that they saw you return on a ship from Kenchreai, two days after Dardanis was found dead. We can call up witnesses from the ports who remember you asking for any word of Eumares as well as any sighting of Dardanis regularly over the years. There can be no question that you made every effort to find your cousin.'

That had been an unlooked-for blessing bestowed by Athena, Apollo, Poseidon or whatever other gods were determined to see justice done as Menekles had blistered his feet traipsing around the docks. He reckoned that more than made up for not finding the actual ship that had given Alkias passage to Corinth.

The killer wasn't defeated yet. He fought against Menekles' hold, forcing out breathless words. 'You said it yourself. Eumares poisoned his own wine.'

I nodded. 'It's the talk of the Leukonoion taverns. Why by Hades would he do such a thing? Any time we like, we can share what we've learned about that puzzle.

412

That he was given the deadly potion by a whore, who'd been duped by an Athenian, who bought his poisons up on the Acrocorinth. He's a man several people can describe in good detail.'

Alkias wasn't struggling now. He hadn't realised quite how much we knew. For the first time, I saw horror in his eyes. I decided it was time I saw fear.

'We won't only share that in Athens. Eumares was a respected member of the Brotherhood of Bellerophon. What do you suppose his grieving brothers will do when we tell them who we think murdered him?'

'My guess is they'll seek revenge.' Menekles tightened his hold. 'Bellerophon favoured direct action.'

'So what can you do to restore your good name?' I stared at Alkias, unblinking. 'For a start, you can leave us well alone, because if any one of us dies a sudden death, we've all left letters to be delivered far and wide, accusing you and explaining why. Looking forward, you can do your duty to the gods and to Eumares' ghost, by safeguarding Laches' inheritance and managing his Athenian property honestly.'

'And leaving Myrrhine well alone,' growled Menekles.

I smiled cheerily once again. 'Then the people looking sideways at you just now will see that you're an upright and trustworthy citizen. Any suspicions they hear whispered in taverns must be unfounded rumours that no one with sense will believe.'

Menekles leaned close to Alkias' ear once again. 'Unless you give us cause to give them good reasons to believe that you're a killer.'

Almost imperceptibly, I saw Alkias sag against the actor's inexorable forearm, still held firm against his throat. Menekles felt his surrender and released his hold. Alkias fell to his hands and knees on the gravelled road. The only sound was the man's harsh breathing, and the carefree trill of birds flitting between the roadside bushes.

Menekles and I watched Alkias decide what to do next as he stared at the ground. His shoulders tensed, and he braced himself, ready to spring up. Two against one wasn't such bad odds, for a man this desperate.

'I wouldn't,' I advised.

Alkias looked up, and saw that we had an ally.

Ambrakis stared down at him. He didn't say anything. He didn't have to. The big slave's chilling gaze would freeze a water clock solid.

Alkias got slowly to his feet. He turned and, without a word, he began walking back towards Athens. We stood and watched.

'Do you think we convinced him?' Menekles asked, once the man was well out of earshot.

'I sincerely hope so.' I found I was shivering like a man caught in a sudden wind. I rubbed my hands briskly up and down my arms. 'Come on, let's get you home,' I said to Ambrakis.

Aristarchos had insisted on lending us his personal torch-bearer and bodyguard when we'd explained our plan to him. He'd pointed out the advantages of confronting Alkias with someone he couldn't possibly recognise. The man might not have seen Menekles with Apollonides or Lysicrates but it wouldn't take long to learn who the actor was. A complete stranger's presence was another matter all together. We hoped that closed our siege around Alkias completely.

'You're heading back to the city?' Menekles was surprised. 'I thought you were going home.'

I shrugged. 'I changed my mind. There are a couple of things I can do, before Zosime finishes work for the day. We can walk back together.'

'Fair enough.' Menekles started walking.

I fell into step beside him, and Ambrakis brought up the rear.

Chapter Thirty-Two

I parted company with Ambrakis where the road through the city met the Sacred Way leading up to the Acropolis. I had expected to feel relieved after this final encounter with Alkias. Instead, I still felt burdened, and I didn't know why. All I could think to do was appeal to divine Athena, to ask what more she expected of me in order to satisfy the dead man's spirit.

Workmen were still busy around her magnificent new temple, as they had been for the last few years, and doubtless would be for years to come. There was dust on the breeze, and the ringing of chisels on stone, and the murmur of voices. The air was full of hope and purpose as these craftsmen went about replacing the ruins of the city's shrines that the invading Persians had ravaged when my father was much the age I was now.

I found a quiet corner of the terrace where I'd be in nobody's way, and sat down on the ground. I gazed into the empty inner sanctum. There was rumour that Pericles planned to dedicate a magnificent statue when the temple was finished. For now I was content to lay my unease before the unseen goddess. This was where we had worshipped Athena since she first walked among us.

I couldn't say how long I'd been sitting there when a shadow fell across me. I looked up, and was startled to see Aristarchos gazing down.

'Ambrakis said I'd find you here.'

'Do you have more questions about Corinth?' I tried to think what I'd failed to tell him.

'No, no.' Aristarchos surprised me even more by sitting down beside me. 'Ambrakis said you seemed preoccupied. I was wondering if there was anything you'd care to discuss.'

I blessed Athena for sending him to me. Sitting here, I'd been able to unravel the tangle of my thoughts. Now I welcomed his shrewd company as I tackled the questions that remained.

'Have I done all that I can to secure justice for Eumelos, and for his wife and son?'

Aristarchos pursed his lips as he considered this. 'Have you seen his last wishes honoured? Is their future secure, thanks to the silver that's held for the child in Isthmia? Is the boy's claim to inherit wealth and property from both his grandfathers now widely acknowledged?'

'Yes,' I agreed, 'in all respects.'

'Then surely you have done a great deal?' Aristarchos raised his grey brows.

'But not everything.' This was what was irritating me, worse than a louse lurking in my tunic. 'Alkias still walks these streets, free to do as he pleases. We can't bring him before the courts to face punishment.'

'He may walk these streets, but thanks to you, he will

be watched wherever he goes,' Aristarchos countered, 'and well he knows it.'

'For how long? How soon will people's memories fade?' I couldn't help thinking of Alypos Temenid, comfortably sitting out a few years away from Corinth, before he returned to rebuild his power and influence.

'His neighbours will be reminded of the suspicions against Alkias whenever the child Laches comes to Athens to take part in district festivals,' Aristarchos pointed out. 'The Leukonoion officials will see to it that the heir to such substantial property is involved in all the appropriate rites.'

He shifted his position to sit more comfortably, tucking the folds of his long tunic around his ankles.

'As for Alkias, he will answer to the gods of the dead for his crimes, whenever the Fates decide that the day to cut his life's thread has come. He must carry the burden of that knowledge as he goes about his business. Isn't that a more lasting punishment than a swift execution, or even exile among people who don't know of his misdeeds?'

I wasn't convinced.

'Zosime's father, Menkaure, tells me how his people's gods weigh the hearts of those who have died against a divine feather,' I remarked. 'Those whose misdeeds tip the balance the wrong way are devoured by a fearsome monster, condemned to utter oblivion.'

That might suit Egyptians, but as far as I was concerned, Alkias didn't deserve to escape his crimes so easily. I wondered what punishment he would face in the Underworld, giving him eternity to contemplate his vile sins. Something at least as exhausting as Sisyphus endlessly rolling a rock up the Acrocorinth, I sincerely hoped.

'I wish I could believe that Alkias would be burdened by such fears,' I said furiously. 'He seems to have no conscience at all. He calmly devised this despicable plan to poison Eumelos, and then he must have followed him until he saw him stricken with his death agonies. Then he set out to hunt down Dardanis, ready to poleaxe him like a beast for slaughter without turning a hair. What manner of man must he be, to see other people as no more than obstacles on his path to the money and property he wants for his own? How many people has he killed, truly?'

I ticked off the murders we suspected the man of on my fingers. 'Eumelos' first wife and daughter, his own wife, Eumelos himself, Dardanis the slave, the herbalist Hermaios. How can the gods let such a vile man live and thrive?'

'We can only be truly certain that he murdered Eumelos and the slave,' Aristarchos pointed out. 'And divine Athena and the avenging Furies made sure that you were there in Corinth, to see to it that his dark deeds were dragged into the light of day.'

'True enough.' That was some consolation, and I had to admit, it was always possible that Alkias' wife had really been ill. Perhaps her accusations had been the fevered imaginings of a dying woman who had been so badly mistreated. It was possible that Eumelos' first wife and child were living quietly and content somewhere far away, with a new husband and father. All of this was possible, though I still didn't believe any of it.

'Are we too quick to accept the easiest explanations, when someone disappears or dies?' I looked at Aristarchos. 'Too ready to agree that they must have just left the city, been cut down by disease, or eaten spoiled meat, or drunk foul water? Surely all this has shown us that not every murder is as obvious as finding someone standing over a corpse with a bloody knife in hand?'

'True enough.' Aristarchos looked thoughtfully at the gleaming white marble of Athena's new temple rising to crown the Acropolis anew. 'Perhaps that's what our goddess wants of us, now that she's shown us what men like Alkias are capable of. She shows us we have a duty to look more closely at such convenient deaths, and ensure that the guilty are revealed.'

I thought about that and nodded slowly. Here in this sacred space, his words had the ring of divine truth.

Acknowledgements

I remain indebted to the family and friends whose continued support and encouragement have sustained me through writing this second adventure for Philocles and the actors. I am also extremely grateful to those readers, reviewers, booksellers and bloggers who have shared their enthusiasm for Shadows of Athens. There really is no better incentive for a writer.

Max Edwards at Apple Tree Literary continues to champion these books for which I am sincerely grateful. My thanks to Craig Lye, who has seen this story through from first outline to finished text, and to Ben Willis, Alainna Hadjigeorgiou, Lucy Frederick and the rest of the team at Orion Books.

When I started writing Scorpions in Corinth, I did not expect to be thanking Sir Tony Robinson in these acknowledgements, but he definitely merits a grateful mention. Until I read his autobiography, No Cunning Plan, I had no idea that he had been one of the actors behind the masks of the National Theatre's production of The Oresteia in 1981. I was an enthralled Sixth Former in the audience on one unforgettable day, and I would like to thank the entire company for bringing me face to face with the full might and majesty of Ancient Greek drama in performance. Those enduring memories are one of the reasons why my hero is a playwright. More than that, as Philocles takes to the stage himself in this book, Sir Tony's recollections of the physical and artistic challenges of acting in a mask were tremendously useful as I sought to convey that experience to a reader.

Other research for this book has drawn heavily on the work of the American School of Classical Studies at Athens, whose archaeologists have been excavating the ancient city of Corinth and the wider Corinthia since 1896. The papers and reports that they have made available online through JSTOR have been invaluable. The publication in 2018 of their updated site guide to Ancient Corinth, with colour photographs, diagrams, maps and a wealth of detail and references could not have been better timed for my purposes. My sincere thanks go to all involved.

Needless to say, any scholarly errors are mine alone, as is all responsibility for the choices I have made in interpreting archaeological and historical evidence in the ways that will best serve my story.

Credits

JM Alvey and Orion Fiction would like to thank everyone at Orion who worked on the publication of *Scorpions in Corinth* in the UK.

Editorial
Craig Lye
Ben Willis
Lucy Frederick

Copy editor
Joanne Gledhill

Proof reader
Karen Ball

Audio
Paul Stark
Amber Bates

Contracts
Anne Goddard

Paul Bulos
Jake Alderson

Design
Rabab Adams
Helen Ewing
Joanna Ridley
Nick May

Editorial Management
Charlie Panayiotou
Jane Hughes
Alice Davis

Finance
Jasdip Nandra
Afeera Ahmed